ATLANTIS
AND OTHER PLACES

ATLANTIS
AND OTHER PLACES

HARRY
TURTLEDOVE

A ROC BOOK

SF
Turtledo

JAN 2011

ROC
Published by New American Library,
a division of Penguin Group (USA) Inc.,
375 Hudson Street, New York, New York 10014, USA
Penguin Group (Canada), 90 Eglinton Avenue East, Suite 700, Toronto,
Ontario M4P 2Y3, Canada (a division of Pearson Penguin Canada Inc.)
Penguin Books Ltd., 80 Strand, London WC2R 0RL, England
Penguin Ireland, 25 St. Stephen's Green, Dublin 2,
Ireland (a division of Penguin Books Ltd.)
Penguin Group (Australia), 250 Camberwell Road, Camberwell,
Victoria 3124, Australia (a division of Pearson Australia Group Pty. Ltd.)
Penguin Books India Pvt. Ltd., 11 Community Centre,
Panchsheel Park, New Delhi - 110 017, India
Penguin Group (NZ), 67 Apollo Drive, Rosedale, North Shore 0632,
New Zealand (a division of Pearson New Zealand Ltd.)
Penguin Books (South Africa) (Pty.) Ltd., 24 Sturdee Avenue,
Rosebank, Johannesburg 2196, South Africa

Penguin Books Ltd., Registered Offices:
80 Strand, London WC2R 0RL, England

First published by Roc, an imprint of New American Library,
a division of Penguin Group (USA) Inc.

First Printing, December 2010
1   3   5   7   9   10   8   6   4   2

Story copyrights can be found on page 441.

ROC REGISTERED TRADEMARK—MARCA REGISTRADA

LIBRARY OF CONGRESS CATALOGING-IN-PUBLICATION DATA:
Turtledove, Harry.
Atlantis, and other places/ Harry Turtledove.
p.   cm.
ISBN 978-0-451-46364-7
1. Adventure stories, American. I. Title.
PS3570.U76A95   2010
813'.54—dc22   2010029373

Set in Guardi   •   Designed by Elke Sigal

Printed in the United States of America

CONTENTS

AUDUBON IN ATLANTIS

Science fiction writers often read a wide variety of books. I was going through one on the ecology of New Zealand before humans arrived when it noted that New Zealand had drifted away from Australia about 85 million years ago. It occurred to me to wonder what would have happened if the same thing had happened to a large chunk of eastern North America at more or less the same time. Suppose that chunk had no native mammals except for bats. Suppose the Native Americans never found it—it would be in the middle of the Atlantic, after all. When Europeans came along, they'd almost certainly call an immense island right there Atlantis. . . .

$\mathcal{D}$elicate as if walking on eggs, the riverboat *Augustus Cae-sar* eased in alongside the quay at New Orleans. Colored roustabouts, bare to the waist, caught lines from the boat and made her fast. The steam whistle blew several long, happy blasts, telling the world the sternwheeler had arrived. Then black smoke stopped belching from the stacks as the crew shut down the engines.

The deck stopped quivering beneath John Audubon's feet. He breathed a silent sigh of relief; for all the time he'd spent aboard boats and ships, he was not a good sailor, and knew he never would be. Any motion, no matter how slight, could make his stomach betray him. He sighed—a long sea voyage still lay ahead of him.

Edward Harris came up and stood alongside him. "Well, my friend, we're on our way," he said.

"It's true—we are. And we shall do that which has not been done, while it may yet be done." As Audubon always did, he gathered enthusiasm when he thought about the goal and not the means by which he had to accomplish it. His English was fluent, but heavily flavored by the French that was his birthspeech. Even with an accent, he would have spoken more mushily than

3

he liked; he was nearer sixty than fifty, and had only a few teeth left. "Before long, Ed, either the great honkers will be gone from this world or I will."

He waited impatiently till the gangplank thudded into place, then hurried off the *Augustus Caesar* onto dry land, or something as close to dry land as New Orleans offered. He was a good-sized man—about five feet ten—with shoulder-length gray hair combed straight back from his forehead and with bushy gray side whiskers that framed a long, strong-nosed face.

Men and women of every color, wearing everything from rags to frock coats and great hoop skirts, thronged the muddy, puddled street. Chatter, jokes, and curses crackled in Spanish, French, and English, and in every possible mixture and corruption of those tongues. Audubon heard far more English than he had when he first came to New Orleans half a lifetime earlier. It was a French town then, with the Spanish dons hanging on where and as they could. Times changed, though. He knew that too well.

Not far from the Cabildo stood the brick building that housed the Bartlett Line. Edward Harris following in his wake, Audubon went inside. A clerk nodded to them. "Good day, gentlemen," he said in English. A generation earlier, the greeting would surely have come in French. "How may I be of service to you today?"

"I wish to purchase passage to Atlantis for the two of us," Audubon replied.

"Certainly, sir." The clerk didn't bat an eye. "The *Maid of Orleans* sails for New Marseille and Avalon on the west coast in . . . let me see . . . five days. If you would rather wait another week, you can book places on the *Sea Queen* for the east. She puts in at St. Augustine, St. Denis, and Hanover, then continues on to London."

"We can reach the interior as easily from either coast," Harris said.

"Just so." Audubon nodded. "We would have to wait longer to leave for the east, the journey would be longer, and I would not care to set out from Hanover in any case. I have too many friends in the capital. With the kindest intentions in the world, they would sweep us up in their social whirl, and we should be weeks getting free of it. The *Maid of Orleans* it shall be."

"You won't be sorry, sir. She's a fine ship." The clerk spoke with professional enthusiasm. He took out a book of ticket forms and inked his pen. "In whose names shall I make these out?"

"I am John James Audubon," Audubon replied. "With me travels my friend and colleague, Mr. Edward Harris."

"Audubon?" The clerk started to write, then looked up, his face aglow. "*The* Audubon? The artist? The naturalist?"

Audubon exchanged a secret smile with Edward Harris. Being recognized never failed to gratify him: he loved himself well enough to crave reminding that others loved him, too. When he swung back toward the clerk, he tried to make the smile modest. "I have the honor to be he, yes."

The clerk thrust out his hand. As Audubon shook it, the young man said, "I cannot tell you how pleased I am to make your acquaintance, sir. Mr. Hiram Bartlett, the chairman of the shipping line, is a subscriber to your *Birds and Viviparous Quadrupeds of Northern Terranova and Atlantis*—the double elephant folio edition. He sometimes brings in one volume or another for the edification of his staff. I admire your art and your text in almost equal measure, and that is the truth."

"You do me too much credit," Audubon said, in lieu of strutting and preening like a courting passenger pigeon. He was also glad to learn how prosperous Bartlett was. No one but a rich man could afford the volumes of the double elephant folio. They were big enough to show almost every bird and most beasts at life size, even if he had twisted poses and bent necks almost unnaturally here and there to fit creatures onto the pages' Procrustean bed.

"Are you traveling to Atlantis to continue your researches?" the clerk asked eagerly.

"If fate is kind, yes," Audubon replied. "Some of the creatures I hope to see are less readily found than they were in years gone by, while I"—he sighed—"I fear I am less well able to find them than I was in years gone by. Yet a man can do only what it is given to him to do, and I intend to try."

"If they're there, John, you'll find them," Harris said.

"God grant it be so," Audubon said. "What is the fare aboard the *Maid of Orleans*?"

"A first-class cabin for two, sir, is a hundred twenty livres," the clerk said. "A second-class cabin is eighty livres, while one in steerage is a mere thirty-five livres. But I fear I cannot recommend steerage for gentlemen of your quality. It lacks the comforts to which you will have become accustomed."

"I've lived rough. Once I get to Atlantis, I expect I shall live rough again," Audubon said. "But, unlike some gentlemen of the Protestant persuasion"—he fondly nudged Edward Harris—"I don't make the mistake of believing comfort is sinful. Let us travel first class."

"I don't believe comfort is sinful, and you know it," Harris said. "We want to get you where you're going and keep you as healthy and happy as we can while we're doing it. First class, by all means."

"First class it shall be, then." The clerk wrote up the tickets.

Audubon boarded the *Maid of Orleans* with a curious blend of anticipation and dread. The sidewheeler was as modern a steamship as any, but she was still a ship, one that would soon put to sea.

Even going up the gangplank, his stomach gave a premonitory lurch.

He laughed and tried to make light of it, both to Harris and to himself. "When I think how many times I've put to sea in a sailing ship, at the mercy of wind and wave, I know how foolish I am to fret about a voyage like this," he said.

"You said it to the clerk last week: you can only do what you can do." Harris was blessed with both a calm stomach and a calm disposition. If opposites attracted, he and Audubon made a natural pair.

The purser strode up to them. Brass buttons gleamed on his blue wool coat; sweat gleamed on his face. "You gentlemen are traveling together?" he said. "If you would be kind enough to show me your tickets. . . ?"

"But of course," Audubon said. He and Harris produced them.

"I thank you." The purser checked them against a list he carried in one of his jacket's many pockets. "Mr. Audubon and Mr. Harris, is it? Very good. We have you in Cabin 12, the main deck on the starboard side. That's on the right as you look forward, if you haven't gone to sea before."

"I'm afraid I have," Audubon said. The purser took off his cap and scratched his balding crown, but Audubon meant it exactly as he'd phrased it. He nodded to Harris and to the free Negro pushing a wheeled cart that held their baggage. "Let's see what we've got, then."

They had a cabin with two beds, a chest of drawers, and a basin and pitcher on top of it: about what they would have had in an inn of reasonable quality, though smaller. *In an inn, though, I'm not likely to drown*, Audubon thought. He didn't suppose he was *likely* to drown on the *Maid of Orleans*, but if the seas got rough he would wish he were dead.

He gave the Negro half a livre, for the luggage, once unloaded

7

from the cart, filled the cabin almost to the bursting point. Neither Audubon nor Harris was a dandy; they had no extraordinary amount of clothes. But Audubon's watercolors and paper filled up a couple of trunks, and the jars and the raw spirits they would use to preserve specimens took up a couple of more. And each of them had a shotgun for gathering specimens and a newfangled revolver for self-protection.

"Leave enough room so you'll be able to get out and come to the galley when you're hungry," the purser said helpfully.

"Thank you so much." Audubon hoped his sarcasm would freeze the man, but the purser, quite unfrozen, tipped his cap and left the cabin. Audubon muttered in pungent French.

"Never mind, John," Harris said. "We're here, and we'll weigh anchor soon. After that, no worries till we get to Avalon."

No worries for you. But Audubon kept that to himself. Harris couldn't help having a tranquil stomach, any more than the artist could help having a nervous one. Audubon only wished his were calm.

He also wished the *Maid of Orleans* sailed at the appointed hour, or even on the appointed day. *Thursday, the 6th day of April, 1843, at half past 10 in the morning,* the clerk had written on each ticket in a fine round hand. Audubon and Harris were aboard in good time. But half past ten came and went without departure. All of Thursday came and went. Passengers kept right on boarding. Stevedores kept on carrying sacks of sugar and rice into the ship's hold. Only the stuffed quail and artichokes and asparagus and the really excellent champagne in the first-class galley went some little way toward reconciling Audubon to being stuck on the steamship an extra day.

Finally, on Friday afternoon, the *Maid of Orleans'* engine rumbled to life. Its engine had a deeper, stronger note than the one that had propelled the *Augustus Caesar* down the Big Muddy. The deck thrummed under Audubon's shoes.

Officers bawled commands as smoke belched from the steamship's stacks. Sailors took in the lines that secured the ship to the quay. Others, grunting with effort, manned the capstan. One link at a time, they brought up the heavy chain and anchor that had held the sidewheeler in place.

Watching them, Harris said, "One of these days, steam will power the capstan as well as the paddlewheels."

"You could be right," Audubon replied. "The sailors must hope you are."

"Steam is the coming thing. You mark my words," Harris said. "Steamships, railroads, factories—who knows what else?"

"So long as they don't make a steam-powered painter, I'll do well enough," Audubon said.

"A steam-powered painter? You come up with the maddest notions, John." Edward Harris laughed. Slowly, though, the mirth faded from his face. "With a mechanical pantograph, your notion might almost come true."

"I wasn't thinking of that so much," Audubon told him. "I was thinking of this new trick of light-writing people have started using the last few years. If it gave pictures in color, not shades of gray, and if you could make—no, they say *take*—a light-writing picture fast enough to capture motion . . . Well, if you could, painters would fall on thin times, I fear."

"Those are hefty *ifs*. It won't happen soon, if it ever does," Harris said.

"Oh, yes. I know." Audubon nodded. "I doubt I'll have to carry a hod in my fading years. My son will likely make a living as a painter, too. But you were talking about days to come. May I not think of them as well?"

The steamship's whistle screamed twice, warning that she was about to move away from the quay. Her paddlewheels spun slowly in reverse, backing her out into the Big Muddy. Then one wheel stopped while the other continued to revolve. Along with the rudder, that swung the *Maid of Orleans'* bow downstream. Another blast from the whistle—a triumphant one—and more smoke pouring from her stacks, she started down the great river toward the Bay of Mexico. Though she hadn't yet reached the sea, Audubon's stomach flinched.

The Big Muddy's delta stretched far out into the Bay of Mexico. As soon as the *Maid of Orleans* left the river and got out into the bay, her motion changed. Her pitch and roll were nothing to speak of, not to the crew and not to most of the passengers. But they were enough to send Audubon and a few other unfortunates running for the rail. After a couple of minutes that seemed like forever, he wearily straightened, mouth foul and burning, eyes streaming with tears. He was rid of what ailed him, at least for the moment.

A steward with a tray of glasses nodded deferentially. "Some punch, sir, to help take the taste away?"

"*Merci. Mon Dieu, merci beaucoup,*" Audubon said, tormented out of English.

"*Pas de quoi,*" the steward replied. Any man on a ship sailing from New Orleans and touching in the southern parts of Atlantis had to speak some French.

Audubon sipped and let rum and sweetened lemon juice clean his mouth. When he swallowed, he feared he would have another spasm, but the punch stayed down. Reassuring warmth spread from his middle. Two more gulps emptied the glass. "God bless you!" he said.

"My pleasure, sir. We see some every time out." The steward offered restoratives to Audubon's fellow sufferers. They fell on him with glad cries. He even got a kiss from a nice-looking young woman—but only after she'd taken a good swig from her glass of punch.

Feeling human in a mournful way, Audubon walked up toward the bow. The breeze of the ship's passage helped him forget about his unhappy innards . . . for now. Gulls screeched overhead. A common tern dove into the sea and came up with a fish in its beak. It didn't get to enjoy the meal. A herring gull flapped after it and made it spit out the fish before it could swallow. The gull got the dainty; the robbed tern flew off to try its luck somewhere else.

On the southern horizon lay the island of Nueva Galicia, about forty miles southeast of the delta. Only a little steam rose above Mount Isabella, near the center of the island. Audubon had been a young man the last time the volcano erupted. He remembered ash raining down on New Orleans.

He looked east toward Mount Pensacola at the mouth of the bay. Pensacola had blown its stack more recently—only about ten years earlier, in fact. For now, though, no ominous plume of black rose in that direction. Audubon nodded to himself. He wouldn't have to worry about making the passage east during an eruption. When Mount Pensacola burst into flame, rivers of molten rock ran steaming into the sea, pushing the Terranovan coastline a little farther south and east. Ships couldn't come too close to observe the awe-inspiring spectacle, for the volcano threw stones to a distance coast artillery only dreamt of. Most splashed into the Bay of Mexico, of course, but who would ever forget the *Black Prince*, holed and sunk by a flying boulder the size of a cow back in '93?

The *Maid of Orleans* steamed sedately eastward. The waves weren't too bad; Audubon found that repeated doses of rum punch worked something not far from a miracle when it came to settling his stomach. If it did twinge now and again, the rum kept him from caring. And the lemon juice, he told himself, held scurvy at bay.

Mount Pensacola was smoking when the sidewheeler passed

it near sunset. But the cloud of steam rising from the conical peak, like that above Mount Isabella, was thin and pale, not broad and black and threatening.

Edward Harris came up alongside Audubon by the port rail. "A pretty view," Harris remarked.

"It is indeed," Audubon said.

"I'm surprised not to find you sketching," Harris told him. "Sunset tingeing the cloud above the mountain with pink against the deepening blue . . . What could be more picturesque?"

"Nothing, probably." Audubon laughed in some embarrassment. "But I've drunk enough of that splendid rum punch to make my right hand forget its cunning."

"I don't suppose I can blame you, not when *mal de mer* torments you so," Harris said. "I hope the sea will be calmer the next time you come this way."

"So do I—if there is a next time," Audubon said. "I am not young, Edward, and I grow no younger. I'm bound for Atlantis to do things and see things while I still may. The land changes year by year, and so do I. Neither of us will be again what we were."

Harris—calm, steady, dependable Harris—smiled and set a hand on his friend's shoulder. "You've drunk yourself sad, that's what you've done. There's more to you than to many a man half your age."

"Good of you to say so, though we both know it's not so, not any more. As for the rum . . ." Audubon shook his head. "I knew this might be my last voyage when I got on the *Augustus Caesar* in St. Louis. Growing up is a time of firsts, of beginnings."

"Oh, yes." Harris' smile grew broader. Audubon had a good idea which first he was remembering.

But the painter wasn't finished. "Growing up is a time for firsts, yes," he repeated. "Growing old . . . Growing old is a time for endings, for lasts. And I do fear this will be my last long voyage."

"Well, make the most of it if it is," Harris said. "Shall we repair to the galley? Turtle soup tonight, with a saddle of mutton to follow." He smacked his lips.

Harris certainly made the most of the supper. Despite his ballasting of rum, Audubon didn't. A few spoonsful of soup, a halfhearted attack on the mutton and the roast potatoes accompanying it, and he felt full to the danger point. "We might as well have traveled second class, or even steerage," he said sadly. "The difference in cost lies mostly in the victuals, and I'll never get my money's worth at a table that rolls."

"I'll just have to do it for both of us, then." Harris poured brandy-spiked gravy over a second helping of mutton. His campaign with fork and knife was serious and methodical, and soon reduced the mutton to nothing. He looked around hopefully. "I wonder what the sweet course is."

It was a cake baked in the shape of the *Maid of Orleans* and stuffed with nuts, candied fruit, and almond paste. Harris indulged immoderately. Audubon watched with a strange smile, half jealous, half wistful.

He went to bed not long after supper. The first day of a sea voyage always told on him, more than ever as he got older. The mattress was as comfortable as the one in the inn back in New Orleans. It might have been softer than the one he slept on at home. But it was unfamiliar, and so he tossed and turned for a while, trying to find the most comfortable position. Even as he tossed, he laughed at himself. Before long, he'd sleep wrapped in a blanket on bare ground in Atlantis. Would he twist and turn there, too? He nodded. Of course he would. Nodding still, he dozed off.

He hadn't been asleep long before Harris came in. His friend was humming "Pretty Black Eyes," a song popular in New Orleans as they set out. Audubon didn't think the other man even knew he was doing it. Harris got into his nightshirt, pissed in the chamber pot under his bed, blew out the oil lamp Audubon had left burning, and lay down. He was snoring in short order. Harris always denied that he snored—and why not? He never heard himself.

Audubon laughed once more. He tossed and twisted and yawned. Pretty soon, he was snoring again himself.

When he went out on deck the next morning, the *Maid of Orleans* might have been the only thing God ever made besides the sea. Terranova had vanished behind her; Atlantis still lay a thousand miles ahead. The steamship had entered the Hesperian Gulf, the wide arm of the North Atlantic that separated the enormous island and its smaller attendants from the continent to the west.

Audubon looked south and east. He'd been born on Santo Tomás, one of those lesser isles. He was brought to France three years later, and so escaped the convulsions that wracked the island when its colored slaves rose up against their masters in a war where neither side asked for quarter or gave it. Blacks ruled Santo Tomás to this day. Not many whites were left on the island. Audubon had only a few faded childhood memories of his first home. He'd never cared to go back, even if he could have without taking his life in his hands.

Edward Harris strolled out on deck. "Good morning," he said. "I hope you slept well?"

"Well enough, thanks," Audubon answered. *I would have done better without "Pretty Black Eyes," but such is life.* "Yourself?"

"Not bad, not bad." Harris eyed him. "You look . . . less greenish than you did yesterday. The bracing salt air, I suppose?"

"It could be. Or maybe I'm getting used to the motion." As soon as Audubon said that, as soon as he thought about his stomach, he gulped. He pointed an accusing finger at his friend. "There—you see? Just asking was enough to jinx me."

"Well, come have some breakfast, then. Nothing like a good mess of ham and eggs or something like that to get you ready for . . . Are you all right?"

"No," Audubon gasped, leaning out over the rail.

He breakfasted lightly, on toasted ship's biscuit and coffee and rum punch. He didn't usually start the day with strong spirits, but he didn't usually start the day with a bout of seasickness, either. *A good thing, too, or I'd have died years ago*, he thought. *I hope I would, anyhow.*

Beside him in the galley, Harris worked his way through fried eggs and ham and sausage and bacon and maizemeal mush. Blotting his lips with a snowy linen napkin, he said, "That was monstrous fine." He patted his pot belly.

"So glad you enjoyed it," Audubon said tonelessly.

Once or twice over the next three days, the *Maid of Orleans* came close enough to another ship to make out her sails or the smoke rising from her stack. A pod of whales came up to blow nearby before sounding again. Most of the time, though, the sidewheeler might have been alone on the ocean.

Audubon was on deck again the third afternoon, when the sea—suddenly, as those things went—changed from greenish gray to a deeper, richer blue. He looked around for Harris, and spotted him not far away, drinking rum punch and chatting with a personable young woman whose curls were the color of fire.

"Edward!" Audubon said. "We've entered the Bay Stream!"

"Have we?" The news didn't seem to have the effect on Harris that Audubon wanted. His friend turned back to the redheaded woman—who also held a glass of punch—and said, "John is wild for nature in every way you can imagine." Spoken in a different tone of voice, it would have been a compliment. Maybe it still was.

Audubon hoped he only imagined Harris' faintly condescending note.

"Is he?" The woman didn't seem much interested in Audubon one way or the other. "What about you, Eddie?"

Eddie? Audubon had trouble believing his ears. No one had ever called Harris such a thing in his hearing before. And Harris . . . smiled. "Well, Beth, I'll tell you—I am, too. But some parts of nature interest me more than others." He set his free hand on her arm. She smiled, too.

He was a widower. He could chase if that suited his fancy, not that Beth seemed to need much chasing. Audubon admired a pretty lady as much as anyone—more than most, for with his painter's eye he saw more than most—but was a thoroughly married man, and didn't slide from admiration to pursuit. He hoped Lucy was well.

Finding Harris temporarily distracted, Audubon went back to the rail himself. By then, the *Maid of Orleans* had left the cooler waters by the east coast of Terranova behind and fully entered the warm current coming up from the Bay of Mexico. Even the bits of seaweed floating in the ocean looked different now. Audubon's main zoological interests did center on birds and viviparous quadrupeds. All the same, he wished he would have thought to net up some of the floating algae in the cool water and then some of these so he could properly compare them.

He turned around to say as much to Harris, only to discover that his friend and Beth were no longer on deck. Had Harris gone off to pursue his own zoological interests? Well, more power to him if he had. Audubon looked back into the ocean, and was rewarded with the sight of a young sea turtle, not much bigger than the palm of his hand, delicately nibbling a strand of the new seaweed. Next to the rewards Harris might be finding, it didn't seem like much, but it was definitely better than nothing.

———

Like the sun, Atlantis, for Audubon, rose in the east. That blur on the horizon—for a little while, you could wonder if it was a distant cloudbank, but only for a little while. Before long, it took on the unmistakable solidity of land. To the Breton and Galician fishermen who'd found it first, almost four hundred years before, it would have sent the setting sun to bed early.

"Next port of call is New Marseille, sir," the purser said, tipping his cap to Audubon as he went by.

"Yes, of course," the artist replied, "but I'm bound for Avalon."

"Even so, sir, you'll have to clear customs at the first port of call in Atlantis," the other man reminded him. "The States are fussy about these things. If you don't have a New Marseille customs stamp on your passport, they won't let you off the ship in Avalon."

"It's a nuisance, to open all my trunks for the sake of a stamp," Audubon said. The purser shrugged the shrug of a man with right, or at least regulations, on his side. And he told the truth: the United States of Atlantis *were* fussy about who visited them. *Do as we do*, they might have said, *or stay away*.

Not that coming ashore at New Marseille was a hardship. On the contrary. Warmed by the Bay Stream, the city basked in an almost unending May. Farther north, in Avalon, it seemed to be April most of the time. And then the Bay Stream curled north and east around the top of Atlantis and delivered the rest of its warmth to the north of France, to the British Isles, and to Scandinavia. The east coast of Atlantis, where the winds swept across several hundred miles of mountains and lowlands before they finally arrived, was an altogether darker, harsher place.

But Audubon was in New Marseille, and if it wasn't veritably May, it was the middle of April, which came close enough. A glance as he and Harris carted their cases to the customs shed sufficed to tell him he'd left Terranova behind. Oh, the magnolias that shaded some nearby streets weren't much different from the ones he could have found near New Orleans. But the gingkoes on other thoroughfares . . . Only one other variety of ginkgo grew anyplace else in the world: in China. And the profusion of squat cycads with tufts of leaves sprouting from the tops of squat trunks also had few counterparts anywhere in the temperate zone.

The customs official, by contrast, seemed much like customs officials in every other kingdom and republic Audubon had ever visited. He frowned as he examined their declaration, and frowned even more as he opened up their baggage to confirm it. "You have a considerable quantity of spirits here," he said. "A dutiable quantity, in fact."

"They aren't intended for drinking or for resale, sir," Audubon said, "but for the preservation of scientific specimens."

"John Audubon's name and artistry are known throughout the civilized world," Edward Harris said.

"I've heard of the gentleman myself. I admire his work, what I've seen of it," the official replied. "But the law does not consider intent. It considers quantity. You will not tell me these strong spirits *cannot* be drunk?"

"No," Audubon admitted reluctantly.

"Well, then," the customs man said. "You owe the fisc of Atlantis . . . Let me see . . ." He checked a table thumbtacked to the wall behind him. "You owe twenty-two eagles and, ah, fourteen cents."

Fuming, Audubon paid. The customs official gave him a receipt, which he didn't want, and the requisite stamp in his passport, which he did. As he and Harris trundled their chattels back to the *Maid of Orleans*, a small bird flew past them. "Look, John!" Harris said. "Wasn't that a gray-throated green?"

Not even the sight of the Atlantean warbler could cheer Audubon. "Well, what if it was?" he said, still mourning the money he'd hoped he wouldn't have to spend.

His friend knew what ailed him. "When we get to Avalon, paint a portrait or two," Harris suggested. "You'll make it up, and more besides."

Audubon shook his head. "I don't *want* to do that, dammit." When thwarted, he could act petulant as a child. "I grudge the time I'd have to spend. Every moment counts. I have not so many days left myself, and the upland honkers . . . Well, who can say if they have any left at all?"

"They'll be there." As usual, Harris radiated confidence.

"Will they?" Audubon, by contrast, careened from optimism to the slough of despond on no known schedule. At the moment, not least because of the customs man, he was mired in gloom. "When fishermen first found this land, a dozen species of honkers filled it—filled it as buffalo fill the plains of Terranova. Now . . . Now a few may be left in the wildest parts of Atlantis. Or, even as we speak, the last ones may be dying—may already have died!— under an eagle's claws or the jaws of a pack of wild dogs or to some rude trapper's shotgun."

"The buffalo are starting to go, too," Harris remarked.

That only agitated Audubon more. "I must hurry! Hurry, do you hear me?"

"Well, you can't go anywhere till the *Maid of Orleans* sails," Harris said reasonably.

"One day soon, a railroad will run from New Marseille to Avalon," Audubon said. Atlantis was building railroads almost as fast as England: faster than France, faster than any of the new Terranovan republics. But soon was not yet, and he *did* have to wait for the steamship to head north.

Passengers left the *Maid of Orleans*. Beth got off, which made Harris glum. Others came aboard. Longshoremen carried crates and boxes and barrels and bags ashore. Others brought fresh cargo onto the ship. Passengers and longshoremen alike moved too slowly to suit Audubon. Again, he could only fume and pace the mercifully motionless deck. At last, late the next afternoon, the *Maid of Orleans* steamed towards Avalon.

She stayed close to shore on the two-and-a-half-day journey. It was one of the most beautiful routes anywhere in the world. Titanic redwoods and sequoias grew almost down to the shore. They rose so tall and straight, they might almost have been the columns of a colossal outdoor cathedral.

But that cathedral could have been dedicated to puzzlement and confusion. The only trees like the enormous evergreens of Atlantis were those on the Pacific coast of Terranova, far, far away. Why did they thrive here, survive there, and exist nowhere else? Audubon had no more answer than any other naturalist, though he dearly wished for one. *That* would crown a career! He feared it was a crown he was unlikely to wear.

The *Maid of Orleans* passed a small fishing town called Newquay without stopping. Having identified the place on his map, Audubon was pleased when the purser confirmed he'd done it right. "If anything happens to the navigator, sir, I'm sure we'd be in good hands with you," the man said, and winked to show he didn't aim to be taken too seriously.

Audubon gave him a dutiful smile and went back to eyeing the map. Atlantis' west coast and the east coast of North Terranova a thousand miles away put him in mind of two pieces of a world-sized jigsaw puzzle: their outlines almost fit together. The same was true for the bulge of Brazil in South Terranova and the indentation in West Africa's coastline on the other side of the Atlantic. And the shape of Atlantis' eastern coast corresponded to that of western Europe in a more general way.

What did that mean? Audubon knew he was far from the

first to wonder. How could anyone who looked at a map help but wonder? Had Atlantis and Terranova been joined once upon a time? Had Africa and Brazil? How could they have been, with so much sea between? He saw no way it could be possible. Neither did anyone else. But when you looked at the map . . .

"Coincidence," Harris said when he mentioned it at supper.

"Maybe so." Audubon cut meat from a goose drumstick. His stomach was behaving better these days—and the seas stayed mild. "But if it is a coincidence, don't you think it's a large one?"

"World's a large place." Harris paused to take a sip of wine. "It has room in it for a large coincidence or three, don't you think?"

"Maybe so," Audubon said again, "but when you look at the maps, it seems as if those matches ought to spring from reason, not happenstance."

"Tell me how the ocean got in between them, then." Harris aimed a finger at him like a pistol barrel. "And if you say it was Noah's flood, I'll pick up that bottle of fine Bordeaux and clout you over the head with it."

"I wasn't going to say anything of the sort," Audubon replied. "Noah's flood may have washed over these lands, but I can't see how it could have washed them apart while still leaving their coastlines so much like each other."

"So it must be coincidence, then."

"I don't believe it *must* be anything, *mon vieux*," Audubon said. "I believe we don't know what it is—or, I admit, if it's anything at all. Maybe they will one day, but not now. For now, it's a puzzlement. We need puzzlements, don't you think?"

"For now, John, I need the gravy," Harris said. "Would you kindly pass it to me? Goes mighty well with the goose."

It did, too. Audubon poured some over the moist, dark meat on his plate before handing his friend the gravy boat. Harris wanted to ignore puzzlements when he could. Not Audubon.

They reminded him not only of how much he—and everyone else—didn't know yet, but also of how much he—in particular—might still find out.

As much as I have time for, he thought, and took another bite of goose.

Avalon rose on six hills. The city fathers kept scouting for a seventh so they could compare their town to Rome, but there wasn't another bump to be found for miles around. The west-facing Bay of Avalon gave the city that bore its name perhaps the finest harbor in Atlantis. A century and a half before, the bay was a pirates' roost. The buccaneers swept out to plunder the Hesperian Gulf for most of a lifetime, till a British and Dutch fleet drove them back to their nest and then smoked them out of it.

City streets still remembered the swashbuckling past: Goldbeard Way, Valjean Avenue, Cutpurse Charlie Lane. But two Atlantean steam frigates patrolled the harbor. Fishing boats, bigger merchantmen—some steamers, others sailing ships—and liners like the *Maid of Orleans* moved in and out. The pirates might be remembered, but they were gone.

May it not be so with the honkers, Audubon thought as the *Maid of Orleans* tied up at a pier. *Please, God, let it not be so.* He crossed himself. He didn't know if the prayer would help, but it couldn't hurt, so he sent it up for whatever it might be worth.

Harris pointed to a man coming up the pier. "Isn't that Gordon Coates?"

"It certainly is." Audubon waved to the man who published his work in Atlantis. Coates, a short, round fellow with side whiskers even bushier than Audubon's, waved back. His suit was of shiny silk; a stovepipe hat sat at a jaunty angle on his head. Audubon cupped his hands in front of his mouth. "How are you, Gordon?"

"Oh, tolerable. Maybe a bit better than tolerable," Coates replied. "So you're haring off into the wilderness again, are you?" He was a city man to the tips of his manicured fingers. The only time he went out to the countryside was to take in a horse race. He knew his ponies, too. When he bet, he won . . . more often than not, anyhow.

He had a couple of servants waiting with carts to take charge of the travelers' baggage. He and Audubon and Harris clasped hands and clapped one another on the back when the gangplank went down and passengers could disembark. "Where are you putting us up?" asked Harris, who always thought about things like where he would be put up. Thanks to his thoughts about such things, Audubon had stayed in some places more comfortable than those where he might have if he made his own arrangements.

"How does the Hesperian Queen sound?" Coates answered.

"Like a pirate's kept woman," Audubon answered, and the publisher sent up gales of laughter. Audubon went on, "Is it near a livery stable or a horse market? I'll want to get my animals as soon as I can." Harris let out a sigh. Audubon pretended not to hear it.

"Not too far, not too far," Coates said. Then he pointed up into the sky. "Look—an eagle! There's an omen for you, if you like."

The large, white-headed bird sailed off toward the south. Audubon knew it was likely bound for the city dump, to scavenge there. White-headed eagles had thrived since men came to Atlantis. Seeing this one secretly disappointed Audubon. He wished it were a red-crested eagle, the Atlantean national bird. But the mighty raptors—by all accounts, the largest in the world—had fallen into a steep decline along with the honkers, which were their principal prey.

"Well," he said, "the Hesperian Queen."

The last time he was in Avalon, the hotel had had another

name and another owner. It had come up in the world since. So had Avalon, which was visibly bigger, visibly richer than it had been ten years—or was it twelve now?—before.

Harris noticed, too. Harris generally noticed things like that. "You do well for yourselves here," he told Gordon Coates over beefsteaks at supper.

"Not too bad, not too bad," the publisher said. "I'm about to put out a book by a chap who thinks he's written the great Atlantean novel, and he lives right here in town. I hope he's right. You never can tell."

"You don't believe it, though," Audubon said.

"Well, no," Coates admitted. "Everybody always thinks he's written the great Atlantean novel—unless he comes from Terranova or England. Sometimes even then. Mr. Hawthorne has a better chance than some—a better chance than most, I daresay—but not *that* much better."

"What's it called?" Harris asked.

"*The Crimson Brand*," Coates said. "Not a bad title, if I say so myself—and I do, because it's mine. *He* wanted to name it *The Shores of a Different Sea*." He yawned, as if to say authors were hopeless with titles. Then, pointing at Audubon, he *did* say it: "I'd have called your books something else, too, if they weren't also coming out in England and Terranova. *Birds and Critters*, maybe. Who remembers what a quadruped is, let alone a viviparous one?"

"They've done well enough with the name I gave them," Audubon said.

"Well enough, sure, but they might've done better. I could've made you *big*." Coates was a man with an eye for the main chance. Making Audubon *big*—he lingered lovingly over the word—would have made him money.

"I know why folks here don't know quadrupeds from a hole in the ground," Harris said. "Atlantis hardly had any before it got

discovered. No snakes in Ireland, no . . . critters"—he grinned—
"here, not then."

"No *viviparous* quadrupeds." Audubon had drunk enough wine
to make him most precise—but not too much to keep him from
pronouncing *viviparous*. "A very great plenty of lizards and tur-
tles and frogs and toads and salamanders—and snakes, of course,
though snakes lack four legs of quadrupedality." He was proud of
himself for that.

"Sure enough, snakes haven't got a leg to stand on." Harris
guffawed.

"Well, we have critters enough now, by God," Coates said.
"Everything from mice on up to elk. Some of 'em we wanted,
some we got anyway. Try and keep rats and mice from coming
aboard ship. Yeah, go ahead and try. Good luck—you'll need it."

"How many indigenous Atlantean creatures are no more because of them?" Audubon said.

"Beats me," Coates answered. "Little too late to worry about it
now, anyway, don't you think?"

"I hope not," Audubon said. "I hope it's not too late for them.
I hope it's not too late for me." He took another sip of wine. "And I
know the viviparous creature responsible for the greatest number
of those sad demises here."

"Rats?" Coates asked.

"Weasels, I bet," Harris said.

Audubon shook his head at each of them in turn. He pointed
an index finger at his own chest. "Man," he said.

He rode out of Avalon three days later. Part of the time he spent
buying horses and tackle for them; that, he didn't begrudge. The
rest he spent with Gordon Coates, meeting with subscribers and
potential subscribers for his books; that, he did. He was a bet-

ter businessman than most of his fellow artists, and normally wouldn't have resented keeping customers happy and trolling for new ones. If nobody bought your art, you had a devil of a time making more of it. As a younger man, he'd worked at several other trades, hated them all, and done well at none. He knew how lucky he was to make a living doing what he loved, and how much work went into what others called luck.

To his relief, he did escape without painting portraits. Even before he set out from New Orleans, he'd felt time's hot breath at his heels. He felt himself aging, getting weaker, getting feebler. In another few years, maybe even in another year or two, he would lack the strength and stamina for a journey into the wilds of central Atlantis. And even if he had it, he might not find any honkers left to paint.

I may not find any now, he thought. That ate at him like vitriol. He kept seeing a hunter or a lumberjack with a shotgun. . . .

Setting out from Avalon, Audubon might almost have traveled through the French or English countryside. Oh, the farms here were larger than they were in Europe, with more meadow between them. This was newly settled land; it hadn't been cultivated for centuries, sometimes for millennia. But the crops—wheat, barley, maize, potatoes—were either European or were Terranovan imports long familiar in the Old World. The fruit trees came from Europe; the nuts, again, from Europe and Terranova. Only a few stands of redwoods and Atlantean pines declared that the Hesperian Gulf lay just a few miles to the west.

It was the same with the animals. Dogs yapped outside of farmhouses. Chickens scratched. Cats prowled, hoping for either mice—also immigrants—or unwary chicks. Ducks and geese—ordinary domestic geese—paddled in ponds. Pigs rooted and wallowed. In the fields, cattle and sheep and horses grazed.

Most people probably wouldn't have noticed the ferns that

sprouted here and there or the birds on the ground, in the trees, and on the wing. Some of those birds, like ravens, ranged all over the world. Others, such as the white-headed eagle Audubon had seen in Avalon, were common in both Atlantis and Terranova (on Atlantis' eastern coast, the white-tailed eagle sometimes visited from its more usual haunts in Europe and Iceland). Still others—no one knew how many—were unique to the great island.

No one but a specialist knew or cared how Atlantean gray-faced swifts differed from the chimney swifts of Terranova or little swifts from Europe. Many Atlantean thrushes were plainly the same sorts of birds as their equivalents to the west and to the east. They belonged to different species, but their plumages and habits were similar to those of the rest. The same held true for island warblers, which flitted through the trees after insects like their counterparts on the far side of the Hesperian Gulf. Yes, there were many similarities. But . . .

"I wonder how soon we'll start seeing oil thrushes," Audubon said.

"Not this close to Avalon," Harris said. "Not with so many dogs and cats and pigs running around."

"I suppose not," Audubon said. "They're trusting things, and they haven't much chance of getting away."

Laughing, Harris mimed flapping his fingertips. Oil thrushes' wings were bigger than that, but not by much—they couldn't fly. The birds themselves were bigger than chickens. They used their long, pointed beaks to probe the ground for worms at depths ordinary thrushes, flying thrushes, couldn't hope to reach. When the hunting was good, they laid up fat against a rainy day.

But they were all but helpless against men and the beasts men had brought to Atlantis. It wasn't just that they were good eating, or that their fat, rendered down, made a fine lamp oil. The real trouble was, they didn't seem to know enough to run away when a dog or a fox came after them. They weren't used to being hunted by animals that lived on the ground; the only viviparous quadrupeds on Atlantis before men arrived were bats.

"Even the bats here are peculiar," Audubon muttered.

"Well, so they are, but why do you say so?" Harris asked.

Audubon explained his train of thought. "Where else in the world do you have bats that spend more of their time scurrying around on the ground than flying?" he went on.

He thought that was a rhetorical question, but Harris said, "Aren't there also some in New Zealand?"

"Are there?" Audubon said in surprise. His friend nodded. The painter scratched at his side whiskers. "Well, well. Both lands far from any others, out in the middle of the sea. . . ."

"New Zealand had its own honkers, too, or something like them," Harris said. "What the devil were they called?"

"Moas," Audubon said. "I do remember that. Didn't I show you the marvelous illustrations of their remains Professor Owen did recently? The draftsmanship is astonishing. Astonishing!" The way he kissed his bunched fingertips proved him a Frenchman at heart.

Edward Harris gave him a sly smile. "Surely you could do better?"

"I doubt it," Audubon said. "Each man to his own bent. Making a specimen look as if it were alive on the canvas—that I can do. My talent lies there, and I've spent almost forty years now learning the tricks and turns that go with it. Showing every detail of dead bone—I'm not in the least ashamed to yield the palm to the good professor there."

"If only you were a little less modest, you'd be perfect," Harris said.

"It could be," Audubon said complacently, and they rode on.

The slow, deep drumming came from thirty feet up a dying pine. Harris pointed. "There he is, John! D'you see him?"

"I'm not likely to miss him, not when he's the size of a raven," Audubon answered. Intent on grubs under the bark, the scarlet-cheeked woodpecker went on drumming. It was a male, which meant its crest was also scarlet. A female's crest would have been black, with a forward curl the male's lacked. That also held true for its close relatives on the Terranovan mainland, the ivory-bill and the imperial woodpecker of Mexico.

Audubon dismounted, loaded his shotgun, and approached the bird. He could get closer to the scarlet-cheeked woodpecker than he could have to one of its Terranovan cousins. Like the oil thrush, like so many other Atlantean birds, the woodpecker had trouble understanding that something walking along on the ground could endanger it. Ivory-bills and imperial woodpeckers were less naive.

The woodpecker raised its head and called. The sound was high and shrill, like a false note on a clarinet. Audubon paused with the gun on his shoulder, waiting to see if another bird would answer. When none did, he squeezed the trigger. The shotgun boomed, belching fireworks-smelling smoke.

With a startled squawk, the scarlet-cheeked woodpecker tumbled out of the pine. It thrashed on the ground for a couple of minutes, then lay still. "Nice shot," Harris said.

"*Merci,*" Audubon answered absently.

He picked up the woodpecker. It was still warm in his hands, and still crawling with mites and bird lice. No one who didn't handle wild birds freshly dead thought of such things. He brushed his palm against his trouser leg to get rid of some of the vagrants. They didn't usually trouble people, who weren't to their taste, but every once in a while . . .

A new thought struck him. He stared at the scarlet-cheeked woodpecker. "I wonder if the parasites on Atlantean birds are as different as the birds themselves, or if they share them with the birds of Terranova."

"I don't know," Harris said. "Do you want to pop some into spirits and see?"

After a moment, Audubon shook his head. "No, better to let someone who truly cares about such things take care of it. I'm after honkers, by God, not lice!"

"Nice specimen you took there, though," his friend said. "Scarlet-cheeks are getting scarce, too."

"Not so much forest for them to hunt in as there once was," Audubon said with a sigh. "Not so much of anything in Atlantis as there once was—except men and farms and sheeps." He knew that was wrong as soon as it came out of his mouth, but let it go. "If we don't show what it was, soon it will be no more, and then it will be too late to show. Too late already for too much of it." *Too late for me?* he wondered. *Please, let it not be so!*

"You going to sketch now?" Harris asked.

"If you don't mind. Birds are much easier to pose before they start to stiffen."

"Go ahead, go ahead." Harris slid down from his horse. "I'll smoke a pipe or two and wander around a bit with my shotgun. Maybe I'll bag something else you can paint, or maybe I'll shoot supper instead. Maybe both—who knows? If I remember right, these Atlantean ducks and geese eat as well as any other kind, except canvasbacks." He was convinced canvasback ducks, properly roasted and served with loaf sugar, were the finest fowl in the world. Audubon wasn't so sure he was wrong.

As Harris ambled away, Audubon set the scarlet-cheeked woodpecker on the grass and walked over to one of the packhorses. He knew which sack held his artistic supplies: his posing board and his wires, his charcoal sticks and precious paper.

He remembered how, as a boy, he'd despaired of ever portraying birds in realistic poses. A bird in the hand was all very well, but a dead bird looked like nothing but a dead bird. It drooped, it sagged, it cried its lifelessness to the eye.

When he studied painting with David in France, he sometimes did figure drawings from a mannequin. His cheeks heated when he recalled the articulated bird model he'd tried to make from wood and cork and wire. After endless effort, he produced something that might have done duty for a spavined dodo. His friends laughed at it. How could he get angry at them when he wanted to laugh at it, too? He ended up kicking the horrible thing to pieces.

If he hadn't thought of wires . . . He didn't know what he would have done then. Wires let him position his birds as if they were still alive. The first kingfisher he'd posed—he knew he was on to something even before he finished. As he set up the posing board now, a shadow of that old excitement glided through him again. Even the bird's eyes had seemed to take on life again once he posed it the way he wanted.

As he worked with wires now to position the woodpecker as it had clung to the tree trunk, he wished he could summon more than a shadow of the old thrill. But he'd done the same sort of thing too many times. Routine fought against art. He wasn't discovering a miracle now. He was . . . working.

Well, if you're working, work the best you can, he told himself. And practice did pay. His hands knew almost without conscious thought how best to set the wires, to pose the bird. When his hands thought he was finished, he eyed the scarlet-cheeked woodpecker. Then he moved a wire to adjust its tail's position.

It used those long, stiff feathers to brace itself against the bark, almost as if it had hind legs back there.

He began to sketch. He remembered the agonies of effort that went into his first tries, and how bad they were despite those agonies. He knew others who'd tried to paint, and who gave up when their earlier pieces failed to match what they wanted, what they expected. Some of them, from what he'd seen, had a real gift. But having it and honing it . . . Ah, what a difference! Not many were stubborn enough to keep doing the thing they wanted to do even when they couldn't do it very well. Audubon didn't know how many times he'd almost given up in despair. But when stubbornness met talent, great things could happen.

The charcoal seemed to have a life of its own as it moved across the page. Audubon nodded to himself. His line remained as strong and fluid as ever. He didn't have the tremors and shakes that marked so many men's descent into age—not yet. Yet how far away from them was he? Every time the sun rose, he came one day closer. He sketched fast, racing against his own decay.

Harris' shotgun bellowed. Audubon's hand did jump then. Whose wouldn't, at the unexpected report? But that jerky line was easily rubbed out. He went on, quick and confident, and had the sketch very much the way he wanted it by the time Harris came back carrying a large dead bird by the feet.

"A turkey?" Audubon exclaimed.

His friend nodded, face wreathed in smiles. "Good eating tonight!"

"Well, yes," Audubon said. "But who would have thought the birds could spread so fast? They were introduced in the south. . . . It can't be more than thirty years ago, can it? And now you shoot one here."

"They give better sport than oil thrushes and the like," Harris said. "At least they have the sense to get away if they see trouble coming. The sense God gave a goose, you might say—except He didn't give it to all the geese here, either."

"No," Audubon said. Some of Atlantis' geese flew to other lands as well, and were properly wary. Some stayed on the great island the whole year round. Those birds weren't. Some of them flew poorly. Some couldn't fly at all, having wings as small and useless as those of the oil thrush.

Honkers looked uncommonly like outsized geese with even more outsized legs. Some species even had black necks and white chin patches reminiscent of Canada geese. That frankly puzzled Audubon: it was as if God were repeating Himself in the Creation, but why? Honkers' feet had vestigial webs, too, while their bills, though laterally compressed, otherwise resembled the broad, flat beaks of ordinary geese.

Audubon had seen the specimens preserved in the museum in Hanover: skeletons, a few hides, enormous greenish eggs. The most recent hide was dated 1803. He wished he hadn't remembered that. If this was a wild goose chase, a wild honker chase . . . Then it was, that was all. He was doing all he could. He only wished he could have done it sooner. He'd tried. He'd failed. He only hoped some possibility of success remained.

Harris cleaned the turkey and got a fire going. Audubon finished the sketch. "That's a good one," Harris said, glancing over at it.

"Not bad," Audubon allowed—he *had* caught the pose he wanted. He gutted the scarlet-cheeked woodpecker so he could preserve it. Not surprisingly, the bird's stomach was full of beetle larvae. The very name of its genus, *Campephilus*, meant *grub-loving*. He made a note in his diary and put the bird in strong spirits.

"Better than that," Harris said. He cut up the turkey and skewered drumsticks on twigs.

"Well, maybe," Audubon said as he took one of the skewers from his friend and started roasting the leg. He wasn't shy of praise—no, indeed. All the same, he went on, "I didn't come here for scarlet-cheeked woodpeckers. I came for honkers, by God."

"You take what you get." Harris turned his twig so the drumstick cooked evenly. "You take what you get, and you hope what you get is what you came for."

"Well, maybe," Audubon said again. He looked east, toward the still poorly explored heart of Atlantis. "But the harder you work, the likelier you are to get what you want. I hope I can still work hard enough. And"—he looked east once more—"I hope what I want is still there to get."

He and Harris stayed on the main highway for most of a week. The broad, well-trodden path let them travel faster than they could have on narrower, more winding roads. But when Audubon saw the Green Ridge Mountains rising over the eastern horizon, the temptation to leave the main road got too strong to resist.

"We don't want to go into the mountains anywhere near the highway," he declared. "We know no honkers live close to it, or people would have seen them, *n'est-ce pas?*"

"Stands to reason," Harris said loyally. He paused before adding, "I wouldn't mind another couple of days of halfway decent inns, though."

"When we come back with what we seek, the Hesperian Queen will be none too good," Audubon said. "But we go through adversity to seek our goal."

Harris sighed. "We sure do."

On the main highway, fruit trees and oaks and chestnuts and elms and maples thrived. They were all imports from Europe or from Terranova. Audubon and Harris hadn't gone far from the highway before Atlantean flora reasserted itself: ginkgoes and magnolias, cycads and pines, with ferns growing in profusion as an understory. Birdsongs, some familiar, others strange, doubled and redoubled as the travelers moved into less settled country. Atlantean birds seemed more comfortable with the trees they'd lived in for generations uncounted than with the brash newcomers men brought in.

Not all the newcomers clung to the road. Buttercups and poppies splashed the improbably green landscape with color. Atlantean bees buzzed around the flowers that had to be unfamiliar to them . . . or maybe those were European honeybees, carried to the new land in the midst of the sea to serve the plants men needed, wanted, or simply liked. Curious, Audubon stopped and waited by some poppies for a closer look at the insects. They were, without a doubt, honeybees. He noted the fact in his diary. It left him oddly disappointed but not surprised.

"In another hundred years," he said, climbing back onto his horse, "how much of the old Atlantis will be left? Any?"

"In another hundred years," Harries replied, "it won't matter to either of us, except from beyond the Pearly Gates."

"No, I suppose not." Audubon wondered if he had ten years left, or even five, let alone a hundred. "But it should matter to those who are young here. They throw away marvels without thinking of what they're doing. Wouldn't you like to see dodos preserved alive?" He tried not to recall his unfortunate bird model.

"Alive? Why, I can go to Hanover and hear them speechifying," Harris said. Audubon snorted. His friend waved a placating hand. "Let it go, John. Let it go. I take your point."

"I'm so glad," Audubon said with sardonic relish. "Perhaps the authorities here—your speechifying dodos—could set up parks to preserve some of what they have." He frowned. "Though how parks could keep out foxes and weasels and rats and windblown seeds, I confess I don't know. Still, it would make a start."

They slept on the grass that night. The throaty hoots of an Atlantean ground owl woke Audubon somewhere near midnight. He loaded his shotgun by the faint, bloody light of the campfire's embers, in case the bird came close enough for him to spot it. Ground owls were hen-sized, more or less. They could fly, but not well. They hunted frogs and lizards and the outsized katydids that scurried through the undergrowth here. Nothing hunted them—or rather, nothing had hunted them till foxes and wild dogs and men came to Atlantis. Like so many creatures here, they couldn't seem to imagine they might become prey. Abundant once, they were scarce these days.

This one's call got farther and farther away. Audubon thought about imitating it to lure the ground owl into range of his charge. In the end, he forbore. Blasting away in the middle of the night might frighten Harris into an apoplexy. And besides—Audubon yawned—he was still sleepy himself. He set down the shotgun, rolled himself in his blanket once more, and soon started snoring again.

When Audubon woke the next morning, he saw a mouse-sized katydid's head and a couple of greenish brown legs only a yard or so from his bedroll. He swore softly: the ground owl *had* come by, but without hooting, so he never knew. If he'd stayed up . . . *If I'd stayed up, I would be useless today*, he thought. He needed regular doses of sleep much more than he had twenty years earlier.

"I wouldn't have minded if you fired on an owl," Harris said as he built up the fire and got coffee going. "We're here for that kind of business."

"Good of you to say so," Audubon replied. "It could be that I will have other chances."

"And it could be that you won't. You were the one who said

the old Atlantis was going under. Grab with both hands while it's here."

"With the honkers, I intend to," Audubon said. "If they're there to be grabbed, grab them I shall. The ground owl . . . Well, who knows if it would have come when I hooted?"

"I bet it would. I never knew a soul who could call birds better than you." Harris took a couple of squares of hardtack out of an oilcloth valise and handed one to Audubon. The artist waited till he had his tin cup of coffee before breakfasting. He broke his hardtack into chunks and dunked each one before eating it. The crackers were baked to a fare-thee-well so they would keep for a long time, which left them chewier than his remaining teeth could easily cope with.

As he and his friend got ready to ride on, he looked again at the remains of the giant katydid. "I really ought to get some specimens of those," he remarked.

"Why, in heaven's name?" Harris said. "They aren't birds, and they aren't viviparous quadrupeds, either. They aren't quadrupeds at all."

"No," Audubon said slowly, "but doesn't it seem to you that here they fill the role mice play in most of the world?"

"Next time I see me a six-legged chirping mouse with feelers"—Harris wiggled his forefingers above his eyes—"you can lock me up and lose the key, on account of I'll have soused my brains with the demon rum."

"Or with whiskey, or gin, or whatever else you can get your hands on," Audubon said. Harris grinned and nodded. As Audubon saddled his horse, he couldn't stop thinking about Atlantean katydids and mice. *Something* had to scurry through the leaves and eat whatever it could find there, and so many other creatures ate mice . . . or, here, the insects instead. He nodded to himself. That was worth a note in the diary whenever they stopped again.

They rode into a hamlet a little before noon. It boasted a saloon, a church, and a few houses. BIDEFORD HOUSE OF UNIVERSAL DEVOTION, the church declared. Strange Protestant sects flourished in Atlantis, not least because none was strong enough to dominate—and neither was his own Catholic Church.

But the saloon, in its own way, was also a house of universal devotion. Bideford couldn't have held more than fifty people, but at least a dozen men sat in there, drinking and eating and talking. A silence fell when Audubon and Harris walked in. The locals stared at them. "Strangers," somebody said; he couldn't have sounded much more surprised had he announced a pair of kangaroos.

Not surprisingly, the man behind the bar recovered fastest. "What'll it be, gents?" he asked.

Harris was seldom at a loss when it came to his personal comforts. "Ham sandwich and a mug of beer, if you please."

"That sounds good," Audubon said. "The same for me, if you'd be so kind."

"Half an eagle for both of you together," the proprietor said. Some of the regulars grinned. Even without those telltale smiles, Audubon would have known he was being gouged. But he paid without complaint. He could afford it, and he'd be asking questions later on, and priming the pump with more silver. He wanted the locals to see he could be openhanded.

The beer was . . . beer. The sandwiches, by contrast, were prodigies: great slabs of tender, flavorful ham on fresh-baked bread, enlivened by spicy mustard and pickles all but jumping with dill and garlic and something else, something earthy—an Atlantean spice?

Audubon hadn't come close to finishing his—he had to chew slowly—when the man behind the bar said, "Don't see too many strangers here." Several locals—big, stocky, bearded fellows in homespun—nodded. So did Audubon, politely. The tapman went on, "Mind if I ask what you're doing passing through?"

"I am John James Audubon," Audubon said, and waited to see if anyone knew his name. Most places, he would have had no doubt. In Bideford . . . Well, who could say?

"The painter fella," one of the regulars said.

"That's right." Audubon smiled, more relieved than he wanted to show. "The painter fella." He repeated the words even though they grated. If the locals understood he was a prominent person, they were less likely to rob him and Harris for the fun of it. He introduced his friend.

"Well, what are you doing here in Bideford?" the proprietor asked again.

"Passing through, as you said," Audubon replied. "I'm hoping to paint honkers." This country was almost isolated enough to give him hope of finding some here—not quite, but almost.

"Honkers?" Two or three men said it at the same time. A heartbeat later, they all laughed. One said, "Ain't seen any of them big fowl round these parts since Hector was a pup."

"That's right," someone else said. Solemn nods filled the saloon.

"It's a shame, too," another man said. "My granddad used to say they was easy to kill, and right good eatin'. Lots of meat on 'em, too." That had to be *why* no honkers lived near Bideford these days, but the local seemed ignorant of cause and effect.

"If you know of any place where they might dwell, I'd be pleased to pay for the information." Audubon tapped a pouch on his belt. Coins clinked sweetly. "You'd help my work, and you'd advance the cause of science."

"Half now," the practical Harris added, "and half on the way back if we find what we're looking for. Maybe a bonus, too, if the tip's good enough."

A nice ploy, Audubon thought. *I have to remember that one.* The locals put their heads together. One of the older men, his beard streaked with gray, spoke up: "Well, I don't know anything for sure, mind, but I was out hunting a few years back and ran into this fellow from Thetford." *He* knew where Thetford was, but Audubon didn't. A few questions established that it lay to the northeast. The Bideford man continued, "We got to gabbing, and he said he saw some a few years before that, off the other side of his town. Can't swear he wasn't lyin', mind, but he sounded like he knew what he was talking about."

Harris looked a question towards Audubon. The artist nodded. Harris gave the Bideford man a silver eagle. "Let me have your name, sir," Harris said. "If the tip proves good, and if we don't pass this way again on our return journey, we *will* make good on the rest of the reward."

"Much obliged, sir," the man said. "I'm Lehonti Kent." He carefully spelled it out for Harris, who wrote it down in one of his notebooks.

"What can you tell me about the House of Universal Devotion?" Audubon asked.

That got him more than he'd bargained for. Suddenly everyone, even the most standoffish locals, wanted to talk at once. He gathered that the church preached the innate divinity of every human being and the possibility of transcending mere mankind—as long as you followed the preachings of the man the locals called the Reverend, with a very audible capital R. *Universal Devotion to the Reverend*, he thought. It all seemed to him the rankest, blackest heresy, but the men of Bideford swore by it.

"Plenty of Devotees"—another obvious capital letter—"in Thetford and other places like that," Lehonti Kent said. He plainly had only the vaguest idea of places more than a couple of days' travel from his home village.

"Isn't that interesting?" Audubon said: one of the few phrases polite almost anywhere.

Because the Bidefordites wanted to preach to them, he and Harris couldn't get away from the saloon for a couple of hours. "Well, well," Harris said as they rode away. "Wasn't that *interesting*?" He freighted the word with enough sarcasm to sink a ship twice the size of the *Maid of Orleans*.

Audubon's head was still spinning. The Reverend seemed to have invented a whole new prehistory for Atlantis and Terranova, one that had little to do with anything Audubon thought he'd learned. He wondered if he'd be able to keep it straight enough to get it down in his diary. The Devotees seemed nearly as superstitious to him as the wild red Terranovan tribes—and they should have known better, while the savages were honestly ignorant. Even so, he said, "If Lehonti—what a name!—Kent gave us a true lead, I don't mind the time we spent . . . too much."

Thetford proved a bigger village than Bideford. It also boasted a House of Universal Devotion, though it had a Methodist church as well. A crudely painted sign in front of the House said, THE REVEREND PREACHES SUNDAY!! Two exclamation points would have warned Audubon away even if he'd never passed through Bideford.

He did ask after honkers in Thetford. No one with whom he talked claimed to have seen one, but a couple of men did say some people from the town had seen them once upon a time. Harris doled out more silver, but it spurred neither memory nor imagination.

"Well, we would have come this way anyhow," Audubon said as they went on riding northeast. The Green Ridge Mountains climbed higher in the sky now, dominating the eastern horizon. Peering ahead with a spyglass, Audubon saw countless dark valleys half hidden by the pines and cycads that gave the mountains their name. Anything could live there . . . couldn't it? He had to believe it could. "We have a little more hope now," he added, as much to himself as to Harris.

"Hope is good," his friend said. "Honkers would be better."

The words were hardly out of his mouth before the ferns and cycads by the side of the road quivered . . . and a stag bounded across. Audubon started to raise his shotgun, but stopped with the motion not even well begun. For one thing, the beast was gone. For another, the gun was charged with birdshot, which would only have stung it.

"*Sic transit gloria honkeris*," Harris said.

"*Honkeris?*" But Audubon held up a hand before Harris could speak. "Yes, *honker* would be a third-declension noun, wouldn't it?"

Little by little, the country rose toward the mountains. Cycads thinned out in the woods; more varieties of pines and spruces and redwoods took their places. The ferns in the undergrowth seemed different, too. As settlements thinned out, so did splashes of color from exotic flowers. The very air seemed different: mistier, moister, full of curious, spicy scents the nose would not meet anywhere else in the world. It felt as if the smells of another time were wafting past the travelers.

"And so they are," Audubon said when that thought crossed his mind. "This is the air of Atlantis as it was, Atlantis before those fishermen saw its coast loom up out of the sea."

"Well, almost," Harris said. That he and Audubon and their horses were here proved his point. In case it didn't, he pointed to the track down which they rode. The ground was damp—muddy in spots—for it had rained the day before. A fox's pads showed plainly.

"How many birds has that beast eaten?" Audubon said. "How

many ground-dwellers' nests has it robbed?" Many Atlantean birds nested on the ground, far more than in either Europe or Terranova. But for a few snakes and large lizards, there were no terrestrial predators—or hadn't been, before men brought them in. Audubon made another note in his diary. Till now, he hadn't thought about the effect the presence or absence of predators might have on birds' nesting habits.

Even here, in the sparsely settled heart of Atlantis, a great deal had been lost. But much still remained. Birdsongs filled the air, especially just after sunrise when Audubon and Harris started out each day. Atlantis had several species of crossbills and grosbeaks: birds with bills that seemed made for getting seeds out of cones and disposing of them afterwards. As with so many birds on the island, they were closely related to Terranovan forms but not identical to them.

Audubon shot a male green grosbeak in full breeding plumage. Lying in his hand, the bird, with its apple green back, warm cinnamon belly, and yellow eye streak, seemed gaudy as a seventeenth-century French courtier. But on the branch of a redwood, against the green foliage and rusty brown bark, it hadn't been easy to spot. If it weren't singing so insistently, chances were he would have ridden right past it.

At dusk, Harris shot an oil thrush. That wasn't for research, though Audubon did save the skin. The long-billed flightless thrush had more than enough meat for both of them. The flavor put Audubon in mind of snipe or woodcock: not surprising, perhaps, when all three were so fond of earthworms.

Gnawing on a thighbone, Harris said, "I wonder how long these birds will last."

"Longer than honkers, anyhow, because they're less conspicuous," Audubon said, and his friend nodded. He went on, "But you have reason—they're in danger. They're one more kind that nests on the ground, and how can they escape foxes and dogs that hunt by scent?"

Somewhere off in the distance, far beyond the light of the campfire, a fox yelped and yowled. Harris nodded. "There's a noise that wasn't heard here before the English brought them."

"If it weren't foxes, it would be dogs," Audubon said sadly, and Harris' head bobbed up and down once more. Atlantis was vulnerable to man and his creatures, and that was the long and short of it. "A pity. A great pity," Audubon murmured. Harris nodded yet again.

The screech ripped across the morning air. Audubon's horse snorted and tried to rear. He calmed it with hands and voice and educated thighs. "Good God!" Harris said. "What was that?"

Before answering, Audubon listened to the sudden and absolute silence all around. A moment before, the birds were singing their hearts out. As a lion's roar was said to bring stillness to the African plains, so this screech froze the forests of Atlantis.

It rang out again, wild and harsh and fierce. Excitement tingled through Audubon. "I know what it is!" Despite the urgency in his voice, it hardly rose above a whisper. His gaze swung to the shotgun. *Have to charge it with stronger shot*, he thought.

"What?" Harris also whispered, hoarsely. As after a lion's roar, talking out loud seemed dangerous.

"A red-crested eagle, by all the saints!" Audubon said. "A *rara avis* itself, and also, with luck, a sign honkers aren't far away." Maybe the Atlantean national bird was reduced to hunting sheep or deer, but Audubon hadn't seen any close by. If the eagle still sought the prey it had always chosen before the coming of man . . . Oh, if it did!

Harris didn't just look at his shotgun. He reached for it and methodically began to load. After a moment, so did Audubon. Red-crested eagles didn't fear men. They were used to swooping down on tall creatures that walked on two legs. People could die—people had died—under their great, tearing claws, long as a big man's thumb. Nor were their fierce beaks to be despised—anything but.

"Where did the cry come from?" Audubon asked after loading both barrels.

"That way." Harris pointed north. "Not far, either."

"No, not far at all," Audubon agreed. "We have to find it. We *have* to, Edward!" He plunged into the undergrowth, moving quiet as he could. Harris hurried after him. They both carried their shotguns at high port, ready to fire and ready to try to fend off the eagle if it struck before they could.

Call again. Audubon willed the thought toward the red-crested eagle with all his strength. *Call again. Show us where you are.*

And the eagle did. The smaller birds had begun to sing again. Silence came down on them like a heavy boot. Audubon grew acutely aware of how loud his own footfalls were. He tried to stride more lightly, with what success he had trouble judging. Tracking the cry, he swung to the west just a little.

"There!" Harris breathed behind him. His friend pointed and froze, for all the world like a well-bred, well-trained hunting dog.

Audubon's eyes darted this way and that. He did not see. . . . He did not see. . . . And then he did. "Oh," he whispered: more a soft sound of wonder than a word.

The eagle perched near the top of a ginkgo tree. It was a big female, close to four feet long from the end of its low, long bill to the tip of the tail. The crest was up, showing the bird was alert and in good spirits. It was the coppery red of a redheaded man's hair or a red-tailed hawk's tail, not the glowing crimson of a hummingbird's gorget. The eagle's back was dark brown, its belly a tawny buff.

Slowly, carefully, Audubon and Harris drew closer. For all their caution, the bird saw them. It mantled on its perch, spreading its wings and screeching again. The span was relatively small for the eagle's size—not much more than seven feet—but the wings were very broad. Red-crested eagles flapped more than they soared, unlike their white-headed and golden cousins. Naturalists disagreed about which were their closer kin.

"Watch out," Harris whispered. "It's going to fly."

And it did, not three heartbeats after the words left his mouth. Audubon and Harris both swung up their guns and fired at essentially the same instant. The eagle cried out once more, this time a startled squall of pain and fear. It fell out of the sky and hit the ground with a thump.

"Got it!" Harris exulted.

"Yes." Joy and sorrow warred in Audubon. That magnificent creature—a shame it had to perish for the sake of art and science. How many were left to carry on the race? One fewer, whatever the answer was.

This one wasn't dead yet. It thrashed in the ferns, screaming in fury because it couldn't fly. Its legs were long and strong—could it run? Audubon trotted towards it. *It mustn't get away*, he thought. Now that he and Harris had shot it, it had to become a specimen and a subject for his art. If it didn't, they would have knocked it down for nothing, and he couldn't bear the idea.

The red-crested eagle wasn't running. When he came close enough, he saw that a shotgun ball from one of the two charges had broken its left leg. The bird screeched and snapped at him; he had to jump back in a hurry to keep that fearsome beak from carving a chunk out of his calf. Hate and rage blazed in those great golden eyes.

Along with the shotgun, Harris also carried his revolver. He drew it now, and aimed it at the bird. "I'll finish it," he said. "Put it out of its misery." He thumbed back the hammer.

"In the breast, if you please," Audubon said. "I don't want to spoil the head."

"At your service, John. If the poor creature will only hold still for a few seconds . . ."

After more frantic thrashing and another long-neck lunge at the men who'd reduced it from lord of the air to wounded victim, the eagle paused to pant and to gather its waning strength. Harris fired. A pistol ball would have blown a songbird to pieces, but the eagle was big enough to absorb the bullet. It let out a final bubbling scream before slumping over, dead.

"That is one splendid creature," Harris said solemnly. "No wonder the Atlanteans put it on their flag and on their money."

"No wonder at all," Audubon said. He waited a few minutes, lest the eagle, like a serpent, have one more bite in it. Even then, he nudged the bird with a stick before picking it up. That beak, and the talons on the unwounded leg, commanded respect. He grunted in surprise as he straightened with the still-warm body in his arms. "How much would you say this bird weighs, Edward?"

"Let me see." Harris held out his arms. Audubon put the red-crested eagle in them. Harris grunted, too. He hefted the eagle, his lips pursed thoughtfully. "Dog my cats if it doesn't go thirty pounds, easy. You wouldn't think such a big bird'd be able to get off the ground, would you?"

"We saw it. Many have seen it," Audubon said. He took the eagle back from Harris and gauged its weight again himself. "Thirty pounds? Yes, that seems about right. I would have guessed something around there, too. Neither the golden nor the white-headed eagle goes much above twelve pounds, and even the largest African eagle will not greatly surpass twenty."

"Those birds don't hunt honkers," Harris said. His usual blunt good sense got to the nub of the problem in a handful of words. "The red-crested, now, it needs all the muscles it can get."

"No doubt you're right," Audubon said. "The biggest honkers, down in the eastern lowlands, would stand a foot, two feet, taller than a man and weigh . . . What do you suppose they would weigh?"

"Three or four times as much as a man, maybe more," Harris said. "You look at those skeletons, you see right away they were lardbutted birds."

Audubon wouldn't have put it that way, but he couldn't say his companion was wrong. "Can you imagine the red-crested eagle diving down to strike a great honker?" he said, excitement at the thought making his voice rise. "It would have been like Jove's lightning from the sky, nothing less."

"Can you imagine trying to hold them off with pikes and matchlocks and bows, the way the first settlers did?" Harris said. "Better those fellows than me, by God! It's a wonder there were any second settlers after that."

"No doubt that's so," Audubon said, but he was only half listening. He looked down at the red-crested eagle, already trying to decide how to pose it for what would, for all sorts of reasons, undoubtedly prove the last volume of *Birds and Viviparous Quadrupeds of Northern Terranova and Atlantis*. He wanted to show it in a posture that displayed its power and majesty, but the bird was simply too large even for the double elephant folios of his life's work.

What can't be cured . . . , he thought, and carried the bird back to the patiently waiting horses. Yes, it surely weighed every ounce of thirty pounds; sweat streamed down his face by the time he got to them. The horses rolled their eyes. One of them let out a soft snort at the smell of blood.

"There, there, my pets, my lovelies," he crooned, and gave

each beast a bit of loaf sugar. That calmed them nicely; horses were as susceptible to bribery as people—and much less likely to go back on any bargain they made.

He got to work with the posing board—which, though he'd brought the largest one he had, was almost too small for the purpose—and his wires. Watching him, Harris asked, "How will you pose a honker if we find one?"

"*When* we find one." Audubon would not admit the possibility of failure to his friend or to himself. "How? I'll do the best I can, of course, and I trust I will enjoy your excellent assistance?"

"I'll do whatever you want me to. You know that," Harris said. "Would I be out here in the middle of nowhere if I wouldn't?"

"No, certainly not." Again, though, Audubon gave the reply only half his attention. He knew what he wanted to do now. He shaped the red-crested eagle with wings pulled back and up to brake its flight, talons splayed wide, and beak agape as if it were about to descend on a great honker's back.

He found a stick of charcoal and began to sketch. No sooner had the charcoal touched the paper than he knew this would be a good one, even a great one. Sometimes the hand would refuse to realize what the eye saw, what the brain thought, what the heart desired. Audubon always did the best he could, as he'd told Harris. Some days, that best was better than others. Today . . . Today was one of those. He felt almost as if he stood outside himself, watching himself perform, watching *something* perform through him.

When the drawing was done, he went on holding the charcoal stick, as if he didn't want to let it go. And he didn't. But he had nothing left to add. He'd done what he could do, and . . .

"That's some of your best work in a long time, John—much better than the woodpecker, and that was mighty good," Harris said. "I didn't want to talk while you were at it, for fear I'd break the spell. But that one, when you paint it, will live forever. It will be less than life-sized on the page, then?"

"Yes. It will have to be," Audubon said. When he spoke, it also felt like breaking the spell. But he made himself nod and respond as a man would in normal circumstances; you couldn't stay on that exalted plane forever. Even touching it now and again seemed a special gift from God. More words came: "This is *right*. If it's small, then it's small, that's all. Those who see will understand."

"When they see the bird like that, they will." Harris seemed unable to tear his eyes away from the sketch.

And Audubon descended to mundane reality, drawing ginkgoes and pines and ferns for the background of the painting yet to come. The work there was solid, professional draftsmanship; it seemed a million miles away from the inspiration that had fired him only minutes before.

Once he finished all the sketches he needed, he skinned the eagle and dissected it. When he opened the bird's stomach, he found gobbets of half-digested, unusually dark flesh. It had a strong odor that put him in mind of . . . "Edward!" he said. "What does this smell like to you?"

Harris stooped beside him and sniffed. He needed only a few seconds to find an answer, one very much in character:

"Steak-and-kidney pie, by God!"

And not only was the answer in character. It was also right, as Audubon recognized at once. "It does!" he exclaimed, though the homely dish wasn't one of his favorites. "And these bits of flesh have the look of kidney, too. And that means . . ."

"What?" Harris asked.

"From everything I've read, honker kidneys and the fat above them were—*are*—the red-crested eagle's favorite food!" Audubon answered. "If this bird has a belly full of chunks of kidney, then somewhere not far away, somewhere not far away at all, there must be—there *must* be, I say—honkers on which it fed."

"Unless it killed a deer or some such," Harris said. In that moment, Audubon almost hated his friend—not because Harris was wrong, but because he might not be. And dropping a brute fact on Audubon's glittering tower of speculation seemed one of the cruelest things any man could do.

"Well," Audubon said, and then, bucking up, "Well," again. He gathered himself, gathered his stubbornness. "We just have to find out, don't we?"

Two days later, two days deeper into the western foothills of the Green Ridge Mountains, Audubon's sense of smell again came to his aid. This time, he had no trouble identifying the odor a breeze sent his way. "Phew!" he said, wrinkling his nose. "Something's dead."

"Sure is," Harris agreed. "Something big, too, by the stink."

"Something big . . ." Audubon nodded, trying without much luck to control the electric jolt that coursed through him at those words. "Yes!"

Harris raised an eyebrow. "Yes, indeed. And so?"

"There aren't many big creatures in Atlantis," Audubon said. "It could be a dead man, though I hope not. It could be a dead deer or horse or cow, perhaps. Or it could be . . . Edward, it could be . . ."

"A dead honker?" Harris spoke the word when Audubon couldn't make himself bring it past the barrier of his teeth, past the barrier of his hopes, and out into the open air where it might wither and perish.

"Yes!" he said again, even more explosively than before.

"Well, then, we'd better rein in, hadn't we, and see if we can find out?" Harris let out a creaky chuckle. "Never thought I'd turn bloodhound in my old age. Only goes to show you can't tell, doesn't it?"

He and Audubon tied their horses to a pine sapling by the side of the track. Audubon didn't worry about anyone coming along and stealing the animals; he just didn't want them wandering off. As far as he knew, he and his friend were the only people for miles around. This region was settled thinly, if at all. The two men plunged into the woods, both of them carrying shotguns.

A bloodhound would have run straight to the mass of corruption. Audubon and Harris had no such luck. Tracking by sight or by ear, Audubon would easily have been able to find his quarry. Trying to track by scent, he discovered at once that he was no bloodhound, and neither was Harris. They cast back and forth, trying to decide whether the stench was stronger here or there, in this direction or that: a slow, nasty, frustrating business.

And then, from the edge of a meadow, Harris called, "John! Come quick! I've found it!"

"Mon Dieu!" Audubon crashed toward him, his heart thumping and thudding in his chest. "Is it, Edward?" he asked. "Is it a—?"

"See for yourself." Harris pointed out to the curved lump of meat that lay in the middle of the grass and weeds.

"Mon Dieu," Audubon said again, softly this time, and crossed himself. "It is a dead honker. It *is*. And where there are dead ones, there must be live ones as well."

"Stands to reason," Harris said, "unless this one here is the very last of its kind."

"Bite your tongue, you horrible man. Fate wouldn't be so cruel to me." Audubon hoped—prayed—he was right. He walked out to the huge dead bird.

If any large scavengers had been at the corpse, Harris—or Audubon's noisy passage through the woods—had scared them off. Clouds of flies still buzzed above it, though, while ants and beetles took their share of the odorous bounty. Audubon stood upwind, which helped some, but only so much.

This wasn't one of the truly enormous honkers that had wandered the eastern plains before men found Atlantis. It was an upland species, and probably hadn't been as tall as Audubon or weighed much more than twice as much as he did. A great wound in the center of its back—now boiling with maggots—told how it died. That was surely a blow from a red-crested eagle: perhaps the one Audubon and Harris had shot, perhaps another.

"Can you draw from this one?" Harris asked.

Regretfully, Audubon shook his head. "I fear not. It's too far gone." His sensitive stomach heaved. Even with the ground firm under his feet, the stench nauseated him.

"I was afraid you'd say that," Harris said. "Shall we take specimens—bones and feathers and such—so we have *something* to bring back in case we don't run into any live honkers?"

Messing about with the dead, reeking bird was the last thing Audubon wanted to do. "We *will* find live ones," he said. Harris didn't answer. He just stolidly stood there and let Audubon listen to himself and know he couldn't be certain he was right. The artist glared at him. "But I suppose we should preserve what specimens we can, in the interest of science."

Pulling feathers from the honker wasn't too bad. The black ones on its neck and the white patch under the chin testified to its affinity to Canada geese. The feathers on the body, though, were long and shaggy, more hairlike than similar to the plumage of birds gifted with flight.

Getting the meat from the bones and then cleaning them . . . Audubon's poor stomach couldn't stand the strain. He lost his breakfast on the green meadow grass and then dry-heaved helplessly for a while. A little rill ran through the meadow not far away.

Perhaps the honker was going out to drink there when the eagle struck.

Audubon rinsed his mouth with cold, clear water from the rill . . . upstream from where Harris washed rotting flesh from the honker's right femur. The thighbone was larger and stouter than his own. Gathering himself, Audubon went back to the corpse to free the bird's pelvis. He brought it back to the rill to clean it. How long would his hands reek of decay? How long would his clothes? Would he ever be able to wear this outfit again? He doubted it. As he worked, he tried not to look at what he was doing.

His hands, then, told him of something odd: a hole in the bone on the left side of the pelvis that wasn't matched on the right. That did make him look. Sure enough, the hole was there, and a shallow groove leading to it. "See what I have here," he said to Harris.

His friend examined it, then asked, "What do you make of that?"

"Don't you think it comes from the claw of the red-crested eagle?" Audubon said. "You saw the talons on the bird. One could pierce the flesh above the bone, and then the bone itself. This is plainly a very recent wound: notice how rough the bone is all around the edge. It had no chance to heal."

After considering, Harris nodded. "I'd say you're right. I'd say you have to be right. You might almost have seen the eagle flying at the honker."

"I wish I would have!" Audubon held up the still-stinking pelvis. "I'll have to draw this. It holds too much information to be easily described in words."

"Let Mr. Owen look to his laurels, then," Harris said.

"I'll do the best I can, that's all," Audubon said. The detailed scientific illustration would have to be pen and ink, not charcoal or watercolor. It would also have to be unrelentingly precise. He couldn't pose the pelvis, except to show the perforation to best advantage, and he couldn't alter and adjust to make things more dramatic. His particular gift lay in portraying motion and emotion; he would have to eschew them both here. He clicked his tongue against the roof of his mouth. "An artist should be versatile, eh?"

"I know you can do it." Harris showed more confidence in him than he had in himself.

The smell of rotting honker came closer to spooking the horses than the eagle's blood had a couple of days before. The packhorse that carried Audubon's artistic supplies didn't want to let him anywhere near it. It didn't even want sugar from his stinking hand. He counted himself lucky to take what he needed without getting kicked.

He set the honker hipbone in the sun, then started sketching with a pencil. He tried and rubbed out, tried and rubbed out. Sweat ran down his face, though the day was fine and mild. This was ever so much harder—for him, anyway—than painting would have been. It seemed like forever before what he set down on paper bore any resemblance to the specimen that was its model.

When he was finally satisfied, he held up the sketch to show it to Harris, only to discover his friend had gone off somewhere and he'd never noticed. Painting took far less concentration. It left room for artistry. This . . . This was a craft, and one in which he knew himself to be imperfectly skilled.

He'd just inked his pen for the first time when Harris' shotgun boomed. Would that be supper or another specimen? *I'll find out*, Audubon thought, and set about turning his shades of gray into black and white. He had to turn the pelvis to compensate for the way shadows had shifted with the moving sun while he worked.

Harris fired again. Audubon heard the blast, but didn't consciously register it. His hand never twitched. A fine line here, shading there to show a hollow, the exact look of the gouge the eagle's claw had dug before piercing the pelvis where the bone thinned . . .

"We've got supper," Harris said. Audubon nodded to show he heard. Harris went on, "And here's something for you to work on when you're done there."

That made Audubon look up. Along with a plump oil thrush, Harris carried a small, grayish, pale-bellied bird with a black cap. "An Atlantean tit!" Audubon said. The bird was closely allied to the tits of England and Europe and to Terranovan chickadees. Naturalists disagreed about which group held its nearest kin. At the moment, though, he was just glad he would be able to sketch and paint; to feel; to let imprecision be a virtue, not a sin. "Yes, that will be a change—and a relief."

"How's the drawing coming?" Harris asked. Audubon showed him. Harris looked from the paper to the pelvis and back again. After a moment, he silently lifted his broad-brimmed felt hat from his head, a salute Audubon cherished more than most wordier ones.

"Bones are all very well," the artist said, "but I want the chance to draw honkers from life!"

Audubon began to despair of getting what he wanted. He began to believe Harris' gibe was right, and he'd come along just in time to find the last honker in the world moldering in the meadow. Could fate be so cruel?

Whenever he started to fret, Harris would say, "Well, we've got something, anyway. We didn't know for sure we'd get anything at all when we set out." Every word of that was true, and it always made Audubon feel worse, not better.

He spent several days haunting the meadow where his friend found the dead honker, hoping it was part of a flock or a gaggle or whatever the English word for a group of honkers was. No others showed up, though. He found no fresh tracks in the mud by the rill. At last, sorrowfully, he decided the dead bird must have been alone.

"What if it *was* the last one?" he said. "To miss it by a few days . . . Why couldn't we have shot the eagle sooner? Then the honker would still be alive!"

He waited for Harris to be grateful again for what they had. But Harris surprised him, saying, "No use worrying about it. We don't *know* that eagle got that honker, anyhow."

"Well, no," Audubon admitted upon reflection. "Maybe it was some other villainous eagle instead." He got most affronted when Harris laughed at him.

Even though he was forced to admit to himself that honkers weren't going to visit the meadow, he was loath to leave it. He knew at least one live bird had frequented it up until mere days before. About what other spot in all Atlantis—in all the world— could he say the same?

He kept looking back over his shoulder long after he and Harris rode away. "Don't worry," said Harris, the optimist born. "Bound to be better land ahead."

"How do you know that?" Audubon demanded.

Harris surprised him by having an answer: "Because as best I can tell, nobody's ever come this way before. We're on a track now, not a road. I haven't seen any hoofprints besides the ones our horses are leaving for a couple of hours now."

Audubon blinked. He looked around—*really* looked around. *"Nom d'un nom!"* he murmured. "So it would seem." Pines and cycads and ginkgoes crowded close together on either side of the track. The air was fragrant with scents whose like he would find nowhere else. "This might almost be the antediluvian age, or another world altogether. What do you suppose made our trail?"

"Anywhere else, I'd say deer. That may be so here, too, but I haven't seen any sign of them—no tracks, no droppings," Harris said. "Oil thrushes? Some of the other big flightless birds they have here? Maybe even honkers—who knows?"

That was enough to make Audubon dismount and minutely examine the surface of the trail in the hope of finding honker tracks. With their size and with the vestigial webbing between their toes, they were unmistakable. He found none. He did see oil-thrush footprints, as Harris had suggested: they reminded him of those of the European blackbird or Terranovan robin, except for being three or four times as large. And he saw a fox's pads, which stood out against the spiky background of bird tracks. Imported creatures penetrated even here, to the wild heart of Atlantis.

But of course, he thought. *Harris and I are here, aren't we? And we're no less fond of an oil-thrush supper than foxes are.*

A splash of vivid green on the side of a redwood sapling caught his eye as he rode past. At first, he thought it was some strange Atlantean fungus clinging to the trunk. Then, ever so slowly, it moved. "A cucumber slug!" Harris exclaimed.

The slug was almost the size of a cucumber, though Audubon would have fought shy of eating anything of that iridescent hue. Though it was neither bird nor viviparous quadruped, he stopped and sketched it. It was a curiosity, and one little known to naturalists—few of them penetrated to the cool, humid uplands where it lived. Eyestalks waving, it glided along the trunk, leaving behind a thumb-wide trail of slime.

"Maybe we'll come across some of those snails that are almost as big as your fist, too," Harris said.

"A shame to do it now, when we have no garlic butter." Audubon might draw the line at a cucumber slug, but he was fond of *escargots.* Harris, a Terranovan born and bred, made a horrible face. Audubon only laughed.

They rode on. The tracks they followed were never made by

58

man. They twisted this way and that and doubled back on themselves again and again. Whenever Audubon came out into the open, he scanned the stretch of grass ahead with eager hope. How he longed to see honkers grazing there, or pulling leaves from tender young trees! How disappointed he was, again and again!

"Maybe that *was* the last honker in this part of Atlantis," he mourned as he and Harris made camp one night. "Maybe it was the last honker in all of Atlantis."

"Maybe it was," his friend replied. Audubon, toasting an oil-thrush drumstick over the flames, glared at him. The least Harris could do was sympathize. But then he continued, "We've come too far and we've done too much to give up so soon, haven't we?"

"Yes," Audubon said. "Oh, yes."

As the scents were different in this mostly pristine Atlantean wilderness, so too were the sounds. Enormous frogs boomed out their calls an octave lower than even Terranovan bullfrogs, let alone the smaller frogs of Europe. When Audubon remarked on them, Harris said, "I suppose you're sorry about the garlic butter there, too."

"Why, yes, now that you mention it," the painter said placidly. His friend screwed up his face again.

The big green katydids that might almost have been mice were noisier than rodents would have been, though some of their squeaks sounded eerily mouselike. But most of their chirps and trills showed them to be insects after all. Their calls made up the background noise, more notable when it suddenly ceased than when it went on.

Audubon heard birdsongs he'd never imagined. Surely some of those singers were as yet nondescript, new to science. If he could shoot one, sketch it and paint it, bring back a type specimen . . . He did shoot several warblers and finches, but all, so far as he knew, from species already recognized.

Then he heard the scream of a red-crested eagle somewhere far off to the north. He reined in and pointed in that direction. "We go there," he declared, in tones that brooked no argument.

Harris argued anyhow: "It's miles away, John. We can't hope to find just where it is, and by the time we get there it'll be somewhere else anyhow."

"We go north," Audubon said, as if his friend hadn't spoken. "The eagle may fly away, but if honkers are nearby they won't. They can't."

"If." Edward Harris packed a world of doubt into one small word.

"You said it yourself: we've come too far and done too much to give up hope." If that wasn't precisely what Harris had said, Audubon preferred not to be reminded of it. Harris had the sense to recognize as much.

Going north proved no easier than going in any other cardinal direction. Audubon swore in English, French, and occasionally Spanish when game tracks swerved and led him astray. The red-crested eagle had fallen silent after that one series of screeches, so it told him nothing about how much farther he needed to come. *Maybe it's killed again. Maybe it's feasting*, he thought. Even a freshly dead honker might do.

He and Harris came to a stream like a young river. Those Goliath frogs croaked from the rocks. "Can we ford it?" Audubon asked.

"We'd better look for a shallow stretch," the ever-sensible Harris said.

They found one half a mile to the west, and forded the stream without getting the horses' bellies wet. He unfolded a map of northern Atlantis. "Which stream do you suppose this is?" he said. "It should be big enough to show up here."

Harris put on reading glasses to peer at the map. "If it was ever surveyed at all," he said, and pointed. "It might be a tributary of the Spey. That's about where we are."

"I would have guessed it flows into the Liffey myself." Audubon pointed, too.

"Next one farther north? Well, maybe," Harris said. "The way we've been wandering lately, we could be damn near anywhere. Shall we go on?" Without waiting for an answer, he urged his horse forward. Audubon got his mount moving, too.

Not long after the murmur of the stream and the frogs' formidable calls—what Aristophanes would have done with them!—faded in the distance, Audubon heard what he first thought were geese flying by. He'd ridden out onto a grassy stretch a little while before. He looked north to see if he could spot the birds, but had no luck.

Harris was peering in the same direction, his face puzzled. "Geese—but not quite geese," he said. "Sounds like trumpet music played on a slide trombone."

"It does!" For a moment, Audubon simply smiled at the comparison. Then, sudden wild surmise in his eye, he stared at his friend. "Edward, you don't suppose—?"

"I don't know," Harris said, "but we'd better find out. If they aren't honkers, they could be nondescript geese, which wouldn't be bad, either. Audubon's geese, you could call them."

"I could," said Audubon, who'd never had less interest in discovering a new species. "I could, yes, but . . . I'm going to load my gun with buckshot." He started doing just that.

"Good plan." So did Harris.

Keep calling. Please keep calling, Audubon thought, again and again, as they rode through the forest toward the sound. The birds—whatever they were—did keep up the noise, now quietly, now rising to an angry peak as if a couple of males were quarreling over a female, as males were likely to do in spring.

When Audubon thought they'd come close enough, he slid down off his horse, saying, "We'd best go forward on foot now." He carried not only his gun but also charcoal sticks and paper, in case . . . Harris also dismounted. Audubon believed he would have brained him with the shotgun had he argued.

After perhaps ten minutes, Harris pointed ahead. "Look. We're coming to an open space." Audubon nodded, not trusting himself to speak. He too saw the bright sunshine that told of a break in the trees. The birdcalls were very loud now, very near. "Would you call that honking?" Harris asked. Audubon only shrugged and slid forward.

He peered out from in back of a cycad at the meadow beyond . . . at the meadow, and at the honkers grazing on it. Then they blurred: tears of joy ran down his face.

"Blessed art Thou, O Lord, Who hast preserved me alive to see such things," he whispered, staring and staring.

Harris stood behind a small spruce a few feet away. "Isn't that something. Isn't that *something*?" he said, his words more prosaic than his friend's but his tone hardly less reverent.

Eight honkers grazed there, pulling up grass with their bills: two males, Audubon judged, and half a dozen smaller females. The birds had a more forward-leaning posture than did the mounted skeletons in the Hanover museum. That meant they weren't so tall. The males probably could stretch their heads up higher than a man, but it wouldn't be easy or comfortable for them.

And then they both moved toward the same female, and did stretch their necks up and up and up, and honked as loudly as ever they could, and flapped their tiny, useless wings to make themselves seem big and fierce. And, while they squabbled, the female walked away.

Audubon started sketching. He didn't know how many of the sketches he would work up into paintings and how many would become woodcuts or lithographs. He didn't care, either. He was sketching honkers from life, and if that wasn't heaven it was the next best thing.

"Which species are they, do you suppose?" Harris asked.

Once, at least a dozen varieties of honker had roamed Atlantis' plains and uplands. The largest couple of species, the so-called great honkers, birds of the easily accessible eastern lowlands, went extinct first. Audubon had studied the remains in Hanover and elsewhere to be ready for this day. Now it was here, and he still found himself unsure. "I . . . believe they're what's called the agile honker," he said slowly. "Those are the specimens they most resemble."

"If you say they're agile honkers, why then, they are," Harris said. "Anyone who thinks otherwise will have to change his mind, because you've got the creatures."

"I want to be right." But Audubon couldn't deny his friend had a point. "A shame to have to take a specimen, but . . ."

"It'll feed us for a while, too." The prospect didn't bother Harris. "They *are* supposed to be good eating."

"True enough." When Audubon had all the sketches he wanted of grazing honkers and of bad-tempered males displaying, he stepped out from behind the cycad. The birds stared at him in mild surprise. Then they walked away. He was something strange, but they didn't think he was particularly dangerous. Atlantean creatures had no innate fear of man. The lack cost them dearly.

He walked after them, and they withdrew again. Harris came out, too, which likely didn't help. Audubon held up a hand. "Stay there, Edward. I'll lure them back."

Setting down his shotgun, he lay on his back in the sweet-smelling grass, raised his hips, and pumped his legs in the air, first one, then the other, again and again, faster and faster. He'd made pronghorn antelope on the Terranovan prairie curious enough to approach with that trick. What worked with the wary antelope should work for agile honkers as well. "Are they coming?" he asked.

"They sure are." Harris chuckled. "You look like a damn fool—you know that?"

"So what?" Audubon went on pumping. Yes, he could hear the honkers drawing near, hear their calls and then hear their big, four-toed feet tramping through the grass.

When he stood up again, he found the bigger male only a few feet away. The honker squalled at him; it didn't care for anything on two legs that was taller than it. "Going to shoot that one?" Harris asked.

"Yes. Be ready if my charge doesn't bring it down," Audubon said. Point-blank buckshot should do the job. Sometimes, though, wild creatures were amazingly tenacious of life.

Audubon raised the shotgun. No, the agile honker had no idea what it was. This hardly seemed sporting, but his art and science both required it. He pulled the trigger. The gun kicked against his shoulder. The male let out a last surprised honk and toppled. The rest of the birds ran off—faster than a man, probably as fast as a horse, gabbling as they went.

Harris came up beside Audubon. "He's down. He won't get up again, either."

"No." Audubon wasn't proud of what he'd done. "And the other male can have all the females now."

"He ought to thank you, eh?" Harris leered and poked Audubon in the ribs.

"He'd best enjoy them while he can." Audubon stayed somber. "Sooner or later—probably sooner—someone else will come along and shoot him, too, and his lady friends with him."

By then, the rest of the honkers had gone perhaps a hundred yards. When no more unexpected thunder boomed, they settled down and started grazing again. A few minutes later, a hawk soared by overhead—not a red-crested eagle, but an ordinary hawk far too small to harm them. Still, its shadow panicked them more thoroughly than the shotgun blast had. They sprinted for the cover of the trees, honking louder than they did when Audubon fired.

"Would you please bring my wires, Edward?" the artist asked. "No posing board with a bird this size, but I can truss him up into lifelike postures."

"I'll be back directly," Harris said. He took longer than he promised, but only because instead of carrying things himself he led up the packhorses. That gave Audubon not only the wires but also his watercolors and the strong spirits for preserving bits of the agile honker. If he and Harris did what he'd told the customs man they wouldn't do and drank some of the spirits instead of using them all as preservatives . . . Well, how else could they celebrate?

Audubon soon got to work. "This may be the last painting I ever do," he said. "If it is, I want to give my best."

"Don't be foolish. You're good for another twenty years, easy," Harris said.

"I hope you're right." Audubon left it there. No matter what he hoped, he didn't believe it, however much he wished he did. He went on, "And this may be the last view of these honkers science ever gets. I owe it to them to give my best, too."

He wired the dead male's neck and wings into the pose it took when challenging its rival. He had the sketches he'd made from life to help him do that. His heart pounded as he and Harris manhandled the honker. Ten years earlier, or even five, it wouldn't have seemed so hard. No, he didn't think he had twenty more left, or anything close to that.

Live for the moment, then, he told himself. *It's all there is.* His eye still saw; his hand still obeyed. If the rest of him was wearing out like a steamboat that had gone up and down the Big Muddy too many times . . . then it was. When people remembered him, it would be for what his eye saw and his hand did. The rest? The rest mattered only to him.

And when people remembered agile honkers from now on, that too would be for what *his* eye saw and what *his* hand did. Even more than he had with the red-crested eagle, he felt responsibility's weight heavy on his shoulders.

The other honkers came out from the trees and began grazing again. Some of them drew close to where he worked. Their calls when they saw him by the male's body seemed to his ear curious and plaintive. They knew their fellow was dead, but they couldn't understand why Audubon stood near the corpse. Unlike a hawk's shadow, he was no danger they recognized.

The sun was setting when he looked up from his work. "I think it may do," he said. "The background will wait for later."

Harris examined the honker on the paper, the honker vibrant with the life Audubon had stolen from its model. He set a hand on the painter's shoulder. "Congratulations. This one will last forever."

"Which is more than I will. Which is more than the birds will." Audubon looked down at the dead honker, agile no more. "Now for the anatomical specimens, and now for the dark meat. Poor thing, it will be all flyblown by this time tomorrow."

"But your painting will keep it alive," Harris said.

"My painting will keep its memory alive. It's not the same." Audubon thought again about how his heart had beat too hard, beat too fast. It was quieter now, but another twenty years? Not likely. "No, it's not the same." He sighed. "But it's all we have. A great pity, but it is." He drew his skinning knife. "And now for the rest of the job . . ."

BEDFELLOWS

When I was at ComicCon a few years ago, I got to talking with a fine San Diego poet, Terry Hertzler. We agreed that, in an odd way, the then-President and a certain terrorist leader had done more for each other than to each other. Stretch that to its illogical extreme and what you get is "Bedfellows." I owe the title and several other fine suggestions to Gordon van Gelder, who bought it for Fantasy & Science Fiction. *It's not real. Of course it's not real. It could never, ever happen. Nahhh.*

$\mathcal{T}$here are photographers. There are strobing flashes. They know ahead of time there will be. They leave their rented limo and walk across the Boston Common toward the State House hand in hand, heads held high. They're in love, and they want to tell the world about it.

W is tall, in a conservative—compassionate, oh yes, but conservative—gray suit with television-blue shirt and maroon necktie. O is taller, and his turban lends him a few extra inches besides. His *shalwar kamiz* is of all-natural fabrics. He's trimmed his beard for the occasion—just a little, but you can tell.

"How did you meet?" a reporter calls to the two of them.

They both smile. O's eyes twinkle. If that's not mascara, he has the longest eyelashes in the world. Their hands squeeze—W's right, O's left. "Oh, we've been chasing each other for years," W says coyly. Joy fills his drawl.

"It is so. *Inshallah*, we shall be together forever," O says. "Truly God is great, to let us find such happiness."

News vans clog Beacon Street. Cops need to clear a path through the reporters so W and O can cross. A TV guy looking for an angle asks one of Boston's finest, "What do you think of all this?"

"Me?" The policeman shrugs. "I don't see how it's my business one way or the other. The court says they've got the right to do it, so that's what the law is. Long as they stay inside the law, nothing else matters."

"Uh, thank you." The TV guy sounds disappointed. He wants controversy, fireworks. That's what TV news is all about. Acceptance? One word—boring.

The State House. Good visuals. Gilded dome. Corinthian colonnade. The happy couple going up the stairs and inside.

More reporters in there. More camerapersons, too. O raises a hand against the bright television lights. More flashes go off, one after another. "Boy, you'd think we're in the middle of a nucular war or something," W says. He always pronounces it *nucular*.

"Nuclear," O says gently. "It's *nuclear*." You can tell he's been trying to get W to do it right for a long time. Every couple needs a little something to squabble about. It takes the strain off, it really does.

"Can we get a picture of you two in front of the Sacred Cod?" a photographer asks.

"I don't mind." W is as genial as they come.

But O frowns. "Sacred Cod? It sounds like a graven image. No, I think not." He shakes his head. "It would not play well in Riyadh or Kandahar."

"Aw, c'mon, Sam, be a sport." W has a nickname for everybody, even his nearest and dearest. And he really does like to oblige.

But O digs in his heels. "I do not care to do this. It is not why we came here. I know why we came here." He bends down and whispers in W's ear. W laughs—giggles, almost. Of course, maybe O's beard tickles, trimmed or not.

W gives the reporters kind of a sheepish smile. "Sorry, friends.

74

That's one photo op you're not gonna get. Now which way to the judge's office?"

"Chambers. The judge's chambers," O says. You wonder which one was brought up speaking English.

"Whatever." W doesn't care how he talks. "Which way?" There's a big old sign with an arrow ——> showing the way. He doesn't notice till one of the reporters points to it.

He and O start down the hall. A reporter calls after them: "What do you see in each other?"

They stop. They turn so they're face-to-face. They gaze into each other's eyes. Now they have both hands clasped together. Anyone can tell it's love. "We need each other," W says. Even if he doesn't talk real well, he gets the message across.

"My infidel," O says fondly.

"My little terrorist." W's eyes glow.

You've seen couples who say the same thing at the same time? They do it here. "Without him," they both say, each pointing to the other, "I'm nothing." O strokes W's cheek. W swats O on the butt. They're grinning when they go into the judge's chambers.

The justice of the peace looks at the two of them over the top of her glasses. How many times has she done that, with how many couples? "You have your license. I can't stop you. But I do want to ask you if you're sure about what you're doing," she says. "Marriage is a big step. You shouldn't enter into it lightly."

"We're sure, ma'am," W says.

"Oh, yes," O says. "*Oh*, yes."

"Well, you sound like you mean it. That's good," she says. "You're making a commitment to each other for the rest of your lives. You're promising to be there for each other in sickness and in health, in good times and in bad."

"We understand," O says.

"I should say we do." W nods like a bobblehead, up and down, up and down. "We already look out for each other. Why, if it wasn't for Sam here, my poll numbers would be underwater."

O beams down at him. "My friends need infidels to hate, and W makes hating them so easy. Take Abu Ghraib, for instance. You'd think he did it just for me."

"Nope. Wasn't like that at all." Now W's head goes side to side, side to side, as if it's on a spring. "We both had fun there. We share lots of things." He grins at O. "See? I told you I'd bring you to justice."

O laughs. "All right." The corners of the justice of the peace's mouth twitch up in spite of themselves. She doesn't meet devotion like this every day. "Let's proceed to the ceremony, then." She reads the carefully nondenominational words. At last, she gets to the nitty-gritty. "Do you take each other to have and to hold, to love and to cherish, as long as you both shall live?"

"I do." W and O answer together. Proudly.

"Then by the authority vested in me by the Commonwealth of Massachusetts, I now pronounce you man and, uh, man." Even though they're legal, the judge is still new at same-sex marriages. Who isn't? But she recovers well: "You may kiss each other."

They do. In here, it's nothing but a little peck on the lips. They wink at each other. They know what the cameras outside are waiting for.

An explosion, a fusillade of flashes when they come out into the hallway. You can see W's mouth shaping *nucular* again, but you can't hear him—too many people yelling questions at once. You can see O tolerantly nodding, too. He knows W's not about to change.

A guy with a great big voice makes himself heard through the din: "Is it official?"

"It sure is," W says.

"Have you kissed each other yet?" somebody else asks—a woman.

"Well, yeah," W answers. The reporters make disappointed noises. W and O wink at each other again. Sometimes they're like a couple of little kids—they seem to think they've invented what they share. "We could do it again, if you want us to," W says.

The roar of approval startles even him and O. O grabs him, bends him back movie-style, and plants a big kiss right on his mouth. W's arms tighten around O's neck. The kiss goes on and on. Another zillion flashes freeze it in thin slices so the whole world can see.

Everything has to end. At last, the kiss does. "Wow!" a reporter says. "Is that hotter than Madonna and Britney or what?"

"Than who?" O doesn't get out much.

W does. "You betcha," he says. If his grin gets any wider, the top of his head will fall off. Is that a bulge in those conservative gray pants? Sure looks like one.

"Where will you honeymoon?" another reporter calls.

"In the mountains," O says.

"At the ranch," W says at the same time.

Not quite in synch there. They look at each other. They pantomime comic shrugs. They'll work it out.

Still hand in hand, they leave the State House. "Massachusetts is a very nice place," O says. "Very . . . tolerant."

"Well, if they put up with me here, they'll put up with anybody," W says, and gets a laugh.

"Gotta take you to meet the folks," W says as they start back toward the limo.

O raises an eyebrow. "That should be . . . interesting."

"Well, yeah." W sounds kind of sheepish. His folks are very, very straight. Then out of nowhere he grins all over his face. "We can do it like that movie, that waddayacallit I showed you." He snaps his fingers. "*La Cage aux Folles*, that's it." You think W has trouble with English, you should hear him try French. Or maybe you shouldn't. It's pretty bad.

"You *are* joking?" There's an ominous ring in O's voice.

"No, no!" W's practically jumping up and down. He's got it all figured out. He may not be right, but by God he's sure. "We'll put you in a bertha, that's what we'll do!"

"A what?" O says.

"Come on, Sam. *You* know. You ought to. You've seen 'em close up, right? One of those robe things that doesn't show any-thing but your eyes."

"A *burka*?"

"That's what I said, isn't it?" W thinks it is, anyway.

"The *burka* is for women," O says in icy tones. Then he smiles thinly—very thinly. "Oh, I see." He draws himself up to his full height, straight as a rocket-propelled grenade launcher. A cat couldn't show more affronted dignity, or even as much. "No."

And W laughs fit to bust. He howls. He slaps his knee. "Got-cha! I gotcha, Sam! Can't tell me I didn't, not this time. I had you going good." He pokes O in the ribs with a pointy elbow.

"You were joking?" O looks at him. "You *were* joking," he ad-mits. He laughs, too, ruefully. "Yes, you got me. This time you got me."

W gives him a hug. You can't stay mad at W, no matter how much you want to. He just won't let you. "I'm glad I've got you, too," he says.

And O melts. He can't help it. "I'm glad I've got you, too—you troublemaker," he says. They both laugh. O goes on, "But maybe we could meet your parents another time?"

"After the honeymoon?" W says.

"Wherever it is," O says.

"I love you," says W. "You made me what I am today."

"And you me." O kisses W, and they walk off across the Common with their arms around each other's waists.

NEWS FROM THE FRONT

————————

As Larry Niven says, there is a technical term for those who judge writers' politics by what they turn out. That term is idiot. *If you doubt it, remember that I wrote "Bedfellows" and I wrote this one. It wonders how World War II might have gone were the American media in those days as, mm, unconstrained as they are now. I like writing pastiche. This piece let me impersonate both Edward R. Murrow and Ernie Pyle. Can't ask for more than that.*

★

December 7, 1941—*Austin Daily Tribune*

U.S. AT WAR

★

December 8, 1941—*Washington Post*

PRESIDENT ASKS FOR WAR DECLARATION!

Claims Date of Attack Will "Live in Infamy"

★

December 8, 1941—*Chicago Tribune*

CONGRESS DECLARES WAR ON JAPAN!

Declaration Is Not Unanimous

December 9, 1941—*New York Times* editorial

ROOSEVELT'S WAR

Plainly, President Franklin D. Roosevelt has brought this war on himself and on the United States. On July 25 of this year, he froze Japanese assets in the United States. On the following day, he ordered the military forces of the Philippine Islands incorporated into our own—a clear act of aggression. And on August 1, he embargoed export of high-octane gasoline and crude oil to Japan, a nation with limited energy resources of its own. Is it any wonder that a proud people might be expected to respond with force to these outrageous provocations? Are we not in large measure to blame for what has happened to us?

Further proof of Mr. Roosevelt's intentions, if such be needed, is offered by the August 12 extension of the Selective Service Act allowing peacetime conscription. Pulling out all political stops and shamelessly exploiting his party's Congressional majorities, the President rammed the measure through by a single vote in the House, a vote some Representatives certainly now regret. . . .

December 11, 1941—*Boston Traveler*

AXIS, U.S. DECLARE WAR

December 12, 1941—*Los Angeles Times* editorial

TWO-FRONT WAR

Having suffered a stinging setback in the Pacific, we now suddenly find ourselves called upon to fight two European enemies as well. FDR's inept foreign-policy team has much to answer for. Mothers whose sons are drafted may well wonder whether the fight is worthwhile and whether the government that orders them into battle has any idea what it is doing. . . .

December 22, 1941—*The New Yorker*

FIASCO IN THE PACIFIC

War Department officials privately concede that U.S. preparations to defend Hawaii and the Philippines weren't up to snuff. "It's almost criminal, how badly we fouled up," said one prominent officer, speaking on condition of anonymity. "The administration really didn't know what the devil it was doing out there."

He and other sources sketch a picture of incompetence on both the strategic and tactical levels. Ships from the Pacific Fleet were brought into port at Pearl Harbor every Saturday and Sunday, offering the Japanese a perfect chance to schedule their attacks. U.S. patterns became predictable as early as this past February, said a source in the Navy Department who is in a position to know.

Further, U.S. search patterns the morning of the attack were utterly inadequate. Airplanes searched a diamond extending as far as 200 miles west of Pearl Harbor and a long, narrow rectangle reaching as far as 100 miles south of the ravaged base, *and that was all*. There was no search coverage north of the island of Oahu, the direction from which the Japanese launched their devastating attack.

It has also been learned that a highly secret electronic warning system actually detected the incoming Japanese planes half an hour before they struck Pearl Harbor. When an operator at this base in the northern part of Oahu spotted these aircraft, he suggested calling in a warning to Pearl Harbor. His superior told him he was crazy.

The junior enlisted man persisted. He finally persuaded his superior to call the Information Center near Fort Shafter. The man reported "that we had an unusually large flight—in fact, the largest I had ever seen on the equipment—coming in from almost due north at 130-some miles."

"Well, don't worry about it," said the officer in charge there, believing the planes to be B-17s from the U.S. mainland.

A private asked the officer, "What do you think it is?"

"It's nothing," the officer replied. About twenty minutes later, bombs began falling.

In the White House, a tense meeting of Cabinet and Congressional leaders ensued. "The principal defense of the whole country and the whole West Coast of the Americas has been very seriously damaged today," Roosevelt admitted.

Senator Tom Connally angrily questioned Navy Secretary Knox: "Didn't you say last month that we could lick the Japs in two weeks? Didn't you say that our Navy was so well prepared and located that the Japanese couldn't hope to hurt us at all?"

According to those present, Knox had trouble coming up with any answer.

Connally pressed him further: "Why did you have all the ships at Pearl Harbor crowded in the way you did? You weren't thinking of an air attack?"

"No," was all Knox said. Roosevelt offered no further comment, either.

"Well, they were supposed to be on the alert," Connally thundered. "I am amazed by the attack by Japan, but I am still more astounded at what happened to our Navy. They were all asleep. Where were our patrols?"

Again, the Secretary of the Navy did not reply.

In the Philippines, the picture of U.S. ineptitude is no better. It may be worse. Another of these secret, specialized electronic range-finding stations was in place in the northern regions of the island of Luzon. It detected Japanese planes approaching from Formosa, but failed to communicate with airfields there to warn them. Some sources blame radio interference. Others point to downed land lines. Whatever the reason, the warning never went through.

And U.S. bombers and fighters were caught on the ground. Although General MacArthur knew Hawaii had been attacked, our planes were caught on the ground. They suffered catastrophic losses from Japanese bombing and strafing attacks. With a third of our fighters and more than half of our heavy bombers—again, the B-17, the apparently misnamed Flying Fortress—lost, any hope for air defense of the Philippines has also been destroyed. Reinforcement also appears improbable. Our forces there, then, are plainly doomed to defeat. . . .

December 23, 1941—*Washington Post*

FDR DECRIES LEAKS

Claims They Harm National Security

President Roosevelt used a so-called fireside chat last night to condemn the publication in *The New Yorker* and elsewhere of information about U.S. military failings. "We are in a war now," he said, "so the rules change. We have to be careful about balancing the people's need to know against the damage these stories can cause our Army and Navy."

He particularly cited the electronic rangefinder mentioned in the *New Yorker* article. Roosevelt claims the Japanese were ignorant of this device and its potential. (The *Post* has learned that the apparatus is commonly called *radar*—an acronym for RAdio Detecting And Ranging.)

A Republican spokesman was quick to challenge the President. "I yield to no one in my support of our troops," he said. "But this administration's record of incompetence in military preparation and in the conduct of the war to date must be exposed. The American people are entitled to the facts—*all* the facts—from which, and from which alone, they can make a proper judgment."

December 29, 1941—*The New Yorker*

DID WAKE HAVE TO FALL?

More fumbling by officials in Honolulu and Washington led to the surrender of Wake Island to the Japanese last Tuesday. Wake, west of the Hawaiian chain, was an important position. Even disgraced Admiral Husband E. Kimmel, who so recently mismanaged the defense of Hawaii, could see this. In a letter dated this past April which a Navy Department source has made available to me, Kimmel wrote:

> To deny Wake to the enemy, without occupying it, would be difficult; to recapture it, if the Japanese should seize it in the early period of hostilities, would require operations of some magnitude. Since the Japanese Fourth Fleet includes transports and troops with equipment especially suited for land operations, it appears not unlikely that one of the initial operations of the Japanese may be directed against Wake.

He was right about that—he could be right about some things. He also recommended that Wake be fortified. But work there did not begin until August 19, more than three months after his letter. Guns were not emplaced until mid-October. Obsolescent aircraft were flown in to try to help defend the island.

After the first Japanese attack on Wake failed, Kimmel proposed a three-pronged countermove, based on our fast carrier forces. Why he thought they might succeed in the face of already established Japanese superiority may be questioned, but he did. The plan did not succeed.

Bad weather kept one carrier from refueling at sea. Bad intelligence data led to a raid on the Japanese base at Jaluit, which proved not to need raiding. Then sizable Japanese air and submarine forces were anticipated in the area. They turned out not to be there, but it was too late.

The relief force, centered on the *Saratoga*, was within 600 miles of Wake Island when the Japanese launched their second attack. They were able to move quickly and think on their feet; we seemed capable of nothing of the kind. They destroyed our last two fighters with continuing heavy air raids, and landed 2,000 men to oppose 500 U.S. Marines.

At this point, Admiral Pye, who replaced Admiral Kimmel before Admiral Nimitz arrived—another illustration of our scrambled command structure—issued and then countermanded several orders. The result was that the relieving force was recalled, and Wake was lost. The recall order provoked a near mutiny aboard some U.S. ships, but in the end was obeyed.

In another document obtained from Navy Department sources, Admiral Pye wrote, "When the enemy had once landed on the island, the general strategic situation took precedence, and conservation of our naval forces became the first consideration. I ordered the retirement with extreme regret."

How many more retirements will we have to regret—extremely—in days to come?

January 1, 1942—*New York Times* editorial

FREEDOM AND LICENSE

President Roosevelt believes news coverage of the war hampers U.S. foreign policy. Neither Mr. Roosevelt nor any lesser figure in his administration has denied the truth of stories recently appearing in this newspaper and elsewhere. On the contrary. The administration's attitude seems to be, Even though this is true, the people must not hear of it.

Some in the administration have questioned the press' patriotism. They have pointed to their own by contrast. Quoting Samuel Johnson—"Patriotism is the last refuge of a scoundrel"—in this context is almost too easy, but we shall not deny ourselves the small pleasure. By wrapping themselves in the American flag, administration officials appear to believe that they become immune to criticism of their failures, which are many and serious.

We are not for or against anybody. We are for the truth, and for publishing the truth. Once the people have the whole truth in front of them, they can decide for themselves. If our government claims it has the right to suppress any part of the truth, how does it differ from the regimes it opposes?

One truth in need of remembering at the moment is that, just over a year ago, Mr. Roosevelt was running for an unprecedented third term. On October 30, 1940, a week before the election, he categorically stated, "I have said this before, but I shall say it again and again and again: your boys are not going to be sent into any foreign wars."

Did Mr. Roosevelt believe even then that he was telling the truth? Given the disasters and the constant missteps that have bedeviled us since we found ourselves in this unfortunate conflict, would it not be better if he had been?

January 3, 1942—*Los Angeles Times*

FDR'S POLL NUMBERS PLUMMET

Since the outbreak of war last month, Franklin D. Roosevelt's personal popularity with American voters has dramatically faded. So has public confidence in his ability to lead the United States to victory. Newest figures from the George Gallup organization make the slide unmistakably clear.

Last December 15, 63% of Americans polled had a favorable impression of FDR, while 59% thought he was an effective war leader. In a survey conducted on December 29, only 49% of respondents had a favorable impression of the President. Faith in his leadership fell even more steeply. Only 38% of those responding believed him "effective" or "very effective" as commander-in-chief.

These figures are based on a survey of 1,127 Americans of voting age who described themselves as "likely" or "very likely" to cast ballots in the next election. The margin for error is ±3%.

January 5, 1942—*Chicago Tribune*

CAN'T FIGHT WAR WITH POLLS, WHITE HOUSE ALLEGES

A White House spokesman called the latest Gallup Poll figures "irrelevant" and "unimportant." In a heated exchange with reporters, the press secretary said, "It's ridiculous to think you can run a war by Gallup Poll."

This is only the latest in a series of evasions from an administration longer on excuses than results. If Roosevelt and his clique keep ignoring public opinion, they will be punished in a poll that matters even to them: the upcoming November elections.

Reporters also asked why Roosevelt is so sensitive about being photographed in a wheelchair. "Everybody knows he uses one," a scribe said.

"Is he afraid of being perceived as weak?" another added.

The press secretary, a former advertising copywriter, termed these queries "shameless" and "impertinent." He offered no explanation for his remarks. Since the war began, the administration has had few explanations to offer, and fewer that can be believed. . . .

January 8, 1942—*Philadelphia Inquirer*

DEMONSTRATORS CLASH— COPS WADE IN

Accusations of Police Brutality

Pro- and antiwar demonstrators threw rocks and bottles at one another in an incident in front of city hall yesterday. Shouting "Nazis!" and "Fascists!" and "Jap-lovers!" the prowar demonstrators attacked people peacefully protesting Roosevelt's ill-advised foreign adventures.

Police were supposed to keep the two groups separate. The antiwar demonstrators, who carried placards reading SEND JAPAN OIL, NOT BLOOD and U.S. TROOPS OUT OF AUSTRALIA and FDR LIED, did not respond to the provocation for some time. When they began to defend themselves, the cops weighed in—on their opponents' side.

"They were swinging their nightsticks, beating on people—it was terrible," said Mildred Andersen, 27. She had come down from Scranton to take part in the protest. "Is this what America's supposed to be about?"

"The cops rioted—nothing else but," agreed Dennis Pulaski, 22, of Philadelphia. He had a gash above his left eyebrow inflicted by a police billy club. "They're supposed to keep the peace, aren't they? They only made things worse."

Police officials declined comment.

January 15, 1942—*Variety*

ANTIWAR PICS PLANNED

MGM, Fox Race to Hit Theaters First

Major Hollywood talent is getting behind the building antiwar buzz. Two big stars and a gorgeous gal will crank out *The Road to Nowhere*—shooting begins tomorrow. Expect it in theaters this spring.

A new radio program, *Boy, Do You Bet Your Life,* airs Wednesday at 8 on the Mutual Network. Its shlemiel of a hero soon discovers Army life ain't what it's cracked up to be. Yeah, so you didn't know that already.

And a New Jersey heartthrob crooner is putting out a platter called "Ain't Gonna Study War No More." The B side will be "Swing for Peace." Think maybe he's out to make a point? Us, too.

February 5, 1942—newsreel narration

What you are about to see has been banned by the Navy Department. The Navy has imposed military censorship about what's going on at sea on the entire East Coast of the United States. That's one more thing it doesn't want you to know. Our cameraman had to smuggle this film out under the noses of Navy authorities to get it to you so you can see the facts.

On the thirty-first of last month, that cameraman and his crew were on the shore by Norfolk, Virginia, when a rescue ship brought thirty survivors from the 6,000-ton tanker *Rochester* into port. You can see their dreadful condition. Our intrepid interviewer managed to speak to one of them before they were hustled away.

"What happened to you?"

"We got torpedoed. Broad daylight. [Bleep] sub attacked on the surface. We never had a chance. We started going down fast. Next thing I knew, I was in the drink. That's how I got this [bleep] oil all over me."

"Did you lose any shipmates?"

"Better believe it, buddy."

"I'm sorry. I—"

At that point, we had to withdraw, because naval officers were coming up. They would have confiscated this film if they'd been able to get their hands on it. They have confiscated other film, and blocked newspaper reporting, too. The *Rochester* is the seventeenth ship known to be attacked in Atlantic waters since the war began. How many had you heard about? How many more will there be?

And how many U-boats has the Navy sunk? Any at all?

February 9, 1942—*The New Yorker*

DOWN THE TUBES

The Mark XIV torpedo is the U.S. Navy's answer to Jane Russell: an expensive bust. Too often, it doesn't go where our submariners aim it. When it does, it doesn't sink what they aim it at. Why not? The answer breaks into three parts—poor design, poor testing, and poor production.

Some Mark XIVs dive down to the bottom of the sea shortly after launch. Some run wild. A few have even reversed course and attacked the subs that turned them loose. Despite this, on the record Navy Department officials continue to insist that there is no problem. Off the record—but only off the record—they are trying to figure out what all is wrong and how to fix it.

The magnetic exploder is an idea whose time may not have come. It was considered and rejected by the German U-boat service, which has more experience with submarine warfare than anyone else on earth. Still, in its infinite wisdom, FDR's Navy Department chose to use this unproved system.

And, in its infinite wisdom, FDR's Navy Department conducted no live-firing tests before the war broke out. None. Officials were sure the magnetic exploder would perform as advertised. If you're sure, why bother to test?

Combat experience has shown why. Our Mark XIVs run silent and run deep. More often than not, they run *too* deep: under the keels of the ships at which they're aimed and on their merry way. Or, sometimes, the magnetic exploder—which is a fragile and highly temperamental gadget—will blow up before the torpedo gets to its target. Manufacturing quality is not where it ought to be—not even close.

Despite this, Navy Department brass is making submariners scrimp with their "fish." They are strongly urged to shoot only one or two torpedoes at each ship, not a large spread. The brass is sure one hit from a torpedo with a magnetic exploder will sink anything afloat. Getting the hit seems to be the sticking point.

Japan builds torpedoes that work even when dropped from airplanes. Why don't we? The answer looks obvious. We want to save money. Japan wants to win the war. When fighting a foe who shows such fanatical determination, how can we hope to prevail?

February 13, 1942—*Washington Post*

ADMINISTRATION RIPS NAYSAYERS

"We Can Gain Victory," FDR Insists

President Roosevelt used the excuse of Lincoln's Birthday to allege that the United States and its coalition partners might still win the war despite the swelling tide of opposition to his ill-planned adventure.

In a national radio address, Roosevelt said, "Those who point out our weaknesses and emphasize our disagreements only aid the enemy. We were taken by surprise on December 7. We need time to get rolling. But we *can* do the job."

The President seemed ill at ease—almost desperate—as he went on, "These leaks that torment us have got to stop. They help no one but the foes of freedom. It is much harder to go forward if Germany and Japan know what we are going to do before we do it."

In the Congressional response to his speech, a ranking member of the Foreign Affairs Committee said, "The President's speech highlights the bankruptcy of his policies. After promising to keep us out of war, he got us into one we are not ready to fight. Our weapons don't work, and we can't begin to keep our shipping safe. We don't have enough men to do half of what the President and the Secretary of War are trying to do. And even if we did, what they want to do doesn't look like a good idea anyhow."

Peaceful pickets outside the White House demanded that the President bring our troops back to the United States and keep them out of harm's way. The presence of photographers and reporters helped ensure that White House police did not rough up the demonstrators.

February 23, 1942—*Washington Post*

HOUSE REJECTS RATIONING BILL

In an embarrassing defeat for the administration, the House of Representatives voted 241–183 to reject a bill that would have rationed fuel, food, and materials deemed "essential to wartime industries."

"Why should the American people have to suffer for Roosevelt's mistakes?" demanded a Congressman who opposed the bill. "If we rationed these commodities, you could just wait and see. Gas would jump past thirty cents a gallon, and there wouldn't be enough of it even at that price."

A War Department official, speaking off the record, called the House's action "deplorable." The only public comment from the executive branch was that it was "studying the situation." Had it done that in 1940 and 1941 . . .

March 17, 1942—*San Francisco Chronicle*

MACARTHUR BAILS OUT OF PHILIPPINES!

Leaves Besieged Garrison to Fate

General Douglas MacArthur fled the Philippines one jump ahead of the Japanese. PT boats and a B-17 brought him to Darwin, Australia. (Incidentally, Japanese bombers leveled Darwin last month and forced its abandonment.)

"I shall return," pledged MacArthur. But the promise rings hollow for the men he left behind. Trapped on the Bataan Peninsula in a war they do not understand, they soldier on as best they can. Since Japanese forces surround them, the only question is how long they can hold out.

Roosevelt hopes MacArthur can lead counterattacks later in the war. Given the disasters thus far, this seems only another sample of his blind and foolish optimism. . . .

March 23, 1942—*The New Yorker*

CAN WE HUNT THE SEA WOLVES?

German U-boats are taking a disastrous toll on military goods bound for England. In the first three months of the war, subs sank ships carrying 400 tanks, 60 8-inch howitzers, 880 25-pounder guns, 400 2-pounder guns, 240 armored cars, 500 machine-gun carriers, 52,100 tons of ammo, 6,000 rifles, 4,280 tons of tank supplies, 20,000 tons of miscellaneous supplies, and 10,000 tanks of gasoline. A secret War Department estimate calls this the equivalent of 30,000 bombing runs.

And the administration cannot stop the bleeding. Blackout orders are routinely ignored. Ships silhouetted at night against illuminated East Coast cities make easy targets. Businessmen say dimming their lights at night would hurt their bottom line.

Although the Navy Department claims to have sunk several U-boats and damaged more, there is no hard evidence it has harmed even one German sailor.

Britain urges the United States to begin convoying, as she has done. U.S. Navy big shots continue to believe this is unnecessary.

How they can maintain this in the face of losses so staggering is strange and troubling, but they do.

The issue is causing a rift between the United States and one of her two most important allies. Last Wednesday, Roosevelt wrote to Churchill, "My Navy has definitely been slack in preparing for this submarine war off our coast. . . . By May 1 I expect to get a pretty good coastal patrol working."

Churchill fears May 1 will be much too late.

"Those of us who are directly concerned with combatting the Atlantic submarine menace are not at all sure that the British are applying sufficient effort to bombing German submarine bases," said U.S. Admiral Ernest J. King.

As the allies bicker, innocent sailors lose their lives for no good purpose.

March 24, 1942—*New York Times*

NEW YORKER OFFICES RAIDED

Magazine's Publication Suspended

A raid by FBI and military agents shuttered the offices of *The New Yorker* yesterday. The raid came on the heels of yet another article critical of the war and of the present administration's conduct of it.

"We are going to close this treason down," said FBI spokesman Thomas O'Banion. Mr. O'Banion added, "These individuals are spreading stories nobody's got a right to know. We have to put a stop to it, and we will."

He did not dispute the truth of the articles published in *The New Yorker*.

ACLU attorneys are seeking the release of jailed editors and writers. "These are important freedom-of-speech and freedom-of-the-press issues," one of them said. "We're confident we'll prevail in court."

March 26, 1942—*Philadelphia Inquirer*

PEACE SHIPS SAIL

Reaching Out to Germany and Japan

More than fifty American actors, musicians, and authors sailed from Philadelphia today aboard the *Gustavus Vasa*, a Swedish ship. Sweden is neutral in Roosevelt's war. Their eventual destination is Germany, where they will confer with their counterparts and seek ways to lower tensions between the two countries.

Another similar party also sailed today from San Francisco aboard the Argentine ship *Rio Negro*. Like Sweden, Argentina has sensibly stayed out of this destructive fight. After stopping in Honolulu to pick up another antiwar delegation there, the *Rio Negro* will continue on to Yokohama, Japan.

"We have to build peace one person at a time," explained Robert Noble of the Friends of Progress. His Los Angeles–based organization, along with the National Legion of Mothers and Women of America, sponsored the peace initiative. Noble added, "The Japanese did the proper thing under the exigencies of the time when they bombed Pearl Harbor. Now it is all over in the Pacific, and we might as well come home."

Noble has been arrested twice recently, once on a charge of sedition and once on one of malicious libel. The government did not bring either case to trial, perhaps fearing the result.

98

Some of the travelers bound for Germany and Japan have volunteered as human shields against U.S. and British bombing. There is no response yet from the governments under attack to their brave commitment.

Bureaucrats in the Roosevelt administration have threatened not to allow the peaceful performers and intellectuals to return to the United States. Travel to their destinations is technically illegal, though a challenge to the ban is under way in the courts. This vindictiveness against critics is typical of administration henchmen.

April 3, 1942—transcript of radio broadcast

THIS IS LONDON

People in the States ask me how the morale situation is over here. They ask whether the English have as many doubts about which way their leaders are taking them as we do back home.

The answer is, of course they do. If anything, they have more. They've been hit hard, and it shows. Nearly two years ago, Germany offered a fair and generous peace. A sensible government would have accepted in a flash.

But Churchill had seized power a few months earlier in what almost amounted to a right-wing coup. He refused a hand extended in friendship, and his country has taken a right to the chin. London and other industrial cities have been bombed flat. Tens of thousands are dead, more wounded and often crippled for life.

"Look at France," a cabdriver said to me the other day. "They went out early, and they have it easy now. We just keep getting pounded on. I'm tired of it, I am."

Calls for British withdrawal from Malta and North Africa

grow stronger by the day. Sooner or later—my guess is sooner—even Churchill will have to face the plain fact that he has led his country into a losing war. . . .

★

April 5, 1942—AP story

THE PHILIPPINE FRONT

Sergeant Leland Calvert is a regular guy. He was born in Hondo, Texas, and grew up in San Antonio. He is 29 years old, with blond hair, blue eyes, and an aw-shucks grin. He is a skilled metalworker, and plays a mean trumpet. He's a big fellow—six feet two, maybe six feet three. Right now, Leland Calvert weighs 127 pounds.

That is how it is for the Americans stuck on the Bataan Peninsula. That is also how it is for the Philippine troops and civilians crammed in with them. There are far more people than there are supplies, which is at the heart of the problem.

"I don't know who planned this," Calvert said in an engaging drawl. "I don't reckon anybody did. Sure doesn't seem much point to it. Hell, we're licked. Anybody with eyes in his head can see that."

Way back in January, rations for 5,600 men in the 91st Division were 19 sacks of rice, 12 cases of salmon, 3½ sacks of sugar, and four carabao quarters. A carabao is a small, scrawny ox. Well, everybody and everything on the peninsula is scrawny now. Feeding 5,600 people with those supplies makes the miracle of the loaves and fishes look easy as pie.

And that was January. Things are much worse now. Sergeant Calvert has eaten snake and frog—not frog's legs, but frog. "Snake's not half bad," he said. "I drew the line at monkey, though. I saw a little hand cooking in a pot, and I didn't think I could keep

100

it down." I asked him about the monkey's paw story, but he has never heard of it.

Disease? That's another story. Leland has dysentery. He has had dengue fever, but he is mostly over it now. He is starting to get beriberi, which comes from lack of vitamins. Beriberi takes the gas right out of your motor. I ought to know—I have it, too. Leland does not think he has got scurvy, but he knows men who do.

He has got malaria. Most people here have got it. Again, I am one of them. The doctors are out of quinine. They are also out of atabrine, which is a fancy new synthetic drug. And they are plumb out of mosquito nets. Something like 1,000 people are going into the hospital with malaria every day now. Without the medicines, there is not much anyone can do for them.

"If I knew why we were here, I would feel better about things," Leland said. "This all seems like such a waste, though. We're fighting for a little stretch of jungle nobody in his right mind would want. What's the point?"

Seems like a good question to me, too. It doesn't look like anyone here has a good answer. I don't know when I'll see that girl again. I don't know if she'll ever see me again. I wish I could say the effort here is worth the candle. But I'm afraid I'm with Leland Calvert. This all seems like such a waste.

April 14, 1942—*Honolulu Star-Bulletin*

ADMINISTRATION PURSUES VENGEANCE POLICY

According to a Navy Department source, two aircraft carriers and several other warships sailed from Midway yesterday, bound for the Japanese home islands. Aboard one of the carriers, the *Hornet*, are U.S. Army B-25s. Pilots have secretly trained in Florida, learning to take off from a runway as short as a flight deck.

The theory is that the B-25s will be able to strike Japan from farther out to sea than normal carrier-based aircraft could. Most of Roosevelt's theories about the war up till now have been wrong, though. Maybe the planes will go into the drink. Maybe the Japanese will be waiting for them. Maybe some other foul-up will torment us. But who will believe this force can succeed until it actually does?

Given the administration's record to date, in fact, many people will have their doubts even then. As a wise man once said, "Trust everybody—but cut the cards."

April 21, 1942—*Washington Post* editorial

BLAMING THE TOOLS

Everyone knows what sort of workman blames his tools. Franklin Roosevelt claims that, if a Hawaiian newspaper had not publicized the plan of attack against the Japanese islands, it might have succeeded. He also claims we would not have lost a carrier and a cruiser and had another carrier damaged had secrecy not been compromised.

This is nonsense of the purest ray serene. The Navy tried a crackbrained scheme, it didn't work, and now the men with lots of gold braid on their sleeves are using the press as a whipping boy. This effort, if we may dignify it with such a name, was doomed to fail from the beginning.

Reliable sources inform us that the Army pilots involved were not even told they would attempt to fly off a carrier deck till they boarded the *Hornet*. The Japanese have twice our carrier force in the Pacific. Why were we wasting so much of our strength on what was at best a propaganda stunt? Are we so desperate that we need to throw men's lives away for the sake of looking good on the home front?

Evidently we are. If that is so, we should never have got involved in this war in the first place. Our best course now, plainly, is to get out of it as soon as we can, to minimize casualties and damage to our prestige. We have already paid too much for Roosevelt's obsessive opposition to Japan and Germany.

April 25, 1942—*New York Times*

READING THE OTHER GENTLEMAN'S MAIL

U.S., British Code Breakers Monitor Germany, Japan

"Gentlemen do not read each other's mail." So goes an ancient precept of diplomacy. But for some time now, the United States and Britain have been monitoring Germany and Japan's most secret codes.

War Department and Navy Department sources confirm that the U.S. and the U.K., with help from Polish experts, have defeated the German Enigma machine and the Japanese Type B diplomatic cipher machine.

The most important code-breaking center is at Bletchley Park, a manor 50 miles north of London. Other cryptographers work in the British capital, in Ceylon, and in Australia. American efforts are based in Washington, D.C., and in Hawaii.

Purple is the name of the device that deciphers the Type B code. It is not prepossessing. It looks like two typewriters and a spaghetti bowl's worth of fancy wiring. But the people who use it say it does the job.

Getting an Enigma machine to Britain was pure cloak-and-dagger. One was found by the Poles aboard a U-boat sunk in shallow water (not, obviously, anywhere near our own ravaged East Coast) and spirited out of Poland one jump ahead of the Germans at the beginning of the war.

Why better use has not been made of these broken codes is a pressing question. No administration official will speak on the record. No administration official will even admit on the record that we are engaged in code-breaking activity.

Only one thing makes administration claims tempting to believe. If the United States and Britain are reading Germany and Japan's codes, they have little to show for it. Roosevelt dragged this country into war by a series of misconceptions, deceptions, and outright lies. Now we are in serious danger of losing it.

April 26, 1942—*Chicago Tribune*

WHITE HOUSE WHINES AT REVELATIONS

In a news conference yesterday afternoon, Franklin D. Roosevelt lashed out at critics in the press and on the radio. "Every time sensitive intelligence is leaked, it hurts our ability to defeat the enemy," Roosevelt claimed.

As he has before, he seeks to hide his own failings behind the veil of censorship. If the press cannot tell the American people the truth, who can? The administration? FDR sure wants you to think so. But the press and radio newscasters have exposed so many falsehoods and so much bungling that no one in his right mind is likely to trust this White House as far as he can throw it.

★

May 1, 1942—*Los Angeles Times*

FDR'S POLL NUMBERS CONTINUE TO SINK

Franklin D. Roosevelt's popularity is sinking faster than freighters off the East Coast. In the latest Gallup survey, his overall approval rating is at 29%, while only 32% approve of his handling of the war. The poll, conducted yesterday, was of 1,191 "likely" or "very likely" voters, and has an error margin of ±5%.

Poll takers also recorded several significant comments. "He doesn't know what he's doing," said one 58-year-old man.

"Why doesn't he bring the troops home? Who wants to die for England?" remarked a 31-year-old woman.

"We can't win this stupid war, so why fight it?" said another woman, who declined to give her age.

Roosevelt's approval ratings are as low as those of President Hoover shortly before he was turned out of office in a landslide. Even Warren G. Harding retained more personal popularity than the embattled current President.

May 3, 1942—*Washington Post*

VEEP BREAKS RANKS WITH WHITE HOUSE

Demands Timetable for War

In the first public rift in the Roosevelt administration, Vice President Henry Wallace called on FDR to establish a timetable for victory. "If we can't win this war within 18 months, we should pack it in," Wallace said, speaking in Des Moines yesterday. "It is causing too many casualties and disrupting the civilian economy."

Wallace, an agricultural expert, also said, "Even if by some chance we should win, we would probably have to try to feed the whole world afterwards. No country can do that."

Support for Wallace's statement came quickly from both sides of the partisan aisle. Even Senators and Representatives who supported Roosevelt's war initiative seemed glad of the chance to distance themselves from it. "If I'd known things would go this badly, I never would have voted for [the declaration of war]," said a prominent Senator.

White House reaction was surprisingly restrained. "We will not set a timetable," said an administration spokesman. "That would be the same as admitting defeat."

Another official, speaking anonymously, said FDR had known Wallace was "off the reservation" for some time. He added, "When the ship sinks, the rats jump off." Then he tried to retract the remark, denying that the ship was sinking. But the evidence speaks for itself.

May 9, 1942—*Miami Herald*

MORE SINKINGS IN BROAD DAYLIGHT

U-Boats Prowl Florida Coast at Will

The toll of ships torpedoed in Florida waters in recent days has only grown worse. On May 6, a U-boat sank the freighter *Amazon* near Jupiter Inlet. She sank in 80 feet of water.

That same day, also under the smiling sun, the tanker *Halsey* went to the bottom not far away. Then, yesterday, the freighter *Ohioan* was sunk. So was the tanker *Esquire*. That ship broke apart, spilling out 92,000 barrels of oil close to shore. No environmental-impact statement has yet been released.

There is still no proof that the U.S. Navy has sunk even a single German submarine, despite increasingly strident claims to the contrary.

May 11, 1942—*Washington Post*

MOTHER'S DAY MARCH

War Protesters Picket White House

Mothers of war victims killed in the Pacific and Atlantic marched in front of the White House to protest the continued fighting. "What does Roosevelt think he's doing?" asked Louise Heffernan, 47, of Altoona, Pennsylvania. Her son Richard was slain in a tanker sinking three weeks ago. "How many more have to die before we admit his policy isn't working?"

A mother who refused to give her name—"Who knows what the FBI would do to me?"—said she lost two sons at Pearl Harbor. "It's a heartache no one who hasn't gone through it can ever understand," she said. "I don't think anyone else should have to suffer the way I have."

Placards read END THE WAR NOW!, NO BLOOD FOR BRITAIN!, and ANOTHER MOTHER FOR PEACE. Passersby whistled and cheered for the demonstrators.

March 12, 1942—*Los Angeles Times*

JAPAN BATTERS U.S. CARRIERS IN CORAL SEA

The Navy Department has clamped a tight lid of secrecy over the battle in the Coral Sea (see map) last week. Correspondents in Hawaii and Australia have had to work hard to piece together an accurate picture of what happened. The Navy's reluctance to talk shows that it considers the engagement yet another defeat.

One U.S. fleet carrier, the *Lexington*, was sunk. Another, the *Yorktown*, was severely damaged, and is limping toward Hawaii for repair. American casualties in the battle were heavy: 543 dead and a number of wounded the Navy still refuses to admit.

In addition to the carriers, the U.S. lost a destroyer, a fleet oiler, and 66 planes. Japanese aircraft hit American ships with 58% of the bombs and torpedoes they dropped. Prewar predictions of bombing accuracy were as low as 3%.

Navy sources claim to have sunk a Japanese light carrier, and to have damaged a fleet carrier—possibly two. They assert that 77 Japanese airplanes were downed, and say Japanese casualties "had to have been" heavier than ours. Given how much the Navy exaggerates what it has done in the Atlantic, these Pacific figures also need to be taken with an ocean of salt.

May 15, 1942—*St. Louis Post-Dispatch*

WALLACE SAYS FDR LIED

President Expected War, VP Insists

Vice President Henry Wallace broke ranks with Roosevelt again in a speech in Little Rock, Arkansas. "Roosevelt looked for us to get sucked into this war," Wallace said. "He was getting ready for it at the same time as he was telling America we could stay out.

"I see that now," the Vice President added. "If I'd seen it then, I never would have agreed to be his running mate. The USA deserves better. How many women—and men—are grieving today because the President of the United States flat-out lied? And how much more grief do we have to look forward to?"

Stormy applause greeted Wallace's remarks. Arkansas is a longtime Democratic stronghold, but FDR's popularity is plummeting there, as it is across the country. After Wallace finished speaking, shouts of "Impeach Roosevelt!" rang out from the crowd. They were also cheered.

Asked whether he thought Roosevelt should be impeached, Wallace said, "I can't comment. If I say no, people will think I agree with his policies, and I don't. But if I say yes, they will think I am angling for the White House myself. The people you need to talk to are the Speaker of the House and the chairman of the Judiciary Committee."

A reporter also asked Wallace if he would seek peace if he did become President. "A negotiated settlement has to be better than the series of catastrophes we've suffered," he replied. "Why should our boys die to uphold the British Empire and Communist Russia?"

★

May 16, 1942—*Washington Post*

IMPEACHMENT "RIDICULOUS," FDR SAYS

Beleaguered Franklin Roosevelt called talk of impeachment "ridiculous" in a written statement released this morning. "I am doing the best job of running this country I can," the statement said. "That is what the American people elected me to do, and I aim to do it. We can win this war—and we will, unless the ingrates who stand up and cheer whenever anything goes wrong have their way."

Roosevelt's statement also lambasted his breakaway Vice President, Henry Wallace. "He is doing more for the other side than a division of panzer troops," it said.

Wallace replied, "I am trying to tell America the truth. Isn't it about time somebody did? We deserve it."

House Speaker Sam Rayburn declined comment. A source close to the Speaker said he is "waiting to see what happens next."

May 26, 1942—Honolulu Star-Bulletin

YORKTOWN TORPEDOED, SUNK

Loss of Life Feared Heavy

A day before she was to put in at Pearl Harbor for emergency repairs, the carrier *Yorktown* was sunk by a Japanese sub southwest of Oahu. The ship sank quickly in shark-infested waters. Only about 120 survivors have been rescued.

The *Yorktown*'s complement is about 1,900 men. She also carried air crew from the *Lexington*, which went down almost three weeks ago in the Coral Sea. Nearly as many men died with her as did at Pearl Harbor, in other words.

The plan was to quickly fix up the *Yorktown* and send her to defend Midway Island along with the *Hornet* and the *Saratoga*. Midway is believed to be the target of an advancing fleet considerably stronger than the forces available to hold the island. Now the two surviving carriers—one damaged itself—and their support vessels will have to go it alone.

If the Japanese occupy Midway, Honolulu and Pearl Harbor will come within reach of their deadly long-range bombers.

May 28, 1942—*Honolulu Advertiser* editorial

STAR-BULLETIN SHUT DOWN

Censors' Reign of Error

Because bullying Navy and War Department censors unconstitutionally closed down our rival newspaper yesterday, it is up to us to carry on in the *Star-Bulletin*'s footsteps. We aim to tell the truth to the people of Honolulu and to the people of America. If the maniacs with the blue pencils try to silence us, we will go underground to carry on the fight for justice and the First Amendment.

From where we sit, the fat cats in the Roosevelt administration who think they ought to have a monopoly on the facts are worse enemies of freedom than Tojo and Hitler put together. In dragging us into this pointless war in the first place, they pulled the wool over the country's eyes. They thought they had the right to do that, because they were doing it for our own good. They knew better than we did, you see.

Only they didn't. One disastrous failure after another has proved that. Up till now, the USA has never lost a war. Unless we can wheel FDR out of the White House soon, that record won't last more than another few weeks.

May 29, 1942—*Cleveland Plain Dealer*

DEMONSTRATORS CLASH DOWNTOWN

Pro- and Antiwar Factions, Police Battle in Streets

Thousands of protesters squared off yesterday in downtown Cleveland. Police were supposed to keep the passionately opposed sides separate. Instead, they joined the pro-FDR forces in pummeling the peaceful demonstrators who condemn the war and, in increasing numbers, call for Roosevelt's impeachment and removal from office.

Antiwar demonstrators far outnumbered the President's supporters. Those who still blindly back Roosevelt, however, came prepared for violence. They were armed with clubs, rocks, and bottles, and were ready to use them.

"War! War! FDR! Now the President's gone too far!" chanted the peaceful antiwar forces. Another chant soon swelled and grew: "Impeach Roosevelt!"

FDR's supporters attacked the antiwar picketers then. Vicious cops were also seen beating protesters with billy clubs and kicking them on the ground (see photo above this story). Some protesters withdrew from the demonstration. Others fought back, refusing to be intimidated by Roosevelt's thuggish followers or by the out-of-control police.

"This can only help our cause," said a man bleeding from a scalp laceration and carrying a NO MORE YEARS! sign. "When the country sees how brutal that man in the White House really is, it will know what to do. I'm sure of it."

May 31, 1942—*Honolulu Advertiser*

HORNET, SARATOGA SAIL FOR MIDWAY

America's two surviving fleet carriers in the Pacific left Pearl Harbor yesterday. Sources say they are bound for strategic Midway Island, about 1,000 miles to the northwest.

With the carriers sailed the usual accompaniment of cruisers and destroyers. The ships made a brave show. But how much can they hope to accomplish against the disciplined nationalism of Japan and the determined bravery of her soldiers and pilots and sailors?

This strike force seems to be Roosevelt's last desperate effort to salvage something from the war he blundered into. The odds look grim. Japan may be low on scrap metal and oil thanks to FDR, but she is long on guts and stubbornness. If the Navy fails here, as it has failed so often, the outlook for Hawaii and for the west coast of the mainland looks bleak indeed.

June 1, 1942—Official proclamation

HONOLULU ADVERTISER
NO LONGER TO BE PUBLISHED

WHEREAS, it is provided by Section 67 of the Organic Act of the Territory of Hawaii, approved April 30, 1900, that the Governor of that territory may call upon the commander of the military forces of the United States in that territory to prevent invasion; and

WHEREAS, it is further provided by the said section that the Governor may, in case of invasion or imminent danger thereof, suspend the privilege of habeas corpus and place the territory under martial law; and

WHEREAS, the *Honolulu Advertiser* has egregiously violated the terms of censorship imposed on the territory following December 7, 1941;

NOW, THEREFORE, I order the said *Honolulu Advertiser* to suspend publication indefinitely and its staff to face military tribunals to judge and punish their disloyalty.

DONE at Honolulu, Territory of Hawaii, this 1st day of June, 1942.

(SEAL OF THE TERRITORY OF HAWAII)

—Lt. Col. Neal D. Franklin
Army Provost Marshal

June 7, 1942—San Francisco Chronicle

DISASTER AT MIDWAY!

Carriers Sunk—Island Invaded

The Imperial Japanese Navy dealt the U.S. Pacific Fleet a devastating blow off Midway Island three days ago. Though Navy officials are maintaining a tight-lipped silence, reliable sources say both the *Saratoga* and the *Hornet* were sunk by Japanese dive bombers. Several support vessels were also sunk or damaged.

Japanese troops have landed on Midway. The *Yamato*, the mightiest battleship in the world, is bombarding the island with what are reported to be 18-inch guns. Japanese planes rule the skies. Resistance is said to be fading.

When the Japanese succeed in occupying Midway, Hawaii will be vulnerable to their bombers. So will convoys coming from the mainland to supply Hawaii—and so will convoys leaving Hawaii for Australia and New Zealand.

Japanese submarines sailing out of Midway will have an easier time reaching the West Coast. They could even threaten the Panama Canal.

This war has seemed to be an uphill fight from the beginning. For all practical purposes, it is unwinnable now. The only person in the country who fails to realize that, unfortunately, lives at 1600 Pennsylvania Avenue in Washington.

June 8, 1942—*Baltimore News-Post*

ROOSEVELT TEARS INTO PRESS

Blames Leaks for U.S. Defeats

Trying to shore up flagging public support for his war, FDR lashed out at American newspapers in a speech before midshipmen at the Naval Academy in Annapolis yesterday. "How can we fight with any hope of success when they trumpet our doings to the foe?" he complained.

The midshipmen applauded warmly. Whether Roosevelt could have found such a friendly reception from civilians is a different question.

"Reporters seem proud when they find a new secret and print it," he said, shaking his fist from his wheelchair. "If printing that secret means our brave sailors and soldiers die, they don't care. They have their scoop."

According to FDR, the staggering loss at Midway can be laid at the feet of newsmen. Our own military incompetence and Japanese skill and courage apparently had nothing to do with it. However loudly the young, naive midshipmen may cheer, the rest of the nation is drawing other conclusions.

June 9, 1942—*Washington Post* editorial

RESPONSIBILITY

Nothing is ever Franklin D. Roosevelt's fault. If you don't believe us, just ask him. German U-boats are sinking ships up and down the Atlantic coast? It's all the newspapers' fault. The Navy and the Army have suffered a string of humiliating defeats in the Pacific? The papers are to blame there, too.

Throwing rocks at the press may make FDR feel better, but that is all it does. What he really blames the newspapers for is pointing out his mistakes. Now the whole country can take a good look at them. Roosevelt does not care for that at all.

With him, image is everything; substance, nothing. Have you ever noticed how seldom he is allowed to be photographed in his wheelchair? If people aren't reminded of it, they won't think about it. That is how his mind works.

But when it comes to the acid test of war, image is not enough. You need real victories on the battlefield, and the United States has not been able to win any. Why not? No matter what Roosevelt and his stooges say, it is not because the press has blabbed our precious secrets.

The fact of the matter is, whether we read codes from Germany and Japan hardly matters. Even when we have good intelligence, we don't know what to do with it. Example? The Japanese tried out their Zero fighter in China in 1940. General Claire Chennault, who led the volunteer Flying Tigers, warned Washington what it was like. It came as a complete surprise to the Navy anyhow.

Most of our intelligence, though, was incredibly bad. We were sure France could give Germany a good fight. We were just as sure our Navy could whip Japan's with ease. We fatally underestimated German technology and resourcefulness, to say nothing of Japanese drive and élan. Japan and Germany are fighting for their homelands. What are *we* fighting for? Anything at all?

FDR is too sunk in pride to get out of the war he stumbled into while the country still has any chestnuts worth pulling from the fire. He will not—he seems unable to—admit that the many mistakes we have made are his and his henchmen's.

And since he will not, we must put someone in the White House who will. Impeachment may be an extreme step, but the United States is in extreme danger. With this war gone so calamitously wrong, we need peace as soon as we can get it, and at almost any price.

June 11, 1942—*Boston Globe*

WALLACE PLEDGES PEACE, IF . . .

Vice President Henry Wallace said American foreign policy needs to change course. "I'm not the President. I can't make policy," he said last night at a Longshoremen's Union banquet. "Right now, the President doesn't even want to listen to me. But I can see it's time for a change. Only peace will put our beloved country back on track."

Wallace did not speak of the growing sentiment for impeachment. After all, he stands to take over the White House after Roosevelt is ousted. But he left no doubt that he would do everything in his power to pull American troops back to this country. He also condemned the huge deficits our massive military adventure is causing us to run.

With his commonsense approach, he seemed much more Presidential than the man still clinging to power in Washington.

June 16, 1942—*Washington Post*

RAYBURN, SUMNERS CONFER

Articles of Impeachment Likely

House Speaker Sam Rayburn and Judiciary Committee Chairman Hatton Sumners met today to discuss procedures for impeaching President Roosevelt. Both Texas Democrats were tight-lipped as they emerged from their conference.

Sumners offered no comment of any kind. Rayburn said only, "I am sorry to be in this position. The good of the country may demand something I would otherwise much rather not do."

Only one President has ever been impeached: Andrew Johnson in 1868. The Senate failed by one vote to convict him.

Sumners has experience with impeachment. He was the House manager in the proceedings against Judges George English and Halsted Ritter. English resigned; Ritter was convicted and removed from office.

Sumners has also clashed with FDR before. He was the chief opponent of Roosevelt's 1937 scheme to pack the Supreme Court.

Roosevelt's time in office must be seen as limited now. And that is a consummation devoutly to be wished. With a new leader, one we can respect, will surely come what Abraham Lincoln called "a new birth of freedom." It cannot come soon enough.

THE CATCHER IN
THE RHINE

---

*More pastiche here, this time of, well, guess what. I owe this piece to
my middle daughter, Rachel, who was much younger when I wrote
it. Her older sister, Alison, had to read J. D. Salinger's book in a high
school English class. Rachel didn't hear the title right. "The catcher in
the Rhine?" she said. Well, as soon as I heard that, I knew I could do
evil things with it. Which I did, and sold them to Esther Friesner for
one of her* Chicks in Chainmail *books. And, in case you're wondering, yes, Rachel did get her share of the check for the story.*

$\mathcal{I}$ don't know how I got here. Wait. That's not quite right. What I mean to say is, I know how I got to Europe and everything, for Chrissake. They sent me over here to find myself or something after that trouble I had. I'm sure you know about that. I'm certain you know about it. Practically *everybody* knows about it. Some of the biggest phonies in the world think they know more about it than I do. They really think so. It's like they read it in English class or something.

So like I say, I know how I got to Europe. I don't know about this finding myself business, though. I swear to God, if you can't find yourself, you've gotta be some kind of psycho. I mean, you're right *there*, for crying out loud. If you weren't right there, where the hell would you be?

And sending somebody to Europe to find himself has got to be the stupidest thing in the world. You have to be a lousy moron to come up with something like that, you really do. You can't find *any*thing in Europe. Honest to God, it's the truth. You really can't. All the streets go every which way, and they change names every other block, or sometimes in the middle of the block.

Besides, the people don't speak English. Try to have an intellectual conversation with somebody who doesn't know what the hell you're talking about. Go ahead and try. It's a goddam waste of time, that's what it is.

Anyway, I went through France, and some of that was pretty neat, it really was, and all of it was historical as hell—not that I was ever any good at history. What I mean is, every single stinking bit of it happened a long time ago—some of it happened a goddam long time ago—so how am I supposed to get all excited when some phony moron of a teacher stands there and goes on and on about it? It's not easy, I tell you.

After I was done with old France, I went over to Germany because it's next door, you know—and I took this boat trip up the Rhine. I don't know what the hell "Rhine" means in German, but it looks like it oughta mean "sewer." The whole river smells like somebody laid a big old fart, too. It really does. I won't ever complain about the Hudson when I get home, and you can walk across the Hudson, practically.

When I get home. *If* I get home. The boat stopped at this place called Isenstein. It's a real dump, I tell you, but back of it there's a kind of a crag thing with a castle on top. I wasn't gonna get off the boat—I'd paid the fare all the way up to Düsseldorf, wherever that is—but the river just smelled so bad I couldn't stand it any more, so I left. Maybe they'd let me back on the next one. And if they didn't, who cares? I had piles of money and traveler's checks and stuff.

Well, let me tell you, the streets in old Isenstein didn't smell so good, either. That was partly because it was still right *next* to the Rhine, and it was partly because the people there had the most disgusting personal habits in the world. I saw this one guy standing in the street taking a leak against the side of a crumby old dirty brick building, and it wasn't even like he was drunk or anything.

He was just *doing* it. And then he went on his way happy as you please. I wouldn't've believed it if I hadn't seen it with my own eyes, and that's the truth.

They had a church there, so I went inside and looked around. I always tried to look at those cultural things, because who knew when I was ever coming back again? Coming back to Europe, I mean—I wouldn't've come back to Isenstein if you *paid* me, you can bet your bottom dollar on that. But the church was pretty dirty and crumby, too. By the time I got done looking at it, I was feeling pretty goddam depressed. I really was. So I got the hell out of there.

I was feeling pretty goddam *hungry*, too. I was feeling hungry as a sonuvabitch, if you want to know the truth. I didn't exactly want to eat in Isenstein—it really was a filthy place. You have no idea how filthy it was. But I was *there*. Where else was I gonna eat, is what I want to know.

Getting something to eat when you don't speak the language is a royal pain in the ass. If you're not careful, they're liable to give you horse manure on a bun. I'm not kidding. I'm really not. When I was in France, I got a plateful of *snails*, for crying out loud. Real snails, like you step on in a garden somewhere and they go crunch under your shoe. With butter. If you think I ate 'em, you're crazy. I sent 'em back pretty toot sweet. That means goddam fast in French. But whatever they gave me instead didn't look much better, so I got the hell out of *that* place toot sweet myself.

Over across the street from the church in old Isenstein was this joint where you could get beer and food. Nobody in Germany cares if you're twenty-one. They don't give a damn, swear to God they don't. They'd give beer to a *nine*-year-old, they really would. If he asked for it, I mean.

So I got a beer, and the guy sitting next to me at the bar was eating a sandwich that didn't look too lousy—it had some kind of sausage and pickles in it—so I pointed to that and told the bartender, "Give me one of those, too." Maybe it was really chopped-up pigs' ears or something, but I didn't *know* it was, so it was all right if I didn't think about it too much. The guy behind the bar figured out what I meant and started making one for me.

I'd just taken a big old bite—it wasn't terrific but I could stand it, pigs' ears or not—when the fellow sitting next to me on the *other* side spoke up and said to me in English, "You are an American, yes?"

If you want to know the truth, it made me kind of angry. Here I was *starv*ing to death, and this guy wanted to strike up a conversation. I didn't want to talk. I wanted to eat, even if it didn't taste so good. So with my mouth full, rude as anything, I said "Yeah," and then I took another bite, even bigger than the first one.

He didn't get mad. I'd hoped he would, I really had, but no such luck. He was a very smooth, very polite guy. He was a little flitty-looking, as a matter of fact—not too, but a little. Enough to make you wonder, anyhow. He said, "We do not often Americans in Isenstein have." He talked that way on account of he was foreign, I guess. I took another bite out of this sandwich—it probably *was* pigs' ears, it sure tasted like what you'd think pigs' ears'd taste like—and he asked me, "What is your name?"

So I told him, and he damn near—I mean *damn* near—fell off his chair. "Hagen Kriemhild?" he said. Boy, he must've had cabbages in his ears or something, even if I was still kind of talking with my mouth full. "Hagen *Kriemhild?*"

"No," I said, and told him again, this time after I'd swallowed and everything, so he couldn't foul it up even if he tried.

"Ah," he said. *"Ach so,"* which I guess is like "okay" in German. "Never mind. It is close enough."

"Close enough for what?" I said, but he didn't answer me right away. He just sat there looking at me. He looked very *intense*, if you know what I mean, like he was thinking a mile a minute. I couldn't very well ask him what the hell he was thinking about, either, because people always lie to you when you do that, or else they get mad. So instead I said, "What's *your* name?" You can't go wrong with that, hardly.

He blinked. He really did—his eyes went blink, blink. It was like he'd forgotten I was there, he'd been thinking so goddam hard. He'd been thinking like a madman, I swear to God he had. Blink, blink—he did it again. It was crumby to watch, honest. I didn't think he was going to tell me his lousy old name, but he did. He said, "I am called Regin Fafnirsbruder."

Well, Jesus Christ, if you think I even *tried* to say that like he said it, you're crazy. I just said "Pleased to meetcha" and I stuck out my hand. I'm too polite for my own good sometimes, I really am.

Old Regin Fafnirsbruder shook hands with me. He didn't shake hands like a flit, I have to admit it. He said, "Come with me. I will you things in Isenstein show that no American has ever seen."

"Can't I finish my sandwich first?" I said—and I didn't even want that crumby old sandwich any more. Isn't that a hell of a thing?

He shook his head like he would drop dead if I took one more bite. So I went bottoms-up with my beer—they make *good* beer in Germany, and I wasn't about to let *that* go to waste—and out of there we went.

"Whaddaya got?" I said. "Is it—a girl?" Could you be a pimp and a flit at the same time? Would you have any fun if you were? I always wonder about crazy stuff like that. If you're gonna wonder about crazy stuff, you might as well wonder about *sexy* crazy stuff, you know what I mean?

"A girl, *ja*. Like none you have ever met." Old Regin Fafnirsbruder's head went up and down like it was on a spring. "And also

127

other things." He looked back over his shoulder at me, to make sure I was still following him, I guess. His eyes were big and round as silver dollars. I'm not making things up, they honest to God were. So help me.

"Listen," I said, "it's been nice knowing you and everything, but I think I ought to get back to my boat now."

He didn't listen to a word I said. He just kept going, out of Isenstein—which wasn't very hard, because it's not a real big town or anything—and toward that tumbledown castle on the crag I already told you about. And I kept walking along after him. To tell you the truth, I didn't *want* to go back to the boat, or to the smelly old Rhine. The farther away from there I got the better, you bet.

All of a sudden, these really thick gray clouds started rolling in, just covering up the whole goddam sky. It hadn't been any too gorgeous out before, but *these* clouds looked like they meant business, no kidding. "Hey," I said, kind of loud so old Regin Fafnirsbruder would be sure to hear me. "You got an umbrella? It looks like it's gonna pour."

"*Ja,*" he said over his shoulder. Yeah it was gonna pour or yeah he had an umbrella? It wasn't like he *told* me, for crying out loud, the stupid moron. I'll tell you, *I* didn't have any umbrella. Jesus Christ, I didn't even have a crumby *hat*. And my crew cut is so short, it's like I don't have any hair at all up there, and when it rains the water that hits on top of my head all runs down right into my face, and that's very annoying, it really is. It's annoying as hell.

But old Regin Fafnirsbruder started up this crag toward the tumbledown old crumby ruin of a castle, and I kept on following him. By then I was feeling kind of like a goddam moron myself. I was also panting like anything. I haven't got any wind at all, on account of I smoke like a madman. I smoke like a goddam *chim*ney, if you want to know the truth.

Sure as hell, it started to rain. I knew it would. I *told* old Regin Fafnirsbruder it would, but did he listen to me? Nobody listens to you, I swear to God it's the truth. This big old raindrop hit me right square in the eye, so I couldn't see anything for a second or two, and I almost fell off this lousy little path we were walking on, and I would've broken my damn neck if I had, too, because it was a *crag*, remember, and steeper than hell every which way.

"Hey!" I yelled. "Slow down!"

That's when the biggest goddam lightning bolt you ever imagined smashed into me and everything went black, like they say in the movies.

When I woke up, there was old Regin Fafnirsbruder leaning over me, almost close enough to give me a kiss. "You are all right, Hagen Kriemhild?" he asked, all anxious like I was his son or something. I think I'd kill myself if I was, I really do.

"I told you, that's not my name." I was pretty mad that he'd taken me all this way and he couldn't even bother to remember my crumby old name. It's not like it's Joe Doakes or John Smith so you'd forget it in a hurry. I sat up. I didn't want to keep laying there on account of he might try something flitty if he thought I couldn't do anything about it or anything. "What the hell happened?"

Right then was when I noticed things had started turning crazy. Old Regin Fafnirsbruder had asked me how I was in this language that wasn't English, and I hadn't just understood him, I'd *answered* him in it, for Chrissake. Isn't that gorgeous? I figured the lightning had fried my brains but good or something.

Then I realized it wasn't raining any more. There wasn't a cloud in the goddam *sky*, as a matter of fact. Not even one. It was about as sunny a day as old Isenstein ever gets, I bet.

I took a deep breath. I was gonna say "What the hell happened?" again—old Regin Fafnirsbruder hadn't told me or anything—but I didn't. And the reason I didn't is that the breath I took didn't stink. With the nasty old Rhine running right by it, the air in Isenstein always smelled like somebody just laid the biggest fart in the world right under your nose.

But it didn't, not any more. It smelled like grass and water—*clean* water—and pine trees, almost like one of those little air freshener things, if you know what I mean. Too good to be true. It wasn't one of those, though, on account of I could smell cows and pigs and horses, too, somewhere way the hell off in the distance. It was like I wasn't by a town any more, like I'd gone off into the country. But I was still sitting right where that old lightning bolt had clobbered me.

Old Regin Fafnirsbruder started dancing around. I'm not kidding, he really did. He had this grin on his face like he was drunk, and he was kind of halfway between doing an Indian war dance and jitterbugging. Watching the old sonuvabitch shake his can like that was pretty damn funny, it really was.

"I did it!" he yelled, not keeping time with his feet or anything. "My magic worked!" He still wasn't speaking English, but I understood him okay.

"Crap," I said. Actually, I didn't say "crap," actually, but what I said meant the same thing as crap, so that was all right. "What do you mean, your magic?"

He still didn't answer me. He was too busy dancing and hollering and having a high old time. He was a very self-centered guy, old Regin Fafnirsbruder was, egocentric as hell. It made him a real pain in the ass to talk to, to tell you the truth.

"What do you *mean*, your crumby magic?" I said again. I hate it when I have to repeat myself, I really do.

Finally, he remembered I was there. "Look!" he said, and he

gave this wave like he was in the lousiest, corniest movie ever made. I swear to God, this wave was so goddam big that he almost fell off the side of the mountain himself.

So I looked. I didn't want to give him the satisfaction, but I finally went and did. I looked back over my shoulder, and I almost felt like the lightning plowed into me all over again. There was the Rhine, all right, like it was supposed to be, only it was blue, blue as the sky, blue*er* than the goddam sky, not the color the water in a toilet bowl is when somebody gets there *just* in the nick of time. No wonder it didn't stink any more.

And somebody'd taken old Isenstein and stuck it in his back pocket. Instead of a real town, there were these maybe ten houses by the riverside, and they all had roofs made out of straw or something. So maybe old Regin Fafnirsbruder *had* worked magic. If he hadn't, what the hell had he done? I didn't know then and I still don't know now.

When I got done gawking at Isenstein—it took me a while, believe me—I looked up to the crumby old tumbledown castle at the top of the crag. There it was, all right, big as life, but it wasn't crumby or old or tumbledown any more. What it looked like was, it looked like somebody built it day before yesterday. There wasn't a single stone missing—not even a pebble, I swear—and all the edges were so sharp you could've cut yourself on 'em. Maybe not even day before yesterday. Maybe yesterday, and I mean yesterday after*noon*.

Oh, and there was this ring of fire all the way around the castle. I didn't see anything burning up, but I sure as hell saw the flames. I heard 'em, too—they crackled like the ones in your fireplace do, only these were ten or twenty times as big. When I was a little kid, I had this book about Paul Bunyan and Babe the giant Blue Ox. It was a pretty crumby book with really stupid pictures, but I remembered it right then anyway on account of if old Babe had tried to walk through those flames, he'd've been short ribs and steaks in nothing flat, and I mean well-done.

"Now shall you your destiny fulfill." I already told you old Regin Fafnirsbruder talked like that sometimes. He did it even when he wasn't speaking English. He wasn't much of a conversationalist, old Regin Fafnirsbruder wasn't.

"What the hell are you talking about?" I said. "And where the hell did Isenstein go, anyway?"

"That is Isenstein, Isenstein as it is now," he said, and then a whole lot of weird stuff I didn't understand at all, and what language he was talking in didn't matter a goddam bit. Time flows and sorceries and I don't know what. It all sounded pretty much like a bunch of crap to me. It would've sounded even more like a bunch of crap if I hadn't kept looking back at that little handful of houses where old Isenstein used to be. Then he pointed up the hill. "You shall to the castle go. You shall through the flames pass. You shall the shield-maiden Brunhild asleep there find. You shall with a kiss her awaken, and you shall with her happily ever after live."

"Oh, yeah?" I said, and he nodded. Just like before, his head bobbed up and down, up and down, like it was on a spring. If he wasn't the biggest madman in the world, I don't know who was. But he was calling the shots, too. I may not apply myself too much—people always go on and on that I'm not *apply*ing my goddam self till I'm about ready to puke sometimes—but I'm not stupid. I'm really not. Old Regin Fafnirsbruder knew what he was doing here, and I didn't have the faintest idea. So I figured I'd better play along for a while, anyway, till I could figure out what the hell was going on.

"Go up to the castle," he said. "You will it is all as I have said see."

I went on up. Now he followed me. Like I said before, the old castle looked so new, it might've just come out of its box or something. Sure as hell, the fire went all the way around the goddam place. The closer I got, the more it felt like fire, too. I pointed to it. I made damn sure I didn't touch it or anything, though, you bet. "How the hell am I supposed to get through that, huh?"

"Just walk through. You will not harmed be. My magic assures it."

"Oh, yeah?" I said. Old Regin Fafnirsbruder's head bobbed up and down some more. He looked pretty stupid, he really did. "Oh, *yeah*?" I said. He kept right on nodding. "Prove it," I said to him. "You're such a madman of a wizard and everything, let's see *you* go on through there without ending up charbroiled."

All of a sudden, he wasn't nodding so much any more. "The spell is not for me. The spell cannot for me be," he said. "The spell is for you and for you alone."

I laughed at him. "I think you're yellow, is what I think." I figured that'd make him mad. If somebody's a coward, what's he gonna hate more than somebody else coming out and *tell*ing him he's a coward, right?

I guess it worked. I guess it worked a little too goddam well, if you want to know the truth. Because what happened was, old Regin Fafnirsbruder came up and gave me a push, and he *pushed* me right into those old flames.

I screamed. I screamed like hell, as a matter of fact. But I didn't burn up or anything—he was right about that. The fire felt hot, but hot like sunshine, not hot like fire. It hurt a lot more when I fell on my ass from the push, it honestly did.

"What'd you go and do *that* for, you goddam moron?" I yelled, and then I started to go on *out* through the fire. I didn't get very goddam far, though. It wasn't just hot like sunshine any more, let me tell you. It burned the tip of my shoe when I stuck it in there, and it would've burned the rest enough, too, if I'd been dumb enough to give it a chance.

Old Regin Fafnirsbruder was laughing his ass off watching me looking at my toasted toe. "You must what I want do," he said. "Then will you what you want get. When you come out with Brunhild, you may through the fire pass. Until then, you must there stay."

"You dirty, filthy, stinking goddam moron," I said. "I hope you drown in the goddam Rhine."

He just ignored me, the lousy sonuvabitch. He had no consideration, old Regin Fafnirsbruder didn't. I started up toward the fire again, but I didn't stick my foot in it this time—you bet I didn't. I sat down on the ground. I felt so depressed, you can't imagine how depressed I felt.

But after a while I stood up again. What can you do when you're just sitting around on your butt and all? I thought I'd get up and look around a little, anyway. So I did that, and I came to this door. I opened it—what the hell? At least old Regin Fafnirsbruder couldn't keep staring at me through the flames any more. And after I went through, I slammed the hell out of that old door. To tell you the truth, I kind of hoped I'd break it right off the hinges, but no such luck.

I thought I'd end up in this big old hall full of guys making pigs of themselves and getting stinking and pinching the serving girls on the butt the way they did back in medieval times, but that isn't what ended up happening. I walked into this little—bedroom, I guess you'd call it, but it wasn't a bed this girl was laying on, it was more like a little sofa or something.

She was kind of cute, as a matter of fact, if you like big husky blondes. But I'd never seen a girl in chain mail before. To tell you the truth, I'd never seen *any*body in chain mail before, and sure as hell not anybody sleeping. It looked uncomfortable, it really did.

She had on a helmet, too, and a sword on a belt around her waist, and this shield was leaning up against the bed or sofa or whatever the hell it was. I stood there for a while like a crumby old moron. In the fairy tales you're supposed to kiss the princess, right, and she'll wake up and you'll both live happily ever after. That was what old Regin Fafnirsbruder had told me would happen, but you'd have to be a real moron not to see he was playing the game for him and nobody else. And if I kissed this girl and she didn't happen to like it or she thought I was trying to get fresh with her or something, she was liable to *murder* me, for Chrissake.

I wished I could've figured out some other way to get out of there. I hate doing what anybody else tells me to do. I hate it like anything, if you want to know the truth. Even when it's for my own good and everything, I still hate it. It's nobody's goddam business but mine what I do. Not that anybody listens to me. Yeah, fat chance of that. You think old Regin Fafnirsbruder gave a damn about what I thought? Fat chance of that, too.

But I was stuck in this old castle. I was stuck really bad. If Brunhild there couldn't get me the hell out, who could? Nobody. Just nobody. So I leaned down and I gave her this little tiny kiss, just like it *was* a fairy tale or something.

Her eyes opened. I'd expected they would be blue—don't ask me why, except she was a blonde and all—but they were brown. She looked at me like I was dirt and nobody'd invented brooms yet. Then she said, "You are not Siegfried. Where is Siegfried?" She spoke the same language as old Regin Fafnirsbruder, whatever the hell it was.

"I dunno," I said. I bet I sounded really smart. I sounded like a goddam moron, is what I sounded like. "Who's Siegfried?"

Her face went all soft and mushy-like. You wouldn't think anybody who was wearing armor could look so sappy, but old Brunhild did. "He is my love, my husband-to-be," she said. Then she sort of frowned, like she'd forgotten I was there and was all of a sudden remembering—and she didn't look any too goddam happy about it, either. "Or he was to have been my husband. The man who came through the fire can claim my hand, if he so desires."

I've always been backasswards with girls. Here she was practically saying she'd *let* me give her the time, but did that make me want to do it? Like hell it did. What it did was, it scared the crap out of me. I said, "I don't want to marry *any*body, for crying out loud. I just want to get the hell outa here, if you want to know the truth."

Brunhild thought about that for a couple seconds. Then she sat up. The chain mail made little clink-clank noises when she moved—molding itself to her shape, you know? She had a hell of a shape, too, I have to admit it. A really nice set of knockers.

"What is your name?" she said, so I told her. Just like old Regin Fafnirsbruder's had, her eyes got big. "Hagen Kriemhild?"

If you really want to know, I was getting pretty goddam tired of that. I said it again, the right way, louder this time, like you would to somebody who was pretty dumb.

But it went right by her. I could tell. Old Brunhild wasn't much for intellectual conversation. She said, "How came you here, Hagen Kriemhild?"

"That's a goddam good question." I explained it as well as I could. It sounded crazy as hell even to *me*, and I'd been through it. She was gonna think I'd gone right off the deep end.

Only she didn't. When I finally got through, old Brunhild said, "Regin Fafnirsbruder is an evil man. How not, when Fafnir his brother is an evil worm? But I shall settle with him. You need have no doubt of that."

She stood up. She was almost as tall as I was, which surprised me, because I have a lot of heighth and she was a girl and everything. But she really was, so help me God. She took out her sword. It went *wheep* when it came out of the old scabbard, and the blade kind of glowed even though the bedroom wasn't what you'd call bright or anything.

"What are you gonna do with that thing?" I said, which has to be one of the stupidest goddam questions of all time. Sometimes I scare myself, I really do. Am I a goddam moron, too, just like everybody else?

But old Brunhild took it just like any other question. "I am going to punish him for what he did to me, for this humiliation. Come with me, Hagen Kriemhild, and guard my back. He has be-smirched your honor as well as mine."

I don't know what the hell she thought I was gonna guard her back *with*. I had some German money in my pocket, and my traveler's checks and all, and a little leftover French money I'd forgotten to change, and that was about it. I didn't even have a *pock*etknife, for crying out loud, and I'm not what you'd call the bravest guy in the world anyhow. I'm pretty much of a chicken, if you want to know the truth. But I followed old Brunhild outa there just the same. If she could get out through the fire, maybe I could, too. I hoped like hell I could, anyway.

There was old Regin Fafnirsbruder on the other side of the flames. He gave Brunhild the phoniest bow you ever saw in your life. "So good you to see," he said. What he sounded like was, he sounded like the headwaiter at this fancy restaurant where all the rich phonies and all their whory-looking girlfriends go to eat and he has to be nice and suck up to the sonsuvbitches all day long even though he hates their stinking guts. "Does your bridegroom you please?" He laughed this really dirty laugh. Pimps *wish* they could laugh the way old Regin Fafnirsbruder laughed right then, honest to God.

Old Brunhild started yelling and cussing and whooping and hollering like you wouldn't believe. She started waving that god-dam sword around, too. She wasn't very *care*ful with it, either—

she damn near chopped *me* a couple of times, let me tell you. I had to duck like a madman, or I swear to God she would've punctured me.

All old Regin Fafnirsbruder did was, he kept laughing. He was laughing his ass off, to tell you the truth. He really was.

Well, that just made old Brunhild madder. "You will pay for your insolence!" she said, and so help me if she didn't charge right on out through the fire. I halfway thought she'd cook. But she was hotter than the flames, and they didn't hurt her one bit.

Anyway, I figured I'd better try and get outa there, too. Old Regin Fafnirsbruder had said Brunhild was my only chance of doing that, and *she'd* said I was supposed to guard her back even though I didn't know what the hell I was supposed to do if somebody did go and jump on her. So I ran after her. People always say I never listen to *any*body, practically, but that's a goddam lie. Well, it was this time.

I didn't run all that goddam *hard*, though, on account of I didn't *know* for sure if the fire would let me go the way it did for old Brunhild. But it felt like it did when that goddam sonuvabitch moron bastard Regin Fafnirsbruder pushed me through it going the other way—it was hot but not *hot*, if you know what I mean.

Let me tell you, old Regin Fafnirsbruder didn't look any too happy when Brunhild burst out of the ring of fire with me right behind her—not that he paid all that much attention to *me*, the lousy crumby moron. Actually, when you get down to it, I can't blame him for that, to tell you the truth. Here was this ordinary guy, and here was this goddam *girl* with chain mail and this sword coming after him yelling "Now you shall get what you deserve!" and swinging that old sword like she wanted to chop his head off—and she *did*, honest to God.

But old Regin Fafnirsbruder was a lot sprier than he looked.

He ducked and he dodged and she ran right on by him. The sword went *wheet!* a couple times but it didn't cut anything but air. And old Regin Fafnirsbruder laughed his ass off again and said, "*Your blade is my life to drink not fated.*"

Well, old Brunhild was already madder than hell, but that only pissed her off worse. She started swinging that sword like a madman—up, down, sideways, I don't know what all. I swear to God, I don't know how old Regin Fafnirsbruder didn't get himself chopped into dog food, either, I really don't, Hou*di*ni couldn't have gotten out of the way of that sword, but Regin Fafnirs-bruder did. He was a bastard, but he was a *slick* bastard, I have to admit it.

Finally, he said, "This grows boring. I shall another surprise for you one day have." Then he was gone. One second he was there, the next second he wasn't. *I* don't know how the hell he did it. I guess maybe he really was a magician, for crying out loud.

Old Brunhild, she needed like half a minute to notice he'd disappeared, she really did. She just kept hacking and slashing away like there was no tomorrow. She'd already hit the ceiling in fourteen different places, and she wasn't anywhere close to ready to calm down. I wanted to keep the hell out of her way, was all I wanted to do right about then, if you want to know the truth.

Only I couldn't. There was this castle with the ring of fire around it, and there was the slope that headed down towards old Isenstein and the Rhine that didn't stink any more, and there were me and old Brunhild. That was it. Talk about no place to hide. If she decided I was in cahoots with old Regin Fafnirsbruder after all, she'd chop me in half. I didn't know how the hell he'd dodged her, but I knew goddam well *I* didn't have a chance.

Anyway, Brunhild *fi*nally figured out old Regin Fafnirsbruder'd flown the coop. She didn't rub her eyes or go "I can't believe it" or anything like that. She just sort of shrugged her shoulders, so

139

the chain mail went *clink-clank* again, and she said, "Curse his foul sorcery."

Then she remembered I was there. I swear to God, I wouldn't've been sorry if she'd forgotten. She walked over to me, that crazy armor jingling every step she took, and she looked up into my face. Like I said before, she didn't have to look *up* very goddam far, on account of she had almost as much heighth as I did.

"You came through the fire for me," she said. "You did it unwittingly, I think, and aided by Regin Fafnirsbruder's magecraft, but the wherefores matter only so much. What bears greater weight is that you did it."

"Yeah, I guess I did."

Old Brunhild nodded. The sun shone off her helmet like a spotlight off the bell of a trombone in a nightclub. She took this deep breath. "However it was done, it was done. As I said when first you woke me, if you would claim me for your bride, you may." And she looked at me like if I was crumby enough to do it, she'd spit in my eye, honest to God she did.

Isn't that a bastard? Isn't that a bastard and a half, as a matter of fact? Here's this girl—and she's a *pretty* girl, she really is, especially if you like blondes about the size of football players—and she was saying, "Yeah, you can give me the time, all right, and I won't say boo," only I know she'll hate me forever if I do. And when old Brunhild hated somebody, she didn't do it halfway. Ask Regin Fafnirsbruder if you don't believe me, for crying out loud. And she was holding on to that sword so tight, her knuckles were white. They really were.

I said, "When I woke you up back there, in that crazy old castle and all, didn't you tell me you were in there waiting for Sieg—for somebody?" I couldn't even remember what the hell his name was, not to save my life.

"For Siegfried." Old Brunhild's face went all gooey again.

I'd kind of like to have a girl look that way when she says *my* name—or else I'd like to puke, one. I'm not sure which, I swear.

"Well," I said, "in that case maybe you'd better go on back in there and wait some more, dontcha think?"

She swung up that old sword again. I got ready to run like a madman, I'm not kidding. But she didn't do any chopping—it was some kind of crazy salute instead. *"Ja,"* she said, just like old Regin Fafnirsbruder, and then she put the sword back in the sheath. "I will do that." And then she leaned forward and stood up on tiptoe—just a little, on account of she was pretty goddam tall, like I say—and she kissed me right on the end of the nose.

Girls. They drive you nuts, they really do. I don't even think they *mean* to sometimes, but they do anyway.

I wanted to grab her and give her a real kiss, but I didn't quite have the nerve. I'm always too slow at that kind of stuff. Old Brunhild, she nodded to me once, and then she walked on back through the fire like it wasn't even there. I heard the door close. I bet she laid down on that old sofa again and fell asleep waiting for old Sieg-whatever to get done with whatever he was doing and come around to give her a call.

As soon as that door closed, I decided I wanted to kiss her after all. I ran toward the ring of fire, and I damn near—*damn near*—burned my nose off. I couldn't go through it, not any more.

No Brunhild. Damn. I shoulda laid her, or at least *kissed* her. I'm *always* too goddam slow, for crying out loud. I swear to God, it's the story of my life. No Regin Fafnirsbruder, either. I don't know where the hell he went, or when he's coming back, or if he's *ever* coming back.

If he's not, I'm gonna be *awful* goddam late making that Rhine boat connection to old Düsseldorf.

What's left here? A crumby castle I can't get into and that little tiny town down there by the river where Isenstein used to be or will be or whatever the hell it is. That's it. I wish I'd paid more attention in history class, I really do.

Well, what the hell? I started towards old—or I guess I mean new—Isenstein. I wonder if they've invented scotch yet. I swear, I *really* wish I'd paid more attention in history class.

Jesus Christ, they're *bound* to have beer at least, right?

THE DAIMON

This one first appeared in a Roc alternate-history anthology of novellas,
Worlds That Weren't. _In real history, Alkibiades had to abandon
command of Athens' expedition against Syracuse in the Pelopon-
nesian War because of scandal back home. Here, things change because
Sokrates accompanies the force. The world that results is quite different. In a piece like this, trying to get the little details right from a distance of 2,400 years is half the challenge and more than half the fun._

$\mathcal{S}$imon the shoemaker's shop stood close to the southwestern corner of the Athenian agora, near the boundary stone marking the edge of the market square and across a narrow dirt lane from the Tholos, the round building where the executive committee of the Boulê met. Inside the shop, Simon pounded iron hobnails into the sole of a sandal. His son worked with an awl, shaping bone eyelets through which rawhide laces would go. Two grandsons cut leather for more shoes.

Outside, in the shade of an olive tree, a man in his mid-fifties strode back and forth, arguing with a knot of younger men and youths. He was engagingly ugly: bald, heavy-browed, snub-nosed, with a gray beard that should have been more neatly trimmed. "And so you see, my friends," he was saying, "my *daimon* has told me that this choice does indeed come from the gods, and that something great may spring from it. Thus, though I love you and honor you, I shall obey the spirit inside me rather than you."

"But, Sokrates, you have already given Athens all she could want of you," exclaimed Kritias, far and away the most prominent of the men gathered there and, next to Sokrates, the eldest.

"You fought at Potidaia and Delion and Amphipolis. But the last of those battles was seven years ago. You are neither so young nor so strong as you used to be. You need not go to Sicily. Stay here in the polis. Your wisdom is worth more to the city than your spear ever could be."

The others dipped their heads in agreement. A youth whose first beard was just beginning to darken his cheeks said, "He speaks for all of us, Sokrates. We need you here more than the expedition ever could."

"How can one man speak for another, Xenophon?" Sokrates asked. Then he held up a hand. "Let that be a question for another time. The question for now is, why should I be any less willing to fight for my polis than, say, *he* is?"

He pointed to a hoplite tramping past in front of Simon's shop. The infantryman wore his crested bronze helm pushed back on his head, so the cheekpieces and noseguard did not hide his face. He rested the shaft of his long thrusting spear on his shoulder; a shortsword swung from his hip. Behind him, a slave carried his corselet and greaves and round, bronze-faced shield.

Kritias abandoned the philosophic calm he usually kept up in Sokrates' company. "To the crows with Alkibiades!" he burst out. "He didn't ask you to sail with him to Sicily for the sake of your strong right arm. He just wants you for the sake of your conversation, the same way as he'll probably bring along a hetaira to keep his bed warm. You're going for the sake of *his* cursed vanity—no other reason."

"No." Sokrates tossed his head. "I am going because it is important that I go. So my *daimon* tells me. I have listened to it all my life, and it has never led me astray."

"We're not going to change his mind now," one of the young men whispered to another. "When he gets that look in his eye, he's stubborn as a donkey."

Sokrates glanced toward the herm in front of Simon's shop: a stone pillar with a crude carving of Hermes' face at the top and the god's genitals halfway down. "Guard me well, patron of travelers," he murmured.

"Be careful you don't get your nose or your prong knocked off, Sokrates, the way a lot of the herms did last year," somebody said.

"Yes, and people say Alkibiades was hip-deep in that sacrilege, too," Kritias added. A considerable silence followed. Kritias was hardly the one to speak of sacrilege. He was at least as scornful of the gods as Alkibiades; he'd once claimed priests had invented them to keep ordinary people in line.

But, instead of rising to that, Sokrates only said, "Have we not seen, O best one, that we should not accept what is said without first attempting to learn how much truth it holds?" Kritias went red, then turned away in anger. If Sokrates noticed, he gave no sign.

I am the golden one.

Alkibiades looked at the triremes and transports in Athens' harbor, Peiraieus. All sixty triremes and forty transport ships about to sail for Sicily were as magnificent as their captains could make them. The eyes painted at their bows seemed to look eagerly toward the west. The ships were long and low and sleek, lean almost as eels. Some skippers had polished the three-finned, bronze-faced rams at their bows so they were a gleaming, coppery red rather than the usual green that almost matched the sea. Paint and even gilding ornamented curved stemposts and sternposts with fanlike ends.

Hoplites boarded the transports, which were triremes with the fittings for their two lower banks of oars removed to make more room for the foot soldiers. Now and then, before going up the gangplanks and into the ships, the men would pause to embrace kinsmen or youths who were dear to them or even hetairai or wives who, veiled against the public eye, had ventured forth for this farewell.

A hundred ships. More than five thousand hoplites. More than twelve thousand rowers. Mine. Every bit of it mine, Alkibiades thought.

He stood at the stern of his own ship, the *Thraseia*. Even thinking of the name made him smile. What else would he call his ship but *Boldness*? If any one trait distinguished him, that was it.

Every so often, a soldier on the way to a transport would wave to him. He always smiled and waved back. Admiration was as essential to him as the air he breathed. *And I deserve every bit I get, too.*

He was thirty-five, the picture of what a man—or perhaps a god—should look like. He'd been the most beautiful boy in Athens, the one all the men wanted. He threw back his head and laughed, remembering the pranks he'd played on some of the rich fools who wanted to be his lover. A lot of boys lost their looks when they came into manhood. *Not me,* he thought complacently. He remained every bit as splendid, if in a different way—still the target of every man's eye . . . and every woman's.

A hoplite trudged by, helmet on his head: a sturdy, wide-shouldered fellow with a gray beard. He carried his own armor and weapons, and didn't seem to be bringing a slave along to attend to him while on campaign. Even though Sokrates had pushed back the helm, as a man did when not wearing it into battle, it made Alkibiades need an extra heartbeat or two to recognize him.

"Hail, O best one!" Alkibiades called.

Sokrates stopped and dipped his head in polite acknowledgment. "Hail."

"Where are you bound?"

"Why, to Sicily: so the Assembly voted, and so we shall go."

Alkibiades snorted. Sokrates could be most annoying when he was most literal, as the younger man had found out studying with him. "No, my dear. That's not what I meant. Where are you bound *now*?"

"To a transport. How else shall I go to Sicily? I cannot swim so far, and I doubt a dolphin would bear me up, as one did for Arion long ago."

"How else shall you go?" Alkibiades said grandly. "Why, here aboard the *Thraseia* with me, of course. I've had the decking cut away to make the ship lighter and faster—and to give more breeze below it. And I've slung a hammock down there, and I can easily sling another for you, my dear. No need to bed down on hard planking."

Sokrates stood there and started to think. When he did that, nothing and no one could reach him till he finished. The fleet might sail without him, and he would never notice. He'd thought through a day and a night up at Potidaia years before, not moving or speaking. Here, though, only a couple of minutes went by before he came out of his trance. "Which other hoplites will go aboard your trireme?" he asked.

"Why, no others—only rowers and marines and officers," Alkibiades answered with a laugh. "We can, if you like, sleep under one blanket, as we did up in the north." He batted his eyes with an alluring smile.

Most Athenians would have sailed with him forever after an offer like that. Sokrates might not even have heard it. "And how many hoplites will be aboard the other triremes of the fleet?" he inquired.

"None I know of," Alkibiades said.

"Then does it not seem to you, O marvelous one, that the proper place for rowers and marines is aboard the triremes, while the proper place for hoplites is aboard the transports?" Having solved the problem to his own satisfaction, Sokrates walked on toward the transports. Alkibiades stared after him. After a moment, he shook his head and laughed again.

Once the Athenians sneaked a few soldiers into Katane by breaking down a poorly built gate, the handful of men in it who supported Syracuse panicked and fled south toward the city they favored. That amused Alkibiades, for he hadn't got enough men into the Sicilian polis to seize it in the face of a determined resistance. *Boldness*, he thought again. *Always boldness*. With the pro-Syracusans gone, Katane promptly opened its gates to the Athenian expeditionary force.

The polis lay about two-thirds of the way down from Messane at the northern corner of Sicily to Syracuse. Mount Aetna dominated the northwestern horizon, a great cone shouldering its way up into the sky. Even with spring well along, snow still clung to the upper slopes of the volcano. Here and there, smoke issued from vents in the flanks and at the top. Every so often, lava would gush from them. When it flowed in the wrong direction, it destroyed the Katanians' fields and olive groves and vineyards. If it flowed in exactly the wrong direction, it would destroy their town.

Alkibiades felt like the volcano himself after another fight with Nikias. The Athenians had sent Nikias along with the expedition to serve as an anchor for Alkibiades. He knew it, knew it and hated it. He didn't particularly hate Nikias himself; he just found him laughable, to say nothing of irrelevant. Nikias was twenty years older than he, and those twenty years might just as well have been a thousand.

Nikias dithered and worried and fretted. Alkibiades thrust home. Nikias gave reverence to the gods with obsessive piety, and did nothing without checking the omens first. Alkibiades laughed at the gods when he didn't ignore them. Nikias had opposed this expedition to Sicily. It had been Alkibiades' idea.

"We were lucky ever to take this place," Nikias had grumbled. He kept fooling with his beard, as if he had lice. For all Alkibiades knew, he did.

"Yes, my dear," Alkibiades had said with such patience as he could muster. "Luck favors us. We should—we had better—take advantage of it. Ask Lamakhos. He'll tell you the same." Lamakhos was the other leading officer in the force. Alkibiades didn't despise him. He wasn't worth despising. He was just . . . dull.

"I don't care what Lamakhos thinks," Nikias had said testily. "I think we ought to thank the gods we've come this far safely. We ought to thank them, and then go home."

"And make Athens the laughingstock of Hellas?" *And make* me *the laughingstock of Hellas?* "Not likely!"

"We cannot do what we came to Sicily to do," Nikias had insisted.

"You were the one who told the Assembly we needed such a great force. Now we have it, and you still aren't happy with it?"

"I never dreamt they would be mad enough actually to send so much."

Alkibiades hadn't hit him then. He might have, but he'd been interrupted. A commotion outside made both men hurry out of Alkibiades' tent. "What is it?" Alkibiades called to a man running his way. "Is the Syracusan fleet coming up to fight us?" It had stayed in the harbor when an Athenian reconnaissance squadron sailed south a couple of weeks before. Maybe the Syracusans hoped to catch the Athenian triremes beached and burn or wreck them. If they did, they would get a nasty surprise.

But the Athenian tossed his head. "It's not the polluted Syracusans," he answered. "It's the *Salaminia*. She's just come into the harbor here."

"The *Salaminia*?" Alkibiades and Nikias spoke together, and in identical astonishment. The *Salaminia* was Athens' official state trireme, and wouldn't venture far from home except on most important business. Sure enough, peering toward the harbor, Alkibiades could see her crew dragging her out of the sea and up onto the yellow sand of the beach. "What's she doing here?" he asked.

Nikias eyed him with an expression compounded of equal parts loathing and gloating. "I'll bet I know," the older man said. "I'll bet they found someone who told the citizens of Athens the real story, the true story, of how the herms all through the polis were profaned."

"I had nothing to do with that," Alkibiades said. He'd said the same thing ever since the mutilations happened. "And besides," he added, "just about as many of the citizens of Athens are here in Sicily as are back at the polis."

"You can't evade like that," Nikias said. "You remind me of your dear teacher Sokrates, using bad logic to beat down good."

Alkibiades stared at him as if he'd found him squashed on the sole of his sandal. "What you say about Sokrates would be a lie even if you'd thought of it yourself. But it comes from Aristophanes' *Clouds*, and you croak it out like a raven trained to speak but without the wit to understand its words."

Nikias' cheeks flamed red as hot iron beaten on the anvil. Alkibiades would have liked to beat him. Instead, he contemptuously turned his back. But that pointed his gaze toward the *Salaminia* again. Athenians down there on the shore were pointing up to the high ground on which he stood. A pair of men whose gold wreaths declared they were on official business made their way toward him.

He hurried to meet them. That was always his style. He wanted to make things happen, not have them happen to him. Nikias followed. "Hail, friends!" Alkibiades called, tasting the lie. "Are you looking for me? I am here."

"Alkibiades son of Kleinias?" one of the newcomers asked formally.

"You know who I am, Herakleides," Alkibiades said. "What do you want?"

"I think, son of Kleinias, that you know what I want," Herakleides replied. "You are ordered by the people of Athens to return to the polis to defend yourself against serious charges that have been raised against you."

More and more hoplites and rowers gathered around Alkibiades and the men newly come from Athens. This was an armed camp, not a peaceful city; many of them carried spears or wore swords on their hips. Alkibiades smiled to see them, for he knew they were well-inclined toward him. In a loud voice, he asked, "Am I under arrest?"

Herakleides and his wreathed comrade licked their lips. The mere word made soldiers growl and heft their spears; several of them drew their swords. Gathering himself, Herakleides answered, "No, you are not under arrest. But you are summoned to defend yourself, as I said. How can a man with such charges hanging over his head hope to hold an important position of public trust?"

"Yes—how indeed?" Nikias murmured.

Again, Alkibiades gave him a look full of withering scorn. Then he forgot about him. Herakleides and his friend were more important at the moment. So were the soldiers and sailors—much more important. With a smile and a mocking bow, Alkibiades said, "How can any man hope to hold an important position of public trust when a lying fool can trump up such charges and hang them over his head?"

"That's the truth," a hoplite growled, right in Herakleides' ear. He was a big, burly fellow with a thick black beard—a man built like a wrestler or a pankratiast. Alkibiades wouldn't have wanted a man like that growling in his ear and clenching a spearshaft till his knuckles whitened.

By the involuntary step back Herakleides took, he didn't care for it, either. His voice quavered as he said, "You deny the charges, then?"

"Of course I do," Alkibiades answered. Out of the corner of his eye, he noticed Sokrates pushing his way through the crowd toward the front. A lot of men were pushing forward, but somehow Sokrates, despite his years, made more progress than most. Maybe the avid curiosity on his face helped propel him forward. Or maybe not; he almost always seemed that curious. But Sokrates would have to wait now, too. Alkibiades went on, "I say they're nothing but a pack of lies put forward by scavenger dogs who, unable to do anything great themselves, want to pull down those who can."

Snarls of agreement rose from the soldiers and sailors. Herakleides licked his lips again. He must have known recalling Alkibiades wouldn't be easy before the *Salaminia* sailed. Had he known it would be *this* hard? Alkibiades had his doubts. With something like a sigh, Herakleides said, "At the motion of Thettalos son of Kimon, it has seemed good to the people of Athens to summon you home. Will you obey the democratic will of the Assembly, or will you not?"

Alkibiades grimaced. He had no use for the democracy of Athens, and had never bothered hiding that. As a result, the demagogues who loved to hear themselves talk in the Assembly hated him. He said, "I have no hope of getting a fair hearing in Athens. My enemies have poisoned the people of the polis against me."

Herakleides frowned portentously. "Would you refuse the Assembly's summons?"

"I don't know what I'll do right now." Alkibiades clenched

his fists. What he wanted to do was pound the smugness out of the plump, prosperous fool in front of him. But no. It would not do. Here, though, even he, normally so quick and decisive, had trouble figuring out what *would* do. "Let me have time to think, O marvelous one," he said, and watched Herakleides redden at the sarcasm. "I will give you my answer tomorrow."

"Do you want to be declared a rebel against the people of Athens?" Herakleides' frown got deeper and darker.

"No, but I don't care to go home and be ordered to guzzle hemlock no matter what I say or do, either," Alkibiades answered. "Were it your life, Herakleides, such as that is, would you not want time to plan out what to do?"

That *such as that is* made the man just come from Athens redden again. But soldiers and sailors jostled forward, getting louder by the minute in support of their general. Herakleides yielded with such grace as he could: "Let it be as you say, most noble one." He turned the title of respect into one of reproach. "I will hear your answer tomorrow. For now . . . hail." He turned and walked back toward the *Salaminia*. The sun glinted dazzlingly off his gold wreath.

Sokrates stood in line to get his evening rations. Talk of Alkibiades and the herms and the profanation of the sacred mysteries was on everyone's lips. Some men thought he'd done what he was accused of doing. Others insisted the charges against him were invented to discredit him.

"Wait," Sokrates told a man who'd been talking about unholy deeds and how the gods despised them. "Say that again, Euthyphron, if you please. I don't follow your thought, which is surely much too wise for a simple fellow like me."

"I'd be glad to, Sokrates," the other hoplite said, and he did.

"I'm sorry, best one. I really must be dense," Sokrates said when he'd finished. "I still do not quite see. Do you say deeds are unholy because the gods hate them, or do you say the gods hate them because they are unholy?"

"I certainly do," Euthyphron answered.

"No, wait. I see what Sokrates means," another soldier broke in. "You can't have that both ways. It's one or the other. Which do you say it is?"

Euthyphron tried to have it both ways. Sokrates' questions wouldn't let him. Some of the other Athenians jeered at him. Others showed more sympathy for him, even in his confusion, than they did for Sokrates. "Do you have to be a gadfly *all* the time?" a hoplite asked him after Euthyphron, very red in the face, bolted out of the line without getting his supper.

"I can only be what I am," Sokrates answered. "Am I wrong for trying to find the truth in everything I do?"

The other man shrugged. "I don't know whether you're right or wrong. What I do know is, you're cursed *annoying*."

When Sokrates blinked his big round eyes in surprise, he looked uncommonly like a frog. "Why should the search for truth be annoying? Would you not think preventing that search to be a greater annoyance for mankind?"

But the hoplite threw up his hands. "Oh, no, you don't. I won't play. You're not going to twist me up in knots, the way you did with poor Euthyphron."

"Euthyphron's thinking was not straight before I ever said a word to him. All I did was show him his inconsistencies. Now maybe he will try to root them out."

The other soldier tossed his head. But he still refused to argue. Sighing, Sokrates snaked forward with the rest of the line. A bored-looking cook handed him a small loaf of dark bread, a chunk of cheese, and an onion. The man filled his cup with watered wine and poured olive oil for the bread into a little cruet he held out.

"I thank you," Sokrates said. The cook looked surprised. Soldiers and sailors were likelier to grumble about the fare than thank him for it.

Men clustered in little knots of friends to eat and to go on hashing over the coming of the *Salaminia* and what it was liable to mean. Sokrates had no usual group to join. Part of the reason was that he was at least twenty years older than most of the other Athenians who'd traveled west to Sicily. But his age was only part of the reason, and he knew it. He sighed. He didn't *want* to make people uncomfortable. He didn't want to, but he'd never been able to avoid it.

He walked back to his tent to eat his supper. When he was done, he went outside and stared up at Mount Aetna. Why, he wondered, did it stay cold enough for snow to linger on the mountain's upper slopes even on this sweltering midsummer evening?

He was no closer to finding the answer when someone called his name. He got the idea this wasn't the first time the man had called. Sure enough, when he turned, there stood Alkibiades with a sardonic grin on his face. "Hail, O wisest of all," the younger man said. "Good to see you with us again."

"If I am wisest—which I doubt, no matter what the gods may say—it is because I know how ignorant I am, where other men are ignorant even of that," Sokrates replied.

Alkibiades' grin grew impudent. "Other men don't know how ignorant you are?" he suggested slyly. Sokrates laughed. But Alkibiades' grin slipped. "Ignorant or not, will you walk with me?"

"If you like," Sokrates said. "You know I never could resist your beauty." He imitated the little lisp for which Alkibiades was famous, and sighed like a lover gazing upon his beloved.

"Oh, go howl!" Alkibiades said. "Even when we slept under

the same blanket, we only slept. You did your best to ruin my reputation."

"I cannot ruin your reputation." Sokrates' voice grew sharp. "Only you can do that."

Alkibiades made a face at him. "Come along, best one, if you'd be so kind." They walked away from the Athenian encampment on a winding dirt track that led up towards Aetna. Alkibiades wore a chiton with purple edging and shoes with golden clasps. Sokrates' tunic was threadbare and raggedy; he went barefoot the way he usually did, as if he were a sailor.

The sight of the most and least elegant men in the Athenian expedition walking along together would have been plenty to draw eyes even if the *Salaminia* hadn't just come to Katane. As things were, they had to tramp along for several stadia before shaking off the last of the curious. Sokrates ignored the men who followed hoping to eavesdrop. Alkibiades glowered at them till they finally gave up.

"Vultures," he muttered. "Now I know how Prometheus must have felt." He put a hand over his liver.

"Is that what you wanted to talk about?" Sokrates asked.

"You know what I want to talk about. You were there when those idiots in gold wreaths summoned me back to Athens," Alkibiades answered. Sokrates looked over at him, his face showing nothing but gentle interest. Alkibiades snorted. "And don't pretend you don't, either, if you please. I haven't the time for it."

"I am only the most ignorant of men—" Sokrates began. Alkibiades cursed him, as vilely as he knew how. Sokrates gave back a mild smile in return. That made Alkibiades curse harder yet. Sokrates went on as if he hadn't spoken: "So you *will* have to tell me what it is you want, I fear."

"All right. All *right*." Alkibiades kicked at a pebble. It spun into the brush by the track. "I'll play your polluted game. What am I supposed to do about the *Salaminia* and the summons?"

"Why, that which is best, of course."

"Thank you so much, O most noble one," Alkibiades snarled. He kicked another pebble, a bigger one this time. "*Oimoi!* That hurt!" He hopped a couple of times before hurrying to catch up with Sokrates, who'd never slowed.

Sokrates eyed him with honest perplexity. "What else *can* a man who knows what the good is do but that which is best?"

"What *is* the good here?" Alkibiades demanded.

"Why ask me, when I am so ignorant?" Sokrates replied. Alkibiades started to kick yet another pebble, thought better of it, and cursed again instead. Sokrates waited till he'd finished, then inquired, "What do *you* think the good is here?"

"Games," Alkibiades muttered. He breathed heavily, mastering himself. Then he laughed, and seemed to take himself by surprise. "I'll pretend I'm an ephebe again, eighteen years old and curious as a puppy. By the gods, I wish I were. The good here is that which is best for me and that which is best for Athens."

He paused, waiting to see what Sokrates would say to that. Sokrates, as was his way, asked another question: "And what will happen if you return to Athens on the *Salaminia*?"

"My enemies there will murder me under form of law," Alkibiades answered. After another couple of strides, he seemed to remember he was supposed to think of Athens, too. "And Nikias will find some way to botch this expedition. For one thing, he's a fool. For another, he doesn't want to be here in the first place. He doesn't think we can win. With *him* in command, he's likely right."

"Is this best for you and best for Athens, then?" Sokrates asked.

Alkibiades gave him a mocking bow. "It would seem not, O best one," he answered, as if he were chopping logic in front of Simon the shoemaker's.

"All right, then. What other possibilities exist?" Sokrates asked.

"I could make as if to go back to Athens, then escape somewhere and live my own life," Alkibiades said. "That's what I'm thinking of doing now, to tell you the truth."

"I see," Sokrates said. "And is this best for you?"

A wild wolf would have envied Alkibiades' smile. "I think so. It would give me the chance to avenge myself on all my enemies. And I would, too. Oh, wouldn't I just?"

"I believe you," Sokrates said, and he did. Alkibiades was a great many things, but no one had ever reckoned him less than able. "Now, what of Athens if you do this?"

"As for the expedition, the same as in the first case. As for the polis, to the crows with it," Alkibiades said savagely. "It is my enemy, and I its."

"And is this that which is best for Athens, which you said you sought?" Sokrates asked. Yes, Alkibiades would make a formidable enemy.

"A man should do his friends good and his enemies harm," he said now. "If the city made me flee her, she would be my enemy, not my friend. Up till now, I have done her as much good as I could. I would do the same in respect to harm."

A wall lizard stared at Sokrates from a boulder sticking up out of the scrubby brush by the side of the track. He took one step closer to it. It scrambled off the boulder and away. For a moment, he could hear it skittering through dry weeds. Then it must have found a hole, for silence returned. He wondered how it knew to run when something that might be danger approached. But that riddle would have to wait for another time. He gave his attention back to Alkibiades, who was watching him with an expression of wry amusement, and asked, "If you go back with the *Salaminia* to Athens, then, you say, you will suffer?"

"That is what I say, yes." Alkibiades dipped his head in agreement.

"And if you do not accompany the *Salaminia* all the way back to Athens, you say that the polis will be the one to suffer?"

"Certainly. I say that also," Alkibiades replied with a wry chuckle. "See how much I sound like any of the other poor fools you question?"

Sokrates waved away the gibe. "Do you say that either of these things is best for you and best for Athens?"

Now Alkibiades tossed his head. "It would seem not, O best one. But what else can I do? The Assembly is back at the city. It voted what it voted. I don't see how I could change its mind unless. . . ." His voice trailed away. He suddenly laughed out loud, laughed out loud and sprang forward to kiss Sokrates on the mouth. "Thank you, my dear! You have given me the answer."

"Nonsense!" Sokrates pushed him away hard enough to make him stumble back a couple of paces; those stonecutter's shoulders still held a good deal of strength. "I only ask questions. If you found an answer, it came from inside you."

"Your questions shone light on it."

"But it was there all along, or I could not have illuminated it. And as for the kiss, if you lured me out into this barren land to seduce me, I am afraid you will find yourself disappointed despite your beauty."

"Ah, Sokrates, if you hadn't put in that last I think you would have broken my heart forever." Alkibiades made as if to kiss the older man again. Sokrates made as if to pick up a rock and clout him with it. Laughing, they turned and walked back toward the Athenians' encampment.

Herakleides threw up shocked hands. "This is illegal!" he exclaimed.

Nikias wagged a finger in Alkibiades' face. "This is unprecedented!" he cried. By the way he said it, that was worse than anything merely illegal could ever be.

Alkibiades bowed to each of them in turn. "Ordering me home when I wasn't in Athens to defend myself is illegal," he said. "Recalling a commander in the middle of such an important campaign is unprecedented. We have plenty of Athenians here. Let's see what *they* think about it."

He looked across the square in Katane. He'd spoken here to the Assembly of the locals not long before, while Athenian soldiers filtered into the polis and brought it under their control. Now Athenian hoplites and rowers and marines filled the square. They made an Assembly of their own. It probably was illegal. It certainly was unprecedented. Alkibiades didn't care. It just as certainly was his only chance.

He took a couple of steps forward, right to the edge of the speakers' platform. Sokrates was out there somewhere. Alkibiades couldn't pick him out, though. He shrugged. He was on his own anyhow. Sokrates might have given him some of the tools he used, but *he* had to use them. He was fighting for *his* life.

"Hear me, men of Athens! Hear me, *people* of Athens!" he said. The soldiers and sailors leaned forward, intent on his every word. The people of Athens had sent them forth to Sicily. The idea that they might *be* the people of Athens as well as its representatives here in the west was new to them. They had to believe it. Alkibiades had to make them believe it. If they didn't, he was doomed.

"Back in the polis, the Assembly there"—he wouldn't call that *the people of Athens*—"has ordered me home so they can condemn me and kill me without most of my friends—without *you*—there to protect me. They say I desecrated the herms in the city. They say I profaned the sacred mysteries of Eleusis. One of their so-called witnesses claims I broke the herms by moonlight, when everyone knows it was done in the last days of the month, when there was no moonlight. These are the sorts of people my enemies produce against me."

He never said he hadn't mutilated the herms. He never said he hadn't burlesqued the mysteries. He said the witnesses his opponents produced lied—and they did.

He went on, "Even if I went back to Athens, my enemies' witnesses would say one thing, my few friends and I another. No matter how the jury finally voted, no one would ever be sure of the truth. And so I say to you, men of Athens, *people* of Athens, let us not rely on lies and jurymen who can be swayed by lies. Let us rest my fate on the laps of the gods."

Nikias started. Alkibiades almost laughed out loud. *Didn't expect that, did you, you omen-mongering fool?*

Aloud, he continued, "If we triumph here in Sicily under my command, will that not prove I have done no wrong in the eyes of heaven? If we triumph—as triumph we can, as triumph we *shall*—then I shall return to Athens with you, and let these stupid charges against me be forgotten forevermore. But if we fail here . . . If we fail here, I swear to you I shall not leave Sicily alive, but will be the offering to repay the gods for whatever sins they reckon me to have committed. That is my offer, to you and to the gods. Time will show what they say of it. But what say you, men of Athens? What say you, *people* of Athens?"

He waited for the decision of the Assembly he'd convened. He didn't have to wait long. Cries of "Yes!" rang out, and "We accept!" and "Alkibiades!" A few men tossed their heads and yelled things like "No!" and "Let the decision of the Assembly in Athens stand!" But they were only a few, overwhelmed and outshouted by Alkibiades' backers.

Turning to Herakleides and Nikias, Alkibiades bowed once more. They'd thought they would be able to address the Athenian soldiers and sailors after he finished. But the decision was already made. Herakleides looked stunned, Nikias dyspeptic.

With another bow, Alkibiades said to Herakleides, "You will take my answer and the true choice of the people of Athens back to the polis?"

The other man needed two or three tries before he managed to stammer out, "Y-Yes."

"Good." Alkibiades smiled. "Tell the polis also, I hope to be back there myself before too long."

Sokrates settled his helmet on his head. The bronze and the glued-in padded lining would, with luck, keep some Syracusan from smashing in his skull. The walls of Syracuse loomed ahead. The Athenians were building their own wall around the city, to cut it off from the countryside and starve it into submission. Now the Syracusans had started a counterwall, thrust out from the fortifications of the polis. If it blocked the one the Athenians were building, Syracuse might stand. If the hoplites Alkibiades led could stop that counterwall . . . A man didn't need to be a general to see what would happen then.

Sweat streamed down Sokrates' face. Summer in Sicily was hotter than it ever got back home in Attica. He had a skin full of watered wine, and squirted some into his mouth. Swallowing felt good. A little of the wine splashed his face. That felt good, too.

"*Pheu!*" said another hoplite close by. "Only thing left of me'll be my shadow by the time we're done here."

Sokrates smiled. "I like that." He tilted back his helmet so he could drag a hairy forearm across his sweaty forehead, then let the helm fall down into place again. He tapped the nodding crimson-dyed horsehair plume with a forefinger. "This makes me seem fiercer than I am. But since all hoplites wear crested helms, and all therefore seem fiercer than they are, is it not true that the intended effect of the crest is wasted?"

Laughing, the other hoplite said, "You come up with some of the strangest things, Sokrates, Furies take me if you don't."

"How can the search for truth be strange?" Sokrates asked. "Do you say the truth is somehow alien to mankind, and that he has no knowledge of it from birth?"

Instead of answering, the other Athenian pointed to one of the rough little forts in which the Syracusans working on their counterwall sheltered. "Look! They're coming out." So they were, laborers in short chitons or loincloths, with armored hoplites to protect them while they piled stone on stone. "Doesn't look like they've got very many guards out today, does it?"

"Certainly not," Sokrates answered. "The next question to be asked is, why have they sent forth so few?"

Horns blared in the Athenian camp. "I don't think our captain cares why," the other hoplite said, pulling down his helmet so the cheekpieces and nasal protected his face. "Whatever the reason is, he's going to make them sorry for being so stupid."

"But do you not agree that *why* is always the most important question?" Sokrates asked. Instead of answering, the other hoplite turned to take his place in line. The horns cried out again. Sokrates picked up his shield and his spear and also joined the building phalanx. In the face of battle, all questions had to wait. Sometimes the fighting answered them without words.

The Athenian captain pointed toward the Syracusans a couple of stadia away. "They've goofed, boys. Let's make 'em pay. We'll beat their hoplites, run their workers off or else kill 'em, and we'll tear down some of that wall they're trying to build. We can do it. It'll be easy. Give the war-cry good and loud so they know we're coming. That'll scare the shit out of 'em, just like on the comic stage."

"How about the comic stage?" the hoplite next to Sokrates asked. "You were up there, in Aristophanes' *Clouds*."

"I wasn't there in person, though the mask the actor wore looked so much like me, I stood up in the audience to show the resemblance," Sokrates answered. "And it's the Syracusans we want to do the shitting, not ourselves."

"Forward!" the captain shouted, and pointed at the Syracusans with his spear.

Sokrates shouted, *"Eleleu! Eleleu!"* with the rest of the Athenians as they advanced on their foes. It wasn't a wild charge at top speed. A phalanx, even a small one like this, would fall to pieces and lose much of its force in such a charge. What made the formation strong was each soldier protecting his neighbor's right as well as his own left with his shield, and two or three serried ranks of spearheads projecting out beyond the front line of hoplites. No soldiers in the world could match Hellenic hoplites. The Great Kings of Persia knew as much, and hired Hellenes by the thousands as mercenaries.

The Athenians might have made short work of Persians or other barbarians. The Syracusans, though, were just as much Hellenes as they were. Though outnumbered, the soldiers guarding the men building the counterwall shouted back and forth in their drawling Doric dialect and then also formed a phalanx—only four or five rows deep, for they were short of men—and hurried to block the Athenians' descent on the laborers. They too cried, *"Eleleu!"*

As a man will do on the battlefield, Sokrates tried to spot the soldier he would likely have to fight. He knew that was a foolish exercise. He marched in the third row of the Athenians, and the enemy he picked might go down or shift position before they met. But, with the universal human longing to find patterns whether they really existed or not, he did it anyway.

"*Eleleu! Elel—*" *Crash!* Both sides' war cries were lost in what sounded like a disaster in a madman's smithy as the two front lines collided. Spearpoints clattered off bronze corselets and bronze-faced shields. Those shields smacked together, men from each side trying to force their foes to danger. Some spearpoints struck flesh instead of bronze. Shrieks and curses rang through the metallic clangor.

Where the man on whom Sokrates had fixed went, he never knew. He thrust underhanded at another Syracusan, a young fellow with reddish streaks in his black beard. The spearpoint bit into the enemy's thigh, below the bronze-studded leather strips he wore over his kilt and above the top of his greave. Blood spurted, red as the feathers of a spotted woodpecker's crest. The Syracusan's mouth opened enormously wide in a great wail of anguish. He toppled, doing his best to pull his shield over himself so he wouldn't be trampled.

Relying on weight of numbers, the Athenians bulled their way forward, forcing their foes to give ground and spearing them down one after another. Most of the laborers the Syracusans had protected ran back toward the fort from which they'd come. Some, though, hovered on the outskirts of the battle and flung stones at the Athenians. One banged off Sokrates' shield.

And if it had hit me in the face? he wondered. The answer to that was obvious enough, though not one even a lover of wisdom cared to contemplate.

A Syracusan thrust a spear at Sokrates. He turned it aside with his shield, then quickly stepped forward, using the shield as a battering ram. The enemy soldier gave ground. He was younger than Sokrates—what hoplite wasn't?—but on the scrawny side. Broad-shouldered and thick through the chest and belly, Sokrates made the most of his weight. The Syracusan tripped over a stone and went down, arms flailing, with a cry of despair. The Athenian behind Sokrates drove a spear into the fallen man's throat. His blood splashed Sokrates' greaves.

Athenians went down, too, in almost equal numbers, but they still had the advantage. Before long, their foes wouldn't be able to hold their line together. Once the Syracusans fled, all running as individuals instead of fighting together in a single unit, they would fall like barley before the scythe.

But then, only moments before that would surely happen, horns blared from the walls of Syracuse. A gate opened. Out poured more Syracusans, rank upon rank of them, the sun gleaming ruddy from their bronzen armor and reflecting in silvery sparkles off countless iron spearheads. *"Eleleu!"* they roared, and thundered down on the Athenians like a landslide.

"A trap!" groaned a hoplite near Sokrates. "They used those few fellows as bait to lure us in, and now they're going to bugger us."

"They have to have twice the men we do," another man agreed.

"Then we shall have to fight twice as hard," Sokrates said. "For is it not true that a man who shows he is anything but easy meat will often come out of danger safe, where one who breaks and runs is surely lost? I have seen both victory and defeat, and so it seems to me."

The more worried he was himself, the more he wanted to keep his comrades steady. The Syracusans out here by the counterwall had hung together well, waiting for their rescuers. Now the Athenians had to do the same. Sokrates looked around. He saw no rescuers. He shrugged inside his corselet. If the Syracusans wanted him, they would have to drag him down.

"Eleleu!" they cried. *"Eleleu!"*

Screaming like men gone mad, Athenian officers swung their men to face the new onslaught. Nothing was more hopeless, more defenseless, than a phalanx struck in the flank. This way, at least, they would make the enemy earn whatever he got. "Come on, boys!" a captain shouted. "They're only Syracusans. We can beat them."

Sokrates wanted to ask him how he knew. No chance for that. The two phalanxes smashed together. Now it was the Athenians who were outnumbered. They fought to keep from being driven back, and to keep the Syracusans from breaking through or sliding around their front. As men in the first few ranks went down, others shoved forward to take their places.

He found himself facing a Syracusan whose spear had broken. The enemy hoplite had thrown away the shaft and drawn his sword—a good enough emergency weapon, but only an emergency weapon when facing a man with a pike. Sokrates could reach him, but he had no chance to reach Sokrates.

He had no chance, that is, till he hacked at Sokrates' spearshaft just below the head and watched the iron point fly free and thump down on the ground. *"Papai!"* Sokrates exclaimed in dismay. The Syracusan let out a triumphant whoop. A sword might not be much against a spear, but against a spearshaft . . .

A sword proved not so much. In the front line, Sokrates had more room to wield what was left of his weapon than he would have farther back. He swung the beheaded shaft as if it were a club. It thudded against the Syracusan's shield. The next blow would have caved in his skull, helm or no helm, if he hadn't brought the shield up in a hurry. And the third stroke smacked into the side of his knee—he hadn't got the shield down again fast enough. No greave could protect him against a blow like that. Down he went, clutching his leg. In a scene straight from the *Iliad*, the hoplite behind him sprang forward to ward him with shield and armored body till comrades farther back could drag him out of the fight.

Sokrates used the moment's respite to throw down the ruined spear and snatch up one that somebody else had dropped. He dipped his head to the Syracusan across from him. "Bravely done, my friend."

"Same to you, old man," the other soldier answered. "A lot of hoplites would have cut and run when they lost their pikes." He gathered himself. "Brave or not, though, Athenian, I'll kill you if I can." Fast as a striking snake, his spearhead darted for Sokrates' face.

Ducking away from the thrust, Sokrates answered with one of his own. The Syracusan turned it on his shield. They both stepped forward to struggle shield to shield. The Syracusan kept up a steady stream of curses. Panting, winded, Sokrates needed all his breath to fight.

He drew back a couple of paces, not because the enemy hoplite was getting the better of him but because the rest of the Athenians had had to retreat. "Should have stayed, old man," the Syracusan jeered. "I'd have had you then, or my pals would if I didn't."

"If you want me, come and fight me," Sokrates said. "You won't kill me with words." *I might fall dead over of my own accord, though.* He couldn't remember the last time he'd been so worn. Maybe—probably—he'd never been so worn before. *Maybe my friends back in Athens were right, and I should have stayed in the city. War is a young man's sport. Am I young?* He laughed. The Syracusan hoplite who'd been trying to kill him knew the answer to that.

"What's funny, old man?" the Syracusan demanded.

"What's funny, young man? That you are what I wish I were," Sokrates replied.

In the shadowed space between his nasal and cheekpieces, the other man's eyes widened slightly. "You talk like a sophist."

"So my enemies have always— Ha!" Sokrates fended off a sudden spearthrust with his shield. "Thought you'd take me unawares, did you?"

"I am your enemy. I—" Now the Syracusan was the one who broke off. He turned his head this way and that to look about. With his helmet on, a hoplite couldn't move only his eyes. Sokrates looked, too, with quick, wary flicks of the head. He saw nothing. For a moment, he also heard nothing. Then his ears—*an old man's ears, sure enough*, he thought—caught the trumpet notes the Syracusan hoplite must have heard a few heartbeats sooner.

Sokrates looked around again. This time, when he looked . . . he saw. Over the crest of a nearby hill came men on horseback, peltasts—light-armed foot soldiers—and a solid column of hoplites. No possible way to doubt which side they belonged to, either. At the head of the column rode Alkibiades, his bright hair shining in the sun, a chiton all of purple—an outrageous, and outrageously expensive, garment—marking him out from every other man.

Shouting out their war cry, the Athenian newcomers roared down on the Syracusans. "We are undone!" one of the Syracusan hoplites cried. They broke ranks and ran back toward their polis. Some of them threw away spears and even shields to flee the faster.

Other Syracusans—perhaps a quarter of their number—tried to go on against the Athenian phalanx they'd been fighting. One of those was the hoplite who'd tussled so long against Sokrates. "Yield," Sokrates urged. "Yield to me, and I will see to it that you suffer no evil."

"I serve my polis no less than you serve yours, Athenian," the man answered, and hurled himself at Sokrates once more. Now, though, with the Syracusan line melting away like rotting ice, he fought not Sokrates alone but three or four Athenians. He fought bravely, but he didn't last long.

"Forward!" an Athenian officer cried. "Forward, and they break. *Eleleu!*"

Forward the Athenians went. Hoplites in a body had a chance, often a good chance, against peltasts and horsemen, even if they moved more slowly than their foes. Peltasts could only use their bows and slings and fling javelins from a distance. Likewise, cavalry had trouble closing because the riders would pop off over their horses' tails if they drove him a charge with the lance. But the panicked, running Syracusans, also hard-pressed by the Athenian hoplites, went down like trees under carpenters' axes.

Alkibiades at their head, the Athenian horsemen got in amongst the Syracusans. They speared some and felled others with slashes from their long cavalrymen's swords. The peltasts tormented the foe with arrows and leaden sling bullets and javelins. And, now roaring *"Eleleu!"* like men seized by Furies, the Athenian hoplites rolled over the slower and more stubborn Syracusans.

The whole enemy host might have fallen there in front of their polis. But the defenders on the walls saw what was happening to them. The gate from which the Syracusan phalanx had marched forth flew open again. The Syracusans ran for their salvation. The Athenians ran after them—and with them.

Like a lot of veterans, Sokrates saw what that might mean. No matter how winded, no matter how parched, he was, he shouted, "As fast as we can now, men of Athens! If we get into Syracuse among them, the city is ours!" He made his stubby legs twinkle over the ground.

Up ahead, Alkibiades heard his voice. He waved and made his horse rear, clinging to the animal with his knees and with one hand clutching its mane. Then he, too, pointed toward that open gate. The horse came down onto all fours. It galloped forward, bounding past the Syracusans on foot. Other riders saw what was toward and followed.

The first Syracusan hoplites were already inside the polis. In stormed the horsemen. They turned on the gate crew, killing some and scattering others. Some of the Syracusan hoplites tried to haul the gates closed. The cavalrymen fought them, delayed them. Athenian peltasts rushed up to the horsemen's aid. Madness reigned around the gate.

What is madness, Sokrates thought, *save the absence of order?* Still in good order, the Athenian phalanx hammered its way through the chaos—through the chaos, through the gate, and into Syracuse. The Syracusan women and children and old men wailed in horror. The Athenian hoplites roared in triumph.

Sokrates roared with the rest: "Syracuse is ours!"

Women wept. Wounded men moaned. The stinks of smoke and blood and spilled guts filled the air. A drunk Athenian peltast danced the kordax, howling out filthy words to go with the filthy dance. His pecker flipped up to smack against his stomach at every prancing step. It was all bread and fine fish and wine—especially wine—to Alkibiades. He stood in front of—appropriately enough—the temple of Athena, watching chained Syracusan captives shamble past.

Nikias came up to him, looking slightly—no, more than slightly—dazed. Alkibiades gave his fellow general his prettiest bow. "Hail," he said, and then, as if Nikias couldn't see it for himself, "We have Syracuse."

"Er—yes." Nikias might see it, but he seemed hardly able to credit it. "We do."

"Do you believe, then, that the gods have shown I'm innocent of sacrilege?" Alkibiades asked. He wasn't sure he believed that himself; some of the things Sokrates and Kritias had said about the gods made him have even more questions than he would have had otherwise. But it was important that prominent, conservative Nikias should believe it.

And the older man dipped his head. "Why, yes, son of Kleinias, I do. I must. I don't see how any man could doubt it, considering what has happened here in Sicily."

I have to make sure he never talks to Sokrates, Alkibiades thought. *He'd find out exactly how a man could doubt it.* Sokrates was a great one for making anybody doubt anything. But there wasn't much risk that he and Nikias would put their heads together. Sokrates would talk with anyone. Nikias, on the other hand, was a born snob. With another bow, carefully controlled so it didn't seem mocking, Alkibiades asked, "What did you expect to happen on this campaign?"

Nikias' eyes got big and round. "I feared . . . disaster," he said hoarsely. "I feared our men failing when they tried to wall off Syracuse. I feared our fleet trapped and beaten by the Syracusans. I feared our brave soldiers worsted and worked to death in the mines. I had . . . dreams." His voice wobbled.

Grinning, Alkibiades clapped him on the shoulder. "And they were all moonshine, weren't they? These amateurs made a mistake, and we made them pay for it. We'll put the people *we* want into power here—you can always find men who will do what you want—and then, before the sailing season ends, we'll go back and see what we can do about giving the Spartans a clout in the teeth."

At that, Nikias' eyes got bigger and rounder than ever. But he said, "We shall have to be careful here. The men we establish may turn against us, or others may rise up and overthrow them."

He was right. Naïveté and superstition sometimes made him a fool; never stupidity. Alkibiades said, "True enough, O best one. Still, once we're done here, Syracuse will be years getting her strength back, even if she does turn against us. And that's what we came west for, isn't it? To weaken her, I mean. We've done it."

"We have," Nikias agreed wonderingly. "With the help of the gods, we have."

Alkibiades' grin got wider. "Then let's enjoy it, shall we? If we don't enjoy ourselves while we're here on earth, when are we going to do it?"

Nikias sent him a severe frown, the frown a pedagogue might have sent a boy who, on the way to school, paused to stare at the naked women in a brothel. "Is *that* why you staged a *komos* last night?"

"I didn't stage the drinking-bout. It just happened," Alkibiades answered. After a night of revelry like that, his head should have ached as if a smith's hammer were falling on it. It should have, but it didn't. Victory made a better anodyne than poppy juice. He went on, "But if you think I didn't enjoy it, you're wrong. And if you think I didn't deserve it, you're wrong about that, too. If I can't celebrate after taking Syracuse when nobody thought I could"—he didn't say the other general had thought that, though he knew Nikias had—"when *am* I entitled to, by the dog of Egypt?"

Nikias muttered at the oath, which Alkibiades had picked up from Sokrates. But he had no answer. Alkibiades hadn't thought he would.

The Peloponnesos is shaped like a hand, narrow wrist by Corinth in the northeast, thumb and three short, stubby fingers of land pointing south (the little island of Kythera lies off the easternmost finger like a detached nail). Sparta sits in the palm, not far from the base of the middle finger. Having rowed through the night, the Athenian fleet beached itself between the little towns of Abia and Pherai, in the indentation between the middle and westernmost fingers, just as dawn was breaking.

Alkibiades ran from one ship to another like a man possessed. "Move! Move! Move!" he shouted as the hoplites and peltasts and the small force of cavalry emerged from the transports. "No time to wait! No time to waste! Sparta's only a day's march ahead of us. If we strike hard enough and fast enough, we get there before the Spartans can pull enough men together to stop us. They've been ravaging Attica for years. Now it's our turn on their home ground."

To the east, the Taygetos Mountains sawbacked the horizon. But the pass that led to Sparta was visible even from the beach. Alkibiades vaulted onto his horse's back, disdaining a leg-up. Like any horseman, he wished there were some better way to mount and to stay on a beast's back. But there wasn't, or nobody had ever found one, and so, like any horseman, he made the best of things.

"Come on!" he called, trotting out ahead of the hoplites. "All of us against not all of them! How can we help but whip 'em?"

They hadn't gone far before they came across a farmer looking up at the not yet ripe olives on his trees. He wasn't a Spartan, of course; he was a Messenian, a helot—next thing to a slave. His eyes bugged out of his head. He took off running, and he might have beaten the man who'd won the sprint at the last games at Olympia.

"Pity we can't cut down their olive groves, the way they've done to ours in Attica," Alkibiades said to Nikias, who rode not far away.

"No time for that," Nikias answered.

Alkibiades dipped his head. "We'll do what we can with fire," he said. But olives were tough. The trees soon recovered from burning alone; really harming them required long, hard axework.

The ground rose beneath the Athenians' feet. Sweat rivered off the hoplites marching in armor. Alkibiades had made every man carry a jug full of heavily watered wine. Every so often, one of them would pause to swig. Most of the streambeds were dry at this season of the year, and would be till the rain came in winter. When the army found one with a trickle of water in it, men fell out to drink.

"They say the Persian host drank streams dry on the way to Hellas," Alkibiades remarked. "Now we can do the same."

"I do not care to be like the Persians in any way," Nikias said stiffly.

"Oh, I don't know," Alkibiades said. "I wouldn't mind having the Great King's wealth. No, I wouldn't mind that a bit. By the dog, I'd use it better than he has."

Except for the track that led up toward the pass, the country around the Athenians got wilder and wilder. Oaks and brush gave way to dark, frowning pines. A bear lumbered across the track in front of Alkibiades. His horse snorted and tried to rear. He fought it down.

"Good hunting in these woods," Nikias said. "Bear, as you saw. Wild boar, too, and goat and deer."

If I'd gone back towards Athens and then fled as I first planned to do, I suppose I would have ended up in Sparta, Alkibiades thought. *I would have wanted to harm Athens all I could for casting me out, and Sparta would have been the place to do it. I might have hunted through these mountains myself if I hadn't hashed things out with Sokrates. The world would have been a different place.*

He laughed. *I'm still hunting through these mountains. Not bear or boar, though. Not goat or deer. I'm hunting Spartans—better game still.*

No forts blocked the crown of the pass. The Spartans weren't in the habit of defending themselves with forts. They used men instead. *This time, by Zeus, some men are going to use them.* Laughing, Alkibiades called, "All downhill from now on, boys." The Athenians raised a cheer.

A hoplite near Sokrates pointed ahead. "That's *it?*" he said in disbelief. "*That's* the place we've been fighting all these years? That miserable dump? It looks like a bunch of villages, and not rich ones, either."

"You can't always tell by looking," Sokrates said. "If Sparta were to become a ruin, no one would believe how powerful the Spartans really are. They don't go in for fancy temples or walls. This looks more like a collection of villages, as you say, not a proper polis. If Athens were to be deserted, visitors to the ruins would reckon us twice as strong as we really are. And yet, have the Spartans shown they can stand against us for the mastery of Hellas, or have they not?"

"They have," the other hoplite replied. "Up till now."

Now, everything in the valley of the Eurotas that would burn burned: olive groves, fields, houses, the barracks where the full Spartan citizens ate, the relative handful of shops that supported the Spartans and the *perioikoi*—those who lived among them, the second-class citizens on whose labor the Spartans proper depended. A great cloud of smoke rose into the heavens. Sokrates remembered seeing the smudges on the horizon that meant the Spartans were burning the cropland of Attica. Those had been as nothing next to this.

Down through the smoke spiraled the carrion birds—vultures and ravens and hooded crows and even jackdaws. They had not known a feast like this for long and long and long. Most of the dead were those who lived here. The folk of Sparta had tried to attack the Athenians whenever and wherever they could. Not just the men had come at them, but also the Spartan women, the women who were used to exercising naked like men and to throwing the javelin.

No, they'd shown no lack of courage. But the Athenians had stayed in a single compact body, and the Spartans, taken by surprise, had attacked them by ones and twos, by tens and twenties. The only way to beat a phalanx in the open field was with another phalanx. With most of their full citizens, their hoplites, not close enough to their home polis, the Spartans didn't, couldn't, assemble one. And they paid. Oh, how they paid.

Through the roar of the flames, an officer shouted, "We take back no prisoners. None, do you hear me? Nothing to slow us down on the march back to the fleet. If you want these Spartan women to bear half-Athenian children, do it here, do it now!"

The other hoplite said, "A woman like that, you drag her into the dirt, she's liable to try and stab you while you're on top."

"I'm too old to find rape much of a sport," Sokrates replied.

An officer called, "Come on, lend a hand on the ropes, you two! We've got to pull down this barracks hall before we set it afire!"

Sokrates and the other Athenian set down their shields and spears and went to haul on the ropes. The Athenians had guards standing close by, so Sokrates didn't worry about losing his weapons. He pulled with all his might. The corner post crashed down. Half the barracks collapsed. The Athenians cheered. A man with a torch held it to a beam till the flames took hold. When they did, another cheer rose to the heavens with the smoke.

Wearily, Sokrates strode back to pick up his equipment. A little Spartan boy—he couldn't have been more than ten—darted in like a fox to try to grab the shield and spear first. The boy had just bent to snatch them up when a peltast's javelin caught him in the small of the back. He shrieked and fell, writhing in torment. Laughing, the peltast pulled out the throwing spear. "He'll take a while to die," he said.

"That is an evil end," Sokrates said. "Let there be as much pain as war must have, but only so much." He knelt, drew his sword, and cut the boy's throat. The end came soon after that.

An old woman—older than Sokrates, too old for any of the Athenians to bother—said, "Thank you for the mercy to my grandson."

Her Doric drawl and some missing front teeth made her hard to understand, but the Athenian managed. "I did not do it for him," he replied. "I did it for myself, for the sake of what I thought to be right."

Her scrawny shoulders went up and down in a shrug. "You did it. That is what matters. He has peace now." After a moment, she added, "You know I would kill you if I could?"

He dipped his head. "Oh, yes. So the old women of Athens say of the Spartans who despoiled them of a loved one. The symmetry does not surprise me."

"Symmetry. Gylippos is dead, and you speak of symmetry." She spat at his feet. "That's for your symmetry." She turned her back and walked away. Sokrates found no answer for her.

Even before the sun rose red and bloody over the smoke-filled valley of the Eurotas, Alkibiades booted the Athenian trumpeters out of sleep. "Get up, you wide-arsed catamites," he called genially. "Blare the men awake. We don't want to overstay our welcome in beautiful, charming Sparta, now do we?"

Hoplites groaned as they staggered to their feet. Spatters of fighting had gone on all through the night. If the army lingered, the fighting today wouldn't be spatters. It would be a storm, a flood, a sea. *And so*, Alkibiades thought, *we don't linger.*

Some of the men grumbled. "We haven't done enough here. Too many buildings still standing," was what Alkibiades heard most often.

He said, "The lion yawned. We reached into his mouth and gave his tongue a good yank. Do you want to hang on to it till he bites down?"

A lot of them did. They'd lost farmhouses. They'd seen olive groves that had stood for centuries hacked down and burned.

They hungered for as much revenge as they could take. But they obeyed him. They followed him. He'd led them here. Without him, they never would have come. When he told them it was time to go, they were willing to believe him.

They didn't have much to eat—bread they'd brought, bread and porridge they'd stolen, whatever sheep and pigs they'd killed. That alone would have kept them from staying very long. They didn't worry about such things. Alkibiades had to.

Away they marched, back down the trail of destruction they'd left on the way to Sparta, back up toward the pass through the Taygetos Mountains. Even if nobody had pointed the way, the Spartans would have had no trouble pursuing. That didn't matter. The Spartans could chase as hard as they pleased, but they wouldn't catch up.

As he had on the way to Sparta, Nikias rode beside Alkibiades on the way back to the ships. He reminded Alkibiades of a man who'd spent too much time talking with Sokrates (though he hadn't really spent any), or of one who'd been stunned by taking hold of an electric ray. "Son of Kleinias, I never thought any man could do what you have done," he said in amazement. "Never."

"A man who believes he will fail is surely right," Alkibiades replied. "A man who believes he can do great things may yet fail, but if he succeeds . . . Ah, if he succeeds! He who does not dare does not win. Say what you will of me, but I dare."

Nikias stared, shook his head—a gesture of bewilderment, not disagreement—and guided his horse off to one side. Alkibiades threw back his head and laughed. Nikias flinched as if a javelin had hissed past his head.

Halfway up the eastern slope of the mountains, where the woods came down close to the track on either side, a knot of Spartans and perioikoi, some armored, some in their shirts, made a stand. "They want to stall us, keep us here till pursuit can reach us," Alkibiades called. "Thermopylai was a long time ago, though. And holding the pass didn't work for these fellows then, either."

He flung his hoplites at the enemy, keeping them busy. The peltasts, meanwhile, slipped among the trees till they came out on the track behind the embattled Spartans. After that, it wasn't a fight any more. It was a slaughter.

"They were brave," Nikias said, looking at the huddled corpses, at the torn cloaks dyed red so they would not show blood.

"They were stupid," Alkibiades said. "They couldn't stop us. Since they couldn't, what was the point of trying?" Nikias opened his mouth once or twice. Now he looked like nothing so much as a tunny freshly pulled from the sea. Dismissing him from his mind, Alkibiades urged his horse forward with pressure from his knees against its barrel and a flick of the reins. He raised his voice to a shout once more: "Come on, men! Almost halfway back to the ships!"

At the height of the pass through the mountains, he looked west toward the bay where the Athenian fleet waited. He couldn't see the ships, of course, not from about a hundred stadia away, but he looked anyhow. If anything had gone wrong with them, he would end up looking just as stupid as those Spartans who'd tried to slow down the Athenian phalanx.

He lost a few men on the journey down to the seashore. One or two had their hearts give out, and fell over dead. Others, unable to bear the pace, fell out by the side of the road to rest. "We wait for nobody," Alkibiades said, over and over. "Waiting for anyone endangers everyone." Maybe some soldiers didn't believe him. Maybe they were too exhausted to care. They would later, but that would be too late.

Where was Sokrates? Alkibiades peered anxiously at the marching Athenians. The dear old boy could have been father to most of the hoplites in the force. Had he been able to stand the pace? All at once, Alkibiades burst out laughing once more. There he was, not only keeping up but volubly arguing with the younger soldier to his right. Say what you would about his ideas—and Alkibiades, despite listening to him for years, still wasn't sure about those—but the man himself was solid.

As the Athenians descended the western slopes of the Taygetos Mountains, they pointed, calling, *"Thalatta! Thalatta!"*—The sea! The sea!—and, *"Nêes! Nêes!"*—The ships! The ships! Sure enough, the transports and the triremes protecting them still waited there. Alkibiades allowed himself the luxury of a sigh of relief.

Then sand flew up under his horse's hooves. He'd reached the beach from which he and the Athenians had set out early the morning before. "We did our part," he called to the waiting sailors. "How was it here?"

"The Spartans' triremes stuck their noses in to see what we had," a man answered. "When they saw, they turned around and skedaddled."

"Did they?" Alkibiades had hoped they would. The sailor dipped his head. Alkibiades said, "Well, best one, now we shall do the same."

"And then what?" the fellow asked.

"And then what?" Alkibiades echoed. "Why, then we head back to our polis, and we find out just who 'the people of Athens' really are." The sailor grinned. So did Alkibiades.

Down in the hold of his transport, Sokrates could see very little. That being so, he spent as little time as he could down there, and as much as he could up on the narrow strip of decking that ran from bow to stern. "For is it not unreasonable, and clean against nature," he said to a sailor who grumbled about his being up there, "for a man to travel far, and see not a bit of where he has gone?"

"I don't care about unreasonable or reasonable," the sailor said, which made Sokrates flinch. "If you get in our way, we'll chuck you down where you belong."

"I shall be very careful," Sokrates promised.

And so he was . . . for a while. The fleet had come back into the Saronic Gulf, bound for Athens and home. There was the island of Aigina—Athens' old rival—to the left, famous Salamis closer to the port of Peiraieus, with the high headland of Cape Sounion, the southeastern corner of Attica, off to the right. The sun sparkled from myriads of little waves. Seabirds dove for fish and then robbed one another for all the world as if they were men.

Sokrates squatted on the decking and asked a rower, "How is your work here, compared to what you would be doing in a trireme?"

"Oh, it's a harder pull," the fellow answered, grunting as he stroked with the six-cubit oar. "We've only got the one deck of rowers, and the ship's heavier than a trireme would be. Still and all, though, this has its points, too. If you're a thalamite or a zeugite in a trireme—anything but a thranite, up on the top bank of oars—the wide-arsed rogue in front of you is always farting in your face."

"Yes, I've heard Aristophanes speak of this in comedies," Sokrates said.

"Don't have to worry about that here, by Zeus," the rower said. His buttocks slid across his leather cushion as he stroked again.

Up at the bow of the transport, an officer pointed north, toward Peiraieus. "Look! A galley's coming out to meet us."

"Only one, though," a man close by him said. "I wondered if they'd bring out a fleet against us."

"They'd be sorry if they tried," the officer said. "We've got the best ships and best crews right here. They couldn't hope to match us."

"Oh, they could hope," the other man said, "but you're right—they'd be sorry." Now he pointed toward the approaching trireme. "It's the *Salaminia*."

"Haven't seen her since Sicily," the officer said sourly. "I wonder if they've heard the news about everything we did. We'll find out."

The triremes traveled ahead of the transports to protect them, but the ship carrying Sokrates was only a couple of plethra behind the warships: close enough to let him hear shouts across the water. There in the middle of the line of triremes sailed Alkibiades' flagship. The commander of the expeditionary force was easy for the men of the *Salaminia* to spot. His bright hair flashed in the sun, and he wore that purple tunic that had to be just this side of hubris. The ceremonial galley steered toward the *Thraseia*.

"Hail!" Alkibiades called to the *Salaminia* as she drew near.

"Alkibiades son of Kleinias?" someone on the other galley replied.

"Is that you again, Herakleides, who don't know who I am?" Alkibiades answered. Sokrates couldn't make out the other man's reply. Whatever it was, Alkibiades laughed and went on, "Go on back to the harbor and tell those stay-at-home fools the gods have given their judgment. We conquered Syracuse, and a government loyal to Athens rules there now. And on the way home we burned Sparta down around the haughty Spartans' ears."

By the sudden buzz—almost a roar—from the crew of the *Salaminia*, that news *hadn't* reached Athens yet. Even so, the spokesman aboard the ceremonial galley, whether Herakleides or another man, went on, "Alkibiades son of Kleinias, it seems good to the people of Athens"—the ancient formula for an Assembly decree—"for your men not to enter the city in arms, but to lay down their weapons as they disembark from their ships at Peiraieus. And it further seems good to the people of Athens that you yourself should enter the city alone before they go in, to explain to the said people of Athens your reasons for flouting their previous summons."

A rumble of anger went up from all the ships in the fleet close enough for the crews to make out the spokesman's words. "Hear that, boys?" Alkibiades shouted in a great voice. "I won the war for them, and they want to tell me to drink hemlock. *You* won the war for them, and they want to take your spears and your corselets away from you. Are we going to let 'em get away with it?"

"Nooooo!" The great roar came from the whole fleet, or as much of it as Alkibiades' voice could reach. Most of the rowers and the officers—and many of the hoplites, who, being belowdecks, couldn't hear so well—aboard Sokrates' transport joined in it.

"You hear that?" Alkibiades called to the *Salaminia* as aftershocks of outrage kept erupting from the wings of the fleet. "There's your answer. You can take it back to the demagogues who lie when they call themselves the people of Athens. But you'd better hurry if you do, because we're bringing it ourselves."

Being the polis' state trireme, the *Salaminia* naturally had a crack crew. Her starboard rowers pulled normally, while those on the port side backed oars. The galley spun in the water, turning almost in her own length. She also enjoyed the luxury of a dry hull, having laid up in a shipshed most of the time. That made her lighter and swifter than the ships of Alkibiades' fleet, which were waterlogged and heavy from hard service. She raced back toward Peiraieus.

The triremes that had gone to Sicily followed. So did the transports, though a little more sedately. A naked sailor nudged Sokrates. "What do you think, old-timer? We going to have to fight our way in?"

"I have opinions on a great many things," Sokrates replied. "Some of them, I hope, are true opinions. Here, however, I shall not venture any opinion. The unfolding of events will yield the answer."

"You don't know either, eh?" The sailor shrugged. "Well, we'll find out pretty cursed quick."

"I thought I just said that," Sokrates said plaintively. But the other man wasn't listening to him any more.

No triremes came forth from Peiraieus to challenge the fleet's entry. Indeed, Athens' harbor seemed all but deserted; most of the sailors and longshoremen and quayside loungers had fled. A herald bearing the staff of his office stood on a quay and shouted in a great voice, "Let all know that any who proceed in arms from this place shall be judged traitors against the city and people of Athens!"

"We *are* the city and people of Athens!" Alkibiades shouted back, and the whole fleet roared agreement. "We have done great things! We will do more!" Again, soldiers and sailors bellowed to back him up.

That sailor came back to Sokrates. "Aren't you going to arm?" he asked. "That's what the orders are."

"I shall do that which seems right," Sokrates answered, which sent the other man off scratching his head.

Sokrates went below. Down in the hold, hoplites were struggling into their armor, poking one another with elbows and knees, and cursing as they were elbowed in turn. He pushed his way through the arming foot soldiers to his own leather duffel. "Come on!" someone said to him, voice cracking with excitement. "Hurry up! High time we cleaned out that whole nest of polluted catamites!"

"Is it?" Sokrates said. "Are they? How do you know?"

The hoplite stared at him. He saw that he might as well have been speaking Persian. The soldier fixed his scabbard on his belt. He reached around his body with his right hand to make sure he could draw his sword in a hurry if he had to.

Up on deck, the oarmaster shouted *"Oöp!"* and the rowers rested at their oars. Somebody said, "No one's here to make us fast to the pier. Furies take 'em! We'll do it ourselves." The ship swayed slightly as a sailor sprang ashore. Other sailors flung him lines. They thumped on the quays. He tied the transport to the side of the pier.

A moment later, the gangplank thudded into place. Up on deck, an officer shouted, "All hoplites out! Go down the quay and form up on dry land!" With a cheer, the soldiers—almost all of them now ready for battle—did as they were told, crowding toward the transport's stern to reach the gangplank. Duffel over his shoulder, Sokrates returned to Athenian soil, too.

This wasn't the first transport to disembark its men. On the shore, red-caped officers were bellowing, "Form a phalanx! We've got work to do yet, and we'll do it, by Zeus!" As the battle formation took shape, Sokrates started north towards Athens all by himself.

"Here, you!" a captain yelled. "Where do you think you're going?"

He stopped for a moment. "Home," he answered calmly.

"What? What are you talking about? We've got fighting to do yet," the man said.

Sokrates tossed his head. "No. When Athenian fights Athenian, who can say which side has the just cause, which the unjust? Not wishing to do the unjust or to suffer it, I shall go home. Good day." With a polite dip of the head, he started walking again.

Pounding sandals said the captain was coming after him. The man grabbed his arm. "You can't do that!"

"Oh, but I can. I will." Sokrates shook him off. The captain grabbed him again—and then, quite suddenly, found himself sitting in the dust. Sokrates kept walking.

"You'll be sorry!" the other man shouted after him, slowly getting to his feet. "Wait till Alkibiades finds out about this!"

"No one can make me sorry for doing what is right," Sokrates said. At his own pace, following his own will, he tramped along toward the city.

He was going along between the Long Walls, still at his own pace, when hoofbeats and the rhythmic thud of thousands of marching feet came from behind him. He got off the path, but kept going. Alkibiades trotted by on horseback in his purple chiton. Catching Sokrates' eye, he grinned and waved. Sokrates dipped his head again.

Alkibiades and the rest of the horsemen rode on. Behind them came the hoplites and peltasts. Behind *them* came a great throng of rowers, unarmored and armed with belt knives and whatever else they could scrounge. They moved at a fine martial tempo, and left ambling Sokrates behind. He kept walking nonetheless.

"Tyrant!" the men on the walls of Athens shouted at Alkibiades. "Impious, sacrilegious defiler of the mysteries! Herm-smasher!"

"I put my fate in the hands of the gods," Alkibiades told them, speaking for the benefit of his own soldiers as well as those who hadn't gone to Sicily. "I prayed that they destroy me if I were guilty of the charges against me, or let me live and let me triumph if I was innocent. I lived. I triumphed. The gods know the right. Do you, men of Athens?" He raised his voice: "Nikias!"

"Yes? What is it?" Nikias sounded apprehensive. Had he been in the city, he would surely have tried to hold it against Alkibiades. But he was out here, and so he could be used.

"You were there. You can tell the men of Athens whether I speak the truth. Did I not call on the gods? Did they not reward me with victory, as I asked them to do to show my innocence?"

A lie here would make Alkibiades' life much more difficult. Nikias had to know that. Alkibiades would have been tempted—more than tempted—to lie. But Nikias was a painfully honest man as well as a painfully pious one. Though he looked as if he'd just taken a big bite of bad fish, he dipped his head. "Yes, son of Kleinias. It is as you say."

His voice was barely audible to Alkibiades, let alone to the soldiers on the walls of the city. Alkibiades pointed their way, saying, "Tell the men of Athens the truth."

Nikias looked more revolted yet. Even so, he did as Alkibiades asked. *Everybody does as I ask*, Alkibiades thought complacently. Having spoken to the defenders of the city, Nikias turned back to Alkibiades. In a low, furious voice, he said, "I'll thank you to leave me out of your schemes from now on."

"What schemes, O best one?" Alkibiades asked, his eyes going wide with injured innocence. "All I asked you to do was tell the truth to the men there."

"You did it so you could seize the city," Nikias said.

"No." Alkibiades tossed his head, though the true answer was of course *yes*. But he went on, "Even if no one opens a gate to me, I'll hold the advantage soon enough. We draw our grain from Byzantion and beyond. I hold Peiraieus, so nothing can come in by sea. Before too long, if it comes to that, Athens will get hungry—and then she'll get hungrier. But I don't think we need to worry about that."

"Why not?" Nikias demanded. "The whole polis stands in arms against you."

"Oh, rubbish," Alkibiades said genially. "I've got at least half the polis here on the outside of the city with me. And if you think everyone in there is against me, you'd better think again. You could do worse than talk with Sokrates about the whole and its parts." As he'd expected, that provoked Nikias again. Alkibiades hid his smile and looked around. "Where *is* Sokrates, anyway?"

A hoplite standing close by answered, "He went into the city, most noble one."

"*Into* the city?" Alkibiades and Nikias said together, in identical surprise. Recovering first, Alkibiades asked, "By the dog of Egypt, how did he manage that?"

The hoplite pointed to a small postern gate. "He told the soldiers on guard there that he didn't intend to fight anybody, that he thought it was wrong for Athenians to fight Athenians"—as most men of Athens would have, he took a certain cheeky pleasure in reporting that to Alkibiades—"and that he wanted to come in and see his wife."

"To see Xanthippe? I wouldn't have thought he'd been away from home *that* long," Alkibiades said; Sokrates was married to a shrew. "But the gate guards let him in?"

"Yes, sir. I think one of them knew him," the hoplite replied.

Nikias clucked like a hen. "You see, Alkibiades? Even your pet sophist wants no part of civil war."

"He's not my pet. He's no more anyone's pet than a fox running on the hills," Alkibiades said. "And he would say he's no sophist, either. He's never taken even an obolos for teaching, you know."

Nikias went right on clucking. Alkibiades stopped listening to him. He eyed the postern gate. That Sokrates had got into Athens only proved his own point. Not all the soldiers defending the city were loyal to the men who'd tried to execute him under form of law. A little discreet talk, preferably in the nighttime when fewer outside ears might hear, and who could say what would happen next?

Alkibiades thought he could. He looked forward to finding out whether he was right.

Quietly, ever so quietly, a postern gate swung open. At Alkibiades' whispered urging the night before, the guards who held it had anointed with olive oil the posts that secured it to the stone lintel above and the stone set into the ground below. A squeak now would be . . . *very embarrassing*, Alkibiades thought as he hurried toward the gate at the head of a column of hoplites.

"You shouldn't go first," one of them whispered to him. "If it's a trap, they'll nail you straightaway."

"If it's a trap, they'll nail me anyhow," he answered easily. "But if I thought it were a trap, I wouldn't be doing this, would I?"

"Who knows?" the hoplite said. "You might just figure you could talk them around once you got inside."

He laughed at that. "You're right. I might. But I don't. Come on. It's the same with a city as it is with a woman—once you're inside, you've won." The soldiers laughed, too. But Alkibiades hadn't been joking, or not very much.

He carried no spear. His left hand gripped his shield, marked with his own emblem. His right tightened on the hilt of his sword as he went through the gate, through the wall itself, and into Athens. It was indeed a penetration of sorts. *Bend forward, my polis. Here I am, taking you unawares.*

If he wasn't taking the city unawares, if his foes did have a trap waiting for him, they would spring it as soon as he came through. This would be the only moment when they knew exactly where he was. But everything inside seemed dark and quiet and sleepy. Except for his own followers, the only men who moved and talked were the guards who'd opened the gate.

In flowed his soldiers, a couple of hundred of them. He sent bands out to the right and left, to seize other men and let in more men back from Sicily. How long would it be before the defenders realized the city was secure no more? Shouts and the sounds of fighting from another gate said the moment was here.

"Come on," Alkibiades told the rest of the men with him. "We seize the agora, we seize the Akropolis, and the city's ours."

They hurried on through darkness as near absolute as made no difference. Night was a time for sleeping. Here and there, a lamp would glow faintly behind a closed shutter. Once, Alkibiades passed the sounds of flutes and raucous, drunken singing: someone was holding a symposion, civil strife or no civil strife. The streets wandered, twisted, doubled back on themselves, deadended. No one not an Athenian born could have hoped to find his way.

More lights showed when Alkibiades and his comrades got to the agora. Torches flared around the Tholos. At least seventeen members of the Boulê were always on duty there. Alkibiades pointed toward the building. "We'll take it," he said. "That will leave them running around headless. Let's go, my dears. Forward!"

"Eleleu!" the hoplites roared. A handful of guards stood outside the building. When so many men thundered down upon them, they dropped their spears and threw up their hands. A couple of them fell to their knees to beg for mercy.

"Spare them," Alkibiades said. "We shed as little blood as we can."

A voice came from inside the Tholos: "What's that racket out there?"

Alkibiades had never been able to resist a dramatic gesture. Here, he didn't even try. Marching into the building, he displayed the Eros with a thunderbolt on his shield that had helped make him famous—or, to some people, notorious. "Good evening, O best ones," he said politely.

The councilors sprang to their feet. It was even better than he'd hoped. There with them were Androkles and Thettalos son of Kimon, two of his chief enemies—Thettalos had introduced the motion against him in the Assembly. "Alkibiades!" Androkles exclaimed in dismay. He could have sounded no more horrified if he'd seen Medusa standing before him—the last thing he would have seen before gazing upon her turned him to stone. No one else in the Tholos seemed any more delighted.

Bowing, Alkibiades answered, "Very much at your service, my dear. I will have you know that my whole army is in the city now. Those who are wise will comport themselves accordingly. Those who are not so wise will resist, for a little while—and pay the price for resisting."

He bowed again, and smiled his sweetest smile. If his enemies chose to, they could still put up a fight for Athens, and perhaps even win. He wanted them to believe they had no chance, no hope. If they did believe it, their belief would help turn it true.

"Surely you are a kakodaimon, spawned from some pit of Tartaros!" Thettalos burst out. "We should have dealt with you before you sailed for Sicily."

"You had your chance," Alkibiades answered. "When the question of who mutilated the herms first came up, I asked for a speedy trial. I wanted my name cleared before the fleet sailed. You were the ones who delayed."

"We needed to find witnesses who would talk," Thettalos said.

"You needed to invent witnesses who would lie, you mean," Alkibiades answered.

"They aren't lying. They speak the truth," Thettalos said stubbornly.

"I tell you, they lie." Alkibiades cocked his head to one side. Yes, that was the sound of hoplites moving through the city, shields now and then clanking on greaves and corselets. And that was the sound of his name in the hoplites' mouths. He'd told the truth here after all. By all appearances, his soldiers *did* hold Athens. He turned back to the men in the Tholos. "And I tell you this is your last chance to surrender and spare your lives. If you wait till my main force gets here, that will be too late. What do you say, gentlemen of Athens?" He used the title with savage irony.

They said what he'd thought they would: "We yield." It was a glum, grumbling chorus, but a chorus nonetheless.

"Take them away," Alkibiades told the soldiers with him. "We'll put some honest people in the Tholos instead." Laughing and grinning, the hoplites led the men of the Boulê out into the night. Alkibiades stayed behind. He set down his shield and flung his arms wide in delight. *At last!* he thought. *By all the gods—if gods there be—at last! Athens is mine!*

As if nothing had changed in the polis, Simon the shoemaker drove hobnails into the sole of a sandal. As if nothing had changed, a small crowd of youths and young men gathered under the shade of the olive tree outside his shop. And, as if nothing had changed, Sokrates still argued with them about whatever came to mind.

He showed no inclination to talk about what had happened while he was away. After a while, a boy named Aristokles, who couldn't have been above twelve, piped up: "Do you think your *daimon* was right, Sokrates, in urging you to go to the west?"

However young he was, he had a power and clarity to his thought that appealed to Sokrates. He'd phrased his question with a man's directness, too. Sokrates wished he could answer so directly. After some hesitation—unusual for him—he said, "We won a victory in Sicily, which can only be good for the polis. And we won a victory in Sparta, where no foreign foe has ever won before. The Kings of Sparta are treating with Alkibiades for peace even while we speak here. That too can only be good for the polis."

He sought truth like a lover pursuing his beloved. He always had. He always would. Here today, though, he wouldn't have been disappointed to have his reply taken as full agreement, which it was not. And Aristokles saw as much, saying, "And yet you still have doubts. Why?"

"I know why," Kritias said. "On account of Alkibiades, that's why."

Sokrates knew why Kritias spoke as he did—he was sick-jealous of Alkibiades. The other man had done things in Athens Kritias hadn't matched and couldn't hope to match. Ambition had always blazed in Kritias, perhaps to do good for his polis, certainly to do well for himself. Now he saw himself outdone, outdone by too much to make it even a contest. All he could do was fume.

Which did not mean he was altogether wrong. Alkibiades worried Sokrates, and had for years. He was brilliant, clever, handsome, dashing, charming—and, in him, all those traits led to vice as readily as to virtue. Sokrates had done everything he could to turn Alkibiades in the direction he should go. But another could do only so much; in the end, a man had to do for himself, too.

Aristokles' eyes flicked from Sokrates to Kritias (they had a family connection, Sokrates recalled) and back again. "Is he right?" the boy asked. "Do you fear Alkibiades?"

"I fear *for* Alkibiades," Sokrates answered. "Is it not reasonable that a man who has gained an uncommon amount of power should also have an uncommon amount of attention aimed at him to see what he does with it?"

"Surely he has done nothing wrong yet," Aristokles said.

"Yet," Kritias murmured.

The boy ignored that, which most men would have found

hard to do. He said, "Why should we aim uncommon attention at a man who has done nothing wrong, unless we seek to learn his virtues and imitate them?"

Kritias said, "When we speak of Alkibiades, at least as many would seek to learn his vices and imitate *them*."

"Yes, many might do that," Aristokles said. "But is it right that they should?"

"Who cares whether it is right? It is *true*," Kritias said.

"Wait." Sokrates held up a hand, then waved out toward the agora. "Hail, Kritias. I wish no more of your company today, nor that of any man who asks, 'Who cares whether it is right?' For what could be more important than that? How can a man who knows what is right choose what is wrong?"

"Why ask me?" Kritias retorted. "Better you should inquire of Alkibiades."

That held enough truth to sting, but Sokrates was too angry to care. He waved again, more vehemently than before. "Get out. You are not welcome here until you mend your tongue, or, better, your spirit."

"Oh, I'll go," Kritias said. "But you blame me when you ought to blame yourself, for you taught Alkibiades the virtue he so blithely ignores." He stalked off.

Again, that arrow hadn't missed its target. Pretending not to feel the wound, Sokrates turned back to the other men standing under the olive tree. "Well, my friends, where were we?"

They did not break up till nearly sunset. Then Aristokles came over to Sokrates and said, "Since my kinsman will not apologize for himself, please let me do it in his place."

"You are gracious," Sokrates said with a smile. Aristokles was worth smiling at: he was a good-looking boy, and would make a striking youth in two or three years, although broad shoulders and a squat build left him short of perfection. However pleasant he was to see, though, Sokrates went on, "How can any man act in such a way on another's behalf?"

With a sigh, Aristokles answered, "In truth, I cannot. But I wish I could."

That made Sokrates' smile get wider. "A noble wish. You are one who seeks the good, I see. That is not common in one so young. Truth to tell, it is not common at any age, but less so in the very young, who have not reflected on these things."

"I can see in my mind the images—the *forms*, if you like—of perfect good, of perfect truth, of perfect beauty," Aristokles said. "In the world, though, they are always flawed. How do we, how can we, approach them?"

"Let us walk." Sokrates set a hand on the boy's shoulder, not in physical longing but in a painful hope he had almost abandoned. Had he at last met someone whose thoughts might march with his? Even so young, the eagle displayed its claws.

They talked far into the night.

King Agis was a short, muscular man with a scar on the upper lip he shaved in the usual Spartan fashion. His face wore what looked like a permanent scowl. He had to fight to hold the expression, though, because he plainly kept wanting to turn and gape at everything he saw in Athens. However much he wanted to, though, he didn't, which placed him a cut above the usual run of country bumpkins seeing the big city for the first time.

"Hail," Alkibiades said smoothly, holding out his hands. "Welcome to Athens. Let us have peace, if we can."

Agis' right hand was ridged with callus, hard as a rower's. He'd toughened it with swordhilt and spearshaft, though, and not with the oar. "Hail," he replied. "Yes, let us have peace. Boys who were at their mothers' breasts when we began this fight are old enough

to wear armor now. And what have we got for it? Only our homeland ravaged. Enough, I say. Let us have peace." The word seemed
all the more emphatic in his flat Doric drawl.

He said nothing about the way the Spartans had devastated
Attica for years. Alkibiades hadn't expected him to. A man didn't
feel it when he stepped on someone else's toes, only when his
own got hurt.

Confirming that, Agis went on, "I thought no man could do
what you did to my polis. Since you did . . ." He grimaced. "Yes, let
us have peace."

"My terms are not hard," Alkibiades said. "Here in Hellas, let
all be as it was before the war began. In Sicily . . . Well, we won
in Sicily. We will not give back what we won. If you had done the
same, neither would you."

Grimly, Agis dipped his head in agreement. He said, "I can rely
on you to get the people of Athens to accept these terms?"

"You can rely on me to get these terms accepted in this polis,"
Alkibiades answered. How much the people of Athens would
have to do with that, he didn't know. His own position was . . .
irregular. He was not a magistrate. He had been a general, yes, but
the campaign for which he'd commanded was over. And yet, he
was unquestionably the most powerful man in the city. Soldiers
leaped to do his bidding. He didn't want the name of tyrant—
tyrants attracted tyrannicides as honey drew flies—but he had
everything except that name.

"I would treat with no one else," Agis said. "You beat us. You
shamed us. You should have been a Spartan yourself. You should
breed sons on our women, that we might add your bloodline to
our stock." He might have been talking of horses.

"You are gracious, but I have women enough here," Alkibiades said. Inside, he laughed. Would Agis offer his own wife next?
What was her name? Timaia, that was it. If King Agis did, it would

insure that Alkibiades' descendants ruled Sparta. He liked the idea.

But Agis did no such thing. Instead, he said, "If we are to have no more war, son of Kleinias, how shall we live at peace? For both of us aim to rule all of Hellas."

"Yes." Alkibiades rubbed his chin. Agis might be dour, but he was no fool. The Athenian went on, "Hear me. While we fought, who ruled Hellas? My polis? No. Yours? No again. Anyone's? Not at all. The only ruler Hellas had was war. Whereas if we both pull together, like two horses in harness pulling a chariot, who knows where we might go?"

Agis stood stock-still for some little while, considering that. At last, he said, "I can think of a place where we might go if we pull in harness," and spoke one word more.

Now Alkibiades laughed out loud. He leaned forward and kissed Agis on the cheek, as if the King of Sparta were a pretty boy. "Do you know, my dear," he said, "we are not so very different after all."

Kritias strode through the agora in a perfect transport of fury. He might have been a whirlwind trying to blow down everything around him. He made not the slightest effort to restrain himself or keep his voice down. When he drew near the Tholos—in fact, even before he drew very near the Tholos—his words were plainly audible under the olive tree in front of Simon's cobbler's shop. They were not only audible, they were loud enough to make the discussion already under way beneath that olive tree falter.

"Us, yoked together with the Spartans?" Kritias raged. "You might as well yoke a dolphin and a wolf! They will surely turn on us and rend us first chance they get!"

"What do you think of that, Sokrates?" a young man asked.

Before Sokrates could answer, someone else said, "Kritias is just jealous he didn't think of it himself. If he had, he'd be screaming every bit as loud that it's the best thing that could possibly happen to Athens."

"Quiet," another man said in a quick, low voice. "That's Kritias' kinsman over there by Sokrates." He jerked a thumb at Aristokles.

"So?" said the man who'd spoken before. "I don't care if that's Kritias' mother over there by Sokrates. It's still true."

Sokrates looked across the agora at the rampaging Kritias. His former pupil came to a stop by the statues of Harmodios and Aristogeiton near the center of the market square. There under the images of the young men said to have liberated Athens from her last tyranny, his fist pumping furiously, he harangued a growing crowd.

With a sigh, Sokrates said, "How is a man who cannot control himself to see clearly what the good is and what it is not?" Slowly and deliberately, he turned his back on Kritias. "Since he is not *quite* so noisy as he was, shall we resume our own discussion? Is knowledge innate and merely evoked by teachers, or do teachers impart new knowledge to those who study under them?"

"You have certainly shown me many things I never knew before, Sokrates," a man named Apollodoros said.

"Ah, but did I show them to you for the first time, or did I merely bring them to light?" Sokrates replied. "That is what we need to . . ."

He stopped, for the others weren't listening to him any more. That irked him; he had an elegant demonstration planned, one that would use a slave boy of Simon's to show that knowledge already existed and merely wanted bringing forth. But no one was paying any attention to him. Instead, his followers stared out into the agora, toward the statues of Harmodios and Aristogeiton and toward Kritias.

Part of Sokrates didn't want to look, not when he'd already turned away. But he was no less curious than any other Hellene—was, indeed, perhaps more curious about more different things than any other Hellene. And so, muttering curses under his breath like the stonecutter he had been for so long, he looked back into the market square himself.

Three men, he saw, had come up out of the crowd and surrounded Kritias. "They wouldn't dare," somebody—Sokrates thought it was Apollodoros, but he wasn't sure—said just as Kritias shoved one of the men away from him. Things happened very quickly after that. All three men—they wore only tunics and went barefoot, as sailors usually did—drew knives. The sun sparkled off the blades' sharp edges. They stabbed Kritias, again and again. His bubbling shriek and the cries of horror from the crowd filled the agora. As he fell, the murderers loped off. A few men started to chase them, but one of them turned back to threaten the pursuers with his now-bloody weapon. They drew back. The three men made good their escape.

With a low wail, Aristokles dashed out toward his fallen relative. Sokrates hurried after the boy to keep anything from happening to him. Several of the other men who frequented the shade in front of Simon's shop trailed along behind them.

"Make way!" Aristokles shouted, his voice full of command even though it had yet to break. "Make way, there! I am Kritias' kinsman!"

People *did* step aside for him. Sokrates followed in his wake, but realized before he got very close to Kritias that Aristokles could do nothing for him now. He lay on his back in a still-spreading pool of his own blood. He'd been stabbed in the chest, the belly, and the throat—probably from behind as well, but Sokrates couldn't see that. His eyes were wide and staring and unblinking. His chest neither rose nor fell.

Aristokles knelt beside him, careless of the blood. "Who did this?" he asked, and then answered his own question: "Alkibiades." No one contradicted him. He reached out and closed Kritias' eyes. "My kinsman was, perhaps, not the best of men, but he did not deserve—this. He shall be avenged." Unbroken voice or not, he sounded every bit a man.

The Assembly never met to ratify Alkibiades' peace with Sparta. His argument—to the degree that he bothered making an argument—was that the peace was so self-evidently good, it needed no formal approval. That subverted the Athenian constitution, but few people complained out loud. Kritias' murder made another sort of argument, one prudent men could not ignore. So did the untimely demise of a young relative of his who might have thought his youth granted his outspokenness immunity.

Over the years, the Athenians had called Sokrates a great many things. Few, though, had ever called him lacking in courage. A couple of weeks after Kritias died—and only a couple of days after Aristokles was laid to rest—Sokrates walked out across the agora from the safe, comfortable shade of the olive tree in front of Simon the shoemaker's toward the statues of Harmodios and Aristogeiton in the heart of the market square. Several of his followers came along with him.

Apollodoros tugged at his chiton. "You don't have to do this," he said in a choked voice, as if about to burst into tears.

"No?" Sokrates looked around. "Men need to hear the truth. Men need to speak the truth. Do you see anyone else doing those things?" He kept walking.

"But what will happen to you?" Apollodoros wailed.

"What will happen to Athens?" Sokrates answered.

He took his place where Kritias must have stood. Blood still stained the base of Aristogeiton's statue. Blocky and foursquare, Sokrates stood and waited. The men and youths who listened to him formed the beginnings of an audience—and the Athenians recognized the attitude of a man about to make a speech. By ones and twos, they wandered over to hear what he had to say.

"Men of Athens, I have always tried to do the good, so far as I could see what that was," he began. "For I believe the good is most important to man: more important than ease, more important than wealth, more important even than peace. Our grandfathers could have had peace with Persia by giving the Great King's envoys earth and water. Yet they saw that was not good, and they fought to stay free.

"Now we have peace with Sparta. Is it good? Alkibiades says it is. Someone asked that question once before, and now that man is dead, as is his young kinsman who dared be outraged at an unjust death. We all know who arranged these things. I tell no secrets. And I tell no secrets when I say these murders were not good."

"You were the one who taught Alkibiades!" someone called.

"I tried to teach him the good and the true, or rather to show him what was already in his mind, as it is in all our minds," Sokrates replied. "Yet I must have failed, for what man, knowing the good, would willingly do evil? And the murder of Kritias, and especially that of young Aristokles, was evil. How can anyone doubt that?"

"What do we do about it, then?" asked someone in the crowd—not one of Sokrates' followers.

"We are Athenians," he replied. "If we are not a light for Hellas to follow, who is? We rule ourselves, and have for a century, since we cast out the last tyrants, the sons of Peisistratos." He set his hand on the statue of Aristogeiton, reminding the men who listened why that statue stood here. "The sons of Peisistratos were the last tyrants before Alkibiades, I should say. We Athenians beat the Persians. We have beaten the Spartans. We—"

"Alkibiades beat the Spartans!" somebody else yelled.

"I was there, my good fellow. Were you?" Sokrates asked. Sudden silence answered him. Into it, he went on, "Yes, Alkibiades led us. But we Athenians triumphed. Peisistratos was a fine general, too, or so they say. Yet he was also a tyrant. Will any man deny that? Alkibiades the man has good qualities. We all know as much. Alkibiades the tyrant . . . What qualities can a tyrant have, save those *of* a tyrant?"

"Do you say we should cast him out?" a man called.

"I say we should do what is good, what is right. We are men. We know what that is," Sokrates said. "We have known what the good is since before birth. If you need me to remind you of it, I will do that. It is why I stand here before you now."

"Alkibiades won't like it," another man predicted in a doleful voice.

Sokrates shrugged broad shoulders. "I have not liked many of the things he has done. If he does not care for my deeds, I doubt I shall lose any sleep over that."

Bang! Bang! Bang! The pounding on the door woke Sokrates and Xanthippe at the same time. It was black as pitch inside their bedroom. "Stupid drunk," Xanthippe grumbled when the racket went on and on. She pushed at her husband. "Go out there and tell the fool he's trying to get into the wrong house."

"I don't think he is," Sokrates answered as he got out of bed.

"What are you talking about?" Xanthippe demanded.

"Something I said in the market square. I seem to have been wrong," Sokrates said. "Here I am, losing sleep after all."

"You waste too much time in the agora." Xanthippe shoved

him again as the pounding got louder. "Now go give that drunk a piece of your mind."

"Whoever is out there, I do not think he is drunk." But Sokrates pulled his chiton on over his head. He made his way out through the crowded little courtyard where Xanthippe grew herbs and up to the front door. As he unbarred it, the pounding stopped. He opened the door. Half a dozen large, burly men stood outside. Three carried torches. They all carried cudgels. "Hail, friends," Sokrates said mildly. "What do you want that cannot keep till morning?"

"Sokrates son of Sophroniskos?" one of the bruisers demanded.

"That's Sokrates, all right," another one said, even as Sokrates dipped his head.

"Got to be sure," the first man said, and then, to Sokrates, "Come along with us."

"And if I don't?" he asked.

They all raised their bludgeons. "You will—one way or the other," the leader said. "Your choice. Which is it?"

"What does the idiot want, Sokrates?" Xanthippe shrilled from the back of the house.

"Me," he said, and went with the men into the night.

Alkibiades yawned. Even to him, an experienced roisterer, staying up into the middle of the night felt strange and unnatural. Once the sun went down, most people went to bed and waited for morning. Most of the time, even roisterers did. The little lamps that cast a faint, flickering yellow light over this bare little courtyard and filled it with the smell of burning olive oil were a far cry from Helios' bright, warm, cheerful rays.

A bat fluttered down, snatched a moth out of the air near a

lamp, and disappeared again. "Hate those things," muttered one of the men in the courtyard with Alkibiades. "They can't be natural."

"People have said the same thing about me," Alkibiades answered lightly. "I will say, though, that I'm prettier than a bat." He preened. He might have had reason to be, but he *was* vain about his looks.

His henchmen chuckled. The door to the house opened. "Here they are," said the man who didn't like bats. "About time, too."

In came Sokrates, in the midst of half a dozen ruffians. "Hail," Alkibiades said. "I wish you hadn't forced me to this."

Sokrates cocked his head to one side and studied him. He showed only curiosity, not fear, though he had to know what lay ahead for him. "How can one man force another to do anything?" he asked. "How, especially, can one man force another to do that which he knows not to be good?"

"This is good—for me," Alkibiades answered. "You have been making a nuisance of yourself in the agora."

"A nuisance?" Sokrates tossed his head. "I am sorry, but whoever told you these things is misinformed. I have spoken the truth and asked questions that might help others decide what is true."

Voice dry, Alkibiades said, "That constitutes being a nuisance, my dear. If you criticize me, what else are you but a nuisance?"

"A truth-teller, as I said before," Sokrates replied. "You must know this. We have discussed it often enough." He sighed. "I think my *daimon* was wrong to bid me accompany you to Sicily. I have never known it to be wrong before, but how can you so lightly put aside what has been shown to be true?"

"True, you showed me the gods cannot be as Homer and Hesiod imagined them," Alkibiades said. "But you have drawn the wrong lesson from that. You say we should live as if the gods were there watching us, even though they are not."

"And so we should, for our own sake," Sokrates said.

"But if the gods are not, O best one, why not grab with both hands?" Alkibiades asked. "This being all I have, I intend to make the most of it. And if anyone should stand in the way . . ." He shrugged. "Too bad."

The henchman who didn't like bats said, "Enough of this chatter. Give him the drug. It's late. I want to go home."

Alkibiades held up a small black-glazed jar with three horizontal incised grooves showing the red clay beneath the glaze. "Hemlock," he told Sokrates. "It's fairly quick and fairly easy—and a lot less messy than what Kritias got."

"Generous of you," Sokrates remarked. He stepped forward and reached out to take the jar. Alkibiades' henchmen let him advance. Why not? If he'd swallow the poison without any fuss, so much the better.

But, when he got within a couple of paces of Alkibiades, he shouted out, *"Eleleu!"* and flung himself at the younger man. The jar of hemlock smashed on the hard dirt of the courtyard. Alkibiades knew at once he was fighting for his life. Sokrates gave away twenty years, but his stocky, broad-shouldered frame seemed nothing but rock-hard muscle.

He and Alkibiades rolled in the dirt, punching and cursing and gouging and kneeing and kicking each other. This was the pankration, the all-in fight of the Olympic and Panathenaic Games, without even the handful of rules the Games enforced. Alkibiades tucked his head down into his chest. The thumb that would have extracted one of his eyes scraped across his forehead instead.

Back when he was a youth, he'd sunk his teeth into a foe who'd got a good wrestling hold on him. "You bite like a woman!" the other boy had cried.

"No, like a lion!" he'd answered.

He'd bitten then because he couldn't stand to lose. He bit now to keep Sokrates from getting a meaty forearm under his chin and strangling him. Sokrates roared. His hot, salty blood filled Alkibiades' mouth. Alkibiades dug an elbow into his belly, but it might have been made from the marble that had gone into the Parthenon.

Shouting, Alkibiades' henchmen ran up and started clubbing Sokrates. The only trouble was, they hit Alkibiades nearly as often. Then, suddenly, Sokrates groaned and went limp. Alkibiades scrambled away from him. The hilt of a knife stood in the older man's back. The point, surely, had reached his heart.

Sokrates' eyes still held reason as he stared up at Alkibiades. He tried to say something, but only blood poured from his mouth. The hand he'd raised fell back. A stench filled the courtyard; his bowels had let go in death.

"*Pheu!*" Alkibiades said, just starting to feel his aches and bruises. "He almost did for me there."

"Who would've thought the old blabbermouth could fight like that?" one of his followers marveled, surprise and respect in his voice.

"He was a blabbermouth, sure enough." Alkibiades bent down and closed the staring eyes. Gently, as a lover might, he kissed Sokrates on the cheek and on the tip of the snub nose. "He was a blabbermouth, yes, but oh, by the gods, he was a man."

Alkibiades and King Agis of Sparta stood side by side on the speakers' platform in the Pnyx, the fan-shaped open area west of the agora where the Athenian Assembly convened. Since Alkibiades had taken the rule of Athens into his own hands, this wasn't really a meeting of the Assembly. But, along with the theater of Dionysos, the Pnyx still made a convenient place to gather the citizens so he—and Agis—could speak to them.

Along with the milling, chattering Athenians, several hundred Spartans who had come up from the Peloponnesos with Agis occupied a corner of the Pnyx. They stood out not only for their red cloaks and shaven upper lips: they stayed in place without movement or talk. Next to the voluble locals, they might almost have been statues.

Nor were they the only Hellenes from other poleis here today. Thebes had sent a delegation to Athens. So had Corinth. So had the Thessalians, from the towns in the north of Hellas proper. And so had the half-wild Macedonians. Their envoys kept staring every which way, especially back toward the Akropolis. Nodding toward them, Alkibiades murmured to Agis, "They haven't got anything like this up in their backwoods country."

"We have nothing like this, either," Agis said. "I doubt whether so much luxury is a good thing."

"It hasn't spoiled us or made us soft," Alkibiades replied. *As you have reason to know*. He didn't say that. It hung in the air nonetheless.

"Yes," Agis said laconically.

What Alkibiades did say was, "We've spent enough time—too much time—fighting among ourselves. If Athens and Sparta agree, if the rest of Hellas—and even Macedonia—follows . . ."

"Yes," Agis said again. This time, he added, "That is why I have come. This job is worth doing, and Sparta cannot do it alone. Neither can Athens."

Getting a bit of your own back? Alkibiades wondered. It wasn't as if Agis were wrong. Alkibiades gestured to a herald who stood on the platform with him and the Spartan. The man stepped up and called in a great voice, "People of Hellas, hear the words of Alkibiades, leader of Hellas, and of Agis, King of Sparta."

Leader sounded ever so much better than *tyrant*, even if they amounted to the same thing. Alkibiades took a step forward.

He loved having thousands of pairs of eyes on him, where Agis seemed uncomfortable under that scrutiny. Agis, of course, was King because of his bloodline. Alkibiades had had to earn all the attention he'd got. He'd had to, and he'd done it.

Now he said, "People of Hellas, you see before you Athenian and Spartan, with neither one quarreling over who should lead us Hellenes in *his* direction." *Of course we're not quarreling,* he thought. *I've won.* He wondered how well Agis understood that. Such worries, though, would have to wait for another time. He went on, "For too long, Hellenes have fought other Hellenes. And while we fought among ourselves, while we spent our own treasure and our own blood, who benefited? Who smiled? Who, by the gods, laughed?"

A few of the men in the audience—the more clever, more alert ones—stirred, catching his drift. The rest stood there, waiting for him to explain. *Sokrates would have understood.* The gouge on Alkibiades' forehead was only a pink scar now. *Sokrates would have said I'm pointing the Athenians in a new direction so they don't look my way. He would have been right, too. But now he's dead, and not too many miss him. He wasn't a nuisance only to me.*

Such musing swallowed no more than a couple of heartbeats. Aloud, Alkibiades continued, "In our grandfathers' day, the Great Kings of Persia tried to conquer Hellas with soldiers, and found they could not. We have men in Athens still alive who fought at Marathon and Salamis and Plataia."

A handful of those ancient veterans stood in the crowd, white-bearded and bent and leaning on sticks like the last part of the answer to the riddle of the Sphinx. Some of them cupped a hand behind an ear to follow him better. What they'd seen in their long lives!

"Since then, though, Hellenes have battled other Hellenes and forgotten the common foe," Alkibiades said. "Indeed, with all his gold, Great King Dareios II has sought to buy mastery of Hellas, and has come closer to gaining it than Kyros and Xerxes did with their great swarms of men. For enmities among us suit Persia well. She gains from our disunion what she could not with spears and arrows.

"A lifetime ago, Great King Xerxes took Athens and burnt it. We have made it a finer polis, a grander polis, since, but our ashes are yet unavenged. Only when we Hellenes have burnt Persepolis to the ground can we say we are, at last, even with the Persians."

Some fellow from Halikarnassos had written a great long book about the struggles between Hellenes and Persians. The burning of Athens was the least of it; he'd traced the conflict back even before the days of the Trojan War. What was his name? Alkibiades couldn't recall. It didn't matter. People knew Athens had gone up in flames. The rest? Long ago and far away.

Almost everyone in the Pnyx saw where he was going now. A low, excited murmur ran through the crowd. He continued, "We've shown one thing, and shown it plainly. *Only Hellenes can beat other Hellenes.* The Great King knows as much. That's why he hires mercenaries from Hellas. But if all our poleis pull together, if all our poleis send hoplites and rowers and ships against Persia, not even those traitors can hope to hold us back.

"Persia and the wealth of Persia will be ours. We will have new lands to rule, new lands to settle. We won't have to expose unwanted infants any more. They will have places where they can live. The Great King's treasury will fall into *our* hands. Now we starve for silver. Once we beat the Persians, we'll have our fill of gold."

No more low, excited murmur. Now the people in the Pnyx burst into cheers. Alkibiades watched the Spartans. They were shouting as loud as the Athenians. The idea of a war against Persia made them forget their usual reserve. The Thebans cheered, too, as did the men from the towns of Thessaly. During Xerxes' invasion, they'd given the Persians earth and water in token of submission.

And the Macedonians cheered more enthusiastically still, pounding one another and their neighbors on the back. Seeing that made Alkibiades smile. For one thing, the Macedonians had also yielded to the Persians. For another, he had no intention of using them to any great degree in his campaign against Persia. Their King, Perdikkas son of Alexandros, was a hill bandit who squabbled with other hill bandits nearby. Macedonia had always been like that. It always would be. Expecting it to amount to anything was a waste of time, a waste of hope.

Alkibiades stepped back and waved King Agis forward. The Spartan said, "Alkibiades has spoken well. We owe our forefathers revenge against Persia. We can win it. We should win it. We *will* win it. So long as we stand together, no one can stop us. Let us go on, then, on to victory!"

He stepped back. More cheers rang out. In his plain way, he had spoken well. An Athenian would have been laughed off the platform for such a bare-bones speech, but standards were different for the Spartans. *Poor fellows,* Alkibiades thought. *They can't help being dull.*

He eyed Agis. Just how dull *was* the Spartan King? *So long as we stand together, no one can stop us.* That was true. Alkibiades was sure of it. But how long *would* the Hellenes stand together? Long enough to beat Great King Dareios? Fighting a common foe would help.

How long *after* beating the Persians would the Hellenes stand together? *Till we start quarreling over who will rule the lands we've won.* Alkibiades eyed Agis again. Did he see that, too, or did he think they would go on sharing? He might. Spartans could be slow on the uptake.

I am alone at the top of Athens now, Alkibiades thought. *Soon I will be alone at the top of the civilized world, from Sicily all the way to India. This must be what Sokrates'* daimon *saw. This must be why it sent him to Sicily with me, to smooth my way to standing here at the pinnacle. Sure enough, it knew what it was doing, whether he thought so or not.* Alkibiades smiled at Agis. Agis, fool that he was, smiled back.

FARMERS' LAW

Historian, fantasy writer, and historical mystery writer par excellence Sharan Newman asked me for a story for a collection of historical mystery pieces. This one draws on my academic background in the most literal way. I fought my way through the Nomos Georgikos *(Farmers' Law) in the original Byzantine Greek in a seminar conducted by Professor Speros Vryonis, Jr. This probably isn't the way he expected me to use it, but I was starting to sell fiction about the same time as I was finishing my grad-school career. This story probably also makes it clear I'm no enormous threat to Sharan at her game.*

Abrostola suited Father George well. The village lay only five or six miles north of Amorion, the capital of the Anatolic theme. That was close enough for George and his little flock to take refuge behind Amorion's stout walls when the Arabs raided Roman territory—and far enough away for them to go unnoticed most of the time.

Going unnoticed also suited Father George well. What with Constantine V following in the footsteps of his father, Leo III, and condemning the veneration of icons, a priest wanted to draw as little notice from Constantinople as he could. That was all the more true if he found the Emperor's theology unfortunate, as Father George did.

Every so often, officials would ride through Abrostola on their way from Amorion up to Ankyra, or from Ankyra coming down to Amorion. They never bothered to stop at the little church beside which George and his wife, Irene, lived. Because they never stopped, they never saw that the images remained in their places there. George never brought it to their attention, nor did any of the other villagers. They had trouble enough scratching a living from the thin, rocky soil of Asia Minor and worrying about the Arabs. They didn't care to risk Constantine's displeasure along with everything else.

George was eating barley bread and olive oil and drinking a cup of wine for breakfast when someone pounded on the door. "Who's that?" Irene asked indignantly from across the table.

"Who's that?" their daughter, Maria, echoed. Rather than indignant, the three-year-old sounded blurry—she was trying to talk around a big mouthful of bread.

"I'd better find out." George rose from his stool with grace surprising in so big a man: he was almost six feet tall, and broad as a bull through the shoulders. The pounding came again, louder and more insistently.

"Oh, dear God," Irene said. "I hope that doesn't mean Zoe's finally decided to run off with somebody."

"Alexander the potter should have got her married off years ago," George said, reaching for the latch. Zoe was the prettiest maiden in the village, and knew it too well.

But when George opened the door, it wasn't Alexander standing there, but a weedy little farmer named Basil. "He's dead, Father!" Basil cried. "He's dead!"

Automatically, the priest made the sign of the cross. Then he asked, "Who's dead?" Nobody in the village, so far as he knew, was even particularly sick. Rumor said plague was loose in Constantinople again, but—*God be praised*, George thought—it hadn't come to Abrostola.

"Who's dead?" Basil repeated, as if he couldn't believe his ears. "Who's dead?" He'd always had a habit of saying things twice. "Why, Theodore, of course." He stared at Father George as if the priest should have already known that.

"Theodore?" George crossed himself again. Theodore couldn't have been more than thirty-five—not far from his own age—and was one of the two or three most prosperous farmers in the village. If any man seemed a good bet to live out his full threescore and ten, he was the one. But, sure enough, the sound of women wailing came from the direction of his house. George shook his head in slow wonder. "God does as He would, not as we would have Him do."

But Basil said, "Not this time." He went on, "God didn't have anything to do with it. Nothing. I'd borrowed an ax from him, to chop some firewood with, and I brought it back to him at sunup, just a little while ago. You know how Theodore is—was. He lets you borrow things, sure enough, but he never lets you forget you did it, either."

"That's so," George admitted. Theodore hadn't overflowed with the milk of human kindness. The priest tried to make the peasant come to the point: "You went to give the ax back to Theodore. And. . . ?"

"And I found him laying there by his house with his head smashed in," Basil said. "Didn't I tell you that?"

"As a matter of fact, no," Father George said. Though he was wearing only the light knee-length tunic in which he'd slept, he hurried out the door and toward Theodore's house. Dust scuffed up under his bare feet. Basil had to go into a skipping half-trot to keep up with him.

A crowd was already gathering. Theodore's wife, Anna, and his two daughters, Margarita and Martina, stood over the body shrieking and tearing at their tunics, which reached down to the ground. Some of Theodore's neighbors stood there, too: Demetrios the smith and a couple of other farmers, John and Kostas. Demetrios' wife, Sophia, came out and began to wail, too; her brother was married to Theodore's sister.

George shouldered his way through them. He looked down at Theodore and crossed himself once more. The prosperous peasant stared up at the sky, but he wasn't seeing anything, and wouldn't ever again. Blood soaked into the ground from the blow that had smashed in the right front of his skull from the eye socket all the way back to above the ear. Flies were already buzzing around the body.

John grabbed Theodore's arm. "Murder!" he said hoarsely, which set everyone exclaiming and wailing anew. What had happened was obvious enough, but naming it somehow made it worse.

"What are we going to do?" Basil asked. "Send down to Amorion, so the *strategos* commanding the theme can order a man up here to find out who did it?"

That was what they should have done. They all knew it. But Lankinos, the governor of the Anatolic theme, was as much an iconoclast as the Emperor Constantine himself. Any man he sent to Abrostola would likely be an iconoclast, too. If he stepped into the church and saw the holy images of Christ and the saints still on the iconostasis . . .

"We can't do that to Father George!" Demetrios the blacksmith exclaimed. "We can't put our own souls in danger doing that, either."

Theodore's wife—no, his widow now—spoke for the first time: "We can't let a murderer walk free." She drew herself straight and wiped her tear-stained face on a tunic sleeve. "I will have vengeance on the man who killed my husband. I *will*, by the Mother of God."

Father George wouldn't have sworn an oath of vengeance in the Virgin's name, but he knew Anna wasn't thinking so clearly as she might have been. Her older daughter, Margarita, said, "Why would anyone want to hurt Father? Why?" She sounded bewildered.

The question made people stir awkwardly. "Why?" Basil

echoed. "Well, on account of he was rich, for starters, and—*ow!*" Father George didn't see what had happened, but guessed somebody'd stepped on Basil's foot.

"If we don't send down to Amorion, how will we find out who killed Theodore?" the farmer named Kostas asked.

No one answered, not in words. No one said anything at all, in fact, though Margarita and Martina kept weeping quietly. But everyone, including Theodore's daughters, looked straight at Father George.

"*Kyrie, eleison!*" the priest said, making the sign of the cross yet again. "*Christe, eleison!*"

"No one had mercy on my husband," Anna said bitterly. "Not the Lord, not Christ, not whoever killed him. No one."

She stood with George beside Theodore's corpse in the parlor of the house that had been the farmer's. She and her daughters had washed the body and wrapped it in white linen and bent Theodore's arms into a cross on his chest. He held a small, rather crudely painted icon showing Christ and Peter. He lay facing east on a couch by the bricks of the north wall, so the caved-in ruin that was the right side of his head showed as little as possible. Candles and incense burned by him.

"You heard nothing when he went out yesterday morning?" Father George asked.

"Nothing," Theodore's widow replied. "I don't know whether he went outside to ease himself or to see what he needed to do first in the morning, the way he sometimes did. Whatever the reason was, he hadn't been gone long enough for me or the girls even to think about it. Then Basil pounded on the door, shouting that he was dead."

"He must have come to me right afterwards," the priest said.

Anna nodded. Father George plucked at his thick black beard. "He didn't tell you he saw anyone running away?"

"No." Anna looked down at her husband's body. "What will become of us? We were doing so well, but now, without a man in the house . . . Hard times."

"I'll pray for you." Father George grimaced as soon as the words were out of his mouth. They were kindly meant, but felt flat and inadequate.

"Catch the man who did this to him—did it to all of us," Anna said. "He must have thought he would profit by it. Don't let him. Don't let Theodore go unavenged." Tears started streaming down her face again.

Gently, Father George quoted Romans: " 'Vengeance is mine; I will repay, saith the Lord.' "

But Anna quoted Scripture, too, the older, harder law of Exodus: " 'Eye for eye, tooth for tooth, hand for hand, foot for foot.' "

And George found himself nodding. He said, "No one heard anything. Basil didn't see anyone running off. No one else did, either, or no one's come forward. Whoever slew your husband got out of sight in a hurry."

"May he never show himself again, not till Judgment Day," Anna said.

"Here is a question I know you will not want to answer, but I hope you will think on it," Father George said. "Who might have wanted Theodore dead?"

"Half the village," the dead man's widow said at once, "and you know it as well as I do. When Theodore and I married, he was working a miserable little plot, and we almost starved a couple of times. But he worked hard—nobody ever worked harder—and he always had a good eye for land that would yield increase, so he made himself a man to be reckoned with in Abrostola—even a man people had heard of in Amorion. That was plenty to make lazy people jealous of him."

The priest nodded again. Theodore had been a great ox in harness. But not everyone said such gracious things about the land deals he'd made, though Father George didn't tax Anna with that now. He already knew some of those tales; he could learn more later. In the smithy close by, Demetrios' hammer clanged on iron. George said, "I'll leave you to your mourning."

"Find the man who killed my husband," Anna said. "If you don't . . . If you don't, I'll have to go down to Amorion to see if the *strategos* and his henchmen can help me."

"I understand." Father George bit the inside of his lower lip. With any luck, his luxuriant beard kept Theodore's widow from noticing. He couldn't blame her. Of course she wanted the murderer caught and punished. But if men from the capital of the Anatolic theme, men loyal to Constantine the iconoclast, started poking through Abrostola, George would have a thin time of it. The whole village would have a thin time of it, for supporting an iconophile priest. "I'll do everything I can."

Anna just waved him to the door, imperious as if she were an empress, not a peasant's widow. And George's retreat, to his own embarrassment, was something close to a rout. After the gloom of candlelight inside Theodore's house, he blinked in the strong sunshine outside.

He almost ran into Kostas, who was coming toward the house. "Excuse me," he said, and got out of the farmer's way.

Kostas dipped his head. He was a lean gray wolf of a man, with hard, dark eyes and with scars on his cheeks and forearms that showed he'd done plenty of fighting against Arab raiders. "You're the man I came to see, Father George," he said. "Your wife told me you were here."

"Walk with me, then," the priest said, and Kostas did. They

went past Demetrios' blacksmithery. The smith stopped hammering at whatever he was making. He raised his right hand from the tongs with which he held hot metal to the anvil to wave to the two men. Kostas nodded again. Father George waved back. As soon as Demetrios started clanking away with the hammer again, the priest gestured to Kostas. "Please, my friend—go on."

"Thanks." But Kostas didn't say anything right away. He stared at the brickwork houses of the village, some whitewashed, some plain; at their red tile roofs; at the flocks and vineyards and pasturage that lay beyond, as if he'd never seen any of them before. At last, when George was wondering if he'd have to prompt the farmer again, Kostas said, "That business between Theodore and me last year, that wasn't so much of a much, not really."

"Has anyone said it was?" Father George asked.

Kostas ignored that. "I still don't think the plot I got from Theodore was as good as the one I gave him in exchange for it, but I never even reckoned it was worth going to law about, you know. Farmers' Law says I could have, and I think I would've won, too. But nobody wants those nosy buggers from Amorion mucking about here, and that's the Lord's truth."

"Seeing how things are these days, I'm glad you feel that way," George said.

Again, Kostas talked right through him: "If I wouldn't go to law over it, I wouldn't smash in Theodore's head over it, either, now would I?"

"I hope not," Father George answered. "But someone did."

"Not me," Kostas repeated, and walked, or rather loped, away. *A lone wolf, sure enough*, the priest thought. He let out a long sigh. How many more denials would he hear over the next few days? And which villager would be lying like Ananias?

Like anyone else in the village, Father George kept a couple of pigs and some chickens. He was scattering barley for the chickens when Basil sidled up to him. Not even the chickens gave the scrawny little peasant much respect; he had to step smartly to keep them from pecking at his toes, which stuck out between the straps of his sandals.

"Good day, Basil." Father George tossed out another handful of grain.

"Same to you." Basil seemed to like the sound of the words. "Yes, same to you." He stood there watching the chickens for a minute or two, and kicked dirt at a bird that was eyeing his feet again. The hen squawked and fluttered back.

"You wanted something?" George asked.

Basil coughed and, to the priest's surprise, blushed red as a pomegranate. "You recall that business year before last, don't you? You know the business I mean."

"When you were tending Theodore's sheep?"

"That's right." Basil's head bobbed up and down. "People said I milked 'em without telling Theodore, and sold the milk and even sold off a couple of the sheep."

People said that because it was true. He'd got caught selling the milk and the sheep in the market square at Orkistos, more than ten miles northwest of Abrostola. Father George didn't bother mentioning that. With a grave nod, he said, "I remember."

"All right. All right, then," Basil said. "And after that, they gave me a good thumping and Theodore took away my wages. That's what the Farmers' Law says to do, and that's what they did. I got what they said was coming to me, and that's the end. Fair enough, right?"

"So far as I know, no one has troubled you about it since," the priest replied. No one had hired Basil as a shepherd since, either, one more thing George didn't say.

"That's true enough—so it is," the skinny peasant agreed. "But do you know what's going round the village now? Do you know?" He hopped in the air, not because a chicken was after his toes but from outrage. "They're saying I smashed in Theodore's head on account of that business, is what they're saying."

"You found him dead," Father George observed. *Did you find him dead because you killed him?* he wondered. But he kept that to himself, too.

Basil dropped to his knees and clasped the priest's hand. "Not you, too!" he cried. "I couldn't've killed Theodore, not even with a club in my hand! He'd've grabbed it and thrashed me all over again. You know it, too."

"Not if you struck from behind." But George hesitated and shook his head. "No. The blow he got surely came from the front. I saw as much. I daresay he would have cried out against you, at any rate, if he saw you coming with a club in your hand."

"That's right! That's just right!" Basil said fervently. He kissed George's hand in an ecstasy of relief.

Is it? George wasn't so sure. Maybe Theodore wouldn't have taken scrawny Basil seriously till too late. But he lifted the peasant from the dirt and dusted him off. "Go your way. And stay away from sheep."

"Oh, I do," Basil said. And the priest believed him. Nobody in Abrostola let Basil near his sheep. Had Father George had sheep, he wouldn't have let Basil near them, either.

Theodore's funeral felt strange, unnatural. The procession to the burial ground outside the village seemed normal enough at first. Father George and the dead man's relatives led the way, all of them but the priest wailing and keening and beating their breasts. More villagers followed.

Some of them lamented, too. But others kept looking at one another. George knew what lay in their minds. It lay in his mind, too. They were wondering which of their number was a murderer. Was it someone they despised? Or was it a friend, a loved one, a brother? Only one man knew, and they were burying him.

No. Father George grimaced. Someone else knew, too: the killer himself. And he hoped to walk free, to escape human judgment. God would surely send him to hell for eternal torment, but he must have despised that, too.

George chanted psalms over Theodore's body as it lay in the grave, to protect his soul from demons. "Let us pray that he goes from here to a better place, to paradise, to the marriage chamber of the spirit," he said, and he and the mourners and the whole crowd of villagers made the sign of the cross together.

As the funeral ended, they straggled back toward Abrostola. Behind Father George, the gravediggers shoveled the earth down onto Theodore's shrouded body. The priest sighed and shook his head. That was always such a final sound, and worse here today because some wicked man had cut short Theodore's proper span of years.

Later that day, Father George went to the dead man's house to console his widow and daughters. Anna met him at the door and gave him an earthenware cup of wine. She was dry-eyed now, dry-eyed and grim. "We are as well as we can be," she said when he asked. "I'll give you another few days to catch the killer. If you don't, I'm going down to Amorion." She sounded unbendably determined. In that, she'd been a good match for Theodore.

"I'm doing all I can, all I know how to do." George knew he sounded harried. His training was to fight sin, not crime. "If you go to Amorion . . ."

"The holy images are dear to me, too," Anna said. "But justice and vengeance are dearer still."

Father George bowed his head. He had no good answer for that, and no way to stop her if she chose to go. "I'll do all I can," he repeated. He finished the wine, gave her the cup, and turned to go.

Demetrios was already hammering away again. When George walked past his house and the smithy by it, Sophia came out and stopped him. "Have you heard?" the smith's wife asked.

"I don't know," Father George said. "But I expect you'll tell me."

Sophia put her hands on her hips and cocked her head to one side as she studied George. Her dark eyes flashed. She remained one of the prettier, and one of the livelier, women in Abrostola. Fifteen years before, she'd been the prize catch in the village, as Zoe was now. George had eyed her back before she married Demetrios. So had a lot of the young men in Abrostola. She knew it, too, and used it now, making him pay more attention to her than he would have were she plainer. "Why, the lies John's spreading, of course." Her tone was intimate, too, as if she were the priest's wife, not the smith's.

"You'd better tell me more," Father George said. "John hasn't said anything to me." That was true. It didn't mean George hadn't heard anything, though he hoped Sophia would think it did.

She tossed her head. "Oh, no. He wouldn't tell you. That's not his way. He'll put poison in other people's ears, and let them put it in yours."

"I haven't heard any poison I know of," George said.

Sophia went on as if he hadn't spoken: "The mill Demetrios built last year has been sitting idle ever since, because the water it took out of the Lalandos kept Theodore's wheatfields from getting enough."

The priest nodded. "That's what the Farmers' Law says you do if a mill takes too much water out of a river—not that the Lalandos is much of a river, especially in summertime. It's a fair law, I think."

"So do I." Sophia reached out and set a hand on his arm, a startling intimacy. "And so does Demetrios. He never said a word when he had to let it rest idle. And why should he have? We make a good living from the smithy as is." Pride rang in her voice, as Demetrios' hammer rang off hot metal.

"I'm sure you do," George said, truthfully enough: Sophia's earrings were gold, not brass, and her tunic of fine, soft wool from the sheep near Ankyra.

"Well, then—Demetrios wouldn't have any reason to hurt Theodore, and so he couldn't have." Sophia made it sound simple.

Father George wished it were. "By all the signs, nobody had any reason to hurt Theodore. But someone did."

"Someone certainly did," Sophia said sharply. "You might ask John about *his* dealings with Theodore. Yes, you might indeed."

"I intend to," George said. Sophia nodded. For a heartbeat, he thought she would kiss him. For half a heartbeat, he hoped she would. She didn't. She just turned and walked away. Shame filled him. *Whosoever looketh on a woman to lust after her hath committed adultery already with her in his heart.* He repented of his sin, but he would have to do penance for it, too.

As soon as the sun rose the next day, Father George went looking for John. He wasn't astonished to discover John walking toward his house. The farmer nodded to him. Like Kostas, John was a scarred veteran. Unlike Kostas, he was actively bad-tempered. "All right," he said now, by way of greeting. "I know that miserable bitch Sophia's been spreading lies about me, but I don't know what kind yet. I suppose you'll tell me, though."

"You didn't think she was a miserable bitch before she married Demetrios," Father George said. "None of the young men did." *I certainly didn't.* He remembered, and grimaced at, his own desirous thoughts the day before.

John dismissed that with a snort and a wave. "Just tell me what she said."

"That you were going on about Demetrios' mill, and why it's idle," the priest answered.

"By the Virgin, that's the truth," John said. "It's not like what *she's* been doing—talking about that ox of mine Theodore killed three years ago. He said it was in his field, and so he had the right, but the carcass was on *my* land. Farmers' Law says he should have paid me, but he's a big sneeze here. Did I ever see a copper follis? Not me."

"Why tell me this?" George asked. "Do you *want* me to think you bore a grudge?"

"Of I course I bore a grudge." John tossed his head in scorn. "Like I'm the only one in Abrostola who did." George had to nod; he'd already seen as much there. John went on, "I've had it for years. Why should I all of a sudden decide to smash in his stinking, lying head? One of these days, I'd've found a revenge to make his heart burn for years. I want to kill whoever did him in, is what I want to do, on account of now I won't get the chance." He spat in the dirt. "What do you think of that?"

"I believe you." It wasn't what Father George had intended to say, but it was true.

"All right, then. Don't waste your time coming after me. Don't waste your time at all." John stalked off, leaving the priest staring after him.

"He could have done it," Irene said that night, over a supper of hot cheese pie with leeks and mushrooms. "He could be covering his tracks."

"John? I know he could." Father George nodded to his wife. He wasn't so sure about John as he had been that morning. "But so could plenty of other people. The longer Theodore's dead, the more it seems everyone hated him."

"Who hated him enough to kill him?" Irene said. "That's the question."

"I don't know," George said unhappily. "And if I don't find out soon, Anna will go down to Amorion, and the *strategos* or his people will come back up here, and . . ." He sighed. "And Abrostola won't be the same." He didn't dwell on what would happen to him, even if the Emperor Constantine and his officials weren't kind to priests who venerated images.

"It's not fair. It's not right," Irene said. Then she gave a small gasp and grabbed for their daughter, who was helping herself to cheese pie with both hands. "Wash yourself off!" she exclaimed. "You're a horrible mess."

"Mess." Maria sounded cheerful, no matter how glum her parents were. She grabbed a rag and did a three-year-old's halfhearted job of wiping herself off. "There!"

Irene shook her head. "Not good enough. See that big glob of cheese on your left hand?"

Maria looked confused. "My best hand, Mama?"

"No, your *left* hand," Irene said, and cleaned it herself. The two words were close in Greek—*aristos* and *aristeros*. *Aristeros*, the word for left, was a euphemism, Father George knew: in pagan days, the left side had been reckoned unlucky. He looked down at his own left hand, on which he wore a wedding ring—to him, a sign of good luck, not bad.

He stared at the ring in dawning astonishment. Then he crossed himself. And then, solemnly, he kissed his wife and daughter. Maria giggled. Irene looked as confused as Maria had a moment before, till George began to explain.

Abrostola hadn't seen such a procession since Theodore's funeral, and not since Easter before that. Father George led this one, too. Kostas and John followed him like a couple of martial saints: they both carried shields and bore swords in their right hands. Basil capered along behind them. He had a light spear, the sort a shepherd might use against wolves—not that he got much chance to herd sheep these days. Several other villagers, all armed as best they might be, also followed the priest.

They stopped not at the church, but at Demetrios'. As usual, the blacksmith was pounding away at something—a plowshare, by the shape of it. He looked up in surprise, sweat streaming down his face, when Father George and Kostas and John strode into the smith. "What's this?" he demanded.

Sadly, George answered, "We've come to take you to Amorion for trial and punishment for the murder of Theodore."

"Me?" Demetrios scowled. "You've got the wrong man, priest. I figure it's likely John here, if you want to know the truth."

But Father George shook his head. "I'm sorry—I'm very sorry—but I'm afraid not, Demetrios. Theodore wouldn't think anything of seeing you with a hammer or an iron bar in your hand, because you carry one so often. And it would have been in your left hand, too, for the blow that killed him was surely struck by a left-handed man."

Demetrios stood over the anvil, breathing hard. As always, the tongs were in his right hand, the hammer in his left. With a sudden shouted curse, he flung that hammer at Father George. Quick as a cat, Kostas leaped sideways to ward the priest with his oval shield. As the hammer thudded off it, Demetrios ran past Kostas and John and out of the smithy.

John swung his sword, but missed. "Catch him!" he shouted. He and Kostas and Father George all rushed after Demetrios.

The smith hadn't got far. He'd knocked one man aside with the tongs, but the rest of the villagers swarmed over him and bore him to the ground. "Get some rope!" somebody shouted. "We'll tie him up, throw him over a mule's back, and take him to Amorion for what he deserves."

"They'll put him to the sword, sure enough." That was Basil, brandishing his spear so fiercely, he almost stabbed a couple of the men close by him. "Sure enough."

From under the pile of men holding him down, Demetrios shouted, "I gave Theodore what he deserved, the son of a pimp. Thought his turds didn't stink, screwed me out of the profit I deserved for the mill. His soul's burning in hell right now."

"And yours will keep it company." Three or four men said the same thing at the same time.

Kostas patted Father George on the back. "You did well here."

"Did I?" the priest asked. He wondered. Murder didn't come under the Farmers' Law, but this one had sprung from its provisions.

Just then, Sophia came out and started to shriek and wail and try to drag the villagers off her husband. A couple of them pulled her away from the pile, but not till after she'd raked them with her nails.

"What else could you have done?" Kostas asked.

Father George sighed. "That's a different question," he said, and started back toward his house.

232

OCCUPATION DUTY

It seems pretty likely that the area of southwest Asia just north and east of the Sinai Peninsula would be a bone of contention no matter what happened and no matter who lived there. It's too strategically placed not to be. It offers access to Egypt from Syria—or, conversely, depending on who's holding it, it offers access to Syria from Egypt. The breakpoint in this alternate history goes back a long way: more than 3,000 years. But, as Al Stewart says in "Nostradamus," the more it changes, the more it stays the same.

*P*heidas wasn't thrilled about going upcountry from Gaza— who would have been? But when you were a nineteen-year-old conscript serving out your term, nobody gave a curse about whether you were thrilled. You were there to do what other people told you—and on the double, soldier!

He got into the armored personnel carrier with all the enthusiasm of someone climbing into his own coffin. None of the other young Philistinians climbing aboard looked any happier than he did. The reason wasn't hard to figure: there was a small—but not nearly small enough—chance they were doing exactly that.

The last man in slammed the clamshell doors at the rear. The big diesel engine rumbled to life. "Next stop, Hierosolyma," the sergeant said.

"Oh, boy," said Pheidas' buddy Antenor.

He spoke softly, but Sergeant Dryops heard him anyway. "You better hope Hierosolyma's our next stop, kid," the noncom said. "If we stop before we get there, it's on account of we've got trouble with the Moabites. You want trouble with the stinking ragheads? You want trouble with them on their terms?"

Antenor shook his head to show he didn't. That wasn't going to be good enough. Before Pheidas could say as much, Dryops beat him to the punch.

"You want trouble with them on their terms?" he yelled.

"No, Sergeant," Antenor said loudly. Dryops nodded, mollified. And Antenor's reply not only took care of military courtesy, it was also the gods' truth. The Moabites caused too much trouble any which way. As far as they were concerned, their rightful border was the beach washed by the Inner Sea. The Philistinians? Invaders. Interlopers. Never mind that they'd been on the land for more than three thousand years. In the history-crowded Middle East, that wasn't long enough.

They don't even believe in Dagon, Pheidas thought as the APC clattered north and east, one of a long string of armored fighting vehicles. It wasn't that he wanted the miserable Moabites worshiping the same god he did. If that didn't ruin the divine neighborhood, he didn't know what would. But too many Moabites didn't believe Dagon *was* a god. Some thought he was a demon; others denied he was there at all. They felt the same way about the other Philistinian deities, too.

Antenor's mind must have been running in the same direction as Pheidas', for he said, "They're jealous of us. They've always been jealous of us."

"Sure," Pheidas said. You learned that in school. Right from the beginning, the Philistinians had been more progressive than the tribes of the interior. They were the ones who'd first learned how to work iron, and they'd done their best to keep the hill tribes from finding out how to do it. Some things didn't change much. The Moabites were still backward . . . but there were an awful lot of them, and they didn't mind a bit if they died in the service of their own grim tribal gods.

Around Gaza, the land was green and fertile. The Philistinians had always had a knack for making the desert bloom. That was why so many nasty neighbors had coveted their country, almost from the very beginning.

Pheidas nudged Antenor. "Hey!" he said.

"What?" Antenor had been about to light a cigarette. He looked annoyed at getting interrupted.

"You were good in school. What was the name of that guy Lord Goliath knocked off?"

"Oh. Him." Antenor frowned, trying to remember. After a moment, he did—he *had* been good in school. "Tabitas, that's what. Tabitas of the Evraioi."

"*That's* right!" Pheidas nodded. He couldn't have come up with it himself, but he knew it as soon as he heard it. "Crazy, isn't it? Here we are all these years later, going off to do the same cursed job all over again."

"Miserable mountain rats don't go away," Sergeant Dryops said. "They want to make *us* go away, but that ain't gonna happen, either." He paused. "Is it?"

"No, Sergeant!" This time, all the troopers in the APC sang out as loud as they could. Once bitten, twice raucous. Dryops not only nodded, he even smiled a little. Pheidas wondered if the world would end. It didn't. The world was a tough old place.

As he peered out from time to time through the firing port by his head, Pheidas watched it get tougher, too. The people of the hills and the people of the coast had been enemies since the days of Goliath and Tabitas, maybe longer. Sometimes it seemed the landscapes were enemies, too.

Things went from green to brown as soon as the land started climbing and getting rougher—as soon as it went from a place where more Philistinians lived to one where there were more Moabites. Chickens and goats and skinny stray dogs roamed the streets of Moabite villages. The houses and shops looked a million years old despite their rust-streaked corrugated iron roofs. Pheidas wouldn't have wanted to drive any of the ancient, beat-up cars. The sun blasted everything with the force of a tactical nuke.

Spray-painted squiggles in the pothook Moabite script marred whitewashed walls. Pheidas could read it. Learning enough Moabite to get by was part of basic training. PHILS OUT! was the most common graffito. Pheidas didn't mind that one so much. He didn't like the Moabites any better than they liked his people. He would have been happy to stay out if his commanders hadn't told him to go in.

But then he saw one that said CHEMOSH CUTS OFF DAGON'S SCALY TAIL! Chemosh was the Moabites' favorite god. For lots of them, he was the only tribal god. A few even said he was the only god, period. You really had to watch out for fanatics like that. They were the kind who turned terrorist.

The scrawl that really raised his hackles, though, was THE SWORD BUDDHA AND THE FOUR WITH CHEMOSH! The Turks of Babylonia were newcomers to these parts; they'd brought the Sword Buddha down off the steppe hardly more than a thousand years ago. But Aluzza, Allat, Manah, and Hubal had been worshiped in Arabia for a very long time. And Babylonia and Arabia were both swimming in oil, which these days counted for even more than the strength of their gods.

Sergeant Dryops saw that one, too. He muttered into his gray-streaked red mustache. Pheidas couldn't make out all of what he said. From what he *could* understand, he was surprised the steel by Dryops' head didn't melt.

"We've got friends, too," the veteran noncom said when his language grew a little less incandescent. "The Ellenes in Syria don't like the Moabites any better than we do. And they *really* don't like the Turks."

That made Pheidas feel a little better—till Antenor went and spoiled it by saying, "They don't have much oil, though."

Dryops looked at him as if he'd found him on the sole of his marching boot. "Blood's thicker than oil, by the gods," he growled.

Antenor didn't say anything at all. His silence seemed more devastating than speech. There *were* ties between Philistinians and Ellenes, yes. But they were ancient. Some of the Philistinians' ancestors had come from Crete before settling on the mainland here. But the languages now were as different as Galatian and Irish—more different, maybe, because they'd been separate longer. And Babylonia outweighed Syria about three to one.

A couple of Moabite men in headcloths and white cotton robes—good cover against the sun—scowled at the armored column as it clattered past. Scowls were basically honest. As long as nobody did anything more than scowl . . . Pheidas could look out through the firing port instead of shooting through it. That suited him fine.

It wasn't far from Gaza to Hierosolyma, not as the crow flew. But a crow didn't fly back through the years, and Pheidas felt he'd fallen into a different century when his convoy rolled into the hill town. Gaza was a city of steel and glass and reinforced concrete, a city that looked across the Inner Sea to the whole wide world. Hierosolyma, hidden in the hills, was built of golden limestone and wood and brick, and looked as if it had been there forever. Had it seemed much different when the Turks sacked it, when the Romans wrecked it, when Philip of Macedon besieged the Persian garrison there, or when Lord Goliath took it away from the Evraioi? Pheidas had his doubts.

Men in robes and women in long, baggy dresses only made the impression of age stronger. Some of the men did wear modern shirts and trousers, but none of the women—none—chose the skimpy, clinging styles that were all the rage down by the sea. As far as girl watching went, it would be a barren time.

But it wouldn't be dull. Graffiti on whitewashed walls were thicker and fiercer here than they had been in the villages to the southwest. Philistinian soldiers with assault rifles patrolled the narrow, twisting streets. They never traveled in parties smaller than four; the Moabites had assault rifles, too, and other, nastier, toys, and used them whenever they figured they could get away with it.

The APC rattled past a couple of firebombed buildings. A wine bottle full of gasoline with a cloth wick was a low-tech weapon, which didn't mean it wasn't effective. Then Pheidas stopped worrying about gasoline bombs, because something a demon of a lot bigger went off much too close. The APC swayed and shook and almost flipped over. Then it stopped so suddenly, it pitched all the soldiers in the fighting compartment into a heap.

"*Get* off me, Dagon damn you!" Sergeant Dryops shouted. "Open the doors and pile out. Somebody's gonna need help."

As usual, a man with a loud voice and a clear notion of what he wanted stood a good chance of getting it. The soldiers unscrambled themselves. Antenor opened the doors at the back of the carrier. The men jumped out, weapons at the ready.

"Gods!" Pheidas exclaimed. He ran forward, boots thudding on cobblestones that might have known the scritch of hobnailed Roman marching sandals.

Someone had driven a car into the Philistinian column—a car with a bomb inside. Then he'd set it off. The car was nothing but twisted steel and flames, with thick black smoke rising from it. Mixed with the chemical stinks was one that held a certain ghastly appeal—it smelled like burnt roast pork. Pheidas' stomach did a slow lurch: that wasn't pork burning.

The murder bomber hadn't just blown himself up. That

would have been too much to hope for. He'd wrecked a Philistinian command car almost as thoroughly as the one that carried the bomb. Pheidas didn't think anybody in there could be alive. And the blast had overturned an APC and set it on fire. Burned and wounded Philistinian soldiers came stumbling out of it.

"Anybody left inside?" Pheidas shouted. He wouldn't have left a Moabite to cook in there. . . . Well, right this minute, maybe he would.

"Did the driver get away?" asked a soldier bleeding from a cut on the forehead.

"We'll find out." Pheidas and Antenor both dashed around the burning chassis to see. The driver's compartment was separate from the one where the soldiers sat, and had its own escape hatches.

If the driver hadn't got out—and it didn't look as if he had—he never would now. The APC's front end had taken the brunt of the blast. With the best will in the world, try to force your way through those flames and you'd end up like one of the babies the Phoenicians up the coast fed to the fires in the old days—and, some people whispered, even now.

A shriek behind Pheidas made him whirl, rifle at the ready. A Moabite woman lay on the ground, blood pouring from a gash in her thigh. Part of Pheidas hoped she would just bleed out. But that wasn't how he'd been trained. He ran over and yanked up her dress so he could bandage the gash.

"What are you doing to her?" The question came in harsh, guttural Moabite. "Why are you putting hands on her?"

Pheidas glanced up. The Moabite standing over him couldn't have been more than a couple of years older than he was. The fellow had a gash under one eye, but he didn't know or care. He seemed to think Pheidas would drop his pants and start humping the wounded woman any second now.

"I'm going to fix her leg if I can," Pheidas answered, using Moabite himself. Speaking the language always made him feel he had a mouth full of rocks. "If you know first aid, you do it instead."

"Not me. Not me, by Chemosh's white beard!" The young Moabite backed away. "You better not do anything dirty to her, that's all."

"Are you crazy?" Pheidas said, and then he forgot about the kid. He had to tie off a bleeder. He'd learned how to do that, but he'd never actually done it before. He thanked Dagon that he didn't lose his lunch. He pinned the wound closed, gave the woman a pain shot, and put a bandage around everything. When he finished, his hands were all over blood. He wiped them on her dress. It was already so bloody, a little more gore wouldn't matter.

Only then did he look up and see that the young Moabite was still watching him. "You did what you said," the fellow admitted.

Wearily, Pheidas pointed to the burning wreck of the car the murder bomber had driven. "A Philistinian didn't do that to her," he said. "A Moabite did. One of your people, not one of mine."

"If you weren't occupying us, we wouldn't have to do things like that," the Moabite answered.

"If we weren't occupying you, you'd throw us into the sea," Pheidas said.

"You deserve it. You came from the sea. You should go back into it," the Moabite said. "If Dagon is so wonderful, he can take care of you there."

Pheidas swung his assault rifle so it almost bore on the young man. He wasn't especially devout—most Philistinians weren't these days—but he wasn't about to let this fellow mock him. "I didn't say anything about your god," he growled, sounding as much like Sergeant Dryops as he could. "Keep your mouth shut about mine."

"You can't say anything bad about Chemosh," the young man said. "Chemosh is a true god. Chemosh is *the* true god."

Fanaticism rang in his voice, though he would probably just have called it pride. Pheidas gestured with the rifle. "Get lost, punk, or you'll be sorry."

"Ha! You fear the glory of Chemosh! You know Dagon is nothing but a dead statue!" But the Moabite backed off. Unlike the murder bomber, he didn't have the stuff of martyrs in him— right this minute, anyhow.

Another Moabite came up to Pheidas. This one wore somber business clothes under a headscarf. "I am a physician," he said in accented but understandable Philistinian. "I will care for the woman now. Thank you for what you did."

"You're welcome," Pheidas said. "Help the soldiers, too, please. Some of them need it more than she does."

The Moabite doctor hesitated. "I would rather not," he said at last. "Nothing personal, but I could find myself in a dangerous position if it were discovered that I had done such a thing."

"Your own people would kill you, you mean," Pheidas said.

"Yes." The physician nodded. "Unfortunately, that is exactly what I mean."

Pheidas felt like pounding his head on the slates of the sidewalk in despair. "How are we both supposed to live on this land when you feel that way?"

"When one of us is gone, the other will live on this land," the Moabite replied. Pheidas knew exactly what he meant. *When you Philistinians are gone, we will live on it.*

Sandbagged machine-gun nests, barbed wire, and concrete barriers to thwart murder bombers in cars surrounded the Philistinian barracks in Hierosolyma. Pheidas didn't feel particularly safe even after he dumped his pack by a cot. Too easy to set up a mortar on a roof or in the courtyard of a house and lob a few bombs this way. You could disassemble the thing and hide it long before anybody found you.

"All the comforts of home," Antenor said, looking around at the dismal place.

"Sure, if you live in a jail," Pheidas said.

Antenor laughed for all the world as if he were kidding. "This whole country's a jail," he said. "We're stuck in it, and so are the cursed Moabites."

"We're occupying this part of it," Pheidas said. "If the Moabites ever get the upper hand, they'll massacre us."

"They say their god says we deserve it." Antenor's raised eyebrow told what he thought of that.

"Chemosh is king!" Pheidas said in Moabite—a phrase any Philistinian had heard often enough to understand, regardless of whether he knew another word of the language. He returned to his own tongue for a two-word editorial: "Stinking fanatics."

"They are," Antenor agreed glumly. "It gives them an advantage. They really believe in the fight while we . . . just kind of go on."

As usual, Sergeant Dryops heard everything that mattered. "I'll tell you what I believe in," he rasped. "I believe in not letting one of those raghead cocksuckers dry-gulch me on account of I got careless—or on account of I got too trusting. Some dogs shouldn't get even one bite."

"Heh." Pheidas knew his laugh sounded nervous. Like Arabs and Aramaeans and Phoenicians, Moabites had little use for dogs. Call one of them a son of a bitch and you made an enemy—quite possibly a murderous enemy—for life.

Dryops understood why Pheidas was jumpy. "None of those mangy hounds in here," he said. "Cursed well better not be, anyhow." He laughed.

"The way those people—all those peoples—feel about dogs is enough to make you anti-Semitic," Antenor said. After three thousand years on the Middle Eastern mainland, Philistinians had a good deal of Semitic blood in them, too. Pheidas found himself nodding all the same.

"I don't give a rat's ass how they feel about dogs," Sergeant Dryops said. "But when they want to murder me . . . That, I don't like."

He didn't need to feel sure he had Dagon's power behind him. His boundless scorn for the Moabites was plenty to keep him going.

Along with half his squad, Pheidas tramped the narrow, winding streets of Hierosolyma. His eyes went this way, that way, every which way. He registered all the windows, all the balconies, all the rooftops. Every time a Moabite drew near, he tensed. Did the man have a murder belt full of explosives and nails laced around his middle? Was the woman carrying grenades?

Moabite men called names, in their language and in Philistinian. Some of what they said made *dog* and *son of a bitch* seem like endearments. In civilian life, Pheidas might have tried to kill someone for insults like that. As a soldier, he had to keep his finger off the trigger. Even sticks and stones weren't reason enough to open up. So the high command insisted, anyhow.

But the high command wasn't out there. Soldiers—ordinary human beings—were. Somebody a couple of blocks from Pheidas got hit by a rock and an insult at the same time. He did what he would have done if he were still a civilian. A few seconds later, a young Moabite writhed in the street, blood pouring from his head and his chest.

When Pheidas heard the burst of automatic-weapons fire, the muzzle of his own rifle automatically swung toward the sound.

But the screams and shouts and curses that followed weren't close enough to give him any targets. They got louder instead of softer, though. "That's trouble," he said.

"Better believe it," Antenor said.

Then there were more bangs. These came from the Novgorodian assault rifles terrorists used all over the world. More Philistinian guns barked in reply.

Pheidas had heard plenty. "Come on!" he shouted, and ran toward the sound of the firing. His squadmates pounded after him.

"Maybe . . . we can keep . . . the riot . . . from starting," Antenor panted as he ran.

It was already too late. "Death to the Philistinians!" somebody yelled from a second-story window. A wine bottle with a flaming wick flew out and smashed on the cobbles in the street. Flame splashed out in a five-cubit circle. Pheidas sidestepped like a dancer. Behind him, one of the other Philistinian soldiers chucked a grenade through the window from which the incendiary had come. A shriek rang out hard on the heels of the boom. The soldier nodded in grim satisfaction and ran on.

A couple of Philistinians were down. So were more than a couple of Moabites. Pheidas smelled blood and shit and fear. Some of the fear was bound to be his own. Two bullets snapped past his head. He dove into the nearest doorway. When he saw somebody in a headscarf, he fired at him.

The man went down, clutching at his side. "Mesha! My Mesha!" a woman screeched, and then, "Murder!"

More and more Moabites converged on the flashpoint. So many of them carried weapons, Pheidas wondered if they weren't waiting for a moment like this. Philistinian soldiers ran toward trouble, too, as they'd been trained. When rocks and firebombs and gunfire met them, they answered with gunfire of their own.

An APC awkwardly turned a tight corner. Its heavy machine

gun and bulletproof sides let it dominate the field—or would have, if a Moabite hadn't set it on fire with another bottle full of gasoline. Some of the Philistinians inside managed to get out. Pheidas didn't think all of them did.

"Chemosh is king!" The cry rose again and again, ever louder. So did another one: "Death to Dagon!"

Pheidas peered out from the doorway. Somebody in a dun-colored uniform like his was down. A Moabite with a Novgorodian rifle drew a bead on the wounded Philistinian from no more than three cubits away. Pheidas shot the Moabite in the back. He threw out his arms as he toppled, the rifle flying from his hands. Pheidas ran to his countryman. The Philistinian had a big chunk blown out of one calf. "Hurts," he said as Pheidas dragged him back to cover.

"I bet it does." Pheidas gave him a shot and bandaged the wound. He was glad he'd replenished his aid kit after helping the Moabite woman. He wasn't so glad he'd helped her, not any more.

"Death to Dagon!" the Moabites howled. "Chemosh is king!"

Another Moabite with a rifle ran out to try to help his friend the way Pheidas had helped the wounded Philistinian. Pheidas shot him, too. He'd never fired his own weapon in anger till this morning. One of these days, he would have to try to figure out what it all meant. Now he just wanted to stay alive.

"What a mess." Thanks to the shot, the wounded Philistinian sounded dreamy, not tormented.

"Man, you can say that again," Pheidas said. "The Arabs in Amman will be screaming about what we did to their little Semite brothers. So will the Phoenicians, and the Turks in Babylonia. We'll be lucky if we don't wind up in another real war."

"Yeah." The wounded man didn't seem to care. That was the drug talking—the drug and the fact that he wouldn't be doing any more fighting for a while no matter what.

An ambulance rolled up, lights flashing and sirens wailing. The Moabites threw rocks at it even though it had the Green Waves painted on the doors. They didn't recognize that symbol of mercy; their ambulances, like most in the Middle East, used the Green Sun instead. Parthians used the Green Lion, while most of the world preferred the Green Hammer.

Pheidas waved to the ambulance driver, who stopped the vehicle. A couple of medics got out and picked up the man who'd been shot. They both had pistols on their hips. Medics were supposed to be noncombatants, but the Moabites didn't care about leaving them alone, so they protected themselves as best they could.

The ambulance screamed away. "Over here!" somebody shouted in Philistinian. "Quick!"

Pheidas caught the slight guttural accent. "Sit tight! He's a fraud!" he yelled. What did the Moabites have waiting? Snipers? A machine gun? Grenades?

A tank fired. The boom of the cannon and the blam of the bursting shell came almost too close together to separate into two noises. Screams followed a moment later. Pheidas hoped some of them came from the Moabite who'd tried to trap his buddies.

"You all right?" That was Antenor's voice.

"So far, yeah. You?" Pheidas called back.

"I'm not bleeding, anyway," his friend said. "Don't know what the demon I'm supposed to do, though."

"Stay alive. Shoot the ragheads if they get too close. What else is there?" Pheidas said.

"There should be something." Antenor sounded desperately unhappy. Pheidas hoped he wouldn't think too much. If you did, you were liable to give the bad guys a chance to punch your ticket when you could have punched theirs instead.

To them, of course, you were the bad guys. The Moabites

were surer they were right than Pheidas' own folk were. *Now who's thinking too much?* Pheidas wondered.

"To me! To me!" That was an unmistakable Philistinian voice. Pheidas dashed out of the doorway. He sprayed a quick burst to make any Moabites in the neighborhood keep their heads down. The Philistinian shouted again. He was inside a grocery. Pheidas ran over and jumped through the blown-out front window.

"What's up?" he asked, flopping down flat.

The Philistinian who'd called wore a captain's three dragons on each shoulder strap. "I've got a captive here, and I want to make sure we get him out in one piece," he answered, keeping his rifle trained on a plump, most dejected-looking man. "I think he's one of those Sword Buddha maniacs from Babylonia, here to stir up the Moabites."

"Great," Pheidas said, peering out to make sure nobody was getting ready to rush the grocery.

"My name is Chemoshyatti," the man said in flawless Moabite. "I have run this grocery for years. By my god, Philistinian, you mistake me."

"My left one," the captain said. "I found the tracts in your register's cash drawer." He didn't turn his head away from Chemoshyatti, but addressed his next words to Pheidas: "The usual garbage."

"Uh-huh," Pheidas said. In the Middle Kingdom and Southeast Asia, Buddhism was a peaceful faith. But the variant the Turks brought down off the steppe preached that nirvana came through killing foes. You didn't even have to be a Buddhist yourself to gain it if you took enough enemies with you. Babylonia fostered terrorists as far as its acolytes could reach.

Antenor and another Philistinian soldier warily approached the grocery. Pheidas raised up enough to let them see him in helmet and uniform, then ducked down again. The captain urged them on, saying, "Now we've got enough men to make sure we can get this guy to the people who need to ask him questions."

That wouldn't be much fun, not for the fellow who had to do the answering. Chemoshyatti, or whatever his real name was, must have decided the same thing. One second, he stood there looking innocent and sorry for himself. The next, he flung himself across the five or six cubits that separated him from the Philistinian officer. He was good; nothing gave the move away till he made it.

But the captain was good, too. He hadn't let the man he'd caught come too close, and he hadn't let the fellow's nondescript appearance lull him. Before the grocer who said he was a Moabite could reach him, the captain squeezed off a neat four-round burst, just the way he'd learned to do it in basic. The rounds stitched across the plump man's chest. The captain sidestepped. Chemoshyatti crashed down and didn't get up.

He choked out a few words that weren't Moabite: *"Om mani . . . padme hum."* Then he slumped over, dead. A latrine stink filled the grocery as his bowels let go.

"Sword Buddhist, sure as demons from the afterworld," the captain said grimly.

"Why don't they leave us alone?" Pheidas said. "The Moabites would be bad enough without the Turks stirring them up."

"That's what the Turks live for, though," the officer said. "Maybe we'll have to pay some more unofficial calls on Babylonia." Philistinian planes had wrecked a Babylonian nuclear pile a few years back; the idea of Sword Buddhists with atomic bombs gave politicians all over the world the galloping jimjams. None of the big powers wanted to do anything about it, though, for fear of offending others and starting the war they wanted to head off. The Philistinians, in a tradition that dated back to the days of Crete, took the bull by the horns. Babylonian bonzes often came down with sudden and unexplained cases of loss of life, too. Officially, Philistinia denied everything. But the captain hadn't talked about anything official.

He scooped out the propaganda pamphlets he'd mentioned. They were of the usual sort, preaching the glories of murder and martyrdom in punchy text and bright pictures. One headline grabbed Pheidas' eyes and didn't want to let go. CHEMOSH WANTS PHILISTINIANS DEAD! it screamed.

"Know what I heard, sir?" Pheidas said.

"What's that?" the captain asked.

"That there are Sword Buddhists in Philistinia, too. They want to get us to murder Moabites. They don't care who kills who, as long as somebody's killing somebody."

"I've heard the same thing. You wouldn't want to think that kind of nonsense could take hold in modern, educated people, but it does, curse it. It does." The captain scowled. "I'll bet some of them get driven round the bend because of the things the Moabites do."

"Wouldn't be surprised." Pheidas nodded. Another burst of gunfire not far away made him spin back toward the window, but he decided halfway through the motion that the shooting wasn't close enough to be dangerous. He went on, "And the ragheads say the same thing about us. How did it all get started? How do we make it stop?"

"It goes back to the days when we first came to Philistinia," the captain said, "all those years ago. Maybe it'd be different now if things were different back then. I don't know. I don't know how to get off the wheel, either, any more than anybody else does. And as long as we're on it, we'd better keep winning."

"Yes, sir," Pheidas said.

THE HORSE OF BRONZE

This one came out in The First Heroes, _an anthology of Bronze Age stories I was lucky enough to coedit with the scholar, writer, and underwater archaeologist Noreen Doyle. I wrote it in the spring of 2002. The timing was serendipitous. I had been invited as guest of honor to the British national SF convention that year. After the con was over, my wife and I stayed in England for a week to explore. We made a day trip from London to Stonehenge, not least because I knew it would figure in the story here. I think the writing, which came only a few days later, is unusually fresh because of that. The jackdaws and the wind are authentic. Stonehenge itself, of course, is rather fresher in the story than for real. Too bad!_

I knew, the last time we fought the sphinxes, this dearth of tin would trouble us. I knew, and I was right, and I had the privilege—if that is what you want to call it—of saying as much beforehand, so that a good many of the hes in the warband heard me being clever. And much grief and labor and danger and fear my cleverness won for me, too, though I could not know *that* ahead of time.

"Oh, copper will serve well enough," said Oreus, who is a he who needs no wine to run wild. He brandished an ax. It gleamed red as blood in the firelight of our encampment, for he had polished it with loving care.

"Too soft," Hylaeus said. He carried a fine old sword, leaf-shaped, as green with patina as growing wheat save for the cutting edge, which gleamed a little darker than Oreus' axe blade. "Bronze is better, and the sphinxes, gods curse them, are bound to have a great plenty of it."

Oreus brandished the ax once more. "Just have to hit harder, then," he said cheerfully. "Hit hard enough, and anything will fall over."

With a snort, Hylaeus turned to me. "Will you listen to him, Cheiron? Will you just listen? All balls and no sense."

If this does not describe half our folk—oh, far more than half, by the Cloud-Mother from whom we are sprung—then never have I heard a phrase that does. "Hylaeus is right," I told Oreus. "With tin to harden their weapons properly, the sphinxes will cause us more trouble than they usually do."

And Oreus turned his back on me and made as if to lash out with his hinder hooves. All balls and no brains, sure enough, as Hylaeus had said. I snatched up my own spear—a new one, worse luck, with a head of copper unalloyed—and would have skewered him as he deserved had he provoked me even a little more. He must have realized as much, for he flinched away and said, "We'll give the sphinxes some of *this*, too." Then he did kick, but not right in my direction.

In worried tones, Hylaeus said, "I wonder if what they say about the Tin Isle is true."

"Well, to the crows with me if I believe it's been overrun by monsters," I replied. "Some things are natural, and some just aren't. But *something's* gone wrong, or we wouldn't have had to do without tin shipments for so long."

Looking back on it, thinking about the Tin Isle while we were camped out not far from the sphinxes' stronghold, in the debatable land north and east of their river-valley homeland, seems strange. This is a country of broiling sun, and one that will never match or even approach the river valley in wealth, for it is as dry as baked straw. Only a few paltry folk dwell therein, and they pay tribute to the sphinxes who hold the land as a shield for their better country. Those folk would pay tribute to us, too, if only we could drive away the sphinxes.

They found us the next morning. Keeping our camp secret from them for as long as we had struck me as something of a miracle. With their eagle-feathered wings, they can soar high over a battlefield, looking for a fight. And so this one did. Hideous, screeching laughter came from it as it spied us. They have faces that put me in mind of our own shes, but lengthened and twisted into a foxlike muzzle, and full of hatred—to say nothing of fangs.

"Now we're for it," I said, watching the accursed thing wing off to southward, listening to its wails fade in the distance. "They'll come by land and air, bedeviling us till we're like to go mad."

Nessus strung his great bow. When he thrummed the bowstring, he got a note like the ones he draws from a harp with a sound box made from the shell of a tortoise. "Some of them will be sorry they tried," he said. Nessus can send an arrow farther than any male I know.

"Some of us will be sorry they tried, too," I answered. I had not liked this expedition from the beginning, and never would have consented to it had I not hoped we might get on the scent of a new source of tin. That seemed more unlikely with each league farther south we traveled. Wherever the sphinxes got the metal to harden their bronze, it was not there.

But we were there, and we were about to pay the price for it. I had put out sentries, though our folk are far from fond of being so forethoughtful. One of them cried, "The sphinxes! The sphinxes come!"

We had enough time to snatch up our weapons and form the roughest sort of line before they swarmed upon us like so many lions. They are smaller and swifter than we. We are stronger. Who is fiercer . . . Well, that is why they have battles: to find out who is fiercer.

Sometimes the sphinxes will not close with us at all, but content themselves with shooting arrows and dropping stones and screeching curses from afar. That day, though, they proved eager enough to fight. Our warbands seldom penetrate so far into their land. I suppose they thought to punish us for our arrogance—as if they have none of their own.

The riddle of the sphinxes is why, with their wings and fangs and talons, they do not rule far more of the land around the Inner Sea than in fact they hold. The answer to the riddle is simplicity itself: they are sphinxes, and so savage and vile and hateful they can seldom decide what to do next or make any other folk obey them save through force and fear. On the one hand, they hold the richest river valley the gods ever made. On the other, they could be so much more than they are. As well they do not see it themselves, I suppose.

But whether they see it or not, they had enough and to spare that day to send us home with our plumed tails hanging down in dismay. Along with their ferocity and their wings, their bronze weapons won the fight for them. Oreus practiced his philosophy, if you care to dignify it with such a word, when he hit one of the sphinxes' shields as hard as he could with his copper-headed axe. The metal that faced the shield was well laced with tin, and so much harder than the blade that smote it that the ax head bent to uselessness from the blow. Hit something hard enough and . . . This possibility had not entered into Oreus' calculations. Of course, Oreus is not one who can count above fourteen without polluting himself.

Which is not to say I was sorry he was part of our warband. On the contrary. The ax failing of the purpose for which it was intended, he hurled it in the startled sphinx's face. The sphinx yowled in pain and rage. Before it could do more than yowl, Oreus stood high on his hinder pair of legs and lashed out with his forehooves. Blood flew. The sphinx, screaming now rather than yammering, tried to take wing. He snatched it out of the air with his hands, threw it down, and trampled it in the dirt with all four feet.

"Who's next?" he cried, and none of the sphinxes had the nerve to challenge him.

Elsewhere in the field, though, we did not do so well. I would it were otherwise, but no. Before the day was even half done, we streamed north in full retreat, our hopes as dead as that lake of wildly salty water lying not far inland from where we were. The sphinxes pursued, jeering us on. I posted three hes beneath an overhanging rock, so they might not be easily seen from the air. They ambushed the sphinxes leading the chase as prettily as you might want. That, unfortunately, was a trick we could play only once, and one that salved the sore of our defeat without curing it.

When evening came, I took Oreus aside and said, "Now do you see why we need tin for our weapons?"

He nodded, his great chest heaving with the exertion of the fight and the long gallop afterwards and the shame he knew that that gallop had been away from the foe. "Aye, by the gods who made us, I do," he replied. "It is because I am too strong for copper alone."

I laughed. Despite the sting of a battle lost, I could not help laughing. "So you are, my dear," I said. "And what do you propose to do about that?"

He frowned. Thought never came easy for him. At length, he said, "We need tin, Cheiron, as you say. If I'm going to smash the sphinxes, we need tin." His thought might not have come easy, but it came straight.

I nodded. "You're right. We do. And where do you propose to get it?"

Again, he had to think. Again, he made heavy going of it. Again, he managed. "Well, we will not get it from the sphinxes. That's all too plain. They've got their supply, whatever it is, and they aren't about to give it up. Only one other place I can think of that has it."

"The Tin Isle?" I said.

Now he nodded. "The Tin Isle. I wonder what's become of it. We paid the folk there a pretty price for their miserable metal. Why don't their traders come down to us any more?"

"I don't know the answer to that, either," I said. "If we go there—and if the gods are kind—we'll find out, and bring home word along with the tin."

Oreus frowned at that. "And if the gods are unkind?"

With a shrug, I answered, "If the gods are unkind, we won't come back ourselves. It's a long way to the Tin Isle, with many strange folk between hither and yon." That only made Oreus snort and throw up his tail like a banner. He has his faults, does Oreus, and no one knows them better than I—certainly not he, for lack of self-knowledge is conspicuous among them—but only a fool would call him craven. I went on, "And whatever has befallen the folk who grub the tin from the ground may meet us, too."

His hands folded into fists. He made as if to rear, to stamp something into submission with his forehooves. But there was nothing he could smite. He scowled. He wanted to smash frustration, as he wants to smash everything. Another fault, without a doubt, but a brave fault, let it be said. "Anything that tries to befall me will rue the day," he declared. Idiocy and arrogance, you are thinking. No doubt. Yet somehow idiocy and arrogance of a sort that cheered me.

And so we built a ship, something centaurs seldom undertake. The *Chalcippus*, we named her—the *Horse of Bronze*. She was a big, sturdy craft, for centaurs are a big, sturdy folk. We need more space to hold enough rowers to drive a ship at a respectable turn of speed. Sphinxes, now, can pack themselves more tightly than we would dream of doing.

But the valley in which the sphinxes dwell has no timber

worth the name. They build their ships from bundled sheaves of papyrus plants. These strange vessels serve them well enough on their tame river, less so when they venture out onto the open waters of the Inner Sea.

We have fine timber in our country. The hills are green with pine and oak. We would have to cut and burn for years on end to despoil them of their trees. I do not like to think the dryads would ever thus be robbed of their homes. Not while the world remains as it is, I daresay, shall they be.

Once the wood was cut into boards and seasoned, we built the hull, joining planks edge to edge with mortise and tenon work and adding a skeleton of ribs at the end of the job for the sake of stiffening against the insults of wave and wind. We painted bright eyes, laughing eyes, at the bow that the ship might see her way through any danger, and the shes wove her a sail of linen they dyed a saffron the color of the sun.

Finding a crew was not the difficult matter I had feared it might be. Rather, my trouble was picking and choosing from among the swarm of hes who sought to sail in search of the Tin Isle. Had I not named Oreus among their number, I am sure he would have come after me with all the wild strength in him. Thus are feuds born. But choose him I did, and Hylaeus, and Nessus, and enough others to row the *Chalcippus* and to fight her: for I felt we would need to fight her before all was said and done.

Sail west to the mouth of the Inner Sea, then north along the coast of the strange lands fronting Ocean the Great—thus in reverse, it was said, the tin came down from the far northwest. What folk dwelt along much of the way, what dangers we would meet—well, why did we make the voyage, if not to learn such things?

Not long before we set out, Oreus sidled up to me. In a low voice, he said, "What do you think, Cheiron? On our travels, do you suppose we'll find—wine?" He whispered the last word.

Even if he had spoke more softly still, it would have been too loud. Wine is . . . Wine is the most wonderful poison in all the world, as any of us who have tasted it will attest. It is a madness, a fire, a delight beyond compare. I know nothing hes or shes would not do to possess it, and I know nothing they might not do after possessing it. As well we have never learned the secret of making the marvelous, deadly stuff for ourselves. Gods only know what might become of us if we could poison ourselves whenever and however we chose.

I said, "I know not. I do not want to find out. And I tell you this, Oreus: if you seek to sail on the *Horse of Bronze* for the sake of wine and not for the sake of tin, sail you shall not."

A flush climbed from where his torso rose above his forelegs all the way to the top of his head. "Not I, Cheiron. I swear it. Not I," he said. "But a he cannot keep from wondering. . . ."

"Well, may we all keep wondering through the whole of the voyage," I said. "I have known the madness of wine, known it and wish I had not. What we do when we have tasted of it—some I do not remember, and some I wish I did not remember. Past that, I will say no more."

"Neither will I, then," Oreus promised. But he did not promise to forget. I wish I could have forced such a vow from him, but the only thing worse than a promise broken is a promise made or forced that is certain to be broken.

We set out on a fine spring day, the sun shining down brightly from the sky. A wind off the hills filled my nostrils with the spicy fragrance of pines. It also filled the saffron sail, which pulled the *Horse of Bronze* across the wine-dark sea (an omen I should have taken, but I did not, I did not) fast enough to cut a creamy wake in the water.

The Inner Sea was calm. In spring and summer, the Inner Sea usually is. The *Chalcippus'* motion was as smooth and gentle as an easy trot across a meadow. This notwithstanding, several strong hes leaned over the rail and puked up their guts all the way to the horse in them. Some simply cannot take the sea, do what they will.

I am not one who suffers so. I stood at the stern, one hand on each steering oar. Another he called the stroke. He set the speed at my direction, but I did not have to do it myself. I was captain aboard the *Chalcippus*, yes, but among us he who leads must have a light hand, or those he presumes to lead will follow no more. Not all hes see this clearly, which is one reason we have been known—oh, yes, we have been known—to fight among ourselves.

But all was well when we first set out. The wind blew strongly, and from a favorable direction. We did not have to row long or row hard. But I wanted the hes to get some notion of what they would need to do later, if the wind faltered or if we fell in with enemies. They still reckoned rowing a sport and not a drudgery, and so they worked with a will. I knew that was liable to change as readily as the wind, but I made the most of it while it lasted.

Some of the hes muttered when we passed out of sight of land. "Are you foals again?" I called to them. "Do you think you will fall off the edge of the earth here in the middle of the Inner Sea? Wait till we are come to Ocean the Great. Then you will find something worth worrying about."

They went on muttering, but now they muttered at me. That I did not mind. I feared no mutiny, not yet. When I set my will against theirs in any serious way, then I would see. A captain who does not know when to let the crew grumble deserves all the trouble he finds, and he will find plenty.

Oreus came up to me when new land heaved itself up over the western horizon. "Is it true what they say about the folk of these foreign parts?" he asked. He was young, as I have said; the failed attack against the sphinxes had been his first time away from the homeland.

"They say all manner of things about the folk of foreign parts," I answered. "Some of them are true, some nothing but lies. The same happens when other folk speak of us."

He gestured impatiently. "You know what I mean. Is it true the folk hereabouts"—he pointed to the land ahead—"are cripples? Missing half their hindquarters?"

"The fauns? Cripples?" I laughed. "By the gods who made them, no! They are as they are supposed to be, and they'll run the legs off you if you give them half a chance. They're made like satyrs. They're half brute, even more so than satyrs, but that's how they work: torso and thinking head above, horse below."

"But only the back part of a horse?" he persisted. When I nodded, he gave back a shudder. "That's disgusting. I can stand it on goaty satyrs, because they're sort of like us only not really. But these faun things—it's like whoever made them couldn't wait to finish the job properly."

"Fauns are not mockeries of us. They are themselves. If you expect them to behave the way we do, you'll get a nasty surprise. If you expect them to act the way they really do, everything will be fine—as long as you keep an eye on them."

He did not like that. I had not expected that he would. But then, after what passed for reflection with him, he brightened. "If they give me a hard time, I'll bash them."

"Good," I said. It might not be good at all—it probably would not be good at all, but telling Oreus not to hit something was like telling the sun not to cross the sky. You could do it, but would he heed you?

I did not want to come ashore among the fauns at all. But rowing is thirsty work, and our water jars were low. And so, warily, with archers and spearers posted at the bow, I brought the *Chalcippus* toward the mouth of a little stream that ran down into the sea.

As I say, fauns are brutes. They scarcely know how to grow crops or work copper, let alone bronze. But a stone arrowhead will let the life out of a he as well as any other. If they gave us trouble, I wanted to be ready to fight or to trade or to run, whichever seemed the best idea at the time.

It turned out to be trade. Half a dozen fauns came upon us as we were filling the water jars—and, being hes on a lark, splashing one another in the stream like a herd of foals. The natives carried spears and arrows, which, sure enough, were tipped with chipped stone. Two of them also carried, on poles slung over their shoulders, the gutted carcass of a boar.

"Bread?" I called to them, and their faces brightened. They are so miserable and poor, they sometimes grind a mess of acorns up into flour. Real wheaten bread is something they seldom see. For less than it was worth, I soon got that lovely carcass aboard the *Horse of Bronze*. My crew would eat well tonight. Before we sailed, before the fauns slipped back into the woods, I found another question to ask them: "Are the sirens any worse than usual?"

They could understand my language, it being not too far removed from their own barbarous jargon. Their chief—I think that is what he was, at any rate; he was certainly the biggest and strongest of them—shook his head. "No worser," he said. "No better, neither. Sirens is sirens."

"True," I said, and wished it were a lie.

An island lies west of the land west of ours. Monsters haunt the strait between mainland and island: one that grabs with tentacles for ships sailing past, another that sucks in water and spits it out to make whirlpools that can pull you down to the bottom of the sea.

We slipped past them and down the east coast of the island. The gods' forge smoked, somewhere deep below the crust of the world. What a slag heap they have built up over the eons, too, so tall that snow still clings to it despite the smoke issuing from the vent.

The weather turned warm, and then warmer, and then hot. We stopped for water every day or two, and to hunt every now and again. There are fauns also on the island, which I had not known and would not have if we had not rushed by them while coursing after deer. Next to them, the fauns of the mainland are paragons of sophistication. I see no way to embarrass them more than to say that, yet they would not be embarrassed if they knew I said it. They would only take its truth for granted. They have not even the sophistication to regret that which is.

Maybe they were as they were because they knew no better. And maybe they were as they were because the sirens hunt them as we hunted that stag through the woods. We would not be as we are, either, not with sirens for near neighbors.

I wish we would have had nothing to do with them. What a he wishes and what the gods give him are all too often two different things. What the gods gave us was trouble. Hylaeus, Nessus, and I had just killed a deer and were butchering it when a siren came out of the woods and into the clearing where we worked. She stood there, watching us.

I have never seen a siren who was not a she. I have never heard of a siren who was a he. How there come to be more sirens is a mystery of the gods. The one we saw was quite enough.

In their features, sirens might be beautiful shes. Past that, though, there is nothing to them that would tempt the eye of even the most desperately urgent he. They are, not to put too fine a point on it, all over feathers, with arms that are half wings and with tail feathers in place of a proper horse's plume. Their legs are the scaly, skinny legs of a bird, with the grasping claws of a bird of prey.

But the eye is not the only gateway to the senses. The siren asked, "What are you doing here?" A simple question, and I had all I could do not to rear up on my hind legs and bellow out a challenge to the world.

Her voice was all honey and poppy juice, sweet and tempting at the same time. I looked at the other two hes. Hylaeus and Nessus were both staring back at me, as if certain I would try to cheat them out of what was rightfully theirs. They knew what they wanted, all right, and they did not care what they had to do to get it.

I glanced over at the siren. Her eyes had slit pupils, like a lion's. They got big and black as a lion's when it sights prey as she watched us. That put me on my guard, where maybe nothing else would have. "Careful, friends," I said. "She does not ask because she wishes us well." Roughly, I answered the siren: "Taking food for ourselves and our comrades."

By the way she eyed me, we had no need of food; we *were* food. She said, "But would you not rather share it with me instead?"

That voice! When she said something might be so, a he's first impulse was to do all he could to make it so. I had to work hard to ask the siren, "Why should we? What payment would you give us?"

I have lived a long time. One of the things this has let me do is make a great many mistakes. Try as I will, I have a hard time remembering a worse one. The siren smiled. She had a great many teeth. They all looked very long and very sharp. "What will I do?" she crooned. "Why, I will sing for you."

And she did. And why I am here to tell you how she sang . . . That is not so easy to explain. Some small beasts, you will know, lure their prey to them by seeming to be something the prey wants very much. There are spiders colored like flowers, but woe betide the bee or butterfly who takes one for a flower, for it will soon find itself seized and poisoned and devoured.

Thus it was with the siren's song. No she of the centaur folk could have sung so beautifully. I am convinced of it. A she of our own kind would have had many things on her mind as she sang: how much she cared about the hes who heard her, what she would do if she did lure one of them—perhaps one of them in particular—forward, and so on and so on.

The siren had no such . . . extraneous concerns. She wanted us for one thing and one thing only: flesh. And her song was designed on the pattern of a hunting snare, to bring food to her table. Any doubts, any second thoughts, that a she of our kind might have had were missing here. She drew us, and drew us, and drew us, and . . .

And, if one of us had been alone, she would have stocked centaur in her larder not long thereafter. But, in drawing Nessus and Hylaeus and me all with the same song, she spread her magic too thin to let it stick everywhere it needed to. Nessus it ensnared completely, Hylaeus perhaps a little less so, and me least of all. Why this should be, I cannot say with certainty. Perhaps it is simply because I have lived a very long time, and my blood does not burn so hotly as it did in years gone by.

Or perhaps it is that when Nessus made to strike at Hylaeus, reckoning him a rival for the charms of the sweetly singing feathered thing, the siren was for a moment distracted. And its distraction let me move further away from the snare it was setting. I came to myself, thinking, *Why do I so want to mate with a thing like this? I would crush it and split it asunder.*

That made me—or rather, let me—hear the siren's song with new ears, see the creature itself with new eyes. How eager it looked, how hungry! How those teeth glistened!

Before Nessus and Hylaeus could commence one of those fights that can leave a pair of hes both badly damaged, I kicked out at the siren. It was not my strongest blow. How could it be, when part of my blood still sang back to the creature? But it dislodged a few of those pearly feathers and brought the siren's song to a sudden, screeching stop.

Both my comrades jerked as if waking from a dream they did not wish to quit. They stared at the siren as if not believing their eyes. Perhaps, indeed, they did not believe their eyes, their ears having so befooled them. I kicked the siren again. This time, the blow landed more solidly. The siren's screech held more pain than startlement. More feathers flew.

Hylaeus and Nessus set on the siren then, too. They attacked with the fury of lovers betrayed. So, I daresay, they imagined themselves to be. The siren died shrieking under their hooves. Only feathers and blood seemed to be left when they were done. The thing was lighter and more delicately made than I would have thought; perhaps it truly was some sort of kin to the birds whose form and feathers it wore.

"Back to the ship, and quick!" I told the other two hes. "The whole island will be roused against us when they find out what happened here."

"What do you suppose it would have done if you hadn't given it a kick?" Hylaeus asked in an unwontedly small voice.

"Fed," I answered.

After that one-word reply, neither Hylaeus nor Nessus seemed much inclined to argue with me any more. They carried away the gutted stag at a thunderous gallop I had not thought they had in them. And they did not even ask me to help bear the carcass. As he ran, Nessus said, "What do we do if they start—singing at us again, Cheiron?"

"Only one thing I can think of," I told him.

We did that one thing, too: we took the *Horse of Bronze* well out to sea. Soon enough, the sirens gathered on the shore and began singing at us, began trying to lure us back to them so they could serve us as we had served one of them. And after they had served us thus, they would have served us on platters, if sirens are in the habit of using platters. On that last I know not, nor do I care whether I ever learn.

We could hear them, if only barely, so I ordered the hes to row us farther yet from the land. Some did not seem to want to obey. Most, though, would sooner listen to me than to those creatures. When we could hear nothing but the waves and the wind and our own panting, I had the whole crew in my hands once more.

But we had not altogether escaped our troubles. We could not leave the island behind without watering the ship once more. Doing it by day would have caused us more of the trouble we had escaped thus far by staying out of earshot of the sirens. For the creatures followed us along the coast. Had some foes come to our shores, slain one of our number, and then put to sea once more, I have no doubt we should have relentlessly hounded them. The sirens did the same for this fallen comrade of theirs. That she had tried to murder us mattered to them not at all. If they could avenge her, they would.

As the sun god drove his chariot into the sea ahead of us, I hoisted sail to make sure the sirens on the shore could see us. Then I swung the *Chalcippus'* bow away from the island and made as if to sail for the mainland lying southwest.

"You are mad," Oreus said. "We'll bake before we get there."

"I know that," I said, and held my course.

Oreus kept on complaining. Oreus always complains, especially when he cannot find something to trample, and not least because he never looks ahead. *It could be that he will learn one day*, I thought. *It could also be that he will never learn, in which case his days will be short.* To my sorrow, I have seen such things before, more often than I would wish.

A few of the other hes likewise grumbled. More, though, paid me no small compliment: they gave me credit for knowing what I was about. Now I had to prove I had earned their trust.

The sun set. Blue drowned pink and gold in the west. Black rose out of the east, drowning blue. Stars began to shine. There was no moon. Her boat would not sail across the sky until later. "Raise the sail to the yard, then lower the yard," I said, and pulled the steering oars so that the *Chalcippus* swung back to starboard.

"Very nice," said Nessus, who seemed to understand what I was doing.

"Is it? I wonder," I replied. "But we have need, and necessity is the master of us all." I raised my voice, but not too loud: "Feather your oars, you rowers. We want to go up to the shore as quietly as we can. Think of a wild cat in the forest stalking a squirrel."

At that, even Oreus understood my plan. He was loud in his praise of it. He was, as is his way, too cursed loud in his praise of it. Someone must have kicked him in the hock, for he fell silent very abruptly.

In the starlight, the sea was dark and glimmering. An owl hooted, somewhere on the land ahead. I took the call as a good omen. Perhaps the sirens did as well, the owl being like them a feathered hunting creature. I have never understood omens, not in fullness. I wonder if ever I shall, or if that lies in the hands of the gods alone.

From the bow came a hiss: "Cheiron! Here's a stream running out into the sea. This is what you want, eh?"

"Yes," I said. "This is just what I want." Few folk are active by night. Fewer still are active both day and night. I hoped we could nip in, fill our empty jars, and escape the sirens without their ever realizing we were about.

What I hoped for and what I got were two different things. Such is the way of life for those who are not gods. I have said as much before, I believe. Repeating oneself is a thing that happens to those who have lived as long and seen as much as I have. And if you believe I have troubles in this regard, you should hear some of the gods I have known. Or, better, you should not. A god will tell the same story a hundred times, and who that is not a god will presume to let him know what a bore he is making of himself? Only one of great courage or one of even greater foolishness, for gods are also quick to anger. And, however boring they may be, they are also powerful. Power, after all, is what makes them gods.

My hes scrambled out of the *Horse of Bronze*. They set to work in as sprightly a way as any captain could have wanted. But they had not yet finished when another owl hooted. As I have remarked, owls crying in the night are said to be birds of good omen, but not this one, for his cries alerted the sirens. I *do* not understand omens. I have said that before, too, have I not?

The sirens rushed towards us, fluttering their winglike arms and then—far more dangerous—commencing to sing. For a bad moment, I thought they would instantly ensorcel all of us, dragging us down to doleful destruction. But then, as if a god—not, for once, a boring god—had whispered in my ear, I called out to my fellow hes: "Shout! Shout for your lives! If you hear yourselves, you will not hear the sirens! Shout! With all the strength that is in you, shout!"

And they did—only a few of them at first, but then more and more as their deep bellow drowned out the sirens' honeyed voices and released other hes from their enchantment. Shouting like mad things, we rushed at the sirens, and they broke and fled before us. Now they did not sing seductively, but squalled out their dismay. And well they might have, for we trod more than one under our hooves, and suffered but a few bites and scratches in the unequal battle.

"Back to the ship," I said then. "We have done what we came to do, and more besides. The faster we get away now, the better."

Those sirens had nerve. They could not close with us, but they tried to sing us back to them as we rowed away. But we kept on shouting, and so their songs went for naught. We pulled out to sea, until we were far enough from land to hear them no more.

"That was neatly done, Cheiron," Oreus said, as if praise from him were what I most sought in life.

Well, this once maybe he was not so far wrong. "I thank you," I said, and let out the long, weary sigh I had held in for too long. "I wonder what other things we shall have to do neatly between here and the Tin Isle—and when we have got there, and on the way home."

We were not tested again until we left the Inner Sea and came out upon the heaving bosom of Ocean the Great. Heave that bosom did. Anyone who has sailed on the Inner Sea will have known storms. He will have known them, yes, but as interludes between longer stretches of calm weather and good sailing. On the Ocean, this business is reversed. Calms there are, but the waters more often toss and turn like a restless sleeper. Sail too close to land and you will be cast up onto it, as would never happen in the calmer seas our ships usually frequent.

The day after we began our sail upon Ocean the Great, we beached ourselves at sunset, as we almost always did at nightfall on the Inner Sea. When the sun god drove his chariot into the water, I wondered how he hoped to return come morning, for

Ocean seemed to stretch on to westward forever, with no land to be seen out to the edge of the world. I hoped we would not sail out far enough to fall off that edge, which had to be there somewhere.

But for our sentries, we slept after supping, for the work had been hard—harder than usual, on those rough waters. And the sentries, of course, faced inland, guarding us against whatever strange folk dwelt in that unknown land. They did not think to look in the other direction, but when we awoke *someone had stolen the sea.*

I stared in consternation at the waters of Ocean the Great, which lay some cubits below the level at which we had beached the *Chalcippus*. I wondered if a mad god had tried to drink the seabed dry through a great rhyton and had come closer than he knew to success.

We tried pushing the ship back into the sea, but to no avail: she was stuck fast. I stood there, wondering what to do. What *could* we do? Nothing. I knew it all too well.

As the sun rose higher in the east, though, the sea gradually returned, until we were able to float the *Horse of Bronze* and sail away as if nothing had happened. It seemed nothing had—except to my bowels, when I imagined us trapped forever on that unknown shore. Little by little, we learned Ocean the Great had a habit of advancing and withdrawing along the edge of the land, a habit the Inner Sea fortunately fails to share. Ocean is Ocean. He does as he pleases.

Here we did not go out of sight of land, not at all. Who could guess what might happen to us if we did? Better not to find out. We crawled along the coast, which ran, generally speaking, north and east. Were we the first centaurs to see those lands, to sail those waters? I cannot prove it, but I believe we were.

We did not see other ships. Even on the Inner Sea, ships are scarce. Here on the unstable waters of Ocean the Great, they are scarcer still. And Ocean's waters proved unstable in another way as well. The farther north we sailed, the cooler and grayer they grew—and also the wilder. Had we not built well, the *Horse of Bronze* would have broken her back, leaving us nothing but strange bones to be cast up on an alien shore. But the ship endured, and so did we.

We had thought to travel from island to island on our way to the Tin Isle. But islands proved few and far between on the Ocean. We did sail past one, not long before coming to the Tin Isle, from which small cattle whose roan coats were half hidden by strange tunics—I know no better word—stared out at us with large, brown, incurious eyes.

Some of the sailors, hungry for meat, wanted to put ashore there and slaughter them. I told them no. "We go on," I said. "They may be sacred to a god—those garments they wear argue for it. Remember the Cattle of the Sun? Look what disaster would befall anyone who dared raise a hand against them. And these may not be cattle at all; they may be folk in the shape of cattle. Who can say for certain, in these strange lands? But that is another reason they might be clothed. Better we leave them alone."

And so we sailed on, and entered the sleeve of water separating the Tin Isle from the mainland. That was the roughest travel we had had yet. More than a few of us clung to the rail, puking till we wished we were dead. Had the day not been bright and clear, showing us the shape of the Tin Isle blue in the distance, we might have had to turn back, despairing of making headway against such seas. But we persevered, and eventually made landfall.

Oreus said, "Like as not, Ocean will steal the ship when our backs are turned. What would we do then, Cheiron?"

"Build another," I answered. "Or would you rather live in this gods-forsaken place the rest of your days?"

Oreus shivered and shook his head. I did not know, not then, how close I came to being right.

Something was badly amiss in the Tin Isle. That I realized not long after we landed there and made our way inland. The Isle proved a bigger place than I had thought when setting out. Simply landing on the coast did not necessarily put us close to the mines from which the vital tin came.

The countryside was lovely, though very different from that around the Inner Sea. Even the sky was strange, ever full of fogs and mists and drizzles. When the sun did appear, it could not bring out more than a watery blue in the dome of heaven. The sun I am used to will strike a centaur dead if he stays out in it too long. It will burn his hide, or the parts of it that are not hairy. Not so on those distant shores. I do not know why the power of the sun god is so attenuated thereabouts, but I know that it is.

Because of the fogs and mists and the endless drizzle, the landscape seemed unnaturally—indeed, almost supernaturally—green. Grass and ferns and shrubs and trees grew in such profusion as I have never seen in all my days. Not even after the wettest winter will our homeland look so marvelously lush. High summer being so cool in those parts, however, I did wonder what winter might be like.

Hard winters or no, though, it was splendid country. A he could break the ground with his hoof and something would grow there. But no one and nothing appeared to have broken the ground any time lately. That was the puzzlement: the land might as well have been empty, and it should not have been.

I knew the names of the folk said to dwell in those parts: piskies and spriggans and especially nuggies, who were said to dig metal from the ground. Those names had come to the Inner Sea along with the hide-wrapped pigs of tin that gave this land its fame there. What manner of folk these might be, though, I could not have said—nor, I believe, could anyone from my part of the world. I had looked forward to finding out. That would have been a tale to tell for many long years to come.

It would have been—but the folk did not come forth. I began to wonder if they *could* come forth, or if some dreadful fate had overwhelmed them. But even if they had been conquered and destroyed, whatever folk had defeated them should have been in evidence. No one was.

"We should have brought shes with us and settled here," Nessus said one day. "We'd have the land to ourselves."

"Would we?" I looked about. "It does seem so, I grant you, but something tells me we would get little joy from it."

Oreus looked about, too, more in bewilderment than anything else. Then he said one of the few things I have ever heard him say with which I could not disagree, either then or later: "If the folk are gone out of the land, no wonder the tin's stopped coming down to the Inner Sea."

"No wonder at all," I said. "Now, though, we have another question." Confusion flowed across his face until I posed it: "*Why* have the folk gone from this land?"

"Sickness?" Nessus suggested. I let the word lie there, not caring to pick it up. It struck me as unlikely, in any case. Most folk are of sturdy constitution. We die, but we do not die easily. I had trouble imagining a sickness that could empty a whole countryside.

Then Oreus said his second sensible thing in a row. Truly this was a remarkable day. "Maybe," he said, "maybe their gods grew angry at them, or tired of them."

A cool breeze blew down from the north. I remember that very well. And I remember wondering whether it was but a breeze, or whether it was the breath of some god either angry or tired. "If

279

that be so," I said, "if that be so, then we will not take tin back to the Inner Sea, and so I shall hope it is not so."

"What if it is?" Nessus asked nervously, and I realized I was not the only one wondering if I felt a god's breath.

I thought for a moment. With that breeze blowing, thought did not come easily, and the moment stretched longer than I wished it would have. At last, I said, "In that case, my friend, we will do well enough to go home ourselves, don't you think?"

"Do our gods see us when we are in this far country?" Oreus asked.

I did not know the answer to that, not with certainty. But I pointed up to the sun, which, fortunately, the clouds and mist did not altogether obscure at that moment. "He shines here, too," I replied. "Do you not think he will watch over us as he does there?"

That should have steadied him. But such was the empty silence of that countryside that he answered only, "I hope so," in tones suggesting that, while he might hope, he did not believe.

Two days—or rather, two nights—later, a nuggy came into our camp. I would not have known him from a piskie or a spriggan, but a nuggy he declared himself to be. I had sentries out around our fires, but he appeared in our midst without their being any the wiser. I believe he tunneled up from under the ground.

He looked like one who had seen much hardship in his time. I later learned from him that was the true aspect of nuggies, but he owned he had it more than most. He was ill-favored, a withered, dried-up creature with a face as hard and sharp as an outcropping of flint. In other circumstances, his tiny size might have made it hard for me to take him seriously; he was no larger in the head and torso than one of us would have been at two years, and had only little bandy legs below, though his arms were, in proportion to the rest of him, large and considerably muscled.

His name, he said, was Bucca. I understood him with difficulty. We did not speak the same language, he and I, but our two tongues held enough words in common to let us pass meaning back and forth. His rocky face worked with some mixture of strong emotion when he came before me. "Gods be praised!" he said, or something much like that. "Old Bucca's not left all alone in the dark!" And he began to weep, a terrible thing to see.

"Here, now. Here, now," I said. I gave him meat and bread. Had we had wine, I would have given him that as well. But for us to carry wine would have been like stags carrying fire with which to roast them once they were slain.

He ate greedily, and without much regard for manners. Though he was so small, he put away a startling amount. Grease shone on his thin lips and his chin when he tossed aside a last bone and said, "I hoped some folk would come when the tin stopped. I prayed some folk would come. But for long and long, no folk came. I drew near to losing hope." More tears slid down the cliffsides of his cheeks.

"Here now," I said again, wanting to embrace him yet fearing I would offend if I did. Only when he came over and clung to my foreleg did I take him up in my arms and hold his small chest against my broad one. He was warm and surprisingly hard; his arms, as they embraced me, held even more strength than I would have guessed. At last, when he seemed somewhat eased, I thought I could ask him, "Why did the tin stop?"

He stared at me, our two faces not far apart. Moonlight and astonishment filled his pale eyes. "You know not?" he whispered.

"That is the truth: I know not," I replied. "That is why I came so far, that is why we all came so far, in the *Horse of Bronze*—to learn why precious tin comes no more to the Inner Sea."

"Why?" Bucca said. "I will tell you why. Because most of us are dead, that is why. Because where *they* are, we cannot live."

I did not believe all Bucca told me. If I am to speak the whole truth here, I did not want to believe what the nuggy told me. And so, not believing, I told a party of hes to come with me so that we might see for ourselves what truth lay in his words—or rather, as I thought of it, so that we might see he was lying.

"You big things are bold and brave," Bucca said as we made ready to trot away. "You will have grief of it. I am no bolder or braver than I have to be, and already I have known griefs uncounted."

"I grieve for your grief," I told him. "I grieve for your grief, but I think things will go better for us."

"It could be," Bucca replied. "Yes, it could be. You big things still believe in yourselves, or so it seems. We nuggies did not, not after a while. And when we did not believe, and when *they* did not believe . . . we died."

"How is it that you are left alive, then?" I asked him. This question had burned in my mind since the night when he first appeared amongst us, though I had not had the heart to ask him then. Now, though, it seemed I might need the answer, if answer there was.

But Bucca only shrugged those surprisingly broad shoulders of his. "I think I am too stubborn to know I should be dead."

That, then, meant nothing to me. I have learned more since than I once knew, however. Even then, I wanted nothing more than to get away from the nuggy. And away we went, rambling east into one of the more glorious mornings the gods ever made.

It was cool. It was always cool on the Tin Isle, except when it was downright cold. A little mist clung to the hillsides. The sun had trouble burning it off. This too is a commonplace of that country. But oh! the greens in that northern clime! Yes, I say it again. Nothing round the Inner Sea can match them, especially not in summertime. And those hills were not stark and jagged, as are the hills we know, but smooth and round, some of them, as a she's breast. The plains are broad, and roll gently. Their soil puts to shame what goes by that name in our land. Yet it grew no wheat or barley, only grass. Indeed, this might have been a countryside forever without folk.

As we trotted east, we left the hills behind us. The plain stretched out ahead, far broader than any in our own homeland. But only a cold, lonely wind sighed across it. "Plague take me if I like this place," Oreus said.

"We need not like it," I answered. "We need but cross it."

Though I might say such things to Oreus, before long the stillness came to oppress me, too. I began to have the feeling about this plain that one might have about a centaurs' paddock where no one happens to be at a particular time: that the folk are but gone for a moment, and will soon return. About the paddock, one having such a feeling is generally right. About this plain, I thought otherwise.

There I proved mistaken.

I found—the entire band of hes found—I was mistaken some little while before actually realizing as much. We hurried through the tall grass of the plain, making better time than we had before, and did not think to wonder why until Hylaeus looked down and exclaimed in sudden, foolish-sounding surprise: "We are following a trail."

All of us stopped then, staring in surprise at the ground under our hooves. Hylaeus was quite correct, even if we had not noticed up until that time. The earth was well trodden down, the grass quite sparse, especially compared to its rich lushness elsewhere.

Nessus asked the question uppermost in all our minds: "Who made it?"

What he meant was, had the trail survived from the days when folk filled this land—days Bucca recalled with fond nostalgia—or was it new, the product of whatever had driven the nuggies and so many other folk to ruin? One obvious way to find the answer crossed my mind. I asked, "How long has it been since any but ourselves walked this way?"

We studied the ground again. A trail, once formed, may last a very long time; the ground, pounded hard under feet or hooves, will keep that hardness year after year. Grass will not thrive there, not when it can find so many easier places close by to grow. And yet . . .

"I do not think this trail is ancient," Hylaeus said. "It shows too much wear to make that likely."

"So it also seems to me," I said, and waiting, hoping someone—anyone—would contradict me. No one did. I had to go on, then: "This means we may soon learn how much of the truth Bucca was telling."

"It means we had better watch out," Nessus said, and who could tell him he was wrong, either?

But for the trail, though, the land continued to seem empty of anything larger than jackdaws and rooks. It stretched on for what might have been forever, wide and green and rolling. Strange how the Tin Isle should show a broader horizon than my own home country, which, although part of the mainland, is much divided by bays and mountains and steep valleys.

There were valleys in this country, too, but they were not like the ones I knew at home, some of which are sharp enough at the bottom to cut yourself on if you are not careful. The valleys that shaped this plain were low and gently sloping. The rivers in them ran in the summertime, when many of the streams in my part of the world go dry.

And I will tell you something else, something even odder.

While we were traveling across that plain, black clouds rolled across the sun. A cold wind from the north began to blow. Rain poured down from the sky, as if from a bucket. Yes, I tell you the truth, no matter how strange it might seem. I saw hard rain—not the drizzle and fogs we had known before—in summertime, when all around the Inner Sea a lizard will cook if it ventures out in the noonday sun. By the gods, it is so.

Truly I was a long way from home.

"Is it natural?" Hylaeus asked, rain dripping from his nose and the tip of his beard and the tip of his tail till he flicked it about, at which point raindrops flew from it in all directions. "Can such a thing be natural?"

"Never!" Oreus said. His tail did not flick. It lashed, back and forth, back and forth, as if it had a life of its own. "This surely must be some evil sorcery raised against us. Perhaps it is akin to whatever caused the nuggies to fail."

"I think you may be mistaken," I told him. He glared at me—until a raindrop hit him in the eye, at which point he blinked, tossed his head, and spluttered. I went on, "Look how green the land is all around us," emphasizing my words with a broad wave of my arm. "Could it be what it is unless rain came down now and again—or more than now and again—in the summertime to keep it so?"

Oreus only grunted. Nessus considered the greenery and said, "I think Cheiron may be right."

"Whether he is or not, we'll be squelching through mud if this goes on much longer." As if to prove Oreus' point, his hoof splashed in a puddle—a puddle that surely had not been there before the rain began.

The hard-packed trail helped more than somewhat, for it did not go to muck nearly so fast as the looser-soiled land to either side. We could go on, if not at our best clip, while the rain continued.

Little by little, the steady downpour eased off to scattered showers. The wind shifted from north to east and began to blow away some of the clouds. When we forded a stream, we paused to wash ourselves. I was by then muddy almost all the way up to my belly, and my comrades no cleaner. Washing, though, proved a business that tested my hardiness, for the stream, like every stream I encountered in the Tin Isle, ran bitterly cold.

In a halfhearted way, the sun tried to come out once more. I was glad of that. Standing under it, even if it seemed but a pale imitation of the blazing disk of light I had known around the Inner Sea, helped dry the water clinging to my coat of hair and also helped give me back at least a little warmth.

I was, then, reluctant to leave the valley in which that stream lay, and all the more so since it was rather deeper and steeper than most of the rest in the plain. "No help for it, Cheiron," said Hylaeus, who of the other hes had the most sympathy for my weariness.

"No, I suppose not," I said sadly, and set my old bones to moving once more. Some of the other centaurs went up the eastern slope of the valley at a pace no better than mine. Oreus, on the other hand, was filled with the fiery impetuosity of youth, and climbed it at the next thing to a gallop. I expected him to charge across the flat land ahead and then come trotting back to mock the rest of us for a pack of lazy good-for-nothings.

I expected that, but I was wrong. Instead, he stopped in his tracks at the very lip of the valley, which stood somewhat higher than the western slope. He stopped, he began to rear in surprise or some other strong emotion, and then he stood stock-still, as if turned to stone by a Gorgon's appalling countenance, his right arm outstretched and pointing ahead.

"What is it?" I called grumpily. I had no great enthusiasm for rushing up there to gape at whatever had seized foolish Oreus' fancy.

286

But he did not answer me. He simply stood where he was and kept on pointing. I slogged up the slope, resolved to kick him in the rump for making such a nuisance of himself.

When at last I reached him, my resolve died. Before I could turn and lash out with my hind feet, my eyes followed his index finger. And then, like him, I could do nothing for long, long moments but stare and stare and stare.

How long I stood there, I am not prepared to say. As long as the wonder ahead deserved? I doubt it, else I might be standing there yet.

The great stone circle loomed up out of nothing, there on the windswept plain. Even in summertime, that wind was far from warm, but it was not the only thing that chilled me. I am not ashamed to say I was awed. I was, in fact, amazed, wondering how and why such a huge thing came to be, and what folk could have raised it.

The sphinxes brag of the monuments they have built, there beside their great river. I have never seen them, not with my own eyes. Centaurs who have visited their country say the image of one of their own kind and the enormous stone piles nearby are astonishing. But the sphinxes, as I have said, dwell in what must be the richest country any gods ever made. This . . . this stood in the middle of what I can best describe as nothing. And the sphinxes had the advantage of their river to haul stone from quarries to where they wanted it. No rivers suitable for the job here. And these blocks of stone, especially the largest in the center of the circle, the ones arranged in a pattern not much different from the outline of my hoof, were, I daresay, larger than any the sphinxes used.

Some of this—much of this, in fact—I learned later. For the

time being, I was simply stunned. So were we all, as we came up the side of the valley one after another to stare at the amazing circle. We might have been under a spell, a spell that kept us from going on and bid far to turn us to stone ourselves.

Brash Oreus, who had first seen the circle of standing stones, was also the one who broke that spell, if spell it was. Sounding at that moment not at all brash, he said, "I must see more." He cantered forward: an oddly stylized gait, and one that showed, I think, how truly impressed he was.

Seeing him move helped free me from the paralysis that had seized me. I too went toward the stone circle, though not at Oreus' ceremonial prance.

As I drew closer, the wind grew colder. Birds flew up from the circle, surprised and frightened that anyone should dare approach. "Chaka-chaka-chak!" they called, and by their cries I knew them for jackdaws.

I do not believe I have ever seen stonework so fresh before. The uprights and the stones that topped them might have been carved only moments before. No lichen clung to them, and I had seen it mottling boulders in the plain. Hylaeus noted the same thing at almost the same time. Pointing ahead as Oreus had done before, he said, "Those stones could have gone up yesterday."

"Yesterday," I agreed, "or surely within the past few years." And all at once, a chill colder even than the breeze pierced me to the root. That was the time in which the tin failed.

Again, Hylaeus was not far behind me. "This is a new thing," he said slowly. "The passing of the folk of the Tin Isle is a new thing, too."

"Chaka-chaka-chak!" the jackdaws screeched. Suddenly, they might have been to my mind carrion crows, of which I had also seen more than a few. And on what carrion had those crows, and the jackdaws, and the bare-faced rooks, and the ravens, on what carrion had they feasted? The wind seemed colder yet, wailing out of the north as if the ice our bones remember lay just over the horizon. But the ice I felt came as much from within me as from without.

Oreus said, "Who made this circle, then, and why? Is it a place of magic?"

Nessus laughed at that, even if the wind blew his mirth away. "Could it be anything but a place of magic? Would any folk labor so long and so hard if they expected nothing in return?"

Not even quarrelsome Oreus could contend against such reasoning. I shivered yet again. Magic is a curious business. Some folk choose to believe they can compel their gods to do their bidding by one means or another, rather than petitioning them in humble piety. What is stranger still is that some gods choose to believe they can be so compelled—at least for a while. Sometimes, later, they remember they are gods, and then no magic in the world can check them. Sometimes . . . but perhaps not always.

I looked at the stone circle again, this time through new eyes. Centaurs have little to do with magic, nor have we ever; it appears to be a thing contrary to our nature. But I believed Nessus had the right of it. Endless labor had gone into this thing. No one would be so daft as to expend such labor without the hope of some reward springing from it.

What sort of reward? Slowly, I said, "If the other folk of the Tin Isle fail, who will take the land? Who will take the mines?"

Once more, I eyed the stone circle, the uprights capped with a continuous ring of lintel stones, the five bigger trilithons set in the hoof-shaped pattern within. Of itself, my hand tightened on the copper-headed spear I bore. I thought I could see an answer to that. Had much power sprung from all this labor?

Chip, chip, chip. I turned at the sound of stone striking stone. Oreus had found a hard shard and was smacking away at one of the uprights. Before I could ask him what he was about, Nessus beat me to it.

"What am I doing? Showing we were here," Oreus answered, and went on chipping.

After watching him for a while, I saw the shape he was making, and I could not help but smile. He was pounding into that great standing stone the image of one of our daggers, broad at the base of the blade and with hardly any quillons at all. When he had finished that, he began another bit of carving beside it: an ax head.

"Not only have you shown we were here, but also for what reason we came to the Tin Isle," I said. Oreus nodded and continued with his work.

He had just finished when one of our hes let out a wordless cry of warning. The centaur pointed north, straight into the teeth of that wind. As I had with Oreus' before, I followed that outflung, pointing arm. There coming towards us were the ones who, surely, had shaped the circle of standing stones.

If dogs had gods, those they worshiped would wag their tails and bark. If sheep had gods, they would follow woolly deities who grazed. As the world is, almost all folk have many things in common, as if the gods who shaped them were using certain parts of a pattern over and over again.

Think on it. You will find it holds much truth. Centaurs and sirens and sphinxes and fauns and satyrs all have faces of an essential similarity. Nor were our features so much different from those of Bucca the nuggy on this distant shore. The differences, such as they are, are those of degree, not of kind.

Again, hands are much alike from one folk to another. How could it be otherwise, when we all must grasp tools and manipulate them? Arms are also broadly similar, one to another, save when a folk needs must use them for flying. Even torsos have broad likenesses amongst us, satyrs and fauns, nuggies, and, to a lesser extent, sirens as well.

The folk striding towards us through the green, green grass might have been the pattern itself, the pattern from whose rearranged pieces the rest of us had been clumsily reassembled. As bronze, which had brought us here, is an alloy of copper and tin, so I saw that sirens were an alloy of these folk and birds, sphinxes of them and birds and lions, satyrs of them and goats, fauns of them and horses. And I saw that we centaurs blended these folk and horses as well, though in different proportions, as one bronze will differ from another depending on how much is copper and how much tin.

Is it any wonder, then, that, on seeing this folk, I at once began to wonder if I had any true right to exist?

And I began to understand what Bucca meant. As a nuggy, he was no doubt perfectly respectable. Next to these new ones, he was a small, wrinkled, ugly *thing*. Any of us, comparing ourselves to them, would have felt the same. How could we help it? We were a mixture. They were the essence with which our other parts were mixed. They might have been so many gods approaching us.

Nessus shivered. It might have been that cutting wind. It might have been, but it was not. "When I look at them, I see my own end," he murmured.

Because I felt the same way, I also felt an obligation to deny it. "They are bound to be as surprised by us as we are by them," I said. "If we have never seen their kind, likewise they have never seen ours. So long as we keep up a bold front, they will know nothing of . . . whatever else we may feel."

"Well said, Cheiron," Hylaeus told me. Whether it would likewise be well done remained to be seen.

"I will go forward with two others, so they may see we come in peace," I said. "Who will come with me?" Hylaeus and Oreus both strode forward, and I was glad to have them (gladder, perhaps, of the one than the other). The reason I offered was plausible, but it was not the only one I had. If I went forward with only two bold companions, the new folk would have more trouble noticing how so many of my hes wavered at the mere sight of them.

We three slowly went out ahead of the rest of the band. When we did, the strangers stopped for a moment. Then they also sent three of their number forward. They walked so straight, so free, so erect. Their gait was so *natural*. It made that of fauns or satyrs seem but a clumsy makeshift.

Two of them carried spears, one a fine leaf-shaped sword of bronze. The one with the sword, the tallest of them, sheathed his weapon. The other two trailed their spears on the ground. They did not want a fight, not then. We also showed we were not there to offer battle.

"Can you understand me?" I called.

Their leader frowned. "Can you understand *me*?" he called back in a tongue not far removed from the one Bucca used. I could, though it was not easy. I gather my language was as strange in his ears.

"Who are you? What is your folk?" I asked him, and, pointing back toward the stone circle, "What is this place?"

"I am Geraint," he answered. "I am a man"—a word I had not heard before. He looked at my companions and me. "I will ask you the same questions, and where you are from, and why you have come here."

I told him who I was, and named my kind as well. He listened attentively, his eyes—eyes gray as the seas thereabouts—alert. And I told him of our desire for tin, and of how we had come from the lands around the Inner Sea to seek it.

He heard me out. He had a cold courtesy much in keeping with that windswept plain. When I had finished, he threw back his head and laughed.

If I needed it, I could have brought up my ax very quickly. "Do you think I jest?" I asked. "Or do you aim to insult me? If you want a quarrel, I am sure we can oblige you."

Geraint shook his head. "Neither, although we will give you all the fight you care for if that is what you want. No, I am laughing because it turns out those funny little digging things were right after all."

"You mean the nuggies?" I asked.

Now he nodded. "Yes, them," he said indifferently. "I thought they dug because they were things that had to dig. But there really is a market for tin in this far corner of the world that has none of its own?"

"There is," I said. "We have trade goods back at the *Horse of Bronze*, our ship. We will pay well."

"Will you?" He eyed me in a way I had never seen before: as if I had no right to exist, as if my standing there on four hooves speaking of trade were an affront of the deadliest sort. Worse was that, when I looked into those oceanic eyes, I more than half believed it myself.

Oreus, always quick to catch a slight, saw this perhaps even before I did. "I wonder if this man-thing has any blood inside it, or only juice like a gourd," he said.

Geraint should not have been able to follow that. He should not have, but he did. His eyes widened, this time in genuine surprise. "You are stronger than the nuggies," he said. "Do any of them yet live?"

"Yes," I said, not mentioning that we had seen only Bucca. "Will you trade tin with us? If not, we will try to mine it ourselves." I did not look forward to that. We had not the skills, and the nuggies' shafts would not be easy for folk with our bulk to negotiate.

But Geraint said, "We will trade. What do you offer?"

"We will trade what we have always sent north in exchange for tin," I answered. "We will give you jewelry of gold and precious stones. We will give olive oil, which cannot be made here. We will give wheat flour, for fine white bread. Wheat gives far better bread than barley, but, like the olive, it does not thrive in this northern clime." I was sure the olive would not grow here. I was less sure about wheat, but Geraint did not need to know that.

"Have you wine?" Geraint asked. "If you have wine, you may be sure we will make a bargain. Truly wine is the blood of the gods." The mans with him nodded.

"We have no wine," I said. "We did not bring any, for it is not to the nuggies' taste." That was true, but it was far from the only reason we had no wine. I said not a word of any other reasons. If Geraint wanted to ferret out our weaknesses, he was welcome to do so on his own. I would not hand them to him on a platter.

I wondered what weaknesses the mans had. Seeing him there, straight and erect and godlike in his all-of-one-pieceness, I wondered if mans had any weaknesses. Surely they did. What those weaknesses might be, though, I had no idea. Even now, I am less certain of them than I wish I were.

I said, "You must leave off killing the nuggies who grub the tin from the ground. They have done you no harm. That will be part of the bargain."

One of the mans with Geraint did not understand that. He repeated it in their language, which I could follow only in part. I did not think he turned it into a joke or a bit of mockery, but the mans laughed and laughed as if it were the funniest thing in the world.

To me, he said, "You misunderstand. We did not kill the nug-gies and the other folk hereabouts. They see us, and then they commonly die."

"Of what?" I asked.

He told me. I was not sure I followed him, and so I asked him to say it again. He did: "Of embarrassment."

I refused to show him how much that chilled me. These mans embarrassed me, too, merely by their existence. I thought of Bucca, who was somehow tougher than his fellows. I wondered who among us might have such toughness. I was not sorry these mans dwelt so far from our homeland.

Another question occurred to me: "Did you make this great stone circle?"

"We did," Geraint answered.

"Why?" I asked.

I thought he would speak to me of the gods these mans worshiped, and of how those gods had commanded his folk to make the circle for some purpose of their own. I would not have been surprised that he and the other mans had no idea what the purpose was. That is often the way of gods: to keep those who reverence them guessing, that they themselves might seem the stronger. And I would not have been surprised to hear him say right out that the purpose of the circle was to bring a bane down upon the other folk dwelling in those parts.

But he answered in neither of those ways. And yet his words *did* surprise me, for he said, "We raised this circle to study the mo-tions of the sun and moon and stars."

"To study their motions?" I frowned, wondering if I had heard rightly and if I had understood what I heard.

Geraint nodded. "That is what I said, yes."

I scratched my head. "But . . . why?" I asked. "Can you hope to change them?"

He laughed at that. "No, of course not. Their motions are as the gods made them."

"True," I said, relieved he saw that much. These mans were so strange, and so full of themselves, he might easily have believed otherwise. "This being so, then, what is the point of, ah, studying these motions?"

"To know them better," Geraint replied, as if talking to a fool or a foal.

For all his scorn, I remained bewildered. "But what good will knowing them better do you?" I asked.

"I cannot tell you. But knowledge is always worth the having." Geraint spoke with great conviction. I wondered why. No sooner had I wondered than he tried to explain, saying, "How do you know you need tin to help harden copper into bronze? There must have been a time when folk did not know it. Someone must have learned it and taught it to others. There must have been a time when folk did not know of wonderful wine, either, or of this fine wheat flour you brag you have brought to trade. Someone must have learned of them."

His words frightened me more even than his appearance. He carved a hole in the center of the world. Worse yet, he knew not what he did. I said, "Assuredly the gods taught us these things."

His laugh might have been the embodiment of the cold wind blowing across that cold plain. "No doubt the gods set the world in motion," he said, "but is it not for us to find out what rules they used when they did it?"

"Gods need no rules. That is why they are gods," I said.

"There are always rules." Geraint sounded as certain as I was. "At the winter solstice, the sun always rises in the same place." He pointed to show where. "At the summer solstice, in another place, once more the same from year to year." He pointed again. "The moon likewise has its laws, though they are subtler. Why, even eclipses have laws."

He was mad, of course, but he sounded very sure of himself. Everyone knows eclipses show the gods are angry with those whose lands they darken. What else could an eclipse be but the anger of the gods? Nothing, plainly. Quarreling with a lunatic is always a risky business, and all the more so in his own country. I did not try it. Instead, I answered, "Let it be as you say, friend. Will you come back to the *Horse of Bronze* and trade tin for our goods?"

"I will," he answered, and then smiled a very unpleasant smile. "We are many in this land—more all the time. You are few, and no more of your kind will come any time soon. Why should we not simply take what we want from you?"

"For one thing, we would fight you, and many of your hes would die," I said. "I do not deny you would win in the end, but it would cost you dear. And if you rob us and kill us, no more of our folk will come to this shore. You will have one triumph, not steady trade. Which do you want more?"

The man thought it over. By his expression, he had never before had to weigh such considerations. I wondered whether one orgy of slaughter *would* count for more with him than years of steady dealing. Some folk care nothing for the future. It might as well not be real to them. Were Geraint and his kind of that sort? If so, all we could do was sell ourselves as dear as possible.

In due course, he decided. "You have given me a thought of weight, Cheiron," he said. He pronounced my name oddly. No doubt his in my mouth was not fully to his liking, either. Our languages were close cousins, but not quite brothers. He went on, "Trade is better. Robbery is easier and more fun, but trade is better. Our grandsons and their grandsons can go on trading if we do well here."

"Just so," I said, pleased he could look past himself. Maybe all his talk of rules, rules even in the heavens, had something to do with it. "Aye, just so. Come back to the ship, then, and we shall see what sort of bargains we may shape."

We clasped hands, he and I. Though his body could not match mine for speed, his grip was strong. He and his followers turned and went off toward the rest of the mans, who were waiting for them. Oreus and Hylaeus and I trotted back to our fellow centaurs. "It is agreed," I called. "We will trade. All is well."

A jackdaw flew up from the stone circle. "Chaka-chaka-chak!" it cried. It seemed as if it was laughing at me. What a fool I was, to let a little gray-eyed bird prove wiser than I.

As I have said, we centaurs were quicker than mans. But Geraint's folk showed surprising endurance. We could do more in an hour. Over a day's journey, the difference between us was smaller, for the mans would go on where we had to pause and rest.

We did all we could to take their measure, watching how they hunted, how they used their bows and spears. They, no doubt, were doing the same with us. How folk hunt tells much about how they will behave in a fight. I learned nothing spectacular from the mans, save that they were nimbler than I would have guessed. With our four feet and larger weight, we cannot change directions so readily as they do. Past that, there was little to choose between them and us.

No, I take that back. There was one thing more. I had seen it even before I saw the mans themselves. The other folk of the Tin Isle could not abide their presence. I wondered if Bucca would call on us while we were in Geraint's company. He did not, which left me saddened but unsurprised. And of the other nuggies, or of the spriggans and piskies, we found not a trace.

Hylaeus noted the same thing. "Maybe the man spoke true when he said they died of embarrassment," he said worriedly. "Will the same begin to happen to us?"

"If it will, it has not yet," I answered. "We are stronger-willed than those other folk; no one would doubt that."

"True." But Hylaeus did not sound much relieved. "But I cannot help thinking they are all of what we are only in part. Does that not give them more of a certain kind of strength than we have?"

I wished that thought had not also occurred to me. Still, I answered, "What difference does it make? What difference *can* it make? We will trade with them, we will load the *Chalcippus* with tin till she wallows like a pregnant sow, and then we will sail home. After that, how can the mans' strength matter?"

Now he did seem happier, saying, "True, Cheiron, and well thought out. The sooner we are away from the Tin Isle, the gladder I shall be."

"And I," I said. "Oh, yes. And I."

Geraint sent some of his mans off to gather the tin: whether to dig it from the ground themselves or to take it from stocks the nuggies had mined before failing, I could not have said. They brought the metal in the usual leather sacks, each man carrying one on his back. They had no shame in using themselves as beasts of burden. And the sacks of tin did not much slow them. They still kept up with us.

As with our home country, no part of the Tin Isle is very far from any other part. We soon returned to the *Horse of Bronze*. The hes we had left behind to guard the ship were overjoyed to see us and bemused to see the mans. Anyone of any folk seeing mans for the first time is bound to be bemused, I do believe.

The trading went well: better than I had expected, in fact. Geraint was clever, no doubt about that. But he had little practice at dickering. I gather, though I am not certain, that he was much more used to taking than to haggling. To him, the tin he gave us was almost an afterthought, nothing to worry about. He wanted what we had.

When the dealing was done, when we had loaded the sacks of tin aboard the *Chalcippus* and his mans had carried off the trade goods, he said, "Let us have a feast, to celebrate the hour of our meeting."

"You are kind and generous," I said, meaning it at least in part. The countryside belonged to the mans. If there was to be a feast, the burden of fixing it would fall on them. I did add, "But let it not be long delayed. The season advances. Ocean the Great was harsh enough on the northward voyage. I would not care to sail in a time when storms grow more likely."

"As you say, so shall it be," Geraint replied, and so, indeed, it was. Mans brought cows and sheep and pigs to the seashore for slaughtering as the sun went down. Others had slain deer and ducks and geese. Shes of the man kind—womans, Geraint called them—came to tend to the cooking. Many of them were as pleasing in face and upper body as any of the shes we had left behind so long ago. Below . . . Below is always a mystery. The mystery here was to discover whether one part would fit with another. Some of us, I am told, made the experiment, and found it not altogether unsatisfactory. I doubt we would have, were our own shes close by. But they were not, and so. . . .

I do wonder if any issue resulted, and of what sort. But that is something I shall never know.

Along with roasting meat, the womans baked barley cakes and others from different grains they grow in that northern clime. Those were edible, but oats and rye are not foods on which I should care to have to depend. And the womans baked bread from the good wheat flour we had brought from our own home.

The soft chewiness and fine flavor of the loaves occasioned much favorable comment from the mans.

In that part of the world, they use less pottery than we. Being rich in forests, they make wooden barrels in place of our amphorae. The mans brought several of them to the feast. I asked Geraint, "What do these hold?"

"Why, cerevisia, of course," he answered in surprise. "We brew it from barley. Do you not know it?"

"No, though we sometimes use barley-water as a medicine," I said.

He laughed. "Even as we do with cerevisia. Drink of it, then, and be . . . cured." He laughed again.

Some of the womans broached a barrel of cerevisia and used a wooden dipper to pour the stuff into mugs, most of them of wood; some of pottery; and a few, for the leaders, of gold. The stuff in the barrel was thin and yellow. It looked, to be honest, more like what we expend after drinking than anything we would have wanted to drink. But the mans showed no hesitation. In fact, they were eager. I also saw that the womans sneaked mugs of cerevisia for themselves when they thought no one was looking.

Geraint, then, had not brought this stuff forth with the intention of poisoning us. He could not possibly have given so many mans an antidote ahead of time, and he could not have known in advance which womans would drink and which would not. He had a mug of cerevisia himself, a golden mug. He lifted it to me in salute. "Your good health!" he said, and drank it down.

A woman brought me a mug of my own, a golden mug similar to Geraint's. Cerevisia sloshed in it. I sniffed the brew. We centaurs have keener noses than many other folk. It had a slightly sour, slightly bitter odor. I did not see how anyone could care to drink it for pleasure, but I did not see how it could hurt me, either.

As Geraint had done, I raised my mug. "And yours!" I said. I too drank down the cerevisia.

It was not quite so nasty as I had thought it would be from the smell, but it was definitely an acquired taste—and one I had not acquired. Still, for courtesy's sake I made shift to empty the mug. I even managed to smile at the woman who poured it full again. She was, I own, worth smiling at. I had made no surreptitious experiments with these womans. With this one . . . Well, I might even get used to the idea that she had no tail.

Looking around, I saw I was not the only centaur drinking cerevisia. Some of the hes who had sailed up to the Tin Isle took to it with more enthusiasm than I could muster myself.

A woman also refilled Geraint's mug. He drank deep once more. When he nodded to me, his face seemed redder than it had. "What do you think?" he asked.

"Of cerevisia?" I tried to be as polite as I could, for it was clear the mans were giving us the best they had. "It is not bad at all."

"Not bad at all?" As I might have known, that was not praise enough to suit him. "It is some of the finest brew we have ever made. I have drunk enough to know." But then he caught himself and began to laugh. "I forget. You who live by the Inner Sea are used to wine, and to those who have drunk only wine cerevisia, even the finest, must seem nothing special."

I drained the golden mug once more. The cerevisia truly was not bad at all as the second serving slid down my throat. The woman smiled at me when she filled the mug again. My brain seemed to buzz. My whole body seemed to buzz, if the truth be known. I told myself it was the woman's smile that excited me so. On the Tin Isle, I told myself any number of things that were not true.

One of the centaurs let out a great, wild whoop. Another he howled out a similar cry a moment later. The buzzing that coursed through me grew stronger. I tossed back the mug of cerevisia. No, it was not bad. In fact, it was quite good. Without my asking, the woman gave me more. And the more I drank, the better it seemed.

Geraint had said something. I needed to remember what it was. It had mattered, or so I thought. But thought was . . . not so much difficult, I would say, as unimportant. I managed, however, and laughed in triumph. "Cerevisia and wine!" I said, though my tongue seemed hardly my own or under my will. "Why do you speak of cerevisia and wine together?"

I was not the only one who laughed. Geraint all but whinnied, he found that so funny. "You should know," he told me when he could speak again.

"What mean you?" I was having trouble speaking, or at least speaking clearly, myself. Drinking cerevisia was easier and more enjoyable. Yet another mug's worth glided down my gullet.

Geraint laughed once more "Why, they are the only brews I know that will make a man drunk," he replied. "And I see they will make your folk drunk as well. In truth, they must mount straight to your head, for the cerevisia makes you drunk far faster than it does with us."

"Cerevisia . . . makes for drunkenness?" I spoke with a certain helpless horror. I knew then what was toward, and knew myself powerless to stop it.

"Why, of course." Geraint seemed tempted to laugh yet again, this time at my foolishness. And I had been a fool, all right. The man asked, "Did you not know this?"

Sick with dread, I shook my head. The buzzing in my veins grew ever higher, ever shriller. Many folk around the Inner Sea make wine, drink wine, enjoy wine. We centaurs fight shy of it. We have good reason, too. Wine does not make us drunk, or not as it makes them drunk. Wine makes us mad. And cerevisia seemed all too likely to do the same.

I tried to say as much, but now my tongue and lips would not obey the orders I gave them. Not far away, a woman squealed. Oreus—I might have known it would be Oreus—had slung her over his shoulder and was galloping off into the darkness with her.

"What is he doing?" Geraint exclaimed. I knew perfectly well what he was doing (as did Geraint, no doubt), but I could not have told him. The man drew his sword, as if to stop Oreus, even though Oreus was now gone. I could not speak, but my hands and hooves still obeyed my will. I dealt Geraint a buffet that stretched him on the ground. When he started to get to his feet, I trampled him. He did not rise after that. No one, not from any folk, could have after that.

The woman who had served me screamed. I trotted toward her. Would I have served her as Oreus was surely serving the other woman? I suppose I would have, but I found myself distracted. There stood the barrel of cerevisia, with the dipper waiting for my hand. I drank and drank. The woman could wait. By the time I thought of her again, she had—quite sensibly—fled.

All over the feasting ground, madness reigned. Centaurs fought mans. Centaurs fought other centaurs. I do not know if mans fought other mans, but I would not be surprised.

A man speared a centaur in the barrel. The centaur, roaring, lifted the man and flung him into a pit of coals where a pig was cooking. The savor of roasting meat got stronger, but did not change its essential nature. Man's flesh on the fire smells much like pork.

Some centaurs did not bother taking womans into the darkness before taking them. The mans attacked these very fiercely. With madness coursing through them, the centaurs fought back with an animal ferocity I had rarely known in us before.

Shrieks and screams and howls of rage from both sides profaned the pleasant seaside feasting ground. There were more mans than centaurs, but the centaurs were bigger and stronger—and, as I say, madder. We cared nothing for wounds, so long as we could wound the enemy in return. We drove the mans wailing into the night, the few we did not slay.

Then we were alone on the beach, along with those wonderful barrels of cerevisia. To the victors, the spoils of battle. For us, these were enough, and more than enough.

I came back to myself thinking I had died—and that the gods of the afterlife were crueler than I had imagined. The pale sun of the Tin Isle beat down as if on the valley of the sphinxes. By the way my head pounded, some demented smith was beating a hammerhead into shape just above my eyes. The taste in my mouth I will not dignify with a name. Like as not, it has none.

The sun was just rising. It showed me not all the horror, not all the nightmare, dwelt within me. Mans and womans and centaurs lay sprawled and twisted in death. The blood that had poured from them was already turning black. Flies buzzed about the bodies. Rooks and carrion crows and ravens hopped here and there, pecking at eyes and tongues and other exposed dainties.

Not many centaurs had died. This, I think, was not only on account of our advantage in size but also because we had been full of the strength and vitality of madness. Looking around, I saw ovens overturned, barrels smashed, and much other destruction for the sake of destruction. This is not our usual way. It is not the usual way of any decent folk. But when the madness of wine— and, evidently, also the madness of cerevisia—struck us, what was usual was forgotten.

Other centaurs were stirring, rousing, from what had passed the night before, even as was I. By their groans, by the anguish in their voices and on their faces, they knew the same pain I did.

305

Awakening from madness can never be easy, or sweet. You always know what you are and, worse, what you were.

My fellows gazed on the devastation all around as if they could not believe their eyes. Well, how could I blame them, when I had as much trouble believing as the rest of them? Nessus said, "Surely we did no such thing. Surely." His voice was as hoarse a croak as any that might burst from a raven's throat. Its very timbre gave his hopeful words the lie.

"Surely we did not," I said, "except that we did." I wish I could claim I sounded better than Nessus. In fact, I can. But claiming a thing does not make it true. How I wish it did!

He turned his tail on the chaos, the carnage, the carrion. It was as if he could not bear to see himself mistaken. Again, blaming him is not easy. Who would wish to be reminded of . . . that?

"Did we slay all the mans?" Hylaeus asked.

"I think not." I shook my head, which sent fresh pangs shooting through it. "No, I know not. Some of them fled off into the night."

"That is not good," Nessus said. "They will bring more of their kind here. They will seek vengeance."

There, he was bound to be right. And the mans would have good reason to hunger for revenge. Not only had we slain their warriors, we had also outraged and slain their shes. Had some other folk assailed us so, we too would have been wild to avenge.

I looked inland. I saw nothing there, but I knew the mans did not yet thickly settle this part of the Tin Isle, the other folk who had lived hereabouts having only recently died out. I also knew this did not mean vengeance would not fall upon us, only that it might be somewhat delayed.

"We would do well not to be here when more mans come," I said. "We would do well to be on our way back toward the Inner Sea."

"There is a coward's counsel!" Oreus exclaimed. "Better we should fight these miserable mans than run from them."

"Can you fight five mans by yourself? Can you fight twenty mans by yourself?" I asked him, trying to plumb the depths of his stupidity.

It ran deeper than I had dreamt, for he said, "We would not be alone. The other folk of this land would fight with us, would fight for us."

"What other folk?" I inquired of him. "When the other folk of this land meet mans, they perish." Perhaps the madness of the cerevisia had not worked altogether for ill for us. Mad with drink, we had not fretted over our place in the scheme of things and that of the strange folk who sought to find rules (rules!—it chills me yet) in the gods' heavens.

Oreus would have argued further, but Nessus kicked him, not too hard, in the flank. "Cheiron is right," he said. "Maybe one day we can sail back here in greater numbers and try conclusions with these mans. For now, though, we would be better gone."

The thought that we might return one day mollified the young, fiery he. Nessus knew better than I how to salve Oreus' pride. "Very well, let us go, then," Oreus said. "The mans will not soon forget us."

Nor we them, I thought. But I did not say that aloud. Instead, I helped the rest of us push the *Horse of Bronze* into the sea, which luckily lay almost under her keel. With all those sacks of tin in her, the work still was not easy, but we managed it. The gods sent us a fair wind out of the east. I ordered the yard raised on the mast and the sail lowered from it. We left the Tin Isle behind.

Our homeward journey was neither easy nor swift. If I speak of it less than I did of the voyage outward, it is because so many of the hazards were the same. For the first two days after we left the Tin Isle, I do admit to anxiously looking back over my tail every now and again. I did not know for a fact whether the mans had mastered the art of shipbuilding. If they had, they might have pursued. But evidently not. We remained alone on the bosom of Ocean the Great, as far as my eyes could tell.

Sailing proved no worse—and possibly better—than it had on our northward leg. We stayed in sight of land when we could, but did not stay so close that we risked being forced onto a lee shore by wind and wave rolling out of the west. And *rolling* is truly the word, for we saw waves on Ocean the Great that no one who has sailed only the Inner Sea can imagine.

With the *Chalcippus* more heavily laden than she had been while we were outward bound, I did not like to bring her up on the beach every night. I had learned to respect and to fear the rise and fall of the waters against the land, which seems to happen twice a day in the regions washed by the Ocean. If the waters withdrew too far, we might not be able to get the galley back into the sea. To hold that worry at arm's length, we dropped anchor offshore most nights.

That too, of course, came with a price. Because we could not let the ship's timbers dry out of nights, they grew heavy and waterlogged, making the *Horse of Bronze* a slower and less responsive steed than she would otherwise have been. Had a bad storm blown up, that might have cost us dear. As things were, the gods smiled, or at least did not frown with all the grimness they might have shown, and we came safe to the Inner Sea once more.

As we sailed east past the pillars said to hold up the heavens, I wondered once more about the mans, and how *they* escaped the gods' wrath. Most folk—no, all folk I had known up until then—are content to live in the world the gods made, and to thank them for their generous bounty. What the gods will, lesser folk accept, as they must—for, as I have remarked, the essence of godhood is power. Were I as powerful as a god, what would I be? A god myself, nothing else. But I am not so powerful, and so am no god.

Nor are these mans gods. That was plain. In our cerevisia-spawned madness, we slew them easily enough. Yet they have the arrogance, the presumption, to seek out the gods' secrets. And they have the further arrogance and presumption to believe that, if they find them, they can use them.

Can a folk not given godlike powers arrogate those powers to itself? The mans seem to think so. How would the gods view such an opinion? If they did take it amiss, as I judged likely, how long would they wait to punish it?

Confident in their own strength, might they wait too long? If a folk did somehow steal godlike power, what need would it have of veritable gods? Such gloomy reflections filled my mind as we made our way across the Inner Sea. I confess to avoiding the sirens' island on the homeward journey. Their temper was unpleasant, their memories doubtless long. We sailed south of them instead, skirting the coast where the lotus-eaters dwell. I remember little of that part of the voyage; the lotus-eaters, I daresay, remember less.

I do remember the long sail we had up from the land of the lotus-eaters to that of the fauns. The sail seemed the longer because, as I say, we had to keep clear of the island of the sirens. We filled all the water jars as full as we could. This let us anchor well off the coast of their island as we traveled north. We also had the good fortune of a strong southerly breeze. We lowered the sail from the yard, then, and ran before the wind. Our hes were able to rest at the oars, which meant they did not grow thirsty as fast as they would have otherwise. We came to the land of the fauns with water still in the jars—not much, but enough.

That breeze had held for us all the way from the land of

the lotus-eaters to that which the fauns call home. From this, I believe—and I certainly hope—the gods favored our cause and not the sirens'. This I believe and hope, yes. But I have not the gall to claim it *proves* the gods favored us, or to use it to predict that the gods would favor us again in the same way. I am not a man. I do not make stone circles. I do not believe a stone circle can measure the deeds and will of the gods.

By what has befallen the other folk on the Tin Isle besides the mans, I may be mistaken.

From the easternmost spit of the fauns' homeland to ours is but a short sail. Yet the *Horse of Bronze* came closer to foundering there than anywhere on turbulent Ocean the Great. A storm blew up from nowhere, as it were. The *Chalcippus* pitched and rolled and yawed. A wave crashed over the bow and threatened to swamp us. We all bailed for our lives, but another wave or two would have stolen them from us.

And then, as abruptly as it had sprung to life, the storm died. What conclusion was I to draw from this? That the gods were trying to frighten me to death but would spare me if they failed? That drawing conclusions about what the gods intend was a risky business, a fool's game? I had already known as much. I was not a man, to require lessons on the subject.

We came home not only to rejoicing but to astonishment. Most of the hes we left behind on setting sail in the *Chalcippus* had expected to see us no more. Many of the shes we left behind also expected to see us no more. That led to several surprises and considerable unpleasantness, none of which deserves recounting here.

It often seemed as if the tin we brought home was more welcome than we were. Few cared to listen to our tales of the great stone circle or of the strange mans who had built it. The fauns, the sirens, the lotus-eaters we centaurs already knew. The stay-at-homes were glad enough to hear stories about them.

Certainly the smiths welcomed the tin with glad cries and with caracoles of delight. They fell to work as if made of bronze themselves. We have a sufficiency of copper—more than a sufficiency, for we trade it with folk whose land gives them none. But tin is far less common and far more dear; were it otherwise, we would not have needed to fare so far to lay hold of it.

Spearheads and shields and swords and helms began to pile up, ready for use against the sphinxes or whoever else should presume to trouble us. Now we could match bronze against bronze, rather than being compelled to use the softer copper unalloyed. Some of the younger hes quite looked forward to combat. That far I would not go. I have seen enough to know that combat too often comes whether we look for it or not; what point, then, to seeking it?

The smiths also made no small stock of less warlike gear. I speak of that less not because I esteem it less, but only because, when bronze is not measured against bronze, its hardness as compared to copper's is of less moment.

Not too long after our return, I learned that we in the *Chalcippus* were not the only band of centaurs to have set out in search of tin. A he named Pholus had led a band north by land. There are mountains in those parts that yield gold and silver, and Pholus hoped he might happen upon tin as well.

Although those mountains are not far as the raven flies, our folk seldom go there. The folk who live in those parts are strange, and strangely fierce and formidable. They come out only at night, and are often in the habit of drinking the blood of those they kill. And they are persistent of life, though sunlight, curiously enough, is alleged to slay them.

This Pholus affirmed for me, saying, "After we caught a couple of them and staked them out for the sunrise, the others proved less eager to see if they could sneak up and murder us by the light of the moon."

311

"Yes, I can see how that might be so," I told him. "Good for you. But I gather you found no tin?"

"I fear me we did not," he agreed. "It is a rich country. Were it not for these night skulkers, we could do a great deal of trade with it. They care nothing for bargaining, though. All they want is the taste of blood in their mouths." His own mouth twisted in disgust.

"Many good-byes to them, then," I said. "Maybe we ought to send a host up that way, to see how many we could drag out for the sun to destroy."

"Maybe." But Pholus did not sound as if he thought that a good idea. "If we did not get rid of them all, they would make us pay. And besides—" He did not go on.

"Besides, what?" I asked when I saw he would not on his own.

He did not answer for a long time. I wondered if he would. At long last, he said, "I swore my hes to secrecy, Cheiron. I did not take the oath myself, for I thought there was no need. I knew I could keep a secret. Perhaps the gods foresaw that I would need to speak one day, and did not want me forsworn. I know you can also hold a secret close at need. The need, I think, is here. I have heard somewhat of your voyage, and of the peculiar folk you met on the Tin Isle."

"The mans?" I said, and he nodded. "Well, what of them?"

"That is the secret we are keeping," Pholus replied. "Up in the mountains, we met some of what I think must be the same folk ourselves. They were coming down from the north, as much strangers in those parts as we were. They did not call themselves mans, though; they had another name."

"Why did you keep them a secret?" I asked.

He shivered. Pholus is bold and swift and strong. I had never thought to see him afraid, and needed a moment to realize that I had. "Because they are . . . what we ought to be," he answered after another long hesitation. "What we and the satyrs and the sphinxes and those troublesome blood-drinkers ought to be. They are . . . all of a kind, with more of the stuff of the gods and less of the beast in them than we hold."

I knew what he meant. I knew so well, I had to pretend I knew not. "More of the gall of the gods, if they truly are like the mans I met," I said.

"And that," he agreed. The hard, bright look of fear still made his eyes opaque. "But if they are coming down from the north— everywhere from the north—how shall any of the folk around the Inner Sea withstand them?"

I had wondered that about the mans, even on the distant Tin Isle. If they had also reached the mountains north of our own land, though, there were more of them than I had dreamt, and the danger to us all was worse. I tried to make light of it, saying, "Well, the blood-drinkers may bar the way."

Pholus nodded, but dubiously. "That is the other reason I would not go after the blood-drinkers: because they might shield us. But I do not think they will, or not for long. The new folk have met them, and have plans of their own for revenge. Do you think the night-skulking blood-drinkers can oppose them?"

"Not if they are mans of the same sort I knew," I said. "Are you sure they are the same? What *did* they call themselves?"

"Lapiths," he answered. The name meant nothing to me then. But these days the echoes of the battle of Lapiths and centaurs resound round the Inner Sea. We are scattered to the winds, those few left to us, and the Lapiths dwell in the land ours since the gods made it. And Pholus knew whereof he spoke. The Lapiths *are* mans. They remain sure to this day that they won simply because they had the right to win, with no other reason needed.

They would.

THE GENETICS LECTURE

This small, silly piece sprang from an e-mail correspondence I got into with the paleontologist Simon Conway Morris, whose work I very much admire. It ran as a "Probability Zero" feature in Analog. *I wouldn't say the probability is zero, exactly, but I doubt it's very high.*

$\mathcal{J}$t was lovely outside, too lovely for the student to want to stay cooped up in here listening to a lecture on genetics. The sun shone brightly. Bees buzzed from flower to flower. Butterflies flitted here and there. The air smelled sweet with spring.

And the professor droned on. The student made himself take notes. This stuff would be on the midterm—he was sure of that. Even so, staying interested enough to keep writing wasn't easy.

If only the prof weren't so . . . old-fashioned. Oh, he was impressive enough in a way: tall and straight, with big blue eyes. But his suit wouldn't have been stylish in his father's day, and those glasses clamped to the bridge of his beak . . . *Nobody* wore those anymore. Except he did.

"This complex of Hox genes, as they're called, regulates early bodily development," he said. The student scribbled. However old-fashioned the prof was, he was talking about stuff on the cutting edge. "Like all insects, the fruit fly has eight Hox genes. The amphioxus, a primitive chordate, has ten."

He picked up a piece of chalk and drew on the blackboard. "The amphioxus is sometimes called a lancelet from its scalpel-like shape, which you see here," he said. "In reality, the animal is quite small. Now where was I? Oh, yes. Hox genes.

"All animals seem to share them from a long-extinct Proterozoic ancestor. There is a correspondence between the orientation of the gene complex and that of the animal. The first Hox gene in both the fruit fly and the amphioxus is responsible for the head end of each animal, the last for the abdomen and tail, respectively.

"And let me tell you something still more remarkable. We have created, for example, mutant fruit flies that are eyeless. If we transfer this *eyeless* gene to an amphioxus, its progeny will be born without their usual eye spots. Note that the normal *expression* of the gene, as we say, is vastly different in the two animals. The amphioxus has only light-sensitive pigment patches at the head end, where the fruit fly has highly evolved compound eyes."

"What about us, Professor?" another student asked. "Why are we so much more complex than fruit flies and the waddayacallit?"

"The amphioxus?" The professor beamed at her. "I was just coming to that. We're more complex because our Hox genes are more complex. It's that simple, really. Instead of a single set of eight or ten Hox genes, we have four separate sets, each with up to thirteen genes in it. The mutations that give rise to this duplication and reduplication took place in Cambrian and Ordovician times, on the order of four hundred million years ago. We are what we are today because our ancient ancestors suddenly found themselves with more genes than they knew what to do with." He beamed again. "Animal life as we know it today, and especially the development of our own phylum, would have been impossible without these mutations."

That intrigued the student almost in spite of himself. When the lecture was over, he went up to the front of the classroom. "Ask you something, Professor?"

"Of course, of course." Even with those silly glasses, the prof wasn't such a bad guy.

"Mutations are random, right? They can happen any old place, any old time?"

"On the whole, yes." The prof was also cautious, as a good academic should be.

"Okay." That *on the whole* was all the student needed. "What if, a long time ago, these Hox genes got doubled and redoubled in arthropods instead of us? Or even in, uh, chordates instead of us?" He was damned if he'd try to say *amphioxus*.

"Instead of in us mollusks? I think the idea is ridiculous— ridiculous, I tell you. We were preadapted for success in ways this sorry little creature's ancestors never could have been." As if to show what he meant, the professor reached out with one of the eight tentacles that grew around the base of his head, snatched up the eraser, and wiped the picture of the lancelet off the board with three quick strokes.

The student flushed a deep green with embarrassment. "I'm sorry, Professor Cthulhu. I'll try not to be so silly again."

"It's all right, Nyarlathotep," the professor said gently—he did calm down in a hurry. "Go on now, though. Have a nice day."

SOMEONE IS STEALING
THE GREAT THRONE ROOMS
OF THE GALAXY

---

*The theme of the 2006 Worldcon in Los Angeles (well, actually in
Anaheim, but billed as L.A.con IV neverthenonetheless) was space cadets. Frankie Thomas, of the original* Space Cadets *TV show, would
have been the media guest of honor (sadly, he died just before the convention). Mike Resnick edited an anthology of space-cadet stories to
be sold as a souvenir book at the con. When I told him what I was
going to perpetrate, he said he'd buy it before he even saw it, which is
the first, last, and only time an editor ever said that to me. I hope he
doesn't regret it too much.*

*W*hen thieves paralyzed the people—well, the saurian human-oids—inside the palace on the main continent of Gould IV and made off with the famous throne room (and the somewhat less famous antechamber), it made a tremendous stir all over the continent.

When pirates paralyzed the people—well, the ammonia/ice blobs—inside the palace on the chief glacier of Amana XI and made off with the magnificent throne room (and the somewhat less magnificent antechamber), it raised a tremendous stink all over the planet.

When robbers paralyzed the people—well, the highly evolved and sagacious kumquats—inside the palace on the grandest orchard of Alpharalpha B and made off with the precociously planted throne room (and the somewhat less precocious antechamber), it caused a sour taste in mouths all over the sector.

And when brigands paralyzed the people—well, the French—inside the palace of Versailles in a third-rate country on a second-rate continent with a splendid future behind it and made off with the baroque throne room (and the somewhat less baroque antechamber), it caused shock waves all over the Galaxy.

As Earth has always been, it remains the sleazy-media center of the Galactic Empire. Anything that happens there gets more attention than it deserves, just because it happens there. And so there was an enormous hue and cry.

Something Must Be Done!

Who got to do it?

Why, the Space Patrol, of course. Specifically, Space Cadet Rufus Q. Shupilluliumash, a Bon of Bons, a noble of nobles . . . a fat overgrown hamster with delusions of gender. And when Cadet Rufus Q. Shupilluliumash (last name best sung to the tune of "Fascinatin' Rhythm") got the call, he was, as fate and the omniscient narrator would have it, massively hungover from a surfeit of fermented starflower seeds.

The hero who gave him the call, Space Patrol Captain Erasmus Z. Utnapishtim (last name best sung to the tune of "On, Wisconsin"), was a member of the same species, and so understood his debility. This is not to say the illustrious Space Patrol captain—another fat overgrown hamster—sympathized. Oh, no. "You're a disgrace to your whiskers, Shupilluliumash," he cheebled furiously.

"Sorry, sir," Rufus Q. Shupilluliumash answered. At that particular moment, he rather hoped his whiskers, and the rest of his pelt, would fall out.

Captain Utnapishtim knew there was only one way to get to the bottom of things: the right way, the proper way, the regulation way, the Space Patrol way. "Go find out who is stealing the great throne rooms of the Galaxy," he ordered. "Find out why. Arrest the worthless miscreants and make the mischief stop."

"Right . . . sir," Cadet Shupilluliumash said miserably, wishing Utnapishtim were dead or he himself were dead or the omniscient narrator were dead (no such luck, Shup baby)—any way at all to escape from this silly story and the pain in his pelt. "Where do I start . . . sir?"

"Start on Earth," Captain Utnapishtim told him. "Earth is the least consequential planet in the Galaxy, and all the inhabitants talk too bloody much. If you can't find a clue there, you're not worth your own tail."

"Like you, sir, I am a fat overgrown hamster," the space cadet replied with dignity. "I have no tail."

"Well, if I remember my briefings, neither do Earthmen," the Space Patrol officer said. "Now get your wheel rolling."

"Yes, sir," Shupilluliumash said resignedly, and headed off to check out a Patrol speedster, the P.S. *Habitrail*.

Now you should know that there are many kinds of space drives to span the parsecs of the Galaxy. You should, yes, but since you don't—you can't fool the omniscient narrator (otherwise he wouldn't be omniscient)—you have to sit through this expository lump. There is the hyperspace drive: traditional, but effective. There is the hop-skip-and-a-jump drive: wearing, but quick. There is the overdrive. There is the underdrive. There is the orthodontic drive, which corrects both overdrive and underdrive but is hellishly expensive. There are any number of others—oh, not *any* number, but, say, forty-two. And, particularly for fat overgrown hamsters, there is the wheel drive.

The wheel drive translates rotary motion into straight-ahead FTL by a clever mechanism with whose workings the omniscient narrator won't bore you (the O.N. knows you have a low boredom threshold, and you won't sit still for two expository lumps in a row). Suffice to say that Space Cadet Shupilluliumash jumped in his wheel, ran like hell, and almost before he'd sweated out the last of his hangover he found himself landing outside of Paris—sort of like Lindbergh long before, but much fuzzier.

He got full cooperation from the French authorities. Once local Galactic officials secured his release from jail, he went to Versailles to view the scene of the crime. "This is a very ugly building," he said with the diplomacy for which his race was so often praised.

After local Galactic officials secured his release from jail again—it took longer this time—they told him, "The French tend to be emotional."

"So do I," Rufus Q. Shupilluliumash said. "Especially about the food in there—it's terrible."

"And such small portions," the Galactic officials chorused.

"How did you know?" Shup asked in genuine surprise. "Or do they bust everybody?"

"Never mind," the officials said, not quite in harmony. "Go back to Versailles. Observe. Take notes. For God's sake, don't talk."

"Oh, all right," the hamster space cadet grumbled.

Go back he did. Observe he did. Take notes he did. Talk he didn't, for God's sake. Except for two missing rooms and an enormous RD spray-painted on the side of the palace, nothing seemed out of the ordinary.

Frustrated, Rufus Q. Shupilluliumash hopped into his wheel and departed for Alpharalpha B, home of the sagacious kumquats. "So what kind of jam are you in?" he asked them.

After local Galactic officials secured his release from the thornbush, he proceeded with his investigation. "You see what they have done!" a sagacious kumquat cried, showing him the ruins of the royal palace.

"Looks like the throne room and the antechamber are gone, all right," Shup agreed . . . sagaciously. "What are those big squiggles on the wall there?"

"They stand for the characters you would call RD," the kumquat replied.

"They do, do they? Looks like it might be a clue." Rufus Q. Shupilluliumash's sagacity score went right off the charts with that observation—in which direction, it is better to specu late than never. The Space Patrol didn't raise any dummies, but sometimes it found one and took him in and made him its own.

"What will you do? You must get the sacred structures back!" the kumquat keened. "How will our sovereign root in peace without them?"

"Somebody did something pretty seedy to you, all right," the space cadet said.

After local Galactic officials secured his release from the thornbush again—it took longer this time—they told him, "Perhaps it would be better if you pursued your investigations somewhere else. Otherwise, the kumquats warn, they will soon be pursuing you."

"Some people—well, highly evolved and sagacious kumquats—are just naturally sour," Rufus Q. Shupilluliumash complained. Neverthenonetheless, and entirely undisirregardless of the slavering mob of fruit salad at his furry heels, he made it into the Patrol speedster and got the hatch shut just in the proverbial Nicholas of time.

Even with the wheel drive, it's a long, long way from Alpharalpha B to Amana XI. Our intrepid space cadet put the time to good use, but after a while even porn began to pall and he decided to do some research instead. He Googled RD. How he could get online while far beyond the normal limits of space and time may well be known to the omniscient narrator (I mean, after all, what isn't?), but he ain't talking. What the space cadet found . . . you'll see. Eventually. Keep your shirt on.

Before climbing out of the airlock on Amana XI, Rufus Q. climbed into his coldsuit. Otherwise, all he would have needed was a stick shoved up the wazoo to become the Galaxy's first

Hamstersicle. But he would have been too damn frozen to shove a stick where it needed to go, so it's just as well he remembered the suit.

"Tell me," he said to one of the ammonia/ice blobs awaiting his arrival at the spaceport, "are your females frigid?"

Once local Galactic officials had secured his release from the hotbox . . . the space cadet was rather vexed at them. The ammonia/ice blobs of Amana XI tormented convicts by subjecting them to heat well above the freezing point of water, and were also inblobane enough to make them endure an oxygen-enhanced atmosphere. Some of the munchies were stale, but it was the best digs ol' Rufus Q. could've found on the whole planet.

He got back into his coldsuit for a whirlwind tour of the devastated palace. Once the whirlwind subsided, he saw on the icy wall now exposed to the elements—and compounds—some writing in an alien script he couldn't begin to read. "What's that say?" he asked.

"In your symbology, it would stand for RD," the nearest ammonia/ice blob answered.

"Probably doesn't mean *Research and Development*, then," Rufus Q. Shupilluliumash sighed. "That'll teach me to hit the 'I Feel Lucky' button, even if I did."

"What are you going to do?" the blob demanded. "Do you not see the magnificence despoiled?"

"Reminds me more of the inside of a root freezer without the goddamn roots," the forthright space cadet replied. He was, by then, quite looking forward to seeing the inside of the hotbox once more. The ammonia/ice blobs appeared overjoyed to oblige him, too. His only real complaint was that the seeds they fed him still weren't of the freshest. He stuffed his cheek pouches full even so.

Once local Galactic officials had secured his release from the hotbox again, they gently suggested his investigation might proceed more promisingly elsewhere. He was inclined to agree with them; he'd discovered that spitting seed casings inside a coldsuit was an exercise in sloppy futility.

Thus it was that Cadet Rufus Q. Shupilluliumash reboarded the redoubtable *Habitrail*, spun the wheel up to translight speed, and sped off to Gould IV and its saurian humanoids. Past walking on their hind legs, they didn't particularly remind him of Frenchmen. Of course, they were even less hamsteroid, which might have colored his opinion. As far as he was concerned, anything with a long scaly tail at one end and a big mouth full of sharp teeth at the other was not to be trusted.

One of the saurians at the spaceport eyed him and remarked, "You look like you'd go down well with drawn butter."

Shup drew not butter but his trusty blaster. "You look like you'd look good on my wall," he replied cheerfully. "In this Galaxy, nothing is certain but death and taxidermy."

He belonged to the Patrol. He had the right to carry any weapon he chose. If he killed, he was assumed to know what he was doing. The Galaxy, as you will have figured out, was in deep kimchi, but this isn't that kind of story. This is the kind of story where the saurians would have jugged him not for toting lethal hardware but as punpunishment. And since it is that kind of story, you may rest assured they did.

Once local Galactic officials had pulled the cork from the jug, a somewhat chaster (he was alone, after all, and not even bull-hamster horniness could make the saurians sexy) but unchastened Rufus Q. Shupilluliumash emerged. He didn't even have to draw his blaster again—which was just as well, since he was no artist—to get the saurians to take him to their royal palace so he could view the missing throne room and antechamber (or rather, view that they *were* missing—he couldn't very well *view* them *while* they were missing, could he?) and what he was coming to think of as the inevitable graffiti.

There seemed to be rather more of them this time. "What do they say?" he inquired of his guide, a stalwart, shamrock-green Gouldian named Albert O'Saurus.

Albert seemed to have inherited a full set of teeth from each parent, and a set from each grandparent, too, maybe for luck. "'Royal Drive,'" he answered. "'Next stop—Galactic Central!'"

Sinister organ chords rang out in the background, or at least in the space cadet's perfervid imagination. "A clue!" quoth he.

"Faith, what a brilliant deduction," Albert O'Saurus said—the Gouldians didn't find sarcasm illegal, immoral, or fattening. "And how did you come up with it, now?"

Rufus Q. Shupilluliumash eyed the saurian. "Well, it's not exactly a cloaca-and-dagger operation," he replied.

Once local Galactic officials had pulled the cork from the jug again—it took longer this time, as second offenses, and offensive offenses, were commonly punpunished by devourment—they encouraged him to spread his talents widely across the sea of stars. "If you stay here any longer," one of them said, "the Gouldians *will* eat you. With mustard."

The hamster space cadet made a horrible, incisor-filled face. "Can't stand mustard," he said. "Ta-ta! I'm off! Me and the baked beans."

"Where will you go?" the official inquired.

"Galactic Central, I do believe," Rufus Q. Shupilluliumash answered.

Ah, Galactic Central! I could go on for pages, or even reams— the disadvantage of being an omniscient narrator. But this isn't *that* kind of story, either, and I will pause while you thank your local deity or demon that it isn't. . . . There. Are you finished now? Good. We can go on.

What you do need to know about the fabulous Galactic Central, and what you will most likely (probability, 87.13%—how's that for omniscient?) have figured out for yourself, is that it boasts the grandest and spiffiest palace in all the Galaxy, that being where the Galactic Emperor and Empress hang out. Said palace boasts the most garish and over-the-top—excuse me, most colorful and extravagant—throne room in all the Galaxy, and also the most likewise and likewise—excuse me, most likewise and likewise—antechamber in all the et cetera.

"I bet the bad guys are going to try and steal them for the Royal Drive," Shup said as he powered up the *Habitrail's* wheel. Then he said, "What the hell *is* the Royal Drive?" Except for the graffiti on Gould IV, he'd never heard of it.

Google had never heard of it, either. Rufus Q. Shupilluliumash wondered whether he was accessing the Chinese system. But no. It was—cue the portentous music again—Something New.

Though his electronic aids failed him, the dedicated space cadet persevered. He had one major advantage over the others whom Erasmus Z. Utnapishtim (remember him?) might have chosen to save the Galaxy . . . or at least its throne rooms and antechambers. Not only was he a hamster, he was a punster as well, as he had proved to the dismay and discomfiture of ammonia/ice blobs and shamrock-green saurian humanoids alike.

And as he neared Galactic Central, he suddenly slowed on the wheel in astonishment—and almost pitched the P.S. *Habitrail* back into normal space in an abnormal place. That wouldn't have been good—so he didn't actually *do* it.

What he did do was cry out, "Eureka!" Why the name of a not very large city in northern California should have become the cry for discovering something, Rufus Q. Shupilluliumash did not know, but it had. The Patrol could be a tradition-bound—even a tradition-gagged—outfit sometimes.

He spun the wheel up to an almost blistering pace. Then, when his feet and little front paws started to hurt, he slowed down again—but not so much, this time, as to endanger his speedster. He thought furiously, which was odd, because he wasn't particularly furious.

"It must work that way," he said. "This story won't run long enough for a lot of wrong guesses." If he'd guessed wrong there, he might have found himself trapped in a novel, but the speedster wasn't a Fforde, so he escaped that fate, anyhow. He shook his head and snuffled his whiskers at the iniquity of the throne-room (and antechamber) thieves. "I must foil them," he declared, and checked his supplies of aluminum, tin, and silver.

He was so transfixed by his fit of analytical brilliance that he almost wheeled right past Galactic Central and back out into the Galactic Boonies. But he didn't—this story won't run long enough for a lot of mistakes, either.

Being a space cadet helped him get through the entry formalities in jig time—which, since he didn't dance, was more than a little challenging. A day and a half later, the freedom of Galactic Central was his, as long as the GPS and radiological tracking devices surgically implanted near his wazoo gave answers the powers that be approved of. Otherwise, the tiny nuke implanted near that very same sensitive place would sadly spoil our upcoming dénouement, to say nothing of half a city block. So we won't.

He hopped on the closest available public transport, discovered it was going the wrong way (see?—we did have room for a mistake after all), hopped off, and got on, this time, as luck (and the necessities of plotting) would have it, going toward the sublime (or something) residence of the beloved (or something) Galactic Emperor and Empress.

No sooner had he arrived—talk about timing! I mean, really!—than a giant chainsaw suddenly appeared in the sky and started carving away at (are you surprised?) the throne room . . . and the antechamber. People screamed. People ran. People coughed from flying sawdust. People of several different flavors got turned into hamburger of several different flavors. People inside the palace, caught by the paralyzer ray that went with the saw, didn't do much of anything.

Guards outside the palace started shooting at the parts of the chainsaw crunching through the walls. Quick-thinking Rufus Q. Shupilluliumash fired at the power button instead: a dot a centimeter wide three kilometers up in the air. Being a Patrol-trained markshamster and luckier than Lucky Pierre, he hit it dead-on, the very first try.

The chainsaw stopped chain-sawing. It fell out of the sky and smashed one of the ritziest neighborhoods—actually, several of the ritziest neighborhoods, because that was a big mother of a chainsaw—of Galactic Central to cottage cheese. Our bold space cadet cared nothing for that, though. He was doing his duty, and he was damned if he'd let common sense stand in his way.

Dashing toward the chainsaw's survival capsule (How did he know where it was? He just knew. This is *that* kind of story.), he was Rufus Q. Shupilluliumash on the spot when a saurian humanoid, an ammonia/ice blob in a hotsuit, a kumquat, and a Frenchman came staggering out.

"You're under arrest!" he shouted, covering them with his ever-reliable blaster. "Suspicion of firing a chainsaw without a license and operating an unauthorized space drive within city limits. Don't nobody move!"

Nobody didn't move . . . or something like that. "What do you know about the Royal Drive?" the Frenchman sneered. "How do you know it's unauthorized?"

"It must be unauthorized, because I couldn't Google it. And I know the Royal Drive uses the hellacious energy output from mixing"—our space cadet paused to build the moment, for he was indeed punster as well as hamster—"chamber and antechamber to propel your spacecraft across the Galaxy in pursuance of your nefarious ends. But now you're busted, space scum!"

The Frenchman, the kumquat, and the saurian humanoid blanched. Rufus Q. Shupilluliumash presumed the ammonia/ice blob did, too—it is, after all, what self-respecting villains do under such circumstances—but the hotsuit kept him from being sure. Palace guards came up behind him. "What do we do with them, sir?" they asked respectfully.

"Take them away," the hamster replied grandly. "They will trouble the spaceways no more."

Your omniscient narrator also has the pleasure to report that, shortly thereafter, Space Cadet Rufus Q. Shupilluliumash became Ensign Rufus Q. Shupilluliumash, with all the rights and privileges appertaining thereto. (Of course, he knew that would happen. Didn't you?) Our space cadet's actions in this case were deemed to be in the highest tradition of the Space Patrol.

UNCLE ALF

Because of everything that's happened since, we don't remember that World War I, and what did and didn't happen then, set the stage for the rest of the crowded and bloody twentieth century. Had the century's first great war turned out differently, we would not be living in the same world today, or anything like it. If the Kaiser's troops had made it to Paris, some people now altogether unknown would be famous, and some now famous would never have got the chance to play a big part on history's stage. Would the world be better? Worse? I have no idea. But it certainly would be different.

My very dear Angela,

You will have seen, I am sure, from the stamp and the postmark that I am now in Lille. I have not seen this place for almost fifteen years, but I well remember the pounding we gave it when we drove out the damned Englishmen. They fought hard, but they could not hold back the All-Highest's victorious soldiers. And even to this day, I find, the lazy Frenchmen have not bothered to repair all the damage the town suffered at that time.

But the Frenchmen, of course, are never too lazy to make trouble for the Kaiser and for the German Empire. That is why the Feldgendarmerie sent me here. When they want results, what do they do? They call on your uncle, that is what. They know I get the job done, come what may. And I aim to do it here, too, though I do not think it will be easy. Of course, if it were easy, they would send an ordinary fool.

Here in Lille, they call Feldgendarmerie men *diables verts*—green devils—on account of the tall green collars on our uniform tunics. I tell you for a fact, darling, I intend to send some of them straight to hell. They deserve nothing less. They lost the war, which proves how naturally inferior they are to good German men, but now they think they can reverse the inescapable verdict of history with tricks and plots and foolery. I am here to show them how wrong they are.

You can write to me at the address on this envelope. I hope all goes well for you, and that you never have to trouble your lovely little head about the schemes of these degenerate Frenchmen. I send you many kisses, and wish I could give them to you in person. With much love, I remain your—

Uncle Alf

9 May 1929

My dearest sweet Angela,

It is worse here than I imagined. No wonder they sent for me. Lille is one of the most backward cities in France. Dazzling riches and loathsome poverty alternate sharply. Side by side with commercial wealth dwell the homeless in gloom and mud. And, though it shames me to do so, I must tell you that at least half the Feldgendarmerie men here are as corrupt as any Frenchman.

I suppose it is inevitable that this should be so. Many of these men have been in their places in Lille since the days of the war. I am not lying or exaggerating a bit when I say they have become more French than German themselves.

They live off the fat of the land. They have taken French mistresses and forgotten the good German wives they left back home.

Such degeneracy should be punished. Such degeneracy must be punished! I have made my views on this subject very clear. If only I held rank higher than Feldwebel, something might be done. But a small, ruthless clique of officers has shamelessly held back my advancement. When I think I turned forty last month with no more to show for my life than this, I know how unjust the world is. If only I had been allowed to show what I might do, everyone would hold his breath and make no comment. Of that you may be certain!

Still, I serve the German Empire with a loyal and honest heart. It is the last and best hope of mankind. French revanchism must be, shall be, mercilessly stamped out. Heads will roll here in Lille, and I shall rejoice to see it.

Meanwhile, I hope your own pretty head back there in Munich is happy and content. I send you kisses and hugs, and I will try to send you and your mother some smoked duck as well. You would be healthier without it, though. This I truly believe. It is one of my cardinal principles, and I shall go on trying to persuade you till the day I die. Meanwhile, in this as in all things, my honor remains true. I am, fondly, your—

Uncle Alf

11 May 1929

Sweet darling Angela,

I hope to hear from you. In this miserable place, a letter would mean a very great deal indeed. Your love and kisses and the thought of you in my embrace could help me forget what a hole Lille is and what a pathetic lot of bunglers the local Feldgendarmerie men have proved to be.

They look ever so impressive as they strut through the town with big, fierce Alsatians on a leash at their sides. But here is the truth: the dogs are braver than all of them and smarter than most of them. They see nothing. They want to see nothing, to know nothing. So long as they can get through the day without noticing anything, they are content. Then in the evening they settle down to cigars and to wine or foul apple brandy from one of the local estaminets, of which, believe me when I tell you, there are a great many. Men with more disgusting habits would be difficult to imagine.

Yet these are the ones who are supposed to root out treason! It would be laughable if it were not so dreadful. No wonder they had to call in someone whose belly does not hang out half a kilometer over his belt! Gott mit uns, our belt buckles say. With these men, their bulging bellies hide God from the world, and surely the Lord on high does not much care to look at them, either.

With them all so fat and sluggish and useless, it is up to me to go into the workers' districts and sniff out the treason growing here. And I will sniff it out, and we will cut it out, and the Second Reich will go on ruling Europe, as it was destined to do.

And when I have done my duty, how I look forward to

seeing you again, to hugging you against me, to running my hands through your golden hair. Truly the reward of the soldier for doing what he must is sweet. The thought of coming home to you makes me struggle all the harder here, so I may speed the day.

Also tell your mother I remain her affectionate half brother, and that I will write to her as soon as I find time. As always, I am your loving—

Uncle Alf

My darling and beloved Angela,

By now I had hoped to receive at least one letter from you, yet the field post brings me nothing. Without word that you still feel kindly towards me, life seems very empty indeed. I do my duty—I always do my duty, for the enemies of the German Empire must be rooted out wherever they are found—but it is, I must tell you, with a heavy heart.

The French, though . . . Gott im Himmel, they are and shall always be our most implacable foes. The hatred on their faces when they see us go by! They may act polite when we are in earshot, but how they wish they had another chance to fight us! You can tell by the looks they give us that they believe the result would be different in a second match. The essence of German policy here is to make sure that second match never comes.

How I thank God that General von Schlieffen was so resolute during the war, and kept the right wing of our advance through Belgium and France strong, stronger, strongest despite the unexpectedly quick Russian invasion of our eastern provinces. Once we wheeled behind Paris, knocked the English out of the war, and made the mongrel Third Republic sue for peace, we easily regained the bits of territory the Czar's hordes stole from us. Soon enough we bundled the Slavic subhumans out of the Fatherland and back to the steppes where they belong! We still have not exploited Russia so fully as we should, but that day too will come. I have no doubt of it; those Cossack hordes must not be allowed to threaten civilized Europe ever again.

But to return to the French. Here in Lille, as elsewhere in this country, endless schemes of revenge bubble and trickle and fume. I must get to the bottom of them before they grow too poisonous. I shall not find much help here—that seems plain. But I am confident regardless. The superior man carries on to victory, alone if necessary, and lets nothing obstruct him in the slightest. This shall be my plan here in Lille.

I wish I would hear from you. Knowing that you feel towards me as I do towards you would steel my resolve in the death struggle against the enemies of the Volk and of the Kaiser. May we soon see each other again. I would like to take you out to a quiet supper and walk with you in the moonlight and kiss you until we both are dizzy. I shall look forward to my hero's homecoming while holding off Reds and Jews and others who so vilely plot against the Fatherland here on foreign soil. With all my love and patriotic duty, I remain your—

Uncle Alf

UNCLE ALF

17 May 1929

Dear lovely Geli,

So good to hear from you at last! When I got your letter, I first and foremost kissed the postage stamp, knowing it had touched your sweet lips but two days before. I am glad all is well in Munich, although I do not know that I ought to be glad you sang in a café. This does not strike me as being completely respectable, even if it might have been, as you say, "fun." Duty and discipline and order first, always. The people lacking them is surely doomed. These Frenchmen were frivolous before the war. Now they pay the price for their folly, and they deserve to pay it.

Which is not to say they are much less frivolous now. Walk into any of dozens of clubs and cafés here in Lille and you will see things that would never be allowed—would never be imagined!—in Germany. I shall say no more, drawing instead a merciful veil of silence over brazen French degeneracy.

But I do begin to make progress. In one of these smoky dens, while saxophones brayed out American music straight from the jungle and while dancers cavorted in ways I shall not—I dare not—discuss further, I heard two Frenchmen speaking of a certain Jacques Doriot, who has come to visit this town.

He is the man I principally seek, for he has been schooled by the vile Russian Reds who tried to overthrow Czar Nicholas in 1916. Had the Kaiser not swiftly sent soldiers to his cousin's aid, those devils might have succeeded in their criminal scheming, and then who knows what a mess this sorry world would find itself in now. But a whiff of grapeshot is always the best answer to such vermin. If the Czar had hanged a few hundred more of them after the troubles of 1905, he would have been spared his later difficulties, but he was and is only a woolly-headed fool of a Russian.

Meanwhile I listened as never before. I cannot speak French without showing myself a foreigner, but I understand it quite well. I had better, after so long tracking down enemies of the Kaiser! At any rate, I heard his name, so now I know he is indeed here in Lille spreading his filth. If I have anything to do with it—and I do—he will not spread it long. Good riddance to bad rubbish, I say.

After I return to Munich, perhaps you will sing for me— just for me. And who knows, my darling, what I might do for you? I am a young man yet. Anyone who says forty is old, forty is not vigorous, is nothing but a liar. I will show you what a man of forty can do, you may rest assured of that. My hair is still dark, my heart is still full of love and resolve, and I am still, and shall always be, your loving—

Uncle Alf

Dear sweet kindly lovely Geli,

Still only one letter from you, and now I have been in Lille almost two weeks. It makes me sad. It makes me terribly sad. I would have hoped for so much more. A lonely soldier needs all the help from those behind the front he can possibly get. And I am, I must tell you, a lonely soldier indeed.

There are those who call me a white crow, a monkey in a jacket, because I do not fit in well with the other men of

334

the Feldgendarmerie. They let so many things get in the
way of their duty: their hunger for gross food and tobacco
and strong drink, their coarse lust for the Frenchwomen
with whom they defile their pure and vital German manhood, and sometimes—too often, I fear!—their venal appetite for money in exchange for silence.

None of these distractions holds the least appeal for me.
You may be sure of that, darling! I live and work only to do
harm to the foes of the German Empire. The others in this
service, the worthless and shiftless ones, know it and envy
me my dedication. They resent me because I do not care
to pollute myself as they have polluted themselves. They
resent me, yes, and they envy me, too. I am sure of that.

I went to the commandant. Brigadier Engelhardt and I
go back some years now. When he was making observa-
tions at the front in 1914, a fellow named Bachmann and I
stood in front of him to shield him from British machine-
gun bullets (he was but a lieutenant-colonel then). None
struck us, but that is the sort of thing a man of honor will
remember. And so he saw me in his office, though I am
but an underofficer.

I spoke my mind. I left nothing out, not a single thing. I
told him exactly what I think of the sad state of affairs now
obtaining in Lille. We might have been two brothers rest-
ing side by side in a trench during the Great War. And he
listened to me. He heard every word I said, as though our
respective ranks meant nothing. And they did not, not for
that little while.

When I was through, he looked at me for a long time
without saying anything. At last, he muttered, "Ade, Ade,
Ade, what shall I do with you?"

"Hear me!" I said. "Do what needs doing! Drive the

money changers from the Temple! Be a thorn in the eyes of those who would stand against the Kaiser. Not just Frenchmen, sir—the Feldgendarmerie, too!"

"They are men, Ade. They have the failings of men. They do good work, taken all in all," he said.

"They consort with Frenchmen. They consort with Frenchwomen. They take money to look the other way when the French want to smuggle. They ignore almost every regulation ever drafted." I grew more furious by the moment.

Brigadier Engelhardt saw as much. He tried to calm me down. "Don't chew the carpet at me, Ade," he said. "I tell you again, they mostly do good work. They don't have to follow every jot and tittle of the rules to manage that."

"But they should! They must!" I said. "We must have order in the ranks, obedience and order! Obedience and order are the pillars of the Second Reich! Without them, we perish!"

"We do have them here—enough of them," Engelhardt replied. Can he be corrupt, too? It makes me sad, terribly sad, even to imagine it. Shaking his head as if he were the font of righteousness, he went on, "Ade, you can't expect to bring the conditions of the front, where everything was an emergency, to an occupation that has gone on for fifteen years and may go on for another fifty."

Corrupt! So corrupt! A whited sepulcher of a man! Rage and indignation rose up in me. Only fools, liars, and criminals can hope for mercy from the enemy. Endless plans chased one another through my head. Furiously, I demanded, "If your precious men are as wonderful as you say, why was I sent for? Couldn't you track down this Red devil of a Doriot with your own green devils?"

He flushed. I knew I had struck home with a deadly shot. Then, with what might have been a sigh, he answered, "For special purposes, we need a special man." A special man! Even though, at that moment, he was far from my friend—was, in fact, much closer to being not only my enemy but an enemy of the Kaiserreich—he named me a special man! Recognizing my qualities, he continued, "This Doriot has a strong streak of fanaticism in him. It could be you are the right one to hunt him."

"We all need to be fanatics in service to the Kaiser," I declared: an obvious truth. "Moderation in the pursuit of Germany's enemy is no virtue, while iron determination to see the Fatherland thrive is no vice."

"All right, Ade," Brigadier Engelhardt said with a sigh. He did not like having an enlisted man outargue him. But, no doubt for old times' sake, he did not shout at me for insubordination, as he might have done. "Bring me Jacques Doriot. You may say whatever you like then, for you will have earned the right. Meanwhile, you are dismissed."

"Yes, sir!" I said, and saluted, and left. That is the superior's privilege: to end a discussion when he is not having the better of it.

Give me the chance, my dear, when I come home to Munich, and I will show you just what a special man is your loving—

Uncle Alf

23 May 1929

My sweet beloved Angela,

It pours rain here in Lille. And there is rain in my spirit as well, for I have still had no new letter from you. I hope that all is well, and that you will bring me up to date on what you have been doing back in the civilized and racially pure and unpolluted Fatherland.

Here, everyone is gloomy: Feldgendarmerie, Frenchmen, Flemings. There are more Flemings—of excellent Germanic stock—here in the northeast of France than one might think. Regardless of whether they speak the Flemish tongue, all those whose names begin with van or de show by this infallible sign their ancient Germanic lineage. A priest hereabout, l'abbé Gantois, has some excellent views on this subject. Few, though, seem to wish to lose their French and reacquire the Flemish of their long-ago forbears. It is a great pity.

Few people out and about today—certainly few of the so-called diables verts, who might catch cold, poor darlings, if they went out in the rain! So you would think, at any rate, to hear them talk. But I tell you, and you may take it as a fact, that rain in a city, even a sullen French industrial city, is as nothing beside rain in a muddy trench, such as I endured without complaint during the Great War.

And so I sally forth as usual, with an umbrella and with the collar of my greatcoat turned up. It is a civilian coat. I am not such a fool as to go out into Lille dressed as a German Feldgendarmerie man. One does not hunt ducks by dressing as a zebra! This is another truth some of my comrades have trouble grasping. They are fools, men unworthy of the trust the Kaiser has placed in them.

I sallied forth, I say, into a working-class district of Lille. It is in such places that Doriot spews his poison, his lies, his hateful slanders against the Kaiser, the Crown Prince, and the Second Reich. There are, no doubt, also French agents pursuing this individual, but how can the German Empire rely on Frenchmen? Will they truly go after the likes of Doriot with all their hearts? Or will they, as is more likely, go through the motions of the chase with no real hope or intention of capturing him?

I have nothing to do with them. I reckon them more likely to betray me than to do me any good. I feel the same way about the Feldgendarmerie in Lille, I must say, but I have no choice except working with them to some degree. Thus ordinary folk try to tie the hands of the superior man!

What a smoky, grimy, filthy city Lille is! Soot everywhere. A good steam cleaning might work wonders. Or, on the other hand, the place might simply fall to pieces in the absence of the dirt holding everything together. In any case, steaming these Augean stables will not happen soon.

I can look like a man of the working class. It is not even difficult for me. I wander the streets with my nose to the ground, listening like a bloodhound. I order coffee in an estaminet. My accent for the one word does not betray me. I stop. I sip. I listen.

I find . . . nothing. Have I been betrayed? Does Doriot know I am here? Has my presence been revealed to him? Is that why he is lying low? Has someone on my own side stabbed me in the back? I would give such a vile subhuman a noose of piano wire, if ever he fell into my hands, and smile and applaud as I watched him slowly die.

Hoping to hear again from you soon, I kiss your hands,

your neck, your cheek, your mouth, and the very tip of
your . . . nose. With much love from—

Uncle Alf

⸺

25 May 1929

Dearest adorable Geli,

What a special man, what a superior man, your uncle
is! Despite having to carry on in the face of your disap-
pointing silence, I relentlessly pursue the Red criminal,
Doriot. And I have found a lead that will infallibly betray
him into my hands.

One thing you must know is that the folk of Lille are
most fond of pigeons. During the early days of the war,
we rightly confiscated these birds, for fear of their aiding
enemy espionage. (Some of these pigeons, I am told, ended
up on soldiers' tables. While I hold no brief for meat-eating,
better our men should enjoy them than the French.)

Now, though, we have in France what is called peace.
The Frenchmen are once more permitted to have their
birds. La Societé colombophile lilloise—the Lille Society
of Pigeon-fanciers—is large and active, with hundreds, it
could even be thousands, of members, and with several
meeting halls in the proletarian districts of the city. And
could not these pigeons still be used for spying and the
conveying of intelligence? Of course they could!

I know something of these birds. I had better—as a run-
ner in the war, did I not often enough see my messages
written down and sent off by pigeon? I should say I did!

And so I have been paying visits to the pigeon-fanciers' clubhouses. There I am Meinheer Koppensteiner—a good family name for us!—from Antwerp, a pigeon-lover in Lille on business. My accent will never let me pass for a Frenchman, but a Fleming? Yes, that is easy enough for them to believe.

"Things are still hard in Antwerp," I tell them. "The green devils will take away a man's birds on any excuse or none."

This wins me sympathy. "It is not so bad here," one of them answers. "The Boches"—this is what they call us, the pigdogs—"are very stupid."

Nods all around. Chuckles, too. They think they are so clever! Another Frenchman says, "The things you can get away with, right under their noses!"

But then there are coughs. A couple of fellows shake their heads. This goes too far. I am a stranger, after all, and what sounds like a Flemish accent could be German, too. I am too clever to push hard. I just say, "Well, you are lucky, then—luckier than we. With us, if a bird is caught carrying a message, for instance, no matter how innocent it may be, this is a matter for the firing squad."

They make sympathetic noises. Things must be hard there, they murmur. By the way a couple of them wink, I am sure they deserve a blindfold and a cigarette, the traitors! And maybe they will get one, too! But not yet. I sit and bide my time. They talk about their birds. Meinheer Koppensteiner says a couple of things, enough to show he knows a pigeon from a goose. Not too much. He is a stranger, a foreigner. He does not need to show off. He needs only to be accepted. And he is. Oh, yes—he is.

Before long, Meinheer Koppensteiner will appear at

other clubhouses, too. He will not ask many questions. He will not say much. But he will listen. Oh, my, yes, he will listen. If I were back in Munich, I would rather listen to you. But then, after all, I am not Meinheer Koppensteiner. Thinking of the kisses I shall give you when I see you again, I am, in fact, your loving—

Uncle Alf

⌁

28 May 1929

Dear sweet adorable lovely Angela,

Three weeks now in Lille and only two letters from you! This is not the way I wish it would be, not the way it should be, not the way it must be! You must immediately write again and let me know all your doings, how you pass your days—and your nights. You must, I say. I wait eagerly and impatiently for your response.

Meanwhile, waiting, I visit the other pigeon-fanciers' clubhouses. And I make sure to return to the first one, too, so people can see Meinheer Koppensteiner is truly interested in these birds. And so he is, though not for the reasons he advertises.

The workers babble on about the pigeons. They drink wine and beer and sometimes apple brandy. As a Fleming, Meinheer Koppensteiner is expected to drink beer, too. And so I do, sacrificing even my health in the service of the Kaiser. At one of the clubs, I hear—overhear, actually—quiet talk of a certain Jacques. Is it Doriot? I am not sure. Why is this pestilential Frenchman not named

Jean-Hérold or Pascal? Every third man in Lille is called Jacques! It is so frustrating, it truly does make me want to chew the carpet!

And then someone complained about les Boches—the charming name the Frenchmen have for us, as I told you in my last letter. A sort of silence ensued, in which more than a few eyes went my way. I pretended to pay no particular attention. If I had shouted from the rafters, I am Belgian, not German, so say whatever you please!—well, such noise only makes the wary man more so. A pose of indifference is better.

It worked here. Indeed, it could not have worked better. Quietly, sympathetically, someone said, "Don't worry about him. He's from Antwerp, poor fellow." In fact, he said something stronger than fellow, something not suited to the ears of a delicate, well-brought-up German maiden.

"Antwerp?" someone else replied. "They've been getting it in the neck from the Boches even longer than we have, and there aren't many who can say that."

This sally produced soft laughter and much agreement. I memorized faces, but for many of them I still have no names. Still, with the help of the immortal and kindly Herr Gott, they too will be caught, and suffer the torments such wretches so richly deserve.

Seeing me make little response—seeing me hardly seem to understand—made them grow bolder. Says one of them, "If you want to hear something about the Boches, my friends . . . Do you know the house of Madame Léa, in the Rue des Sarrasins, by the church of Saints Peter and Paul?"

I suspected this was a house of ill repute, but I proved mistaken. This happens even to me, though not often.

"You mean the clairvoyant?" says another, and the first fellow nods. Madame Léa the clairvoyant? There is a picture for you, eh, my dear? Imagine a fat, mustachioed, greasy Jewess, telling her lies to earn her francs! Better such people should be exterminated, I say.

But to return. After the first pigeon-fancier agrees this is indeed the Madame Léa he has in mind—heaven only knows how many shady kikes operate under the same surely false name in Lille!—he says, "Well, come tomorrow at half past nine, then. She gives readings Friday, Saturday, Sunday, Monday. Other days, other things." He chuckles knowingly.

Tomorrow, of course, is Wednesday. Who knows what sort of treachery boils and bubbles in Madame Léa's house on the days when she does not give readings? No one—no one German—knows now. But after tomorrow, she will be exposed to the world for what she is, for a purveyor and panderer to filth of the vilest and most anti-German sort. Such is ever the way of the Jew. But it shall be stopped! Whatever it is, it shall be stopped! I take my holy oath that this be so.

Maybe it will not be Doriot. I hope it will be. I think it will be. No, it must be! It cannot be anyone, anything, else. On this I will stake my reputation. On this I will stake my honor. On this I will stake my very life!

When the mothers of ancient Greece sent their sons into battle, they told them, "With your shield or on it!" So it shall be for me as I storm into the struggle against the enemies of the German Empire! I shall not flag nor fail, but shall emerge triumphant or abandon all hope of future greatness. Hail victory!

Give me your prayers, give me your heart, give me the reward of the conquering hero when I come home covered in glory, as I cannot help but do. I pause here only to kiss your letters once more and wish they were you. Tomorrow— into the fray! Hail victory! for your iron-willed—

Uncle Alf

⌐

29 May 1929

My dear and most beloved Geli,

Himmelherrgottkreuzmillionendonnerwetter! The idiocy of these men! The asininity! The fatuity! How did we win the war? Were the Frenchmen and the English even more cretinous than we? It beggars the imagination, but it must be so.

When I returned to Feldgendarmerie headquarters after shaking off whatever tails the suspicious pigeon-fanciers might have put on me, I first wrote to you, then at once demanded force enough to deal with the mad and vicious Frenchmen who will surely be congregating at Madame Léa's tonight.

I made this entirely reasonable and logical demand— made it and had it refused! "Oh, no, we can't do that," says the fat, stupid sergeant in charge of such things. "Not important enough for the fuss you're making about it."

Not important enough! "Do you care nothing about serving the Reich?" I say, in a very storm of passion. "Do you care nothing about helping your country?" I shake a finger in his face and watch his jowls wobble. "You are worse than a Frenchman, you are!" I cry. "A Frenchman, however racially degenerate he may be, has a reason for being Germany's enemy. But what of you? Why do you hate your own Fatherland?"

He turned red as a holly berry, red as a ripe tomato. "You are insubordinate!" he booms. And so I am, when to be otherwise is to betray the Kaiserreich. "I shall report you to the commandant. He'll put a flea in your ear—you wait and see."

"Go ahead!" I jeer. "Brigadier Engelhardt is a brave man, a true warrior . . . unlike some I could name." The fat sergeant went redder than ever.

The hour by then being after eleven, the brigadier was snug in his bed, so my being haled before him had to wait until the following morning. You may be certain I reported to Feldgendarmerie headquarters as soon as might be. You may also be certain I wore my uniform, with everything in accordance with regulations: no more shabby cap and tweed greatcoat, such as I had had on the previous night for purposes of disguise.

Of course, the other sergeant was still snoring away somewhere. Did you expect anything different? I should hope not! Such men are always indolent, even when they should be most zealous—especially when they should be most zealous, I had better say.

So there I sat, all my buttons gleaming—for I had paid them special attention—when the commandant came in. I sprang to my feet, took my stiffest brace—my back creaked like a tree in the wind—and tore off a salute every training sergeant in the Imperial Army would have admired and used as an example for his foolish, feckless recruits. "Reporting as ordered, sir!" I rapped out.

"Hello, Sergeant," Brigadier Engelhardt replied in the

forthright, manly way that made him so much admired—so much loved, it would not go too far to say—by his soldiers during the Great War. I still tried to think well of him, you see, even though he had thwarted my will before. He returned my salute with grave military courtesy, and then inquired, "But what is all this in aid of?"

Having only just arrived, he would not yet have seen whatever denunciation that swine-fat fool of a sergeant had written out against me. I had to strike while the sun was hot. "I believe I have run this polecat of a Doriot to earth, sir," I said, "and now I need the Feldgendarmerie to help me make the pinch."

"Well, well," he said. "This is news indeed, Ade. Why don't you come into my office and tell me all about it?"

"Yes, sir!" I said. Everything was right with the world again. Far from being corrupt, the brigadier, as I have known since my days at the fighting front, is a man of honor and integrity. Once I explained the undoubted facts to him, how could he possibly fail to draw the same conclusions from them as I had myself? He could not. I was certain of it.

And, again without a doubt, he would at once have drawn those proper conclusions had he not chosen to look at the papers he found on his desk. I stood to attention while he flipped through them—and found, at the very top, the false, lying, and moronic accusations that that jackass of a local Feldgendarmerie sergeant had lodged against me. As he read this fantastic farrago of falsehoods, his eyebrows rose higher and higher. He clicked his tongue between his teeth—tch, tch, tch—the way a mother will when confronting a wayward child.

"Well, well, Ade," he said when at last he had gone

through the whole sordid pack of lies—for such it had to be, when it was aimed against me and against the manifest truth. Brigadier Engelhardt sadly shook his head. "Well, well," he repeated. "You have been a busy boy, haven't you?"

"Sir, I have been doing my duty, as is expected and required of a soldier of the Kaiserreich," I said stiffly.

"Do you think abusing your fellow soldiers for no good cause is part of this duty?" he asked, doing his best to sound severe.

"Sir, I do, when they refuse to do their duty," I said, and the entire story of the previous evening poured from my lips. I utterly confuted and exploded and made into nothingness the absurd slanders that villain of a Feldwebel, that wolf in sheep's clothing, that hidden enemy of the German Empire, spewed forth against me.

Brigadier Engelhardt seemed more than a little surprised at my vehemence. "You are very sure," he remarks.

"As sure as of my hope of heaven, sir," I reply.

"And yet," says he, "your evidence for what you believe strikes me as being on the flimsy side. Why should we lay on so many men for what looks likely to prove a false alarm? Answer me that, if you please."

"Sir," I say, "why did the Feldgendarmerie bring me here to Lille, if not to solve a problem the local men had proved themselves incapable of dealing with? Here now I have the answer, I have the problem as good as solved, and what do I find? That no one—no one, not even you, sir!—will take me seriously. I might as well have stayed in Munich, where I could have visited my lovely and charming niece." You see, my darling, even in my service to the kingdom you are always uppermost in my mind.

Brigadier Engelhardt frowns like a schoolmaster when you give him an answer he does not expect. It may be a right answer—if you are clever enough to think of an answer the schoolmaster does not expect, it probably will be a right answer, as mine was obviously right here—but he has to pause to take it in. Sometimes he will beat you merely for having the nerve to think better and more quickly than he can. Brigadier Engelhardt, I will say, has not been one of that sort.

At last, he says, "But Ade, do you not see? No one has spoken Doriot's name. You do not know that he will be at Madame Léa's."

"I know there will be some sort of subversion there," I say. "And with Doriot in the city to spread his Red filth, what else could it be?"

"Practically anything," he replies. "Lille is not a town that loves the German Empire. It never has been. It never will be."

"It is Doriot!" I say—loudly. "It must be Doriot!" I lean forward. I pound my fist on the desk. His papers jump. So does a vase holding a single red rose.

Brigadier Engelhardt catches it before it tips over. He looks at me for a long time. Then he says, "You go too far, Sergeant. You go much too far, as a matter of fact."

I say nothing. He wants me to say I am sorry. I am not sorry. I am right. I know I am right. My spirit is full of certainty.

He drums his fingers on the desktop. Another pause follows. He sighs. "All right, Ade," he says. "I will give you exactly what you say you want."

I spring to my feet! I salute! "Thank you, Brigadier! Hail victory!"

"Wait." He is dark, brooding. He might almost be a Frenchman, all so-called intellect, and not a proper German, a man of will, of action, of deed, at all. He points a finger at me. "I will give you exactly what you say you want," he repeats. "You can take these men to this fortune-teller's place. If you bring back Jacques Doriot, well and good. If you do not bring back Jacques Doriot . . . If you do not bring him back, I will make you very, very sorry for the trouble you have caused here. Do you understand me?"

"Yes, sir!" This is it! Victory or death! With my shield or on it!

"Do you wish to change your mind?"

"No, sir! Not in the slightest!" I fear nothing. My heart is firm. It pounds only with eagerness to vanquish the foes of the Reich, the foes of the Kaiser. Not a trace of fear. Nowhere at all a trace of fear, I swear it. Into battle I shall go.

He sighs again. "Very well. Dismissed, Feldwebel."

Now I have merely to wait until the evening, to prepare the Feldgendarmerie men who shall surround Madame Léa's establishment, and then to—to net my fish! You shall see. By this time tomorrow, Doriot will be in my pocket and I will be a famous man, or as famous as a man whose work must necessarily for the most part be done in secret can become.

And once I am famous, what shall I do? Why, come home to my family—most especially to my loving and beloved niece!—and celebrate just as I hope. You are the perfect one to give a proper Hail victory! for your proud, your stern, your resolute—

Uncle Alf

30 May 1929

My very dearest and most beloved sweet Geli,

Hail victory! I kiss you and caress you here in my mind, as I bask in the triumph of my will! Strength and success, as I have always said, lie not in defense but in attack. Just as a hundred fools cannot replace a wise man, a heroic decision like mine will never come from a hundred cowards. If a plan is right in itself, and if thus armed it sets out on struggle in this world, it is invincible. Every persecution will only make it stronger. So it is with me today.

After fifteen years of the work I have accomplished, as a common German soldier and merely with my fanatical willpower, I achieved last night a victory that confounded not only my superiors who summoned me to Lille but also the arrogant little manikins who, because they did not know what I could do or with whom they were dealing, anticipated my failure. All of them are today laughing out of the other side of their mouths, and you had best believe it!

Let me tell you exactly how it happened.

That fat and revolting sergeant had finally reached his post when I came out of Brigadier Engelhardt's office. Laughing in my face, the swine, he says, "I bet the commandant told you where to head in—and just what you deserve, too."

"Not me," I say. "The raid is on for tonight. I am in charge of it. After that, we'll see who gloats."

He gaped at me, gross and disgustingly foolish. Such Untermenschen, even though allegedly German, are worse foes to the Kaiserreich than the French, perhaps even worse than the Jews themselves. They show the Volk can also poison itself and drown in a sewer tide of mediocrity. But I will not let that happen. I will not! It must not!

Would you believe it, that lumpen-sergeant had the infernal and damnable gall to ask Brigadier Engelhardt—Brigadier Engelhardt, whom I protected with my own body during the war!—if I was telling the truth. That shameless badger!

He came back looking crestfallen and exultant at the same time. "All right—we'll play your stupid game," says he. "We'll play it—and then you'll get it in the neck. Don't come crying to me afterwards, either. It'll do you no good."

"Just do your job," I say. "That's all I want from you. Just do your job."

"Don't worry about it," he says gruffly. As though he hadn't given me cause enough for worry, God knows. But I only nodded. I would give him and his men the necessary orders. They had but to obey me. If they did as I commanded, all would be well. I could not be everywhere at once, however much I wanted to. I had discovered the foul Red plot; others would have to help snuff it out.

When the time came that evening, I set out for Madame Léa's. The Lille Feldgendarmerie would follow, I hoped not too noisily and not too obviously. That stinking sergeant could ruin the game simply by letting the vile Marxist conspirators spot him. I hoped he would not, but he could—and, because he was so disgustingly round, there was a great deal of him to spot.

The church of Sts. Peter and Paul is lackluster architecturally, the house Madame Léa infests even more so. A sign in her window announced her as a LISEUSE DE PEN-

SÉE, a thought-reader—and, for the benefit of German troops benighted enough to seek out her services, also as a WAHRSAGERIN, a lady soothsayer. Lies! Foolishness! To say nothing of espionage and treason!

I knocked on the door. A challenge from within: "Who are you? What do you want?"

"I'm here for the lecture," I answered.

"You sound funny," said the man behind the door—my accent proved a problem, as it does too often in France.

"I'm from Antwerp," I said, as I had at the pigeon-fanciers' clubs.

And then Lady Luck, who watched out for me on the battlefields of the war, reached out to protect me once again. If one's destiny is to save the beloved Fatherland, one will not be allowed to fail. I was starting to explain how I had heard of the lecture at La Societé colombo-phile lilloise when one of the men with whom I had spoken there came up and said, "This Koppensteiner fellow's all right. Knows his pigeons, he does. And if you think the Boches don't screw over the Flemings, too, you're daft."

That got them to open the door for me. I doffed my cap to the man who had vouched for me. "Merci beaucoup," I said, resolving to thank him as he truly deserved once he was under arrest. But that could—would have to—wait.

To my disappointment, I did not see Madame Léa there. Well, no matter. We can round her up in due course. But let me go on with the story. Her living room, where I suppose she normally spins her web of falsehood and deceit, is quite large. The wages of sin may be death, but the wages of deceit, by all appearances, are very good. Twenty, perhaps even thirty, folding chairs of cheap manufacture—without a doubt produced in factories run by pestilential

Jews, who care only for profit, not for quality—had been crammed into it for the evening's festivities. About half were taken when I came in.

And there, by the far wall, under a dingy print of a painting I suppose intended to be occult, stood Jacques Doriot. I recognized him immediately, from the photographs on file with the Feldgendarmerie. He is a Frenchman of the worst racial type, squat and swarthy, with thick spectacles perched on a pointed nose. His hair is crisp and curly and black, and shines with some strong-smelling grease I noticed from halfway across the room. I was right all along, you see. I had known it, and now I had proof. I wanted to shout for joy, but knew I had to keep silent.

Several men, some of whom I had seen at one pigeon-fanciers' club or another, went up to chat with him. I marked them in particular: they were likely to be the most dangerous customers in the room. Doriot took no special notice, though, of those who hung back, of whom I was one. Why should he have? Not everyone is a leader. Most men would sooner go behind, like so many sheep. It is true even amongst us Germans—how much more so amongst the mongrelized, degenerate French!

More would-be rebels and traitors continued to come in, until the place was full. We all squeezed together, tight as sardines in a tin. One of the local men did not sit down right away. He said, "Here is Comrade Jacques, who will speak of some ways to get our own back against the Boches."

"Thank you, my friend," Doriot said, and his voice startled me. By his looks, he seemed a typical French ball of suet, and I had expected nothing much from him as a speaker. But as soon as he went on, "We can lick these

German bastards," I understood exactly why he has caused the Kaiserreich so much trouble over the years. Not only are his tones deep and resonant, demanding and deserving of attention, but he has the common touch that distinguishes the politician from the theoretician.

No ivory-tower egghead he! He wasted no time on ideology. Every man has one, but how many care about it? It is like the spleen, necessary but undramatic. Theoreticians always fail to grasp this. Not Doriot! "We can make the Boche's life hell," he said with a wicked grin, "and I'll show you just how to do it. Listen! Whenever you do something for those damned stiff-necked sons of bitches, do it wrong! If you drive a cab, let them off at the wrong address and drive away before they notice. If you wait tables, bring them something they didn't order, then be very sorry—and bring them something else they didn't ask for. If you work in a factory, let your machine get out of order and stand around like an idiot till it's fixed. If it's not working, what can you do? Not a thing, of course. If you're in a foundry . . . But you're all clever fellows. You get the picture, eh?"

He grinned again. So did the Frenchmen listening to him. They got the picture, all right. The picture was treason and rebellion, pure and simple. I had plenty to arrest him right there for spouting such tripe, and them for listening to it. But I waited. I wanted more.

And Doriot gave it to me. He went on, "The workers' revolution almost came off in Russia after the war, but the forces of reaction, the forces of oppression, were too strong. It can come here. With councils of workers and peasants in the saddle, I tell you France can be a great nation once more. France will be a great nation once more!"

"And when she is"—theatrically, he lowered his voice—"when she is, I say, then we truly pay back the Boches. Then we don't have to play stupid games with them any more. Then we rebuild our army, we rebuild our navy, we send swarms of airplanes into the sky, and we put revolution on the march all through Europe! *Vive la France!*"

"*Vive la France!*" the audience cried.

"*Vive la révolution!*" Doriot shouted.

"*Vive la révolution!*" they echoed.

"*Vive la drapeau rouge!*" he yelled.

They called out for the red flag, too. They sprang to their feet. They beat their palms together. They were in a perfect frenzy of excitement. I also sprang to my feet. I also beat my palms together. I too was in a perfect frenzy of excitement. I drew forth my pistol and fired a shot into the ceiling.

Men to either side of me sprang aside. There was no one behind me. I had made sure of that. To make sure no one could get behind me, I put my back against the wall, meanwhile pointing the pistol at Doriot. He has courage, I say so much for him. "Here, my friend, my comrade, what does this mean?" he asked me.

I clicked my heels. "This means you are under arrest. This means I am the forces of reaction, the forces of oppression. À votre service, monsieur." I gave him a bow a Parisian headwaiter would have envied, but the pistol never wavered from his chest.

Indeed, Doriot has very considerable courage. I watched him thinking about whether to rush me, whether to order his fellow traitors to rush me. As I watched, I waited for the men of the Lille Feldgendarmerie post to break down the doors and storm in to seize those Frenchmen. My pistol shot should have brought them on the run. It should have, but where were they, the lazy swine?

So I wondered. And I could see Doriot nerving himself to order that charge. I gestured with the pistol, saying, "You think, monsieur, this is an ordinary Luger, and that, if you tell your men to rush me, I can shoot at the most eight—seven, now—and the rest will drag me down and slay me. I regret to inform you, that is a mistake. I have here a Luger Parabellum, Artilleriemodel 08. It has a thirty-two-round drum. I may not get all of you, but it will be more than seven, I promise. And I will enjoy every bit of it—I promise you that, too." I shifted the pistol's barrel, just by a hair. "So—who will be first?"

And, my sweet, do you want to hear the most delicious thing of all? I was lying! I held only an ordinary Luger. There is such a thing as the Artilleriemodel; it was developed after the war to give artillerymen a little extra firepower if by some mischance they should find they had to defend themselves at close quarters against infantry. I have seen the weapon. The drum below the butt is quite prominent—as it must be, to accommodate thirty-two rounds of pistol ammunition.

A close look—even a cursory look—would have shown the Frenchmen I was lying. But they stood frozen like mammoths in the ice of Russia, believing every word I said. Why? I will tell you why. The great masses of the people will more easily fall victim to a big lie than to a small one, that is why. And I told the biggest lie I could possibly tell just then.

Nevertheless, I was beginning to wonder if more lies— or more gunshots—would be necessary when at last I heard the so-welcome sound of doors crashing down at the front and rear of Madame Léa's establishment. In swarmed the Feldgendarmerie men! Now, now that I had done all the work, faced all the danger, they were as fierce as tigers. Their Alsatians bayed like the hounds of hell. They took the French criminals and plotters out into the night.

That fat, arrogant Feldwebel stayed behind. His jowls jiggled like calves'-foot jelly as he asked me, "How did you know this? How did you hold them all, you alone, until we came?"

"A man of iron will can do anything," I declared, and he did not dare argue with me, for the result had proved me right. He walked away instead, shaking his stupid, empty head.

And, when I return to Munich, I will show you exactly what a man with iron in his will—and elsewhere! oh, yes, and elsewhere!—can do. In the meantime, I remain, most fondly, your loving—

Uncle Alf

---

31 May 1929

To my sweet and most delicious Geli,

Hello, my darling. I wonder whether this letter will get to Munich ahead of me, for I have earned leave following the end of duty today. Nevertheless I must write, so full of triumph am I.

Today I saw Brigadier Engelhardt once more. I wondered if I would. In fact, he made a point of summoning me to his office. He proved himself a true gentleman, I must admit.

When I came in, he made a production of lighting up his pipe. Only after he has it going to his satisfaction does he say, "Well, Ade, you were right all along." A true gentleman, as I told you!

"Yes, sir," I reply. "I knew it from the start."

He blows out a cloud of smoke, then sighs. "Well, I will certainly write you a letter of commendation, for you've earned it. But I want to say one thing to you, man to man, under four eyes and no more."

"Yes, sir," I say again. When dealing with officers, least said is always safest.

He sighs again. "One of these days, Ade, that damned arrogance of yours will trip you up and let you down as badly as it's helped you up till now. I don't know where and I don't know how, but it will. You'd do best to be more careful. Do you understand what I'm telling you? Do you understand even one word?"

"No, sir," I say, with all the truth in my heart.

Yet another sigh from him. "Well, I didn't think you would, but I knew I ought to make the effort. Today you're a hero, no doubt about it. Enjoy the moment. But, as the slave used to whisper at a Roman triumph, 'Remember, thou art mortal.' Dismissed, Ade."

I saluted. I went out. I sat down to write this letter. I will be home soon. Wear a skirt that flips up easily, for I intend to show you just what a hero, just what a conqueror, is your iron-hard—

Uncle Alf

THE SCARLET BAND

Here's another tale of Atlantis for you. Any resemblance between Athelstan Helms and Sh*****k H****s is, of course, purely coincidental. I mean, it must be. This is an alternate world, one in which Sh*****k H****s never existed. There never was any such story as "A Study in Scarlet." And there certainly wasn't any such story as "The Adventure of the Speckled Band." C'mon. You read science fiction and fantasy, don't you? Surely you can suspend that much disbelief—can't you? Please? You've come this far. Give it a try.

stormy November on the North Atlantic. Even a great liner like the *Victoria Augusta* rolled and pitched in the swells sweeping down from the direction of Iceland. The motion of her deck was not dissimilar to that of a restive horse, though the most restive horse rested at last, while the *Victoria Augusta* seemed likely to go on jouncing on the sea forever.

Most of the big ship's passengers stayed in their cabins. Nor was that sure proof against seasickness; the sharp stink of vomit filled the passageways, and was liable to nauseate even passengers who might have withstood the motion alone.

A pair of men, though, paced the promenade deck as if it were July on the Mediterranean. Passing sailors sent them curious looks. "'Ere, now," one of the men in blue said, touching a deferential forefinger to his cap. "Shouldn't you toffs go below? It'll be easier to take, like, if you do."

"I find the weather salubrious enough, thank you," the taller and leaner of the pair replied. "I am glad to discern that we shall soon come into port."

"Good heavens, Helms—how can you know that?" his companion ejaculated in surprise.

Athelstan Helms puffed on his pipe. "Nothing simpler, Doctor. Have you not noted that the waves discommoding our motion are sharper and more closely spaced than they were when we sailed the broad bosom of the Atlantic? That can only mean a shallow bottom beneath us, and a shallow bottom surely presages the coastline of Atlantis."

"Right you are, sir. Sure as can be, you've got your sea legs under you, to feel something like that." The sailor's voice held real respect now. "Wasn't more than fifteen minutes ago I 'eard the chief engineer say we was two, maybe three, hours out of 'Anover."

"Upon my soul," Dr. James Walton murmured. "It all seems plain enough when you set it out, Helms."

"I'm glad you think so," Helms replied. "You do commonly seem to."

Walton chuckled, a little self-consciously. "By now I ought not to be surprised at your constantly surprising me, what?" He laughed again, louder this time. "A bit of a paradox, that, don't you think?"

"A bit," Athelstan Helms agreed, an unaccustomed note of indulgence in his voice.

The sailor stared at him, then aimed a stubby forefinger in the general direction of his sternum. "I know who you are, sir," he said. "You're that detective feller!"

"Only an amateur," Helms replied.

He might as well have left the words unsaid. As if he had, the sailor rounded on Dr. Walton. "And you must be the bloke 'oo writes up 'is adventures. I've read a great plenty of 'em, I 'ave."

"You're far too kind, my good man." Walton, delighted to trumpet Athelstan Helms' achievements to the skies, was modest about his own.

"But what brings the two of you to Atlantis?" the sailor asked. "I thought you stayed in England, where it's civilized, like."

"As a matter of fact—" Dr. Walton began.

Helms smoothly cut in: "As a matter of fact, that is a matter we really should not discuss before conferring with the authorities in Hanover."

"I get you, sir." The sailor winked and laid a finger by the side of his nose. "Mum's the word. Not a soul will hear from me." Away he went, almost bursting with self-importance.

"It will be all over the ship before we dock," Dr. Walton said dolefully.

Athelstan Helms nodded. "Of course it will. But it can't get off the ship before we dock, so that is a matter of small consequence."

"Why didn't you want me to mention the House of Universal Devotion, then?" Dr. Walton asked. "For I saw that you prevented my doing so."

"Indeed." Helms nodded. "I believe the sailor may well be a member of that curious sect."

"Him? Good heavens, Helms! He's as English as Yorkshire pudding."

"No doubt. And yet the House, though Atlantean in origin, has its devotees in our land as well, and in the Terranovan republics and principalities. If the case with which we shall be concerned in the United States of Atlantis did not have ties to our England, you may rest assured I should not have embarked on the *Victoria Augusta*, excellent though she may be." Helms paused as another sailor walked past. When the man was out of earshot, the detective continued, "Did you note nothing unusual about the manner in which our recent acquaintance expressed himself?"

"Unusual? Not really." Dr. Walton shook his head. "A Londoner from the East End, I make him out to be. Not an educated man, even if he has his letters. Has scant respect for his aitches, but not quite a Cockney."

Although Helms' pinched features seemed to have little room for a smile, when one did find a home it illuminated his whole face. "Capital, Walton!" he said, and made as if to clap his hands. "I agree completely. Your analysis is impeccable—well, nearly so, anyhow."

"'Nearly'? How have I gone astray?" By the way Walton said it, he did not believe he'd strayed at all.

"As you are such a cunning linguist, Doctor, I am confident the answer will suggest itself to you in a matter of moments." Athelstan Helms waited. When Walton shook his head, Helms shrugged and said, "Did you not hear the intrusive 'like' he used twice? Most un-English, but a common enough Atlantean locution. Begun by an actor—one of the Succot brothers, I believe—a generation ago, and adopted by the generality. I conjecture this fellow may have acquired it in meetings with his fellow worshipers."

"It could be." Dr. Walton stroked his salt-and-pepper chin whiskers. "Yes, it could be. But not all Atlanteans belong to the House of Universal Devotion. Far from it, in fact. He could have learned that interjection innocently enough."

"Certainly. That is why I said no more than that he might well be a member of the sect," Helms replied. "But I do find it likely, as the close and continuous intercourse amongst members of the House while engaged in worship seems calculated to foster such accretions. And he knew who we were. Members of the House, familiar with the difficulties the Atlantean constabulary is having with this case, may also be on the lookout for assistance from a foreign clime."

"Hmm," Walton said, and then, "Hmm," again. "How could they know the chief inspector in Hanover—"

"Chief of police, they call him," Helms noted.

"Chief of police, then," Walton said impatiently. "How could they know he sought your aid and not that of, say, Scotland Yard?"

"The easiest way to effect that would be to secret someone belonging to the House of Universal Devotion within the Hanoverian police department, something which strikes me as not implausible," Athelstan Helms said. "Other possible methodologies are bound to suggest themselves upon reflection."

By the unhappy expression spreading over Dr. Walton's fleshy countenance, such methodologies did indeed suggest themselves. But before he could mention any of them, a shout from the bow drew his attention, and Athelstan Helms' as well: "Hanover Light! Hanover Light ahead!"

Helms all but quivered with anticipation. "Before long, Doctor, we shall see what we shall see."

"So we shall." Walton seemed less enthusiastic.

Hanover Light was one of the engineering marvels of the age. Situated on a wave-washed rock several miles east of the Atlantean coast, the lighthouse reached more than three hundred feet into the air. The lamps in the upper story guided ships in from far out to sea.

Hanover itself cupped a small enclosed bay that formed the finest harbor on the east coast of Atlantis—a better harbor, even, than Avalon in the more lightly settled Atlantean west. Steam tugs with heavy rope fenders nudged the *Victoria Augusta* to her berth. Sailors tossed lines to waiting longshoremen, who made the ship fast to the pier. The liner's engines sighed into silence.

Dr. Walton sighed, too. "Well, we're here."

Athelstan Helms nodded. "I could not have deduced it more precisely myself," he said. "The red-crested eagle on the flag flying from yonder pole, the longshoremen shouting in what passes for

English in the United States of Atlantis, the fact that we have just completed an ocean voyage . . . Everything does indeed point to our being here."

Walton blinked. Was Helms having him on? He dismissed the notion from his mind, as being unworthy of a great detective. Lighting a cigar, he said, "I wonder if anyone will be here to meet us."

"Assuredly," Helms replied. "The customs men will take their usual interest—I generously refrain from saying, *their customary interest*—in our belongings." Walton began to speak; Helms forestalled him. "But you were about to say, anyone in an official capacity. Unless I am very much mistaken, that excitable-looking gentleman on the planking there will be a Captain La Strada of the Hanover police."

The individual in question certainly did seem excitable. He wore tight trousers, a five-button jacket with tiny lapels, and one of the most appalling cravats in the history of haberdashery. His broad-brimmed hat would have raised eyebrows in London, too. Nor did his face have a great deal to recommend it: he looked like a ferret, with narrow, close-set eyes, a beak of a nose, and a wildly disorderly mustache.

And he was looking for the two Englishmen. "Helms!" he shouted, jumping up and down. "Walton!" He waved and pointed—unfortunately, at two other men halfway along the *Victoria Augusta*'s deck.

"Here we are!" Walton called. Under his breath, he added, "Shocking they let a dago climb so high, bloody shocking."

Inspector La Strada jumped even higher. As if impelled by some galvanic current, his arm swung toward the detective and his medical companion. "Helms! Walton!" he bawled, for all the world as if he hadn't been yelling at those other chaps a moment before. Perhaps he hoped Helms and Walton hadn't noticed him doing it.

He pumped their hands when they came down the gangplank, and undertook to push their trunks to the customs house on one of the low-slung wheeled carts provided for the purpose. "Very kind of you," Walton murmured, reflecting that no true gentleman in London would lower himself to playing the navvy.

As if reading his mind, La Strada said, "Here in Atlantis, we roll up our sleeves and set our hands to whatever wants doing. This is a land for men of action, not sissies who sit around drinking port and playing the fiddle."

"Shall I take my return passage now, in that case?" Helms inquired in a voice rather cooler than the wind off the Greenland ice.

"By no means." La Strada seemed cheerfully unaware he'd given offense. "There's work to be done here, and you are—we hope you are—the man to do it."

Some of the first work to be done would be explaining the pistols in the travelers' baggage—so Dr. Walton anticipated, at any rate. But the customs inspectors took the firearms in stride. They seemed more interested in the reagents Helms carried in a cleverly padded case inside his trunk. At La Strada's voluble insistence that these were essential to the business for which the detective had been summoned to Atlantis, the inspectors grudgingly stamped Helms' passport, and Walton's as well.

La Strada had a coach waiting outside the customs house. "Shall I take you gents to the hotel first, to freshen up after your voyage, or would you rather come to the station and take your first look at what you'll be dealing with?" he asked.

Dr. Walton would have plumped for the manifold virtues of a good hotel, assuming Hanover boasted such a marvelous sanctuary, but Helms forestalled him, saying, "The station, Inspector, by all means. Well begun is half done, as they say, and the sooner we finish our business here, the sooner we can go home again."

"Once you spend a while in Atlantis, Mr. Helms, you may decide you don't care to go home after all," La Strada said.

"I doubt it." Athelstan Helms' reply would have silenced an Englishman and very likely crushed him. Inspector La Strada was made of sterner, or, more likely, coarser stuff. He let out a merry peal of laughter and lit a cheroot much nastier than the fragrant cigar Walton enjoyed.

Lamplighters went through the cobblestoned and bricked streets with long poles, setting the gas jets alight. The buttery glow of the street lights went some way toward mitigating the deepening twilight. Hanover wasn't London—what city was, or could be?—but it did not put its head in its shell with the coming of night, either. The streets and taverns and music halls and even many of the shops remained crowded.

London boasted inhabitants from every corner of the far-flung British Empire. Hanover, the largest urban center in a republic fueled by immigration, had residents from all over the world: Englishmen, Scots, Irish, the French and Spaniards who'd originally settled southern Atlantis, Negro freemen and freedmen and -women, swarthy Italians like La Strada, Scandinavians, stolid Germans, Jews from Eastern Europe, copper-skinned Terranovan aboriginals, Chinese running eateries and laundries advertised in their incomprehensible script, and every possible intermingling of them.

"Pack of mongrels," Dr. Walton muttered.

"What do you say, Doctor?" the inspector inquired. "With the rattle and clatter of the wheels, I fear I did not hear you."

"Oh, nothing. Nothing, really." Walton puffed on his cigar, both to blot out the stench of La Strada's and, perhaps, to send up a defensive smoke screen.

Unlike London, whose streets wandered where they would and changed names when they would, Hanover was built on a

right-angled gridwork. People proclaimed it made navigation easier and more efficient. And it likely did, but Dr. Walton could not
escape the notion that a city needed to be learned, that making it
too easy to get around in reduced it to a habitation for children,
not men.

He had the same low opinion of Atlantis' coinage. A hundred
cents to an eagle—well, where was the challenge in *that*? Four far-
things to a penny, twelve pence to the shilling, twenty shillings the
pound (or, if you were an aristo, twenty-one in a guinea) . . . Foreigners always whined about how complicated English currency
was. To Walton's way of thinking, that was all to the good. Whin-
ing helped mark out the foreigners and let you keep a proper eye
on them.

And as for architecture, did Hanover really have any? A few
Georgian buildings, Greek Revival more pretentious than otherwise, and endless modern utilitarian boxes of smoke-smudged
brick that might once have been red or brown or yellow or even
purple for all anyone could tell nowadays. Some—many—of these
brick boxes were blocks of flats that outdid even London's for
sheer squalidity. The odors of cheap cooking and bad plumbing
wafted from them.

In such slums, the brass-buttoned policemen traveled in
pairs. They wore low caps with patent-leather brims, and carried
revolvers on their belts along with their billy clubs. They didn't
look much like bobbies, and they didn't act much like bobbies,
either.

"Do you find, then, that you need to intimidate your citizenry
to maintain order?" Dr. Walton asked.

Inspector La Strada stared at him, eyes shiny under a gas
lamp. "Intimidate our citizenry?" he said, as if the words were
Chinese or Quechua. Then, much more slowly than he might
have, he grasped what the Englishman was driving at. "God bless

you, Doctor!" he exclaimed, no doubt in lieu of some more pungent comment. "Our policemen don't carry guns to intimidate the citizenry."

"Why, then?" Walton asked in genuine bewilderment.

Athelstan Helms spoke before the Atlantean inspector could: "They wear guns to keep the citizenry from murdering them in its criminal pursuits."

"Couldn't have put it better myself," La Strada said. "This isn't London, you know."

"Yes, I'd noticed that," Dr. Walton observed tartly.

La Strada either missed or ignored the sarcasm. "Thought you might, like," he said. "Anyone but a convicted felon can legally carry a gun here. And the convicted felons do it, too—what have they got to lose? A tavern brawl here isn't one fellow breaking a mug over the other one's head. He pulls out a snub-nosed .42 and puts a pill in the bastard's brisket. And if getting away means plugging a policeman, he doesn't stick at that, either."

"Charming people," the physician murmured.

"In many ways, they are," Helms said. "But, having won freedom through a bloody uprising against the British crown, they labor under the delusion that they must be ready—nay, eager—to shed more blood at any moment to defend it."

"We don't happen to think that is a delusion, sir," La Strada said stiffly.

"No doubt," Athelstan Helms replied. "That does not mean it isn't one. I draw your notice to the Dominion of Ontario, in northeastern Terranova. Ontario declined revolution—despite your buccaneers, I might add, or perhaps because of them—yet can you deny that its people are as free as your own, and possessed of virtually identical rights?"

"Of course I can. They still have a Queen—your Queen." La Strada wrinkled up his nose as if to show he could smell the stench of monarchism across the thousand miles of Hesperian Gulf separating the USA and Ontario.

"We do not find it unduly discommodes us," Helms said.

"The more fools you," La Strada told him. There was remarkably little conversation in the coach after that until it pulled up in front of Hanover's police headquarters.

Dr. Walton had not looked for the headquarters to be lovely. But neither had he looked for the building to be as ugly as it was. A gas lamp on either side of the steps leading up to the entrance showed the brickwork to be of a jaundiced, despairing yellow. The steps themselves were of poured concrete: utilitarian, no doubt, but unequivocally unlovely. The edifice was squat and sturdy, with small rectangular windows; it put Walton in mind of a fortress. The stout iron bars on the windows of the bottom two stories reinforced the impression—and the windows.

After gazing at those, Helms remarked, "They will use this place to house criminals as well as constables." There, for once, the detective's companion had not the slightest difficulty comprehending how his friend made the deduction.

"Come along, gents, come along." La Strada hopped down to the ground, spry as a cricket. Helms and Walton followed. The policeman who drove the carriage, who'd said not a word on the journey from the customs house, remained behind to ensure that their luggage did not decide to tour the city on its own.

The odors greeting the newcomers when they went inside would have told them what sort of place they were finding. Dante might have had such smells in mind when he wrote, *All hope abandon, ye who enter here.* Dampness and mold, bad tobacco, stale sweat infused with the aftereffects of rum and whiskey, sour vomit, chamber pots that wanted emptying, the sharp smell of fear and the less definable odor of despair . . . Dr. Walton sighed. They were no different from what he would have smelled at the Old Bailey.

And, walking past cells on the way to the stairs, Walton and Athelstan Helms saw scenes straight out of Hogarth engravings, and others that, again, might have come straight from the *Inferno*. "Here we go," Inspector La Strada said, politely holding the door open for the two Englishmen. When he closed the stout redwood panel (anywhere but Atlantis, it would have been oak) behind them, he might have put a mile of distance between them and the hellish din behind it.

Another door, equally sturdy, guarded each of the upper floors. Even if, through catastrophe or conspiracy, a swarm of prisoners escaped, the constables could fortify their position and defend themselves for a long time. "You have firing ports, I see," Helms murmured. Dr. Walton, who'd fought in Afghanistan and was one of the lucky few to have escaped that hellhole, slapped at his thigh, annoyed at himself for missing the telling detail.

Inspector La Strada opened one of those fortified portals. A rotund constabulary sergeant with a large-caliber revolver sat just beyond it, ready for any eventuality. Not far away, a technician had a dissipated-looking young man in a special chair, and was measuring his skull and ear and left middle finger and ring finger with calipers and ruler. A clerk wrote down the numbers he called out.

"You still use the Bertillon system for identifying your miscreants, then?" Athelstan Helms inquired.

"We do," La Strada replied. "It's not perfect, but far better than any other method we've found." He thrust out his receding chin as far as it would go. "And I haven't heard that Scotland Yard's got anything better, either."

"Scotland Yard? No." Helms sounded faintly dismissive. "But I am personally convinced that one day—and perhaps one day quite soon—the ridges and crenelations on a man's fingertips will prove more efficacious yet, and with far less labor and less likelihood of error and mistaken identity."

"Well, I'll believe that when I see it, sir, and not a moment before." La Strada picked his way through chaos not much quieter and not much less odorous than that downstairs. He finally halted at a plain—indeed, battered—pine desk. "My home from home, you might say," he remarked, and purloined a couple of cheap, unpadded chairs nearby. "Have a seat, gents, and I'll tell you what's what, like."

Before sitting, Dr. Walton tried to brush something off his chair. Whatever it was, it proved sticky and resistant to brushing. He perched gingerly, on one buttock, rather like the old woman in *Candide*. Either Helms' chair was clean or he was indifferent to any dirt it might have accumulated.

La Strada reached into a desk drawer and pulled out a brown glass bottle and, after some rummaging, three none too clean tumblers. "A restorative, gentlemen?" he said, and started to pour before the Englishmen could say yea or nay.

It wasn't scotch. It was maize whiskey—corn liquor, they called it in Atlantis—and it might have been aged a week, or perhaps even two. "Gives one the sensation of having swallowed a lighted gas lamp, what?" Dr. Walton wheezed when more or less capable of intelligible speech once more.

"It intoxicates. Past that, what more is truly required?" Helms drank his off with an aplomb suggesting long experience—and perhaps a galvanized gullet.

"This here is legal whiskey, gents. You should taste what the homecookers make." La Strada shuddered . . . and refilled his glass. "Shall we get down to business?"

"May we talk freely here?" Helms asked. "Are you certain none of your colleagues within earshot belongs to the House of Universal Devotion?"

"Certain? Mr. Helms, I'm not certain of a damned thing," La Strada said. "If you told me a giant honker would walk up those stairs and come through that doorway there, I couldn't say I was certain you were wrong."

"Aren't honkers as extinct as the dodo?" Dr. Walton asked, sudden sharp interest in his voice: he fancied himself an amateur ornithologist. "Didn't that Audubon chap paint some of the last of them before your slave uprising?"

"The Servile Insurrection, we call it." La Strada's face clouded. Like most Atlanteans his age, he would have served in the fight. "I've got a scar on my leg on account of it. . . . But you don't care about that. Yes, they say honkers are gone, but the backwoods of Atlantis are a mighty big place, so who knows for sure, like . . .? But you don't care about that, either, not really. The House of Universal Devotion."

"Yes. The House of Universal Devotion." Helms leaned forward on his hard, uncomfortable seat.

"Well, you'll know they're killing important men. If you attended to my letter, you'll know they're doing it for no good reason any man who doesn't belong to the House can see. And you'll know they're damned hard to stop, because their murderers don't care if they live or die," La Strada said. "They figure they go straight to heaven if they're killed."

"Like the Hashishin," murmured Walton, who, from his service in the East, was steeped in Oriental lore.

La Strada looked blank. "The Assassins," Athelstan Helms glossed.

"They're assassins, all right," the inspector said, missing most of the point. Neither Englishman seemed to reckon it worthwhile to enlighten him. La Strada went on, "We aim to find a way to make them stop without outlawing them altogether. We have religious freedom here in Atlantis, we do. We don't establish any one church and disadvantage the rest."

"Er, well, despite that, we have it in England, as well," Walton said. "But we don't construe it to mean freedom to slaughter your fellow man in the name of your creed."

"Nor do we," La Strada said. "Otherwise, we wouldn't be trying to stop it, now would we?" He seemed to feel he'd proved some sort of point.

"Perhaps the best way to go about it would be to arrange for a suitable divine revelation from the Preacher," Helms suggested.

"Yes, that would be the best way—if the Preacher could be persuaded to announce that kind of revelation," La Strada agreed. "If, indeed, the Preacher could be found by anyone not a votary of the House of Universal Devotion."

"Do I correctly infer you have it in mind for me to seek him out and discuss with him the possibility and practicability of such a revelation?" Helms asked.

"You are indeed a formidable detective, Mr. Helms," La Strada said. "Your fee will be formidable, too, should you succeed."

"Do you imagine the magnificent Athelstan Helms can fail?" Dr. Walton inquired indignantly.

"Several here have made the attempt. None has reached the Preacher. None, in fact, has survived," Inspector La Strada answered. "So yes, I can imagine your comrade failing. I do not wish it, but I can imagine it."

"Quite right. Quite right," Helms said. "Imagining all that might go wrong is the best preventive. Now, then—can you tell me where the Preacher is likeliest to be found?"

"Wellll . . ." La Strada stretched the word out to an annoying length. "He's in Atlantis. We're pretty sure of that."

"Capital," Helms said without the least trace of irony. "All that remains, then, is to track him down, eh?"

"I'm sure you'll manage in the next few days." La Strada, by contrast . . .

The Golden Burgher, the hotel into which La Strada had booked Helms and Walton, lay only a few blocks from police headquarters, but might have come from a different world. It would not have seemed out of place in London, though the atmosphere put Dr. Walton more in mind of vulgar ostentation than of the genteel luxury more ideally British. And few British hotels would have had so many spittoons—cuspidors, they seemed to call them here—so prominently placed. The brown stains on the white marble squares of the checkerboard flooring (and, presumably though less prominently, on the black as well) argued that there might have been even more.

The room was unexceptional. And, when the travelers went down to the restaurant, they found nothing wrong with the saddle of mutton. Walton did bristle when the waiter inquired whether he preferred his meat with mint jelly or with garlic. "Garlic!" he exploded. "D'you take me for an Italian?"

"No, sir," said the waiter, who might have been of that extraction himself. "But some Atlanteans are fond of it."

"I shouldn't wonder," the physician replied, a devastating retort that somehow failed to devastate. His *amour propre* ruffled, he added, "I'm not an Atlantean, either, for which I give thanks to the Almighty."

"So does Atlantis, sir." The waiter hurried off.

Walton at first took that to mean Atlantis also thanked God. Only after noticing a certain gleam in Athelstan Helms' eye did he wonder if the man meant Atlantis thanked God that he was not an Atlantean. "The cheek of the fellow!" he growled. "Have I been given the glove?"

"A finger from it, at any rate, I should say," Helms told him.

The good doctor intended to speak sharply to the waiter. But he soon made a discovery others had found before him: it was difficult—indeed, next to impossible—to stay angry at a man who was feeding you so well. The mutton, flavorful without being gamy, matched any in England. The mint jelly complemented it marvelously. Potatoes and peas were likewise tasty and well prepared.

"For dessert," the waiter said as a busboy took away dirty plates, "we have several flavors of ice cream made on the premises, we have a plum pudding of which many of our English guests are quite fond, and we also have a local confection: candied heart of cycad with rum sauce." He waited expectantly.

"Plum pudding, by all means," Dr. Walton said.

"I'll try the cycad dessert," Helms said. "Something I'm not likely to find elsewhere." ("And a good thing, too," Walton muttered, his *voce* not quite *sotto* enough.)

The physician had to admit that his plum pudding, like the mutton, lived up to all reasonable expectations. Athelstan Helms consumed the strange, chewy-looking object on his plate with every sign of enjoyment. When he was nearly finished, he offered Walton a bite.

"Thanks, but no," the physician said. "Stuffed. Quite stuffed. I do believe I'd burst if I picked up the fork again."

"However you please." Helms finished the dessert himself. "Not bad at all. I shouldn't be surprised if what they call rum is also distilled from the cycad, although they do grow considerable sugar down in the south."

He left a meticulous gratuity for the waiter; Walton would have been less generous. They went back up to their room. Dr.

Walton struck a match against the sole of his boot and lit the gas lamp.

"I say!" Helms exclaimed. "The plot thickens—so it does. I deduce that someone is not desirous of our company here."

Again, he did not need his richly deserved reputation for detection to arrive at his conclusion. Someone had driven a dagger hilt-deep into the pillow on each bed.

"No, I'm not surprised," Inspector La Strada said. "The House of Universal Devotion casts its web widely here."

"Someone should step on the spider, then, by Jove!" Dr. Walton said.

"Freedom of religion again, I'm afraid," La Strada said. "Our Basic Law guarantees the right to worship as one pleases and the right not to worship if one pleases. We find that a more just policy than yours." Yes, he enjoyed scoring points off the mother country.

Dr. Walton was in a high temper, and in a high color as well, his cheeks approaching the hue of red-hot iron. "Where in the Good Book does it say assassinating two innocent pillows amounts to a religious observance?"

"What the good doctor means, I believe, is that any faith can use the excuse of acting in God's cause to perpetrate deeds those more impartial might deem unrighteous," Athelstan Helms said. Walton nodded emphatically enough to set two or three chins wobbling.

"Any liberty can become license—any policeman who's been on the job longer than a week knows as much," La Strada said. "But the Preacher has been going up and down in Atlantis for more than fifty years now. He may have forgotten."

"Going up and down like Satan in the Book of Job," Walton

growled. "We need to find the rascal so we can give him a piece of our mind."

The Atlantean inspector shifted from foot to foot. "Well, sir, like I told you last night, finding him's a problem we haven't ciphered out ourselves."

"What then?" Dr. Walton was still in a challenging mood. "Shall we walk into the nearest House of Universal Devotion and ask the hemidemisemipagans pretending to be priests where the devil their precious Preacher is? The devil ought to know, all right." No, he was not a happy man.

Athelstan Helms, by contrast, suddenly looked as happy as his saturnine features would allow. "A capital idea, Doctor! Capital, I say. Tomorrow morning, bright and early, we shall do that very thing. Beard the blighters in their den, like." He used the Atlanteanism with what struck Walton as malice, or at least mischief, aforethought.

"You're not serious, Helms?" the doctor burst out.

"I am, sir—serious to the point of solemnity," Helms replied. "What better way to come to know our quarry's henchmen?"

"What better way to end up in an alley with our throats cut?" Dr. Walton said. "I'd lay long odds the blackguards have more knives than the two they wasted on goosedown."

Helms paused long enough to light his pipe, then rounded on La Strada. "What is your view of this, Inspector?"

"I wouldn't recommend it," the policeman said. "I doubt you'd be murdered, not two such famous fellows as you are. They have to know we'd haul their Houses down on top of 'em if they worked that kind of outrage. But I don't reckon you'd learn very much from 'em, either."

"There! D'you see, Helms?" Walton said. "Inspector La Strada's a man of sense."

"By which you mean nothing except that he agrees with you," Helms said placidly. "To the nearest House we shall go."

Hanover had several Houses of Universal Devotion, all of them in poor, even rough, neighborhoods. Devotion was not a faith that appealed to the wealthy, though more than a few Devotees had, through skill and hard work, succeeded in becoming prosperous. "Nothing but a heresy," Dr. Walton grumbled as he and Helms approached a House. "Blacker than Pelagianism. Blacker than *Arianism*, by God, and who would have dreamt it possible?"

"Your intimate acquaintance with creeds outworn no doubt does you credit, Doctor," Helms said. "Here, however, we face a creed emphatically not outworn, and we would do well to remember as much."

The House of Universal Devotion seemed unprepossessing enough, without even a spire to mark it as a church. On the lintel were carved a sun, a crescent moon, several stars, and other, more obscure symbols. "Astrology?" Dr. Walton asked.

"Freemasonry," Helms answered. "There are those who claim the two are one and inseparable, but I cannot agree." His long legs scissored up the stairs two at a time. Walton followed more sedately.

"What do we do if they won't let us in?" Walton inquired.

"Create a disturbance as a ruse, then effect an entrance will they or nill they." Athelstan Helms rather seemed to look forward to the prospect. But when he worked the latch the door swung inward on silent, well-oiled hinges. With a small, half-rueful shrug, he stepped across the threshold, Dr. Walton again at his heels.

Inside, the House of Universal Devotion looked more like a church. There were rows of plain pine pews. There was an altar, with a cross on the wall behind it. If the cross was flanked by the symbols also placed above the entryway, that seemed not so remarkable. I AM THE RESURRECTION AND THE LIFE was written on the south wall, EVERY MAN HATH GOD WITHIN

AND MUST LEARN TO SET HIM FREE on the north, both in the same large block capitals.

"I don't recognize that Scriptural quotation," Walton said, nodding toward the slogan on the north wall. In spite of himself, he spoke in the hushed tones suitable for a place of worship.

"From the Preacher's *Book of Devotions*," Helms said. "If you are a Devotee, you will believe the Lord inspired him to set down chapter and verse through the agency of automatic writing. If you are not, you may conceivably hold some other opinion." Walton's scornful sniff gave some hint as to his views of the matter.

Before he could put them into words—if, indeed, that had been his intention—a man in a somber black suit (not clerical garb in any formal sense of the word, but distinctive all the same) came out from a room off to the left of the altar. "I thought I heard voices here," he said. "May I help you, gentlemen?"

"Yes," Athelstan Helms said. "I should like to meet the Preacher, and as expeditiously as may be practicable."

"As who would not?" returned the man in the black suit.

"You are the priest here?" Walton asked.

"I have the honor to be the rector, yes." The man stressed the proper word. Bowing slightly, he continued, "Henry Praeger, sir, at your service. And you would be—?" He broke off, sudden insight lighting his features. "Are you by any chance Helms and Walton?"

"How the devil did you know that?" Walton demanded.

"I daresay he read of our arrival in this morning's *Hanover Herald*," Athelstan Helms said. "By now, half the capital will have done so. I did myself, at breakfast. Good to know I came here safely, what?"

Dr. Walton spluttered in embarrassment. He had glanced at the newspaper while eating a not quite tender enough beefsteak and three eggs fried hard, but had missed the story in question.

Henry Praeger nodded eagerly. "I did, Mr. Helms, and wondered if you might call at a House, not really expecting mine to be the one you chose, of course. But I am honored to make your acquaintance—and yours, too, Dr. Walton." He could be charming when he chose.

Dr. Walton remained uncharmed. He murmured something muffled to unintelligibility by the luxuriant growth of hair above his upper lip.

"You *can* convey my desire to the Preacher?" Helms pressed. "His views on the present unfortunate situation are bound to be of considerable importance. If he believes that killing off his opponents and doubters will enhance his position or that of the House of Universal Devotion, I must tell you that I shall essay to disabuse him of this erroneous impression."

"That has never been the policy of the House of Universal Devotion, Mr. Helms, nor of the Preacher," Henry Praeger said earnestly. "Those who claim otherwise seek to defame our church and discredit our leader."

"What about the men who assuredly are deceased, and as assuredly did not die of natural causes?" Dr. Walton inquired.

"What about them, sir?" Praeger returned. "Men die by violence all over the world, like. You will not claim the House of Universal Devotion is to blame for all of those unfortunate passings, I hope?"

"Er—no," Walton said, though his tone suggested he might like to.

"When the men in question have either criticized the House or attempted to leave the embrace of its creed, I trust you will not marvel overmuch, Mr. Praeger, if some suspicion falls on the institutions you represent," Athelstan Helms said.

"But I do marvel. I marvel very much," Praeger said. "That suspicion may fall on individuals . . . that is one thing. That it should fall on the House of Universal Devotion is something else again. The House is renowned throughout Atlantis, and in Terranova, and indeed in England, for its charity and generosity toward the poor and downtrodden, of whom there are in this sorry world far too many."

"The House is also renowned for its clannishness, its secrecy, and its curious, shall we say, beliefs, as well as for the vehemence with which its adherents cling to them," Helms said.

"Jews are renowned for the same thing," Henry Praeger retorted. "Do you believe the tales of ritual murder that come out of Russia?"

"No, for they are fabrications. I have looked into this matter, and know whereof I speak," Helms answered. "Here in Hanover, however, and elsewhere in this republic, men are unquestionably dead, as Dr. Walton reminded you a moment before. Also, the Jews have the justification of following custom immemorial, which you do not."

"You are right—we do not follow ancient usages," Praeger said proudly. "We take for ourselves the beliefs we require, and reshape them ourselves to our hearts' desire. That is the modern way. That is the Atlantean way. We are loyal to our country, sir, even if misguided officials persist in failing to understand us."

"You don't say anything about the dead 'uns," Walton remarked.

"I don't know anything about them. Nor do I know how to reach the Preacher." Praeger held up a hand before either Englishman could speak. "I shall talk to certain colleagues of mine. If, through them or their associates, word of your desire reaches him, I am confident that he will in turn be able to reach you." His shrug seemed genuinely regretful. "I can do no more."

"Thank you for doing that much," Helms said. "Tell me one thing more, if you would: what do the symbols flanking the cross to either side signify to you?"

"Why, the truth, of course," Henry Praeger answered.

———

Dr. Walton was happy enough to play tourist in Hanover. Even if the city was young—almost infantile by Old World standards—there was a good deal to see, from the Curb Exchange Building to the Navy Yard to the cancan houses that were the scandal of Atlantis, and of much of Terranova and Europe as well (France, by all accounts, took them in stride). Walton returned from his visit happily scandalized.

Athelstan Helms went to no cancan houses. He set up a laboratory of sorts in their rooms, and paid the chambermaids not to clean it. When he wasn't fussing there with the daggers that had greeted him or the good doctor, he was poring over files of the *Hanover Herald* he had prevailed upon Inspector La Strada to prevail upon the newspaper to let him see.

From sources unknown to Walton, Helms procured a violin, upon which he practiced at all hours until guests in the adjoining chambers pounded on the walls. Then, reluctantly, he was persuaded to desist.

"Some people," he said with the faintest trace of petulance, "have no appreciation for—"

"Good music," Dr. Walton said loyally.

"Well, actually, that is not what I was going to say," Helms told him. "They have no appreciation for the fact that any musician, good, bad, or indifferent, must regularly play his instrument if he is not to become worse. In the absence of any communication from the Preacher, what shall I do with my time?"

"You might tour the city," Walton suggested. "There is, I must admit, more to it than I would have expected."

"It is not London," Athelstan Helms said, as if that were all that required saying. In case it wasn't, he added a still more devastating sidebar: "It is not even Paris."

"Well, no," Walton said, "but have you seen the museum? Astonishing relics of the honkers. Not just skeletons and eggshells, mind you, but skins with feathers still on 'em. The birds might almost be alive."

"So might the men the House of Universal Devotion murdered," Helms replied, still in that tart mood. "They might almost be, but they are not."

"Also a fine selection of Atlantean plants," the good doctor said. "Those are as distinctive as the avifauna, if not more so. Some merely decorative, some ingeniously insectivorous, some from which we draw spices, and also some formidably poisonous."

That drew his particular friend's interest; Dr. Walton had thought it might. "I have made a certain study of the noxious alkaloids to be derived from plants," Helms admitted. "That one from southern Terranova, though a stimulant, has deleterious side effects if used for extended periods. Perhaps I should take advantage of the opportunity to observe the specimens from which the poisons are drawn."

"Perhaps you should, Helms," Walton said, and so it was decided.

The Atlantean Museum could not match its British counterpart in exterior grandeur. Indeed, but for the generosity of a Briton earlier in the century, there might not have been any Atlantean Museum. Living in the present and looking toward the future as they did, the inhabitants of Atlantis cared little for the past. The museum was almost deserted when Walton brought Helms back to it.

Helms sniffed at the exhibit of extinct honkers that had so pleased his associate. Nor did a close-up view of the formidable beak and talons of a stuffed red-crested eagle much impress him. What purported to be a cucumber slug climbing up a redwood got him to lean forward to examine it more closely. He drew back a moment later, shaking his head. "It's made of plaster of Paris, and its trail is mucilage."

"This is a museum, not a zoological garden," Dr. Walton said reasonably. "You can hardly expect a live slug here. Suppose it crawled off to the other side of the trunk, where no one but its keeper could see it?" Helms only grunted, which went some way toward showing the cogency of Walton's point.

Helms could not lean close to examine the poisonous plants; glass separated them from overzealous observers. The detective nodded approvingly, saying, "That is as it should be. It protects not only the plants but those who scrutinize them—assuming they are real. With mushrooms of the genus *Amanita*, even inhaling their spores is toxic."

A folded piece of foolscap was wedged in the narrow gap between a pane of glass and the wooden framing that held it in place. "What's that, Helms?" Dr. Walton asked, pointing to it.

"Probably nothing." But Athelstan Helms plucked it away with long, slim fingers—a violist's fingers, sure enough—and opened it. "I say!" he murmured.

"What?"

Wordlessly, Helms held the paper out to Walton. The doctor donned his reading glasses. "'Be on the 4:27 train to Thetford tomorrow afternoon. It would be unfortunate for all concerned if you were to inform Inspector La Strada of your intentions.'" He read slowly; the script, though precise, was quite small. Refolding the sheet of foolscap, he glanced over to Helms. "Extraordinary! What do you make of it?"

"I would say you were probably observed on your previous visit here. Someone familiar with your habits—and with mine; and with mine!—must have deduced that we would return here together, and that I was likely, on coming to the museum, to repair to the section of most interest to me," Helms replied. "Thus . . . the note, and its placement."

Dr. Walton slowly nodded. "Interesting. Persuasive. It does seem to account for the facts as we know them."

"As we know them, yes. As we are intended to know them." Athelstan Helms took the note from his companion and reread it. "Interesting, indeed. And anyone capable of deducing our probable future actions from those just past is an opponent who bears watching."

"I should say so." Walton took off the spectacles and replaced them in their leather case. "I wonder what we shall find upon arriving in Thetford. The town is, I believe, a stronghold of the House of Universal Devotion."

"I wonder if we shall find anything there," Helms said. Walton raised a bushy eyebrow in surprise. The detective explained: "The missive instructs us to board the train. It does not say we shall be enlightened after disembarking. For all we know now, the Preacher may greet us in the uniform of a porter as soon as we take our seats."

"Why, so he may!" Walton exclaimed gaily. "I'd pay good money to see it if he did, though, devil take me if I wouldn't. The porters on these Atlantean trains are just about all of them colored fellows."

"Well, you're right about that." Helms seemed to yield the point, but then returned to it, saying, "He might black his face for the occasion." He shook his head, arguing more with himself than with Dr. Walton. "But no; that would not do. The Atlantean passengers would notice the imposture, being more casually familiar with Negroes than we are. And the dialect these blacks employ is easier for a white man to burlesque than to imitate with precision. I therefore agree with you: whatever disguise the Preacher should choose—if he should choose any—he is unlikely to appear *in forma porteris*."

"Er—quite," the doctor said. "You intend to follow the strictures of the note, then?"

"In every particular, as if it were Holy Writ," Helms replied. "And in the reckoning of the chap who placed it here, so it may be."

Above the entrance to Radcliff Station was the inscription THE CLAN, NOT THE MAN. Radcliffs (in early days, the name was sometimes spelled with a final *e*) were among the first English settlers of Atlantis. That meant those earliest Radcliff(e)s were nothing but fishermen blown astray, an unfortunate fact the family did its best to forget over the next four centuries. Its subsequent successes excused, if they did not altogether justify, such convenient amnesia.

The station smelled of coal smoke, fried food, tobacco, and people—people in swarms almost uncountable. Dr. Watson's clinically trained nose detected at least one case of imminent liver failure and two pelvic infections, but in those shoals of humanity he could not discern which faces belonged to the sufferers.

He and Athelstan Helms bought their tickets to Thetford and back (round trips, they called them here, rather than return tickets) from a green-visored clerk with enough ennui on his wizened face to make even the most jaded Londoner look to his laurels. "Go to Platform Nine," the clerk said. "Have a pleasant trip." His tone implied that he wouldn't care if they fell over dead before they got to the platform. And why should he? He already had their eagles in his cashbox.

Carpetbags in hand, they made their way to the waiting area. "Better signposts here than there would be in an English station," Helms remarked—and, indeed, only a blind man would have had trouble finding the proper platform.

Once there, Helms and Walton had a wait of half an hour before their train was scheduled to depart. A few passengers already stood on the platform when they arrived. More and more came after them, till the waiting area grew unpleasantly crowded. Dr. Walton stuck his free hand in his left front trouser pocket, where his wallet resided, to thwart pickpockets and sneak thieves. He would not have been a bit surprised if the throng contained several. It seemed a typical Atlantean cross section: a large number of people who would not have been out of place in London leavened by the scrapings of every corner of Europe and Terranova and even Asia. Bearded Jews in baggy trousers gabbled in their corrupt German dialect. Two Italian families screamed at each other with almost operatic intensity. A young Mexican man avidly eyed a statuesque blonde from Sweden or Denmark. Walton frowned at the thought of such miscegenation, but Atlantis did not forbid it. A Chinese man in a flowing robe read—he was intrigued to see—the Bible.

Boys selling sausages on sticks and fried potatoes and coffee and beer elbowed through the crowd, loudly shouting their wares. A sausage proved as spicy and greasy as Walton would have expected. He washed it down with a mug of beer, which was surprisingly good. Athelstan Helms, of more ascetic temperament, refrained from partaking of refreshments.

The train bound for Thetford came in half an hour late. Dr. Walton called down curses on the heads of the Atlantean schedulers. "No doubt you have never known an English train to be tardy," Helms said, which elicited a somewhat shamefaced laugh from his traveling companion.

Instead of seating passengers in small compartments, Atlantean cars put them all in what amounted to a common room, with row after row of paired seats on either side of a long central aisle. Dr. Walton also grumbled about that, more because it was different from what he was used to than out of any inherent inferiority in the arrangement.

NO SMOKING! signs declared, and FINE FOR SMOKING, E10! and SMOKING CAR AT REAR OF TRAIN. The good doctor returned his cigar case to his waistcoat. "I wish they'd collect fines for eating garlic, too," he growled; several people in the car were consuming or had recently consumed that odorous, most un-English comestible.

Athelstan Helms pointed to several open windows in the car, which did little to mitigate the raw heat pouring from stoves at either end. "Never fear, Doctor," he said. "I suspect we shall have our fair share of smoke and more in short order."

Sure enough, as soon as the train started out, coal smoke and cinders poured in through those windows. Passengers sitting next to them forced them closed—all but one, which jammed in its track. The conductor, a personage of some importance on an Atlantean train, lent his assistance to the commercial traveler trying to set it right, but in vain. "Guess you're stuck with it," he said. The commercial traveler's reply, while heartfelt, held little literary merit.

Dr. Walton closely eyed the conductor, wondering if he was the mysterious and elusive Preacher in disguise. Reluctantly, he decided it was improbable; the Preacher's career spanned half a century, while the gent in blue serge and gleaming brass buttons could not have been much above forty.

For his part, Helms stared out the window with more interest than the utterly mundane countryside seemed to Walton to warrant. "What's so ruddy fascinating?" the doctor asked when curiosity got the better of him at last.

"Remnants of the old Atlantis amidst the new," his colleague replied. Walton made a questioning noise. Helms condescended to explain: "Stands of Atlantean pines and redwoods and cycads and ginkgoes, with ferns growing around and beneath them. The unique flora that supported your unique avifauna, but is now being supplanted by Eurasian and Terranovan varieties imported for the comfort and convenience of mankind."

"Curious, what, that Atlantis, lying as it does between Europe and the Terranovan mainland, should have native to it plants and creatures so different to those of either," Dr. Walton said.

"Quite." Athelstan Helms nodded. "The most economical explanation, as William of Occam would have used the term, seems to me to be positing some early separation of Atlantis from northeastern Terranova, to which geography argues it must at one time have adhered, thereby allowing—indeed, compelling—Darwinian selection to proceed here from those forms present then, which would not have included the ancestors of what are now Terranova's commonplace varieties. You *do* reckon yourself a Darwinist, Doctor, do you not?"

"Well, I don't know," Walton said uncomfortably. "His logic is compelling, I must admit, but it flies dead in the face of every religious principle inculcated in me since childhood days."

"Oh, my dear fellow!" Helms exclaimed. "Where reason and childish phantasms collide, which will you choose? In what sort of state would mankind be if it rejected reason?"

"In what sort of state is mankind now?" the good doctor returned.

Helms began to answer, then checked himself; the question held an unpleasant and poignant cogency. At last, he said, "Is mankind in that parlous state because of reason or in despite of it?"

"I don't know," Walton said. "Perhaps you might do better to inquire of Professor Nietzsche, who has published provocative works upon the subject."

Again, Helms found no quick response. This time, a man sitting behind him spoke up before he could say anything at all: "Pardon me, gents, but I couldn't help overhearing you, like. You ask me, Darwin is going straight to hell, and everybody who believes his lies'll end up there, too. The Good Book says it, I believe it, and by God that settles it." He spoke in Atlantean accents, and in particularly self-satisfied ones, too.

"Did God tell you this personally, Mr. . . . ?" Helms inquired.

"My name is Primrose, sir, Henry David Primrose," the man said, ignoring Helms' irony. "God gave me my head to think with and the Bible to think from, and I don't need anything more. Neither does anyone else, I say, and that goes double for your precious Darwin."

Dr. Walton was at first inclined to listen to Henry David Primrose with unusual attention, being struck by the matching initial consonants of his last name and the word *preacher*. He did not need long to conclude, however, that Mr. Primrose was not, in fact, their mysterious and elusive quarry. Mr. Primrose was a crazy man, or, in the Atlantean idiom, a nut. He wasn't even a follower of the House of Universal Devotion—he was a Methodist, which, to the Englishmen, made him a boring nut. The way he used the Bible to justify the ignorant views he already held would have converted the Pope to Darwinism. And he would not shut up.

"I will write a check for a million eagles to either one of you gentlemen if you can show me a single place where the Good Book is mistaken—even a single place, mind you," he said, much too loudly.

Athelstan Helms stirred. He and Walton had had this discussion; both men knew there were such places. Walton, however, was seized by the strong conviction that this was not the occasion to enumerate them. "What say we visit the smoking car, eh, Helms?" he said with patently false joviality.

"Very well," Helms replied. "I am sure Mr. Primrose does not indulge, tobacco being unmentioned in the Holy Scriptures—if not an actual error, surely a grievous omission."

That set Mr. Primrose spluttering anew, but he did not pursue the two Englishmen as they rose and walked down the central aisle. Dr. Walton had accomplished his purpose. "I dread our return," Walton said. "He'll serenade us some more."

"Ah, well," Helms said. "Perhaps he will leave us at peace if we avoid topics zoological and theological."

"And if he doesn't, we can always kill him." Dr. Walton was not inclined to feel charitable.

Despite the thickness of the atmosphere, the smoking car proved more salubrious than the ordinary passenger coach. It boasted couches bolted to the floor rather than the row upon row of hard seats in the other car. Walton lit a cigar, while Athelstan Helms puffed on his pipe. They improved the aroma of the smoke in the car, as most of the gentlemen there smoked harsh, nasty cigarettes.

A stag and a doe watched the train rattle past. They must have been used to the noisy mechanical monsters, for they did not bound off in terror. "More immigrants," Helms remarked.

"I beg your pardon?" his traveling companion said.

"The deer," Helms replied. "But for a few bats—many of them peculiar even by the standards of the Chiroptera—Atlantis was devoid of mammalia before those fishermen chanced upon its shores. In the absence of predators other than men with rifles, the deer have flourished mightily."

"Not an unhandsome country, even if it is foreign," Dr. Walton said—as much praise as any non-English locale this side of heaven was likely to get from him.

"Hard winters on this side of the Green Ridge Mountains, I'm given to understand," Helms said. "We would notice it more if the majority of the trees were deciduous rather than coniferous—bare branches do speak to the seasons of the year."

"That's so," Walton agreed. "I suppose most of the ancestors of the deciduous plants had not yet, ah, evolved when some geological catastrophe first caused Atlantis to separate from Terranova."

"It seems very likely," Helms said. "Mr. Primrose might tell us it was Noah's flood."

Dr. Walton expressed an opinion of Mr. Primrose's intimate personal habits on which he was unlikely to have any exact knowledge from such a brief acquaintance. Athelstan Helms' pipe sent up a couple of unusually large plumes of smoke. Had the great detective not been smoking it, one could almost suspect that he might have chuckled.

Day faded fast. A conductor came through and lit the lamps in the car. Walton's eyes began to sting; his lungs felt as if he were inhaling shagreen or emery paper. Nevertheless, he said, "I don't really care to go back."

"Shall we repair to the dining car, then?" Helms suggested.

"Capital idea," Walton said, and so they did.

Eating an excellent—or at least a tolerable—supper whilst rolling along at upwards of twenty miles an hour was not the least of train travel's attractions. Dr. Walton chose a capon, while Helms ordered beefsteak: both simple repasts unlikely to be spoiled by the vagaries of cooking on wheels. The wines from the west coast of Atlantis they ordered to accompany their suppers were a pleasant surprise, easily matching their French equivalents in quality while costing only half as much.

Halfway through the meal, the train shunted onto a siding and stopped: a less pleasant surprise. When Helms asked a waiter what had happened, the man only shrugged. "I do not know, sir," he replied in a gluey Teutonic accent, "but I would guess an accident is in front of us."

"Damnation!" Walton said. "We shall be late to Thetford."

"We are already late to Thetford. We shall be later," Helms corrected. To the waiter, he added, "Another bottle of this admirable red, if you would be so kind."

———

They sat on the siding most of the night. Word filtered through the train that there had been a derailment ahead. Mr. Primrose was snoring when Helms and Walton returned to their seats. Both Englishmen soon joined him in slumber; sleep came easier when the train stood still. Dr. Walton might have wished for the comfort of a Throckmorton car, with a sofa that made up into a bed and another bunk that swung down from the wall above it, but he did not stay awake to wish for long.

Morning twilight had begun edging night's black certainty with the ambiguity of gray when the train jerked into motion once more. Athelstan Helms' eyes opened at once, and with reason in them. He seemed as refreshed as if he *had* passed the night in a Throckmorton car—or, for that matter, in his hotel room back in Hanover. Walton seemed confused when he first woke. At last realizing his circumstances and surroundings, he sent Helms a faintly accusing stare. "*You're* not a beautiful woman," he said.

"I can scarcely deny it," Helms replied equably. "Why you should think I might be is, perhaps, a more interesting question."

If it was, it was one that his friend, now fully returned to the mundane world, had no intention of answering.

Behind them, Mr. Primrose might have been an apprentice sawmill. They took care not to wake him when they went back to the dining car for breakfast. Walton would have preferred bloaters or bangers, but Atlantean cuisine did not run to such English delicacies. He had to make do with fried eggs and a small beefsteak, as he had back in the capital. Helms' choice matched his. They both drank coffee; Atlantean tea had proved shockingly bad even when available.

They were still eating when the train rolled past the scene

of the crash that had delayed it. Passenger and freight cars and a locomotive lay on their side not far from the track. Workmen swarmed over them, salvaging what they could. "A bad accident, very bad," Walton murmured.

"Do you know how an Atlantean sage once defined an accident?" Helms inquired. When the good doctor shook his head, Helms continued with obvious relish: "As 'an inevitable occurrence due to the action of immutable natural laws.' Mr. Bierce, I believe his name is, is a clear-sighted man."

"Quite," Walton said. "Could you pass me another roll, Helms? I find I'm a peckish man myself this morning."

Little by little, the terrain grew steeper. Stands of forest became more frequent in the distance, though most trees had been cut down closer to the railroad line. Being primarily composed of evergreen conifers, the woods bore a more somber aspect than those of England. Their timbers helped bridge several rivers rushing east out of the Green Ridge Mountains. Other rivers, the larger ones, were spanned with iron and even steel.

"Those streams helped power Atlantis' early factories, even before she was initiated into the mysteries of the steam engine," Helms remarked.

"Helped make her into a competitor, you mean," Dr. Walton said. "The old-time mercantilists weren't such fools as people make them out to be, seems to me."

"As their policies are as dead as they are, it's rather too late to make a fuss over either," Helms said, a sentiment with which his colleague could scarcely quarrel regardless of his personal inclinations.

When Helms and Walton returned to their seats in the passenger car, they passed Henry David Primrose heading for the diner. "Ah, we get a bit more peace and quiet, anyhow," Walton said, and Helms nodded.

By the time Mr. Primrose came back, the train was well up into the mountains. The peaks of the Green Ridge were neither inordinately tall nor inordinately steep, but had formed a considerable barrier to westward expansion across Atlantis because of the thick forest that had cloaked them. Even now, the slopes remained shrouded in dark, mournful green. Only the pass through which the railroad line went had been logged off.

The locomotive labored and wheezed, hauling its cars up after it to what the Atlanteans called the Great Divide. Then, descending once more, it picked up speed. Ferns and shrubs seemed more abundant on the western side of the mountains, and the weather, though still cool, no longer reminded the Englishmen of November in their homeland—or, worse, of November on the Continent.

"I have read that the Bay Stream, flowing up along Atlantis' western coast, has a remarkable moderating effect on the climate on this side of the mountains," Helms said. "That does indeed appear to be the case."

A couple of hours later, the train pulled into Thetford, which had something of the look of an industrial town in the English Midlands. After a sigh of disappointment, Dr. Walton displayed his own reading: "Forty years ago, Audubon says, this was a bucolic village. No more."

"*Mais où sont les neiges d'antan?*" Helms replied.

As he and Walton rose to disembark, Henry David Primrose said, "Enjoyed chatting with you gents, that I did." Helms let the remark pass in dignified, even chilly, silence; the good doctor muttered a polite unpleasantry and went on his way.

A few other people got out with them. Friends and relatives waited on the platform for some of them. Others went off to the baggage office to reclaim their chattels. A gray-bearded sweeper in overalls pottered about, pushing bits of dust about with his broom. A stalwart policeman came up to the Englishmen. Tipping his cap, he said, "You will be Dr. Helms and Mr. Walton. Hanover wired me to expect you, though I didn't know your train would be so very late. I am Sergeant Karpinski; I am instructed to render you every possible assistance."

"Very kind of you," Walton said, and proceeded to enlighten the sergeant as to which title went with which man.

Athelstan Helms, meanwhile, walked over to the sweeper and extended his right hand. "Good day, sir," he said. "Unless I am very much in error, you will be the gentleman who has attained a certain amount of worldly fame under the sobriquet of the Preacher."

"Oh, good heavens!" Dr. Walton exclaimed to Sergeant Karpinski. "Please excuse me. Helms doesn't make mistakes very often, but when he does he doesn't make small ones." He hurried over to his friend. "For God's sake, Helms, can't you see he's nothing but a cleaning man?"

The sweeper turned his mild gray eyes on Walton, who suddenly realized that if anyone had made a mistake, it was he. "I *am* a cleaning man, sir," he said, and his voice put the good doctor in mind of an organ played very softly: not only was it musical in the extreme, but it also gave the strong impression of having much more power behind it than was presently being used. The man continued, "While cleaning train-station platforms is a worthy enough occupation, in my small way I also seek to cleanse men's souls. For your friend is correct: I am sometimes called the Preacher." He eyed Athelstan Helms with a lively curiosity. "How did you deduce my identity, sir?"

"In the police station in Hanover, I got a look at your photograph," the detective replied. "Armed with a knowledge of your physiognomy, it was not difficult."

"Well done! Well done!" The Preacher had a merry laugh. "And here is Sergeant Karpinski," he went on as the policeman trudged over. "Will you clap me in irons for what you call my crimes, Sergeant?"

"Not today, thanks," Karpinski said in stolid tones. "I don't much fancy touching off a new round of riots here, like. But your day will come, and you can mark my words on that."

"Every man's day will come," the Preacher said, almost gaily, "but I do not think mine is destined to come at your large and capable hands." He turned back to Helms and Walton. "You will want to recover your baggage. After that, shall we repair to someplace rather more comfortable than this drafty platform? You can tell me what brought you to the wilds of Atlantis in pursuit of a desperate character like me."

"Murder is a good start," Walton said.

"No, murder is a bad stop," the Preacher said. "I shall pray for you. I shall ask that your soul be baptized in the spirit of devotion to the universal Lord, that you may be reborn a god."

"I've already been baptized, thank you very much," the doctor said stiffly.

"That is only the baptism of the body," the Preacher replied with an indifferent wave. "The baptism of the spirit is a different and highly superior manifestation."

"Why don't you see to our trunks, Walton?" Helms said. "Their contents will clothe only our bodies, but without them Sergeant Karpinksi would be compelled to take a dim view of us in his professional capacity."

Braced by such satire, Dr. Walton hurried off to reclaim the luggage. Karpinski laughed and then did his best to pretend he hadn't. Even the Preacher smiled. After Dr. Walton returned, the Preacher led them out of the station. The spectacle of two well-dressed Englishmen and a uniformed sergeant of police following a sweeper in faded denim overalls might have seemed outlandish but for the dignity with which the Preacher carried himself: he acted the role of a man who deserved to be followed, and acted it so well that he certainly seemed to believe it himself.

So did the inhabitants of Thetford who witnessed the small procession. None of them appeared to be in the least doubt as to the Preacher's identity. "God bless you!" one man called, lifting his derby. "Holy sir!" another said. A woman dropped a curtsy. Another rushed up, kissed the Preacher's hand, and then hurried away again, her face aglow. Sergeant Karpinski had not been mistaken when he alluded to the devotion the older man inspired.

The Preacher did not lead them to a House of Universal Devotion, as Dr. Walton had expected he would. In fact, he walked past not one but two such houses, halting instead at the walk leading up to what seemed an ordinary home in Thetford: one-story clapboard, painted white. "I doubt we shall be disturbed here," he murmured.

Several large, hard-looking individuals materialized as if from nowhere, no doubt to make sure the Preacher and his companions were not disturbed. None was visibly armed; the way Sergeant Karpinski's mouth tightened suggested that a lack of appearances might be deceiving.

Inside, the home proved comfortably furnished; it might have been a model of middle-class Victorian respectability. A smiling and attractive young woman brought a tray of food into the parlor, stayed long enough to light the gas lamps and dispel the gloom, and then withdrew once more. "A handmaiden of the Spirit?" Athelstan Helms inquired.

"As a matter of fact, yes," the Preacher said. "Those who impute any degree of licentiousness to the relationship have no personal knowledge of it."

Dr. Walton was halfway through a roast-beef sandwich made

piquant with mustard and an Atlantean spice he could not name before realizing that was not necessarily a denial of the imputation. "Why, the randy old devil!" he muttered, fortunately with his mouth full.

Helms finished his own sandwich and a glass of lager before asking, "And what of those who impute to you the instigation of a campaign of homicides against backsliders from the House of Universal Devotion and critics of its doctrine and policies?" Sergeant Karpinski raised a tawny eyebrow, perhaps in surprise at the detective's frankness.

That frankness did not faze the Preacher. "Well, what of them?" he said. "We lack the barristers and solicitors to pursue every slanderous loudmouth and every libeler who grinds out his hate-filled broadsheets or spreads his prejudice in some weekly rag."

"You deny any connection, then?" Helms persisted.

"I am a man of God," the Preacher said simply.

"So was the Hebrew king who exulted, 'Moab is my washpot,'" Helms said. "So was the Prophet Mohammed. So were the Crusaders who cried, 'God wills it!' as they killed. Regretfully, I must point out that being a man of God does not preclude violence—on the contrary, in fact."

"Let me make myself plainer, then: I have never murdered anyone, nor did any of the murders to which you refer take place at my instigation," the Preacher said. "Is that clear enough to let us proceed from there?"

"Clear? Without a doubt. It is admirably clear," Helms said, though Dr. Walton noted—and thought it likely his friend did as well—that the Preacher had not denied instigating all murders, only those the detective had mentioned. Helms continued, "You will acknowledge a distinction between clarity and truth?"

"Generally, yes. In this instance, no," the Preacher said.

"Oh, come off it," Sergeant Karpinski said, which came close to expressing Dr. Walton's opinion. "Everybody knows those fellows wouldn't be dead if you'd even lifted a finger to keep 'em breathing."

"By which you mean you find me responsible for my followers' excessive zeal," the Preacher said.

"Damned right I do," the sergeant said forthrightly.

Turning to Athelstan Helms, the Preacher said, "Surely, sir, you must find this attitude unreasonable. You spoke of previous religious episodes. Can you imagine blaming all the excesses of Jesus' followers on Him?" He spread his hands, as if to show by gesture how absurd the notion was. Both his voice and his motions showed he was accustomed to swaying crowds and individuals.

"If you will forgive me, I also cannot imagine you rising on the third day," Helms said.

"To be frank, Mr. Helms, neither can I," the Preacher replied. "But the Atlantean authorities seem so intent on crucifying me, they may afford me the opportunity to make the attempt."

"Well, if you had nothing to do with killing those blokes, how come they're dead?" Dr. Walton demanded. "Who did for 'em?" His indignation increased his vehemence while playing hob with his diction.

"Oh, his little chums put lilies in their fists—no doubt of that," Sergeant Karpinski said. "Proving it's a different story, or he'd've swung a long time ago."

"Perhaps the Preacher will answer for himself," Helms said.

"Yes, perhaps he will," the Preacher agreed, speaking of himself in the third person. "Perhaps he will say that it is far more likely the authorities have eliminated these persons for reasons of their own than that his own followers should have had any hand in it. Perhaps he will also say that he does not believe two distinguished English gentlemen hired by those authorities will take him seriously."

"And why the devil should they, when you spew lies the way a broken sewer pipe spews filth?" Righteous indignation filled Karpinski's voice.

"Gently, Sergeant, gently," Helms said, and then, to the Preacher, "Such inflammatory statements are all the better for proof, or even evidence."

"Which I will supply when the time is ripe," the Preacher said. "For now, though, you will want to settle in after your journey here. I understand you have reserved rooms at the Thetford Belvedere?"

"And how do you come to understand that?" Dr. Walton thundered.

"Sergeant Karpinski mentioned it as we came over here," the Preacher answered. Thinking back on it, Walton realized he was right. The Preacher continued, "I might have recommended the Crested Eagle myself, but the Belvedere will do. I hope to see you gentlemen again soon. Unless the sergeant objects, my driver will take you to the hotel."

In England, the Belvedere would have been a normal enough provincial hotel, better than most, not as good as some. So it also seemed in Thetford, which made Dr. Walton decide Atlantis might be rather more civilized than he had previously believed. If the Preacher's favored Crested Eagle was superior, then it was. The Belvedere would definitely do.

The menu in the dining room showed that he and Helms were not in England any more. "What on earth is an oil thrush?" he inquired.

"A blackbird far too large to be baked in a pie," Athelstan Helms replied. "A large, flightless thrush, in other words. I have read that they are good eating, and intend making the experiment. Will you join me?"

"I don't know." Walton sounded dubious. "Seems as though it'd be swimming in grease, what?"

"I think not. It is roasted, after all," Helms said. "And do you see? We have the choice of orange sauce or cranberry or starberry, which I take to be something local and tart. They use such accompaniments with duck and goose, which can also be oleaginous, so they should prove effective amelioratives here, too."

With a sigh, the good doctor yielded. "Since you seem set on it, I'll go along. Whatever the bird turns out to be, I'm sure I ate worse in Afghanistan, and I was bl— er, mighty glad to have it."

Lying on a pewter tray, the roasted oil thrush smelled more than appetizing enough and looked brown and handsome, though the wings were absurdly small: to Dr. Walton's mind, enough so to damage the appearance of the bird. The waiter spooned hot starberry sauce—of a bilious green—over the bird. "Enjoy your supper, gentlemen," he said, and withdrew.

To Walton's surprise, he did, very much. The oil thrush tasted more like a gamebird than a capon. And starberries, tangy and sweet at the same time, complemented the rich flesh well. "You could make a formidable wine from those berries, I do believe," Walton said. "Nothing to send the froggies running for cover, maybe, but more than good enough for the countryside."

"In the countryside, I'm sure they do," Helms said. "How much of it comes into the city—how much of it comes to the tax collector's notice—is liable to be a different tale."

"Aha! I get you." Walton laid a finger by the side of his nose and looked sly.

Only a few people shared the dining room with the Englishmen. Not many tourists came to Thetford, while the Belvedere was on the grand side for housing commercial travelers. The stout, prosperous-looking gentleman who came in when Helms and Walton were well on their way to demolishing the bird in front of them could have had his pick of tables. Instead, he made a beeline for theirs. One of Dr. Walton's eyebrows rose, as if to say, *I might have known.*

"Can I do something for you, sir?" Athelstan Helms asked, polite as usual but with a touch—just a touch, but unmistakable nonetheless—of asperity in his voice.

"You will be the detectives come to give the Preacher the comeuppance he deserves," the man said. "Good for you, by God! High time the House of Universal Depravity has to close up shop once and for all."

Dr. Walton ate another bite of moist, tender, flavorsome flesh from the oil thrush's thigh—the breast, without large flight muscles, was something of a disappointment. Then, resignedly, he said, "I am afraid you have the advantage of us, Mr. . . . ?"

"My name is Morris, Benjamin Joshua Morris. I practice law here in Thetford, and for some time my avocation has been chronicling the multifarious malfeasances and debaucheries of the House of Universal Disgust and the so-called Preacher. About time the authorities stop trembling in fear of his accursed secret society and root it out of the soil from which it has sprouted like some rank and poisonous mushroom."

"Perhaps you will do us the honor of sitting down and telling us more about it," Helms said.

"Perhaps you will also order a bite for yourself so we don't have to go on eating in front of you." Dr. Walton didn't intend to stop, but could—with some effort—stay mannerly.

"Well, perhaps I will." Morris waved for the waiter and ordered a beefsteak, blood rare. To the Englishmen, he said, "I see you are dining off the productions of the wilderness. Myself, I would sooner eat as if civilization had come to the backwoods here." He sighed. "The case of Samuel Jones, however, inclines me to skepticism."

"Samuel Jones?" Walton said. "The name is not familiar."

"You will know him better as the Preacher, founder and propagator—propagator, forsooth!—of the House of Universal Deviation." Benjamin Morris seemed intent on finding as many disparaging names for the Preacher's foundation as he could. "How many members of the House his member has sired I am not prepared to say, but the number is not small."

"He embraces his mistresses as they embrace his principles," Athelstan Helms suggested.

Morris laughed, but quickly sobered. "That is excellent repartee, sir, but falls short in regard of truthfulness. For the Preacher has no principles, but ever professes that which is momentarily expedient. No wonder his theology, so-called, is such an extraordinary tissue of lies and jumble of whatever half-baked texts he chances to have recently read. That men can become as gods! Tell me, gentlemen: has mankind seemed more godly than usual lately? It is to laugh!" Like a lot of lawyers, he often answered his own questions.

His beefsteak appeared then, and proved sanguinary enough to satisfy a surgeon, let alone an attorney. He attacked it with excellent appetite, and also did full justice to an Atlantean red with a nose closely approximating that of a hearty Burgundy. After a bit, Helms said, "Few faiths are entirely logical and self-consistent. The early Christian controversies pertaining to the relation of the Son and the Father and to the relation between the divine and the human within Jesus Christ demonstrate this all too well, as does the blood spilled over them."

"No doubt, no doubt," Benjamin Morris said. "But our Lord was not a louche debauchee, and did not compose the Scriptures with an eye toward giving himself as wide a latitude for misbehavior as he could find." He told several salacious stories about the Preacher's earlier days. They seemed more suitable to the smoking car of a long-haul train than to this placid provincial dining room.

Even Walton, who did not love the Preacher, felt compelled to remark, "Such unsavory assertions would be all the better for proof."

"I have documentary proof at my offices, sir," Morris said. "As I told you, I have been following this rogue and his antics for years, like. After supper, I shall go there and bring you what I trust will suffice to satisfy the most determined skeptic."

Having made that announcement, he hurried through the rest of his meal, drained a last glass of wine, and, slapping a couple of golden Atlantean eagles on the table, arose and hastened from the dining room.

Less than a minute later, several sharp pops rang out. "Fireworks?" Walton said.

"Firearms," Athelstan Helms replied, his voice suddenly grim. "A large-bore revolver, unless I am much mistaken." In such matter, Walton knew his friend was unlikely to be.

Sure enough, someone shouted, "Is a doctor close by? A man's been shot!"

Still masticating a last savory bite of oil thrush, Walton dashed out into the street to do what he could for the fallen man. Helms, though no physician, followed hard on his heels to learn what he could from the scene of this latest crime. "I hope it isn't that Morris fellow," the good doctor said.

"Well, so do I, but not to any great degree, for it is likely a hope wasted," Helms said.

And sure enough, there lay Benjamin Joshua Morris, with three bullet wounds in his chest. "Good heavens," Walton said. "Beggar's dead as a stone. Hardly had the chance to know what hit him, I daresay."

Sergeant Karpinski popped up out of nowhere like a jack-in-the-box, pistol in hand. Athelstan Helms' nostrils twitched, as if in surprise. "I heard gunshots," Karpinski said, and then, looking down, "Great God, it's Morris!"

"He was just speaking to us of the perfidies of the House of Universal Devotion." Dr. Walton stared at the corpse, and at the blood puddling beneath it on the cobbles. "Here, I should say, we find the said perfidies demonstrated upon his person."

"So it would seem." Sergeant Karpinski scowled at the body, and then in the direction of the house where he and the Englishmen had conversed with the Preacher. "I should have jugged that no-good son of a . . . Well, I should have jugged him when I had the chance. A better man might still be alive if I'd done it."

Dr. Walton also looked back toward that house. "You could still drop in on him, you know."

Gloomily, the policeman shook his head. "Not a chance he'll still be there. He'll lie low for a while now, pop up here and there to preach a sermon, and then disappear again. Oh, I'll send some men over, but they won't find him. I know the man. I know him too well."

Athelstan Helms coughed. "I should point out that we have no proof the House of Universal Devotion murdered the late Mr. Morris, nor that the Preacher ordered his slaying if some member of the House was in fact responsible for it."

Both his particular friend and the police sergeant eyed him as if he'd taken leave of his senses. "I say, Helms, if we haven't got cause and effect here, what have we got?" Walton asked.

"A dead man," the detective replied. "By all appearances, a paucity of witnesses to the slaying. Past that, only untested hypotheses."

"Call them whatever you want," Karpinski said. "As for me, I'm going to try to run the Preacher to earth. I know some of his hidey-holes—maybe more than he thinks I do. With a little luck . . . And I'll send my men back here to take charge of the body." He paused. "Good lord, I'll have to tell Lucy Morris her husband's been murdered. I don't relish that."

"There will be a postmortem examination on the deceased, I assume?" Helms said. When Sergeant Karpinski nodded, Helms continued, "Would you be kind enough to send a copy of the results to me here at the hotel?"

"I can do that," Karpinski said.

"He also spoke of papers in his office, papers with information damaging to the House of Universal Devotion," Walton said. "Any chance we might get an idea of what they contain?"

Now the police sergeant frowned. "A lawyer's private papers after his death? That won't be so easy to arrange, I'm afraid. I'll speak to his widow about it, though. If she's in a vengeful mood and thinks showing them to you would help make the House fall, she might give you leave to see them. I make no promises, of course. And now, if you'll pardon me . . ." He tipped his derby and hurried away.

Athelstan Helms stared after him, a cold light flickering in his pale eyes. "I dislike homicide, Walton," the detective said. "I especially dislike it when perpetrated for the purpose of furthering a cause. *Ideological* homicide, to use the word that seems all the rage on the Continent these days, makes the crime of passion and even murder for the sake of wealth seem clean by comparison."

"And in furtherance of a *religious* ideology!" Walton exclaimed. "Of all the outmoded things! Seems as if it ought to belong in Crusader days, as you told that so-called Preacher yourself."

"Those who have the most to lose are aptest to strike to preserve what they still have," Helms observed.

"Just so." Dr. Walton nodded vigorously. "When Mr. Samuel Jones found out that poor Morris here was conferring with us in aid of his assorted sordid iniquities"—he chuckled, fancying his own turn of phrase—"he must have decided he couldn't afford it, and sent his assassins after the man."

Two policemen, both large and rotund, huffed up. Each wore on his hip in a patent-leather holster a stout brute of a pistol, of the same model as Sergeant Karpinski's—no doubt the standard weapon for the police in Thetford, if not in all of Atlantis. "That's Morris, all right," one of them said, eyeing the body. "There'll be hell to pay when word of this gets out."

"Yes, and the Preacher to pay it," the other man said with a certain grim anticipation.

The first policeman eyed Helms and Walton. "And who the devil are you two, and where were you when this poor bastard got cooled?"

"This is the famous Athelstan Helms," Dr. Walton said indignantly.

"We were dining in the Belvedere when Mr. Morris was shot," Helms continued. "We have witnesses to that effect. We were conversing with him shortly before his death, however."

"If Mr. What's-his-name Helms is so famous, how come I never heard of him?" the local policeman said.

Because you are an ignorant, back-country lout, went through Dr. Walton's mind. Saying that to the back-country lout's face when said lout was armed and also armored in authority struck him as inexpedient. What he did say was, "Inspector La Strada of Hanover brought us from England to assist in the investigation of the House of Universal Devotion."

"About time they give those maniacs their just deserts," the second policeman said.

"Which reminds me, Helms," the good doctor said. "We were interrupted before we could attend to ours."

"I dare hope ours would require another 's,'" Helms said. He nodded to the policemen. "If you will be kind enough to excuse us . . . ?" The blue-uniformed Atlanteans did not say no.

With another polite nod, Helms walked back toward the Belvedere, Dr. Walton at first at his heels and then bustling on ahead of him.

After finishing their desserts—which proved not to come up to the hopes Walton had lavished on them—the Englishmen went up to their rooms. "What puzzles me," Walton said, "is how the Preacher could have known Morris would speak to us then, and had a gunman waiting for him as he emerged."

"He would have done better to dispose of the man before we conversed," Helms replied. "If he had a pistoleer waiting for him, why not anticipate and set the blackguard in place ahead of time?"

"Maybe someone in the dining room belongs to the House and hotfooted away to let him know what was toward," Dr. Walton suggested.

"It could be," Helms said. "I wonder what the post-mortem will show."

"Cause of death is obvious enough," Walton said. "Poor devil got in the way of at least three rounds to the chest."

"Quite," Helms said. "But, as always, the devil is in the details."

"Do you suppose the devil is in Mr. Jones?" Walton asked.

"Well, if we were required to dispose of every man who ever made a sport of, ah, sporting with a number of pretty young women, the world would be a duller and a much emptier place," Athelstan Helms said judiciously. "Indeed, given the Prince of Wales' predilections, even the succession might be jeopardized. Murder, however, is a far more serious business, whether motivated by religious zeal or some reason considerably more secular."

"What would you say if the Preacher appeared on our door-step proclaiming his innocence?" Dr. Walton asked.

"At this hour of the evening? I do believe I'd say, 'Fascinating, old chap. Do you suppose you could elaborate at breakfast tomorrow?'"

The good doctor pulled his watch from a waistcoat pocket. "It *is* late, isn't it? And I know I didn't get much sleep on that wretched train last night. You, though . . . Sometimes I think you are powered by steel springs and steam, not flesh and blood."

"A misapprehension, I assure you. I have never cared for the taste of coal," Helms said gravely.

"Er—I suppose not," Walton said. "Shall we knit up the raveled sleeve of care, then?"

"A capital notion," the detective replied. "And while we're about it, we should also sleep." Walton started to say something in response to that, then seemed to give it up as a bad job. Whether that had been his particular friend's intention did not appear to cross his mind, which, under the circumstances, might have been just as well.

A reasonably restful night, a hearty breakfast, and strong coffee might have put some distance between the Englishmen and Benjamin Morris' murder—had the waiter in the dining room not seated them at the table where they'd spoken with him at supper. Dr. Walton kept looking around as if expecting the attorney to walk in again. Barring an unanticipated Judgment Trump, that seemed unlikely.

"How do you suppose we could reach the Preacher now?" Walton asked. "He surely won't be at that House any more."

"I'll inquire at the closest House of Universal Devotion," Helms answered. "Whether unofficially and informally or not, the preacher there should be able to reach him."

Before the detective and his companion could leave the hotel, a policeman handed Helms an envelope. "The post-mortem on Mr. Morris, sir," he said.

"I thank you." Athelstan Helms broke the seal on the envelope. "Let's see. . . . Two jacketed slugs through the heart, and another through the right lung. Death by rapid exsanguination."

"Rapid? Upon my word, yes! I should say so!" Dr. Walton shook his head. "With wounds like those, he'd go down like Bob's your uncle. With two in the heart and one in the lung, an elephant would."

"Jacketed bullets . . ." Helms turned as if to ask something of the policeman who'd brought the report, but that worthy had already departed.

"Even so, Helms," Walton said. "Granted, they don't mushroom like your ordinary slug of soft lead, but they'll do the job more than well enough, especially in vital spots like that. And they foul the bore much less than a soft slug would."

"I am not ignorant of the advantages," Helms said with a touch of asperity. "I merely wished to enquire . . . Well, never mind." He gathered himself and set his cap on his head. "To the House of Universal Devotion."

The preacher looked at Helms and Walton in something approaching astonishment. "How extraordinary!" he said. "In the past half hour, I've heard from the Preacher, the police, and now you gentlemen."

"What did the Preacher want?" Helms asked.

"Why, I didn't see him. But I have a message from him to you if you came to call."

"And the police?" Walton inquired.

"They wanted to know if I'd heard from the Preacher." The young man in charge of the local House sniffed. "I denied it, of course. None of their business."

"They might have roughed you up a bit," Walton said. They might have done a good deal worse than that. Whatever one thought of the House of Universal Devotion's theology, the loyalty it evoked could not be ignored.

This particular preacher was thin and pale, certainly none too prepossessing. Nevertheless, when he gathered himself and said, "The tree of faith is nourished by the blood of martyrs, which is its natural manure," he made the good doctor believe him.

"And the message from the Preacher was. . . ?" Athelstan Helms prompted.

"That he is innocent in every particular of this latest horrific crime. That it is but another example of the sort of thing of which he spoke to you in person—you will know what that means, no doubt. That an investigation is bound to establish the facts. That those facts, once established, will rock not only Atlantis but the world."

"He doesn't think small!" Walton exclaimed. "Not half, he doesn't."

"If he thought small, he would not have achieved the success that has already been his," Helms said, and then, to the preacher, "Do you know his current whereabouts?"

"No, sir. What I don't know, they can't interrogate out of me, like. And I never saw the fellow who gave me the message before, either. But it's a true message, isn't it?"

"I believe so, yes," Helms replied.

"*I* believe the Preacher would make a first-rate spymaster had he chosen to try his hand at that instead of founding a religion," Dr. Walton said. "He has the principles down pat."

"Do you believe him?" the young preacher asked anxiously.

"Well, that remains to be seen," Helms said. "Such assertions as he has made are all the better for proof, but I can see how he is in a poor position to offer any. My investigations continue, and in the end, I trust, they will be crowned with success."

"They commonly are," Walton added with more than a hint of smugness.

Athelstan Helms allowed himself the barest hint of a smile. "Those who fail are seldom chronicled—the *mobile vulgus* clamors after success, and nothing less will do. A pity, that, when failure so often proves more instructive."

"My failure to publish accounts of your failures has been more instructive than I wish it were," Walton said feelingly.

"Let us hope that will not be the case here, then," Helms said. "Onward!—the plot thickens."

Dr. Walton was not particularly surprised to discover Sergeant Karpinski standing on the sidewalk outside the House of Universal Devotion. "We went in there, too," Karpinski said. "We didn't find anything worth knowing. You?"

"Our investigation continues." Helms' voice was bland. "When we have conclusions to impart, you may rest assured that you will be among the first to hear them."

"And what exactly does that mean?" the sergeant asked.

"What it says," the detective replied. "Not a word more; not a word less."

"If you think you can go poking your nose into our affairs, sir, without so much as a by-your-leave—"

"If Mr. Helms believes that, Sergeant, he's bloody well right," Dr. Walton broke in. "He—and I—are in your hole of a town, in your hole of a country, at the express invitation of Inspector La Strada. Without it, believe me, we should never have come. But we will thank you not to interfere with our performing our duties in the manner we see fit. Good day."

Sergeant Karpinski's countenance was eloquent of discontent. He opened his mouth, closed it, opened it again, and then, shaking his head, walked off with whatever answer he might have given still suppressed.

"Pigheaded Polack," Walton muttered.

"You did not endear yourself to him," Helms said. "The unvarnished truth is seldom palatable—though I doubt whether any varnish would have made your comments appetizing."

"Too bad," the good doctor said, and, if an intensifying participle found its way into his diction, it need not be recorded here.

"I wonder what La Strada will say when word of this gets back to him, as it surely will," Helms remarked.

"The worst he can do is expel us, in which case *I* shall say, 'Thank you,'" Dr. Watson answered.

"I hope that is the worst he can do to us," Helms said.

"He cannot claim we shot Benjamin Morris—we have witnesses to the contrary," Walton said. "Neither can he claim we shot any of the others whom he alleges the House of Universal Devotion slew—we were safely back in England then. And the sooner we are safely back in England once more, the happier I shall be. Of that you may rest assured."

"I begin to feel the same way," Helms replied. "Nevertheless, we are here, and we must persevere. Onward, I say!"

Their course intersected with that of the police on several more occasions. Thetford's self-declared finest eyed them as if they were vultures at a feast. "I do believe we shall be hard-pressed to come by any further information from official sources," Helms said.

"Brilliant deduction!" Dr. Walton said. One of Athelstan Helms' elegant eyebrows rose. Surely the good doctor could not be displaying an ironical side? Surely not. . . .

Gun shops flourished in Thetford. They sold all manner of shotguns and rifles for hunting. That made a certain amount of sense to Walton; the countryside surrounding the city was far wilder than any English woods. Despite the almost certain extinction of honkers, other native birds still thrived there, as did turkeys imported from Terranova and deer and wild boar and foxes brought across the sea from the British Isles and Europe.

The gun shops also sold an even greater profusion of pistols: everything from a derringer small enough to be concealed in a fancy belt buckle to pistols that Dr. Walton, a large, solidly made man, would not have cared to fire two-handed, let alone with only one. "Something like that," he said, pointing to one in the window, "you're better off clouting the other bloke in the head with it. That'd put the quietus on him, by Jove!"

"I daresay," Helms replied, and then surprised his friend by going into the shop.

"Help you with something?" asked the proprietor, a wizened little man in a green eyeshade who looked more like a pawnbroker than the bluff, hearty sort one might expect to run such an establishment.

"If you would be so kind," Helms said. "I'd like to see a police pistol, if you please."

"A .465 Manstopper?" the proprietor said. Walton thought the pistol had an alarmingly forthright name. The man produced one: a sturdy revolver, if not quite so gargantuan as some of the weapons civilians here seemed to carry.

Athelstan Helms broke it down and reassembled it with a practiced ease that made the proprietor eye him with more respect than he'd shown hitherto. "A well-made weapon, sure enough," Helms said. "The action seems a bit stiff, but only a bit. And the ammunition?"

"How keen on getting rid of fouling are you?" the gunshop owner asked.

"When necessary, of course," Helms replied. "I am not averse to reducing the necessity as much as possible."

"Sensible fellow." The proprietor produced a gaudily printed cardboard box holding twenty-five rounds. "These are the cartridges the police use. Sell you this and the pistol for thirteen eagles twenty-five cents."

Dr. Walton expected Helms to decline, perhaps with scorn. Instead, the detective took from his pocket a medium-sized gold coin, three large silver ones, and one medium-sized silver one. "Here you are, and I thank you very much."

"Thank *you*." The proprietor stowed the money in a cash box. "You'll get good use from that pistol, if you ever need it."

"Oh, I expect I shall," Athelstan Helms replied. "Yes, I expect I shall."

"I say, Helms—this is extraordinary. Most extraordinary. Not your usual way of doing business at all," Dr. Walton said, more than a little disapproval in his voice.

"Really?" Helms said. "How is it different?"

Walton opened his mouth for a blistering reply, then shut it again. When he did speak, it was in accusing tones: "You're having me on."

"Am I?" Helms might have been innocence personified but for the hint of a twinkle in his eye and but for the setting: a large lecture hall at Bronvard University, the oldest in Atlantis, a few miles outside of Hanover. The hall was packed with reporters from the capital and from other Atlantean towns with newspapers that maintained bureaus there. Rain poured down outside. The air smelled of wool from the reporters' suits and of the cheap tobacco they smoked in extravagant quantities.

In the middle of the mob of newspapermen sat Inspector La Strada. He stared ruefully at the remains of his bumbershoot, which had blown inside out. Water dripped from the end of his nose; he resembled nothing so much as a drowned ferret.

"Shall we get on with it?" Walton inquired. At Helms' nod, the good doctor took his place behind the lectern more commonly used for disquisitions on chemistry, perhaps, or on the uses of the ablative absolute in Latin. "Gentlemen of the press, I have the high honor and distinct privilege of presenting to you the greatest detective of the modern age, my colleague and, I am lucky enough to say, my particular friend, Mr. Athelstan Helms. He will discuss with you the results of his investigations into the murders of certain opponents of the House of Universal Devotion and of Mr. Samuel Jones, otherwise known as the Preacher, and especially of his investigation into the untimely demise of Mr. Benjamin Morris in Thetford not long ago. Helms?"

"Thank you, Dr. Walton." Helms replaced his fellow Englishman behind the lectern. "I should like to make some prefatory remarks before explicating the solution I believe to be true. First and foremost, I should like to state for the record that I am not now a member of the House of Universal Devotion, nor have I ever been. I consider the House's theology to be erroneous, improbable, and misguided in every particular. Only in a land where democracy flourishes to the point of making every man's judgment as good as another's, wisdom, knowledge, and experience notwithstanding, could such an abortion of a cult come into being and, worse, thrive."

The reporters scribbled furiously. Some of them seemed to gather that he had cast aspersions on the United States of Atlantis. Despite any aspersions, Inspector La Strada sat there smiling as he dripped. Several hands flew into the air. Other reporters neglected even that minimal politeness, bawling out Helms' name and their questions.

"Gentlemen, please," Helms said several times. When that failed, he shouted, *"Enough!"* in a voice of startling volume. By chance or by design, the acoustics of the hall favored him over the reporters. Having won something resembling silence except for being rather louder, he went on, "I shall respond to your queries in due course, I promise. For now, please let me proceed. Perhaps more questions will occur to you as I do."

Dr. Walton knew he would have been ruder than that. To the good doctor, the reporters were nothing but a yapping pack of provincial pests. To Athelstan Helms, almost all of mankind fell into that category, Atlanteans hardly more than Englishmen.

"It seemed obvious from the beginning that the House of Universal Devotion was behind the recent campaign of extermination against its critics," Helms said. "There can be no doubt that the House has responded strongly in the past to any and all efforts to call it to account for its doctrinal and social peculiarities. Thus a simple, obvious solution presented itself—one obvious enough to draw the notice of police officials in Hanover and other Atlantean cities."

He got a small laugh from the assembled gentlemen of the press. Inspector La Strada laughed, too. Why not? Despite sarcasm, Helms had declared the solution the police favored to be the simple and obvious one. Was that not the same as saying it was true?

It was not, as Helms proceeded to make clear: "Almost every puzzle has a solution that is simple and obvious—simple and obvious and, unfortunately, altogether wrong. Such appears to me to be the case here. As best I have been able to determine, there is no large-scale conspiracy on the part of the House of Universal Devotion to rid the world of its critics—and a good thing, too, or the world would soon become an empty and echoing place."

"Well, how come those bastards are dead, then?" a reporter shouted, careless of anything resembling rules of procedure. Inspector La Strada, Dr. Walton noted, was no longer smiling or laughing.

"Please note that I did not say there was no conspiracy," Athelstan Helms replied. "I merely said there was none on the part of the House of Universal Devotion. Whether there was one *against* the said House is, I regret to report, an altogether different question, with an altogether different answer."

Walton saw that keeping the proceedings orderly would be anything but easy. Some of the reporters still seemed eager and attentive, but others looked angry, even hostile. As for La Strada, his countenance would have had to lighten considerably for either of those adjectives to apply. As a medical man, Dr. Walton feared the police official was on the point of suffering an apoplexy.

Impassive as if he were being greeted with enthusiasm and applause, Athelstan Helms continued, "To take the particular case of Mr. Benjamin Morris, his killer was in fact not an outraged member of the House of Universal Devotion, but rather one Sergeant Casimir Karpinski of the Thetford Police Department."

Pandemonium. Chaos. Shouted questions and raised hands. A fistfight in the back rows. One question came often enough to stay clear through the din: "How the devil d'you know that?"

"My suspicions were kindled," Helms said—several times, each louder than the last, until his voice finally prevailed—"My suspicions were kindled, I say, when Karpinski repaired to the scene of the crime with astounding celerity, and also smelling strongly of black-powder smoke, such being the propellant with which the caliber .465 Manstopper is charged. The Manstopper is the Thetford Police Department's preferred arm, and the late Mr. Morris was slain with copper-jacketed bullets, which the police department also uses. But the odor of powder was what truly made me begin to contemplate this unfortunate possibility. The nose is sadly underestimated in detection." He tapped his own bladelike proboscis.

"Sounds pretty goddamn thin to me!" a reporter called. Others shouted agreement. "You have any real evidence besides the big nose you're sticking into our affairs?" The gentlemen of the press and Inspector La Strada nodded vigorously.

"I do," Helms said, calmly still. "Dr. Walton, if you would be so kind . . . ?"

"Certainly." Walton hurried over to the door through which he and his colleague had entered the hall and said, "Bring him in now, if you please."

In came Sergeant Karpinski, a glum expression on his unshaven face, his hands chained together behind him. His escorts were two men even larger and burlier than he was himself: *not* police officers, but men who styled themselves detectives, though what they did for a living was considerably different from Athelstan Helms' definition of the art.

"Here is Casimir Karpinski," Helms said. "He will tell you for himself whether my deductions have merit."

"I killed Benjamin Morris," Karpinski said. "I'm damned if I'd tell you so unless this bastard had the goods on me, but he does, worse luck. I did it, and I'm not real sorry, either. The House of Universal Devotion needs taking down, and this was a way to do it. Or it would have been, if *he* hadn't started poking around."

A hush settled over the lecture hall as the reporters slowly realized this was no humbug. They scribbled furiously. "Why do you think the House needs taking down?" Helms asked.

"It's as plain as the nose on my face. It's as plain as the nose on *your* face, by God," Karpinski replied, which drew a nervous laugh from his audience. "They're a state within a state. They have their own rules, their own laws, their own morals. People are loyal to the Preacher, not to the United States of Atlantis. Time—past time—to bring 'em into line."

"Are these your opinions alone?" the detective inquired.

Karpinski laughed in his face. "I should hope not! Any decent Atlantean would tell you the same."

"The decency of framing the Preacher and his sect for a crime they did not commit I leave to others to expatiate upon," Athelstan Helms said. "But did you act alone, Sergeant, or upon the urging of other 'decent Atlanteans' of higher rank in society?"

"I got my orders from Hanover," Sergeant Karpinski answered. "I got them straight from Inspector La Strada, as a matter of fact."

"That's a lie!" La Strada roared.

"It is not." Helms pulled from an inside jacket pocket a folded square of pale yellow paper. "I have here a telegram found in Sergeant Karpinski's flat—"

Inspector La Strada, his face flushed a deep, liverish red suggestive of extreme choler, pulled from a shoulder holster a large, stout pistol that would have been better carried elsewhere upon his person; even in that moment of extreme tension, Dr. Walton noted that the weapon in question was a Manstopper .465—a recommendation for the model, if one the good doctor would as gladly have forgone. La Strada leveled, or attempted to level, the revolver not at either of the two Englishmen who had uncovered his nefarious machinations, but rather at Sergeant Karpinski, whose testimony could do him so much harm.

He was foiled not by Helms or Walton, but by the reporter sitting to his right. That worthy, possessed of quick wits and quicker reflexes, seized Inspector La Strada's wrist and jerked his hand upward just as the Manstopper discharged. The roar of the piece was astoundingly loud in the enclosed space. Plaster dust drifted down from the ceiling, followed a moment later by several drops of water; the pistol had proved its potency by penetrating ceiling and roof alike.

Another shot ricocheted from the marble floor several feet to Dr. Walton's left and shattered a window as it left the lecture hall. After that, the gentlemen of the press swarmed over the police inspector and forcibly separated him from his revolver; had they been but a little more forceful, they would have separated him from his right index finger as well. The Atlantean policemen in the hall, chagrin and dismay writ large upon their faces, descended to take charge of their erstwhile superior.

"Sequester all documents in Inspector La Strada's office," Athelstan Helms enjoined them. "Let nothing be removed; let nothing be destroyed. The conspiracy against the House of Universal Devotion is unlikely to have sprung full-grown from his forehead, as Pallas Athena is said to have sprung from that of cloud-gathering Zeus."

"Never you fear, Mr. Helms," a reporter called to him. "Now that we know something's rotten in the state of Denmark, like, we'll be able to run it down ourselves." His allusion, if not Homeric, was at least Shakespearean.

"God, what this'll do to the elections next summer!" another reported said. Then he blinked and looked amazed. "Who can guess now *what* it'll do? All depends on where La Strada got his orders from." Although he casually violated the prohibition against ending a sentence with a preposition, his remarks remained cogent.

"Why would anybody need to try to take down the House like that?" yet another man said. "Its members have sinned a boatload of genuine sins. What point to inventing more in the hope that they'll provoke people against the sect?"

"Such questions as those are not so easily solved by detection," Helms replied. "Any remarks I offer are speculative, and based solely on my understanding, such as it is, of human nature. First, the Preacher and his faith continue to attract large numbers of new devotees nearly half a century after he founded the House. His sect, as you rightly term it, is not only a religious force in Atlantis but also a political and an economic force. Those representing other such forces—I name no names—would naturally be concerned about his growing influence in affairs. And a trumped-up killing—or, more likely, a series of them—allows the opposing forces to choose their timing and their presentation of the case against the House, which any possible natural incidents would not. Some of you will perhaps grasp exactly what I mean: those whose papers have been loudest in the cry against the Preacher."

Several reporters looked uncomfortable; one or two might even have looked guilty. One of those who seemed most uncomfortable asked, "If all these charges against the House of Universal Devotion are false, why would Inspector La Strada have brought you over from London? Wasn't he contributing to his own undoing?"

"Why? I'll tell you why, by Jove!" That was the good doctor, not the detective. "Because he underestimated Mr. Athelstan Helms, that's why! He thought Helms would see what he wanted him to see, and damn all else. He thought Helms would give his seal of approval, you might say, to whatever he wanted to do to the House of Universal Devotion. He thought Helms would make it all . . . What's the word the sheenies use?"

"Kosher?" Helms suggested, murmuring, "Under the circumstances, an infelicitous analogy."

Dr. Walton ignored the aside. "Kosher!" he echoed triumphantly. "That's it. He thought Helms' seal of approval would make it all kosher! But he reckoned without my friend's—my particular friend's—brilliance, he did. Athelstan Helms doesn't let the wool get pulled over his eyes. Athelstan Helms doesn't see what other blokes want him to see or mean for him to see. Athelstan Helms, by God, sees what's there!"

Athelstan Helms saw the reporters staring at him as if he were an extinct honker somehow magically restored to life—as if he were a specimen rather than a man. He coughed modestly. "The good doctor does me too much honor, I fear. In this case, I count myself uncommonly fortunate."

"Well, what if you are?" a reporter shouted at him, face and voice full of fury. "What if you are, God damn you? What have you just gone and done to Atlantis? Do you count us uncommonly fortunate on account of it? You've gone and given that bearded maniac of a Preacher free rein for the rest of his worthless life!"

Another man stood up and yelled, "Hold your blasphemous tongue! God speaks through the Preacher, not through the likes of you!"

Someone else punched the Preacher's partisan in the nose. In an instant, fresh pandemonium filled the lecture hall. "I think perhaps we should make our exit now," the detective said.

"Brilliant deduction, Helms!" Walton said, and they did.

Boarding the *Crown of India* for the return voyage came as a distinct relief to Helms and Walton. Behind them, the United States of Atlantis heaved with political passions more French, or even Spanish, than British. The Atlantean authorities also refused to pay the sizable fee La Strada had promised them, and laughed at the signed contract Dr. Walton displayed. Under the circumstances, that was perhaps understandable, but it did not contribute to Walton's regard for the republic they were quitting.

"A bloody good job you insisted on return tickets paid in advance," he told Helms. "Otherwise they'd boot us off the pier and let us swim home—and take pot shots at us whilst we were in the water, too."

"I shouldn't wonder," Helms said. "Well, let's repair to our cabin. If the ocean was rough coming here, it's unlikely to be smoother now."

Walton sighed. "True enough. I have a tolerably strong stomach, but even so. . . . Where have they put us?"

Helms looked at his ticket. "Suite twenty-seven, it says. Well, that sounds moderately promising, anyhow."

When they opened the door to Suite 27, however, they found it already occupied by two strikingly attractive young women, one a blonde, the other a brunette. "Oh, dear," Walton said. "Let me summon a steward. There must be some sort of mistake."

The young women shook their heads, curls swinging in unison. "You are Mr. Helms and Dr. Walton, aren't you?" the golden-haired one said.

"Yes, of course they are," the brunette said. "I'm Polly, and she's Kate," she added, as if that explained everything.

Seeing that perhaps it didn't, Kate said, "We're staying in Suite twenty-seven, too, you see. The Preacher made sure we would."

"I beg your pardon?" Walton spluttered. "The Preacher, you say?"

"You are handmaidens of the Spirit, I presume?" Helms showed more aplomb.

That's right." Polly smiled. "He *is* a clever fellow," she said to Kate.

"But . . . !" Walton remained nonplused. "What are you doing *here*?"

Polly's expression said he wasn't such a clever fellow. It vexed him; he'd seen that expression aimed his way too often while in Athelstan Helms' company. "Well," Polly said, "the Preacher believes—heavens, everyone knows—the spirit and body are linked. We wouldn't be *people* if they weren't."

"Quite right," Helms murmured.

"And"—Kate took up the tale again—"the Preacher's mighty grateful to the two of you for all you did for him. And he thought we might show you *how* grateful he is, like."

"He's *mighty* grateful," Polly affirmed. "All the way to London grateful, he is. We are."

"Is he? Are you? I say!" Dr. Walton *was* sometimes slow on the uptake, but he'd definitely caught on now. "This could be a jolly interesting voyage home, what?"

Athelstan Helms was hanging the DO NOT DISTURB sign on the suite's outer door. "Brilliant deduction, Walton," he said.